ALEXANDER KENDZIORSKI

Every Hunt Shall Be The Last

An African Painted Wolf Novel

This book was professionally typeset on Reedsy.
Find out more at reedsy.com

For the hundreds of wildlife rangers killed while protecting the land, the people, and the wild. What is owed to you is beyond evaluation.

It is up to you now. Defy them all, queen of
the veld.

– Johan Marais

Contents

Acknowledgement

Thanks to veterinarian Theanette Staal and the teachers of Wildlife Act who helped me to understand wildlife behavior and the basics of wildlife management. I am doing my best.

Chapter 1

MOZAMBIQUE

Every moment a negotiation

Hope for one lay in the doom of another.

A hoofbeat, a sledgehammer striking earth, the dull thud swallowed by the arid surrounds.

A lighter footfall behind it, a whisper of a step, teeth flashing in silence.

Each crash of the hind hooves carried the lithe figure of the impala into the air, sailing forward with its rear legs aloft. The graceful pronk announced to all in view that the male was robust, and in his prime.

Slicing through the dust was a spear of black, gold, and white fur, lean musculature churning beneath the wiry coat. Limbs of sprung steel scissored, and claws dug into loose ground, pulling it closer to its prey. The bullet-shaped head of the Painted wolf was held low, large dish-like ears folded back, eyes locked onto the impala's hindquarters.

"Close the chase, Koorsboom!" A high twitter from another wolf close behind encouraged him. "The hunt is yours!"

"The blood river comes, Kurkbos!" The young wolf could not hide his joy.

The dry savanna beneath them awaited its share of the blood promised by the hunt, indifferent of whether it came from predator or prey. For one or the other, every hunt could be the last.

The impala banked into a turn.

The wolf did so in kind, cutting off escape.

Smoky hazel eyes peered forward, his focus absolute on the coming kill. The short grasses, grazed upon through the summer downpours, were now stunted by the reduced rainfall of the approaching dry season. The low foliage did not hinder his tireless machined lope. The impala sailed effortlessly over a tangle of Knob-thorn acacia brush, hind hooves clearing the towering branches by over a meter. The wolf lowered his head further, and closing his eyes only for a moment, plunged into the brush. Branches armed with sharp conical thorns reached out to ensnare him, speared his skin, and ripped open gashes that flecked the dry leaves with crimson. He emerged from the brush having lost no ground on the impala, eyes locked once more on his prey, wounds completely ignored.

The pounding of the hooves no longer obscured the rasp of the antelope, chest heaving as it galloped toward an imagined salvation. On his flank, an old wound inflicted during a failed hunt last season began to tear open. His reserves utterly spent, the impala raced for his life into the sands of the savanna.

The wolf clipped the haunch of the impala. The prey lost his footing briefly, but long enough to forfeit momentum. Koorsboom gripped the side of the antelope, slowing him further. Three other wolves surrounded them, and the race was over. The prey was halted, anchored to the ground.

Koorsboom released his grip on the shoulder, leapt to the fore of the impala, and seized the snout, jaws closing on the upper lip. The other wolves took hold of the limbs, while another ripped open the hide of the belly. Viscera spilled out on the ground in a rapidly expanding pool of blood. Koorsboom glared into the marble blackness of the impala's eyes, filled with pure terror. He did not release or relax, continuing to stare into those eyes. He imagined for an instant being on the other side, and his heart began to hammer briefly before diminishing to a calm.

The black eyes of the impala wavered, and faded into acceptance.

Koorsboom allowed the antelope to fall, and at that the rest of the wolves pulled the carcass into several pieces. Death came in seconds, and the savanna drank its fill of the blood.

"Your hunting prowess resembles your mother's, young one." The larger male gulped down the bulk of the hip muscle. He was brawn across the shoulders for a Painted wolf, and his coarse fur was mostly white swirling across black, with golden tones across his back. Most of that color was now obscured with crimson.

"There is much to be learned before measuring up to that honor, Kurkbos." Koorsboom stepped toward the mangled torso, and buried his head within, unrooting the heart.

"I scent only our musk on the wind." Kurkbos had his nose in the air. "We are safe to eat for now. Quickly—the pups are waiting."

"Have you seen them yet?"

Kurkbos shook his head, spraying the others with clotted blood. "I have caught only a glimpse of our pups—your mother allows no one within the den. Veiled within her sanctuary under the fever tree, she has almost become a rumor, a story told in the evening twilight."

"You are not wrong, come to that." Koorsboom paused. "What she has survived has become a legend for us all."

The wolves ate in silence with blinding speed, packing away meat and organs with the greatest haste. Koorsboom stopped and looked about, satisfied there were no lions waiting to pounce. He hesitated, and before resuming his feed allowed his ears to rise to their erect position. Each swiveled, straining to detect an errant sound above the wind and distant bark of baboon. The water of the nearby pan was receding as the rains became less frequent, leaving behind swaths of emerald grasses. He sniffed the air, detecting only the musk of his hunting party. Before he buried his head in the carcass again, he paused, and nearly stood on hind legs for a moment, sniffing the air.

"Musk, indeed." He twittered to the others, the fluttering chirp sharp and crisp in the air, and the feast stopped on the instant.

"What, then, Koorsboom?" Besembossie, a yearling from the litter of the last dry season, was tensed. Each tendon and muscle were locked in place, ready for war.

"Is there a danger?" Kamassi shook the gore from her head, mouth agape and taking deep breaths in preparation for whatever came.

Overhead, a goshawk glided low over the plain, its white and brown barred underparts apparent as it released its sharp 'quik' call. The wolves took little notice of it.

"We are not alone." Koorsboom stepped away from the kill and toward the distant impenetrable thicket of mimosa. It retained the green of the wet season as the invasive plant sucked the water from the ground. He released another twittering volley, louder this time as he wished for the sound to carry. "You may as well come forth, *bliksem.*"

"Is it Essenhout's pack?" Besembossie was at his side, her voice nearly a whisper.

"No, they are further to the east." Kurkbos stood by the yearling. "Unlike the dead dogs we face now!" His voice rose into a warbling alarm bark that made each of the wolves tense further, at the ready to fight or flee.

Thorned branches of mimosa parted slightly to allow a single wolf through. Its rounded ears were high and alert, hazel eyes meeting those of Koorsboom. Another wolf joined it, and they stood motionless, regarding their adversaries. The air was suffused with an unquiet, and Koorsboom twitched.

"No, *boet*. Wait for it." Kurkbos panted in the heat. "There is more to this than a simple chase."

"Indeed there is." A graveled voice behind them made each of the wolves lurch. "The savanna is more crowded than you realized." The wolf they faced was the largest they had seen. His fur was dark, mostly blackened with swirls of gold and white that seemed to vanish into shadow. His shoulders were hunched forward, as though preparing to leap. His eyes glared balefully, one hazel, the other clouded white, lending him a maniacal appearance.

Kurkbos took a step toward the visitor, his voice remaining even and calm. "You overestimate your menace." He took a deep breath. "Our numbers are greater than your little party... and many more not far hence."

The dark wolf bared his teeth, white daggers against the pink of his throat. "I have not forgotten you, Kurkbos." His voice rumbled. "Our pack was well rid of you, unfavored son." He took another step toward the kill.

Koorsboom tensed further, preparing for the attack.

"And our numbers have only grown since you abandoned us." The dark wolf gestured to the others with his head not to approach.

Kurkbos gasped. He glanced at his pack mates before composing himself. "The far horizon has room enough for us all, Ratel. In this paradise, we could be legion..."

"And now we know you have denned."

Kurkbos stopped breathing.

Ratel lifted a lip, bearing serrated canines. "Penetrated your hide, have I not?" He rasped in what became a chuckle. "You always did speak far quicker than you could think. Never boast of your success—it only reveals that pups are on your mind. Be warned... the hunting grounds are ours to claim."

Kurkbos was a statue, and the silence lingered between them. After a long pause, he spoke. "And you never said much of use at all, Ratel." He took another deep breath. "What say you, Koorsboom? Shall we all cut him down?" His voice wavered as he spoke.

Ratel gave a thin smile in response.

"The lions of the north and the hyenas of the east are spreading their empires. They advance, and shall not yield to us." Ratel addressed the others, ignoring Kurkbos. "Between them all, there will be precious little grounds left to our kind." He fixed his one remaining eye upon Koorsboom. "And my mate, Varkoor, will drive you into the desert to keep it."

Koorsboom did not avert his glare.

"Your threats are empty, unfavored son." Ratel turned his stare back to Kurkbos. "If you had any courage, you would have attacked me already."

His lips drew back, and he hissed through his teeth. "And you would be dead before you hit the ground."

The hulking wolf bounded away without waiting for a response, into the stabbing thorns of the mimosa brush.

"We had best be away." Kurkbos exhaled, perhaps louder than he intended. "We have meat to deliver to our chief."

"And the ominous news of the evening." Koorsboom returned to the impala corpse to take the rest of his fill. One could never tell when a time of plenty will end.

Their return to the den was wordless. Their path carried them across a drying plain dotted with broad-crowned Giraffe-thorn acacia trees now nearly bare of green. A grove of Apple-leaf trees, their grey trunks bent and twisted, provided little shade as the leaves had dropped, leaving behind flat pods on the crooked branches. At last, the phosphorescent green of the fever tree was in view, and the wolves were enveloped in its glow. Another young wolf was waiting in the shade, and bounded out to meet them. "I presume this blood is not yours!" He twittered with joy.

"It is not, Blackthorn." Koorsboom greeted the yearling.

They all clustered around the opening of the abandoned aardvark hole that was their den. Kurkbos eased himself down the opening, a steep decline into a claustrophobic but dry interior.

"You have provided for our pups?" Aalwyn's voice was quiet, rising above the mewling of the small forms about her. Their pug faces were ever frowning, and nosed her belly for milk.

"The savanna rewarded us." He stepped carefully toward her—but not too close—and regurgitated bundles of meat and organ from the impala.

"And what grim news of that savanna lingers in the back of your throat?"

Kurkbos hesitated, unable to meet her stare in the dim light of the burrow. "They have come to warn us. Ratel delivers the threat of Varkoor, their alpha."

"The pack in which you were born has closed the distance." An exhale in the dark stirred the dust at his feet. "Very well. We may need to become the *Dwalen* once more."

"Wanderers?" Kurkbos inquired, unfamiliar with the moniker.

"We wandered for a long time to find this home, before you joined my pack." Aalwyn devoured the food presented to her. "I thought the time might come again." She relished the savor of the meat. "We will need to wean the pups."

"So soon?"

"They will be ready." She nosed one of her pups closer, and it latched onto a teat.

The young body of Koorsboom was crouched by the opening of the den, his snout pointed toward the hole, each ear focused on the echoed whispers inside.

"Something disturbs you."

Koorsboom nearly jumped, and looked back to see Olienhout over his shoulder. "You are as secretive as a leopard, my love." He lapped her muzzle, and she lapped his in kind, eyes closed.

"Kamassi spoke of the pack you faced."

He nodded. "The challenge awaits." His tongue lolled out as he panted, smiling in the way wolves smile. "When it comes, it will meet my teeth, not my tail."

Olienhout frowned toward the quiet within the burrow as the alphas spoke in hushed voices. Her eyes went toward the sky. As the burnished red disk of the sun dipped behind the mountains to the west, a chill wind slipped into the air.

"Another season is upon us."

Chapter 2

Parked in the shade of a Winter-thorn tree, the Land Rover seemed to blend into the savanna. The trunk of greenish-grey bark vaulted high above the vehicle, the leaves retained in the winter providing some sparse cover until they were shed in the summer rains. The faded light brown paint and dirt completed the camouflage. Seated away from the protection of the shade were two rangers, one squatting on the ground peering through a pair of binoculars, the other kneeling next to him. Their gaze was trained on the fever tree distant, where a Painted wolf raised its head just above the grass, glanced about, then lowered its head out of sight.

The older heavyset man peering through the binoculars was clad in green khaki shorts with brown leather work boots and a bicolored khaki shirt, topped with a wide brimmed safari hat. His right hand made notes in a ruled notebook. His left hand, hovering next to the binoculars to make adjustments, was deformed, the middle finger missing with a tangled scar between.

The woman, slightly built, was kitted in khaki pants and a shirt too warm for the climate, with sweat stains still spreading across her clothing. The heat was stifling, but still did not bother her as much as that left hand, from which her gaze would not shift.

Scarcely a word had passed between them all morning, until now.

"An hour. Or less." The older man spoke in a clipped Afrikaans accent, his voice hushed. "The temperature is dropping, so they will soon be off."

"Dropping? I... yes, I had not noticed."

"It has only been a week. You will adapt."

He glanced back to the young woman, and noticed her staring at his left hand.

"What is it, Venter?"

Sonja Venter immediately averted her eyes, and stammered. "Yes, we must—"

"What is on your mind." Johan Marais turned his considerable form toward her, his wide face a blank. His bushy brown mustache concealed his mouth, exaggerating the stoicism of his appearance. Brown eyes, verging on black, gave no indication of his thoughts.

"Was that from the war, Marais?" She immediately frowned and looked toward the ground.

He seemed to notice his mangled hand hovering over the binoculars and immediately withdrew it, massaging the scar with his right. "*Nee.* Puff adder bite." After a moment, he resumed examining the fever tree before him through the binoculars.

"*Ek is jammer.* I was told you were in the Border War."

"I was." He absently stroked his left hand before resuming taking notes.

She thumbed through her new, crisp journal, a book containing photographs of African wild dogs along with behavioral notes. "That must have been hectic. I had read about the *okes* who fought there. Able to kill a man with either end of a gun."

"I spent most of my time repairing the *Casspir.*" He removed his hat for a moment to scratch his head, revealing an unruly crop of brown hair. "The vehicle had a brilliant design to avert mines, but needed constant attention."

Venter looked up from the photographs. "I was in primary school then."

"Fortunate." He adjusted the body of the binoculars, as one set of rounded ears peeked above the line of grass. "War is a waste of everything our species offers. Naturally, it is where we spend most of our efforts."

"In another time." She relaxed. "We seem to be on the edge of a different reckoning today."

"So many conflicts to choose from." Marais sighed.

"Well, in wildlife conservation—"

"Public sentiment about wildlife, land issues borne of colonization, or the actual wars threatening to boil over around us." Marais peered through the binoculars.

"Focusing on wildlife con—"

"If the world allows you to focus."

"—servation, the world is finally recognizing its importance." She picked up her pad. *20-5; 0825 kill impala x1.* Morning for the pack had gone well. "In any case, this is an extraordinary time."

"How so?" Two sets of dish-like ears were visible above the wavering tips of grass.

"Awareness and interest have never been greater." She watched the fever tree ahead, crouched but on her toes, poised and ready to move.

"We are in the middle of a mass extinction, of which mammals are especially hard hit. Wild dogs have been extirpated from nearly their entire range. In twenty years, this work could all be academic, Ms. Venter."

"Wild dogs have not been seen at Gorongosa. Ever. Now we have two, possibly three packs surviving here."

"Perhaps." He flexed his left hand closed, open, closed. "These populations are relatively isolated, as are the populations across Africa. In South Africa, the metapopulation requires intensive management across several game parks to survive. Individuals are moved about in the name of genetic variability at a cost of millions of rand per year."

"Millions provided by donors the world over. All the more reason for hope." She began to pack her notes. "People never cared before. They do now."

"Too little, too late." Marais disconnected the binoculars from the tripod, pocketing the bolt and folding the stand shut. "They were shot on sight for years, by game rangers, no less. Farmers still kill them at will." He stood up, and several sets of ears were moving about. "They are on the move."

"It took the extermination of the passenger pigeon to start the conservation movement." Venter packed her gear in haste. "The tide has turned."

"You must meet a friend of mine." He was up and striding to the Land Rover, moving quickly for one whose physique resembled a building. "Du Plessis. He once discovered a pack of wild dogs that trekked through the Lowveld of South Africa, and his land there. He is a supporter, and an unreasonable optimist like you."

"The Wildlife Trust did not spot any in that region. Not this year."

"We could use more people like Du Plessis." Marais deposited his gear behind the front seat of the Land Rover.

"Hearts and minds." She gave an ineffable smile to Marais, which made him pause.

"A Vietnam War slogan from the losing side."

"Yes." She laughed in spite of herself. "Sorry about the questions."

"Have your people given you an ETA on the Tick?"

"First prototypes are coming in two weeks." She looked toward the fever tree, and the gold, black, and white coats were bounding about in the exultation of the hunting rally. "We must hurry, they are motivated, now, man."

Marais had moved the rest of his equipment to the Land Rover, and positioned his ample frame into the driver's seat. Massive hands wrapped around the steering wheel. His arms were covered with deep scars from years of acacia thorn wounds and gashes from truck repairs.

Venter raced around the other side and slammed the door behind her. The much abused yet fussily kept Land Rover wheezed forth. They gave the fever tree and the den a wide berth, while keeping the rest of the pack in sight.

Marais shifted into second gear as they bounced over the rough ground, plowing through scrub brush. The wild dog pack bounced around as they headed out for the evening hunt.

"I met an *oke* from South Africa, north of Joburg, just before I came out here." She bit down on a smile, looking towards Marais. "He keeps wild animals. He said he knew you."

"Dyk? The idiot who runs a zoo?" Marais rolled his eyes.

She laughed. "He told me he was breeding stock for reserves. And he said 'Tell that *oke* Marais it is not a bloody zoo!'"

"Canned hunting farm. Zoo is too kind a word. I hope he is not still interested in acquiring wild dogs."

"All sorts of people are gaining interest in the Painted wolf." Venter shrugged. "All the same, this is an exciting time."

Marais stabbed the forefinger of his ruined hand against the windshield. "This pack is something special. Look at this one." He pointed toward the lead hunting dog. "This one is always in the lead for the hunt. Always with the same male." Though they barely kept the white tips of the wolf tails within sight, both could see the leader of the hunt. Her distinct black-ringed gold coloration stood out. By her side was a male, and they ran close together. "Both quite young."

"You could argue there are two alpha pairs."

"Well, yes." Marais nodded to her. "Exactly. Only the older alpha breeds, but these two..." He nodded again, his ruined left hand on the gearshift knob. "Unusual for wolves so young to have a leadership role. They will have their own pack just now."

She smiled. "You almost sound optimistic."

"Working with wild dogs requires some optimism." He flexed his left hand. The pain had never gone away from the puff adder bite. "Even if that optimism is poured into a bottomless hole."

Chapter 3

Cold of night faded with the next gleaming dawn, and pairs of hazel eyes opened to greet it. Koorsboom and Olienhout were huddled together, and stood up as one to shake the dew from gold, white, and black wiry fur. The pattern of his coat resembled a swirl of cream dissolving into coffee, white and black whirling about with patches of gold interspersed. Her coat was of more distinct gold splotches ringed in black. On one side, a broad patch of gold was bordered by black in the shape of the western coast of Africa, with a sweep of white where the Benguela current flowed. They lapped one another's muzzles as they padded about the base of the fever tree to shake off their torpor.

Kurkbos was up next, blinking away the sleep. Large rounded ears surveyed the clearing, and heard only the activity of his pack. He nosed Kamassi and Besembossie, yearlings from Aalwyn's last litter. Branddoring crashed into all three of them, and was on her hind legs boxing the others. Blackthorn was the last to join. Wolves lapped muzzles in a frenzy, as though they had been separated for years. As the excitement of the greetings passed from one wolf to the next, a cacophony of twittering rose. Aalwyn bounded out of the den to join them. She walked alongside Kamassi, whose tongue rolled and jaw hung agape.

"Blackthorn—mind the pups carefully while I am away."

The yearling's jaw hung open in shock. "I may meet the new litter?"

"You may. I will introduce the pups to the rest of the pack on our return."

He bowed his head in deference, and ducked into the den. A storm of yipping greeted him as he started licking them clean, one at a time. The pups rolled about, glad of the attention from someone new.

"Olienhout—today I will lead the hunt. We shall move far to the east."

"Your sister's territory?" She dipped her head beneath the matriarch's, and her gesture was accepted.

"The rains have faded since I last saw Essenhout. Her pack has been doing well."

Olienhout paused to greet Besembossie and Kamassi with effusive muzzle-lapping. "I would presume so, as half your yearlings from the last litter made the bulk of her pack. What was the name of her mate?"

"Rukato." She stared toward the sunrise.

"From where did he hail?"

"A nomad, same as us, though he wandered alone for one winter to the next after the rest of his pack died." Aalwyn sprinted to the edge of the clearing, and gave a rapid series of chirps to the others. "Alone for so many seasons. How he survived by himself so long without going mad." Her voice trailed off.

The pack followed her lead, and the *Dwalen* was on the hunt.

* * *

Several figures reclined on the ground, huddled against the cold in filthy blankets of thin cloth. As the dawn cut through the trees around them, one by one the humans opened their eyes. There were yawns and stretching, but little other noise passed save the odd muttered expletive. One stood tall and bent his head back with a crack, dropping his blanket to the dirt. He had slept in his boots. This was as much to retain warmth as it was to prevent having a scorpion or adder take shelter within a boot during the night. He strode over to where a fire still smoldered, picked up a can from an open box, and opened the tab. The can marked *MANICA—Cervejas de Mocambique* was upended, every drop of beer drained, and pitched into the remnants of embers. All of the men were awake now, and they began to greet one another with low murmurs, punctuated by occasional boisterous laughter. Theirs was the easy cadence of men who lived their entire lives together, all from the same village in southern Mozambique.

One walked toward a large truck, the white of its paint obscured by dust and rust. The *SCANIA* chrome letters below the windshield were faded and cracked. Tires covered with dust groaned under the weight of the truck and its load on failing springs. The man hefted a rucksack and repacked its contents. He paused as one of the men called to him: "Augusto!"

He nodded, resumed work, and slid the bag onto the flatbed next to a pile of rhino horns.

The horns were of varying size, some quite small. Each were caked in blood and flesh at the root. Next to these was a chainsaw, also caked in layers of blood and gore, new upon old.

The men bundled their blankets and supplies into the back of the flatbed, three jumping into the cab and the rest in back with the horns.

They were on the hunt.

* * *

Grey bark of a Knob-thorn acacia separated one ecosystem from another. Outside the tree, carnivores chased while herbivores foraged. Just inside the bark, a colony of yellow ants over a million strong swarmed through the meat of the tree. The ants carefully laid silk to coat its tunnels and create a meshwork that sealed off their world from invaders. The delicate, translucent bodies climbed through the silk lattice, tending to the scale insects that harvested sugar from the sap. Their farm did a robust business, allowing the colony to thrive.

This ant colony died the moment the bark was ripped from the surface of the tree, after a fleeing impala dislodged it with a hoof. The exposed population was rapidly invaded by black ants that suddenly awakened to the scent and chemical signals of the silk-weavers. Each yellow ant and the larvae they tended were stung repeatedly, gathered up, and taken back to the black ants' home colony or eaten alive on the spot. Within the hour, nothing remained of that colony but an empty hole.

The impala pounded the dark earth, its nostrils flaring to gather air with straining grunts. Hooves dug into the loose dirt, rear legs pistons that vaulted it forward over a clump of acacia sedge.

Koorsboom scrabbled over the gravel, clawing his way forward. His head was held low, ears flat, mouth shut, a painted arrow that followed its target. Olienhout was on his flank, and she kept the pace. Aalwyn was close behind them, and twittered her calls to the point wolf.

"A disturbance lies ahead! Keep the impala moving in that direction!" She raced forward to take station to Koorsboom's side.

The antelope banked sharply left, and Aalwyn loosed a series of chirps as she closed the distance. This drove the impala back to its original course. It banked right briefly until Olienhout closed that escape as well.

There was a slight crashing ahead, still distant, but this approached rapidly.

"Another hunt is before us. Stay focused on our prey!"

As Aalwyn gave this command, the brush parted to reveal an open plain—and another wolf pack bearing down upon them. Koorsboom and the rest wavered but for a moment, and stayed on task. The lead wolf nipped the rear of the impala, and it stumbled. Olienhout sprinted forward and gripped the snout, while the rest of the pack swarmed over their prize.

Aalwyn ignored the kill and continued forward toward the other wolf pack. They chased an impala of their own, their pack forming a rough horseshoe around their quarry. Aalwyn powered toward them, closing the distance in less than a minute.

Without breaking stride, she met the antelope head-on and seized its throat. Anchoring her feet with claw and muscle, the impala's weight carried it forward, and dragged the throat wide open. It tumbled into the dust, and was surrounded on the instant.

Aalwyn was on hind legs, waving her forepaws, and boxed the rival matriarch. "Essenhout—a gift for your clan!"

"*Ag*, that kill was within our grasp!" Essenhout boxed her sister in kind, with a mock show of aggression. They lapped one another's muzzles with the close affection only siblings can share. "Better return to your prey,

Aalwyn. You have pups to feed." She gestured toward the other impala that Koorsboom and Olienhout dragged down, now dismembered.

"As you soon will, dear sister."

The wolf packs each ate their fill in silent peace.

The bulk of the carcasses were consumed before the first scavengers made an appearance. First to arrive were Lappet-faced vultures, coasting down from their thermals, wings folding slightly to cup the air and slow their descent. The three-meter wingspan quickly folded shut on landing, their dark, nearly black plumage contrasting sharply with the naked pink head. Charging into the kills, the large birds ripped away hide and began to feed.

Additional vultures arrived, most of them White-backed, smaller in size, but bolder as the numbers mounted. One vulture ambled toward an impala kill, only to be chased away in a cloud of feathers by Kurkbos. His teeth bared, he uttered no sounds. The wolf took mouthfuls of flesh when he could, but more vultures crowded the carcass. The *Dwalen* scattered momentarily to chase back the vultures and buy more time. The impala hide was ripped away, the organs eaten, ribcage denuded of muscle. The body was in pieces, the head mostly intact with eyes staring sightlessly into the sky.

By now a hyena had found the double kill. It was a male, and as such was lacking in courage. It bounded far from the wolf packs, unwilling to chance an attack until reinforcements arrived. *Whooop!* The call echoed across the savanna.

Two Black-backed jackals appeared, a male and female that had mated for life. They quietly waited close to Kurkbos for an opportunity.

Another vulture landed on the impala, gripping bone with its talons, sharp beak open. The wolves were startled for a moment, and all abandoned the carcass to chase the raptor away. It escaped with broad sweeps of its wings, soaring in a circle above.

With this disturbance, the jackals raced to the impala and devoured what meat remained from the hip and pelvis.

Kurkbos turned to see the pilferage, and chased the jackals off. "Bloody thieves, they are." He pulled off as much rib meat as he could swallow. "Aalwyn, that is the same pair that took over our last kill."

"Best to leave them be, Kurk. We have taken as much as we can carry."

"They are a threat, Aalwyn." He swallowed with more than a little effort. "And they will take a pup or two if we forget that."

"I have forgotten nothing." She glared at him, annoyed at the needling. "Some threats are more demanding of our attention." She left the carcass to join Essenhout. Koorsboom and Olienhout left as well, reeling slightly from the heavy load they carried undigested in their bellies. The yearlings withdrew, unwilling to defend the impala any longer.

Kurkbos snarled at one vulture, then another. One sharp beak nipped his tail, and he rounded to find nothing behind him, the vulture already having swooped over him to bury its head in the carcass to feed. The jackals returned to the kill, dancing in and out between the scavenging birds to take their share.

Kurkbos glared at the jackal pair and joined his pack once again.

The Lappet-faced vultures gobbled down all the hide they were able to strip away. Once this was gone, they were content to wait until there was seemingly nothing left, and would eat the connective tissue and tendons that the others could not digest.

"My yearlings have grown into eager hunters. I am pleased your family thrives, Essenhout."

"*Droom.* That is the name of our pack."

Aalwyn canted her head to the side. "Dream? Are you all sharing a dream, then?"

"Indeed. The dream has not stopped since we arrived here, in this good land together." She nodded, as though agreeing with an unheard voice. "Even with the loved ones we have lost."

Aalwyn looked to the ground. "It seems a lifetime ago, fighting for our place on this savanna."

"A place well earned, my sister. Blackthorn could not have wished for a greater legacy."

Aalwyn winced visibly at the mention of his name. "I still see him in my sleep."

"That must be why you named one of your pups after him." Essenhout smiled.

Aalwyn nodded, her thoughts drifting.

"I see them all—our parents, our life by the far away river, all of those who have died on the long *trek* here." She sniffed the air. "We may den soon enough." She shook her fur free of the blood from the kill. "Rukato is keen to have a litter."

Aalwyn looked to Essenhout's mate, who raised his head from the carcass at the sound of his name. His muzzle parted, revealing fangs. His smile extended up the side of his head, with flesh still healing from a bullet wound that grazed his skull.

"He is a strong one."

"Fearing nothing." Essenhout nodded. "And a clever hunter."

Kurkbos bounded up to the sisters. "We may as well get back." He grumbled toward the writhing mass of dirty white feathers that appeared to boil over the impala's remains. "If those jackals shadow us back toward the den, we will have another kill today."

"We will be watchful, Kurk." Aalwyn touched noses with him. "For this and other threats."

"Varkoor and the Selous pack." Essenhout emitted a low growl. "Their numbers rival the both of ours combined. Though we have done well here, the dry season will put pressure on them." She looked to the north. "And on the lion prides that have swelled since our arrival."

Aalwyn twittered to her pack. "Our pups await their measure of the kill. Time has come to wean them."

"You will enjoy this, Olienhout." Koorsboom chirped happily. "Wait until those pups feast on meat for the first time. A hunger will begin that shall never be sated."

The two wolf packs separated, and Aalwyn looked back at her sister.

After several bounding steps, Essenhout turned to look back with a lingering gaze. They each resumed their travel, returning to a den that embodied their hopes for the future.

After they completed their scavenging, the jackals followed the *Dwalen* at a polite distance.

***

The truck had stopped, and was idling in the track. The exhaust belched out blackish smoke, filling the area with a sharp, sour odor as the polluted fuel combusted. The men threaded through the brush while Augusto looked around at the rough earth as he paced away from the truck.

Calloused black hands withdrew lengths of wire from pockets. One end of the wire was tied and clamped around acacia brush branches with wire cutters. The rest of the wire was shaped into a large circle and the end looped around and crimped again to the wire itself. This loop could slip along the rest of the wire easily if pulled. The snare would sit, for months or years, awaiting a swiftly moving animal to tangle itself in the wire, which would pull tight and immobilize or strangle the animal. The men would check on these snares if they remembered in time, and they would have food.

Or the animals would be left to die of starvation and rot. If a kill was forgotten, it did not matter. Wire was cheap.

Augusto paused in his walk and crouched down. A large depression the size of a plate was worn into the ground. He walked on, and found another. And another. Finally, through the grass, a giant midden of dung. It had very little scent as far as he could tell, the waste mostly consisting of partially digested grass, and was stomped into a flat pile several meters across. The top layer was fresh, and to the touch, still warm.

"*Ei, pessoal!*" Augusto motioned to his men to return to the truck. "*Rinoceronte!*"

***

Blackthorn raised his head sharply at the sound of the *Dwalen* approaching. He was on his feet, though he could already detect the pattern of twittering, and the sound of his mother's voice.

Aalwyn was the first to reach the fever tree, tongue lolled out in anticipation. She nodded to Blackthorn, and dove headfirst into the den.

Her eyesight rapidly adjusted, and seven rotund figures emerged in the gloom. Each were covered in soft black and white fur, the gold of maturity yet to emerge. At sight of her, they emitted ultrasonic calls, pleading for milk.

Aalwyn emitted a low rumble within, a signal for them to silence. She then regurgitated every scrap of meat she consumed of the impala, a seemingly infinite cascade of blood and gore in a pile at her feet. She stepped back to watch.

The pups at first were incredulous, then ravenous, and they pounced as one on the feast. Small pieces of muscle and organ were swallowed whole. Larger pieces were gripped by one pup, then another, and as they pulled against each other in the dark, the chunk parted. The pups shared a glance, filing away that tactic for lifelong use. As quickly as the meat appeared, it vanished down bottomless throats, leaving only the faintest stain of crimson on the floor of the den. The pups watched expectantly, and none mewled for milk any longer.

"Kurkbos!" She did not look behind her, as the form of her mate darkened the entrance. "Feed your pups. They still hunger." They passed one another in the den, and she left the burrow. Blackthorn consumed his share from Besembossie, and brushed alongside his mother, Aalwyn.

She closed her eyes, whispering his name. *Blackthorn.* Her thoughts drifted to that of her mate, the father of these yearlings. She moved on to Koorsboom and lapped his muzzle. This prompted him to release his store of meat, and they shared the balance. In this way, they ate as a family. She rubbed her head against her son's, whose eyes were closed in the embrace.

They lay together, watching Kurkbos emerge from the den. He boxed Blackthorn for a moment before collapsing in a heap to rest. Aalwyn continued to watch her yearling and whispered his name again, louder than she intended. *"Blackthorn."*

"I miss him as well, mother." Koorsboom nudged her muzzle with his, and noticed her eyes were teared.

"It was the start of the wet season, before the last. When we first found these good lands." Her eyes bored into the young wolf sleeping before them. "Blackthorn was as much my world as you were. Every step of our long *trek* from the great river to the west, through every danger he was *my* wolf. Claw and fang... and a heart he could deliver against any enemy. Until the very last."

Koorsboom laid his head on his forepaws. "I remember his every teaching word. As I do yours."

"You would do well to. Be the father he was." She touched noses with him. "Claw and fang, heart great as the mountain for Olienhout." Her eyes flashed wildly. "The treacherous veld shall demand it. To the very last."

A short distance from the fever tree, hidden in the shadow of *Combretum* shrub, the jackals watched with mounting interest. At the sound of the pup calls that echoed from the den, the male ran a tongue along his chops.

* * *

"Pare o caminhao!"

The brakes were applied, and the large truck ground to a halt. There was no sound nearby for a few minutes. Then a branch broke. Several more.

Augusto murmured to his men, and they crept down to the ground. He removed the key from the ignition, opened his door slowly, and left it open. Reaching behind the seat, in the back of the cab, he retrieved an assault rifle. He resisted the urge to check the clip and chamber a round, as one was already in place, awaiting his command. He flipped the metal safety lever down. His thick, calloused fingers wrapped around the handle, finger away from the trigger for now. His other hand moved aside a branch as he walked past a low-growing Giraffe-thorn acacia shrub. The thorns tugged at his light green shirt, but could not dig in or slow him. Thick black boots stepped through the grass. He snapped his fingers lightly behind him, calling to his men.

He emerged from the acacia to find an adult mother white rhinoceros grazing on the drying grass. Wide, flat lips parted as she dipped her head to the ground, closing on a tussock of grass, pulling it up whole. She chewed on this briefly and swallowed, and lowered her head to take another mouthful.

Augusto brought the rifle butt to his shoulder, and his finger lightly brushed the trigger.

The bulk of the rhinoceros was a dusty white, thick skin like leather armor, as though a holdover from the era of dinosaurs. Two diminutive funnel-like ears swiveled independently to detect sounds of approaching threats. She took a large step, and bent down to take in another mouthful. Her eyes, nearly useless, did not see the hunter.

As Augusto lined up his shot, another branch beyond the mother cracked and gave way. Trotting forward into view was another rhinoceros, the baby. He whined for a moment, and brushed next to his mother. His awkward appearance was made more so by his funnel ears, seeming too large for the body, and oversized padded feet. The wrinkled hide, with stark ridges at the shoulder and hip joints, resembled an off-white sweater that his mother required him to wear with admonishment. The young snorted as he resumed grazing.

Augusto's lips pulled into a wide smile as he noticed that the calf, likely two years old at this point, had a horn. Small, but nonetheless a horn.

With a pull of the trigger, the rifle bucked with the single shot. He pulled several more times in quick succession, and red holes were punched into the rib cage of the mother. She emitted a deep gasp, and strained to take a step. In this she was halted abruptly, pulled roughly to the ground by an overwhelming invisible weight. She groaned deeply, a long exhale as both perforated and torn lungs filled quickly with blood. One of the rifle slugs had penetrated the heart, and she began to die.

The calf had never learned the import of gunfire, and prodded his mother. She did not respond. He whined with desperation, his nudging of her immobile body taking on a quiet fury. He took care not to prod her with his horn, knowing such things can hurt.

Augusto strode toward the calf, and with far less concern about any threat, squeezed several more shots into the baby.

He turned toward his men, not paying attention to whether the young had stopped breathing. *"Venha!"*

The rifle was slung onto his back. *"Pegue a motosserra!"*

One of the men nodded, and jogged back to the truck. From the flatbed he retrieved the rusted chainsaw.

Chapter 4

Death shadowed them, and there would be no escape.

The impala were predators of an immobile prey. Grass and brush leaves were tough and required every waking minute to process the nutrients, staving off starvation for another day.

The carnivores would seek the same, staving off starvation in kind by striking the plant predator down. Every thicket, each tussock of grass could conceal a killer, but there was no avoiding the need to search for food.

The carnivore arrived, the Painted wolf, and she took no effort to hide. Ears folded back, head down low, eyes locked upon the herd before her.

Death hung over her head, and would have its due from herbivore or carnivore, by fang or famine.

Impala were alert now, heads craned toward the wolf, muscles tensed, hooves stamping. Alert, but still chewing on the precious grass. Even the threat of the hunt would not stop the chewing.

The wolf, fur of black, gold, and white, drew closer. Still, none would run. The hunt may yet be aborted, and then all of that work of running would have gone to waste. The distance closed, step by inexorable step. A bark by one of the antelope. Another. Stamping of hoof, another and another. One final coughing bark, and the herd was off, the carnivores having broken an invisible perimeter.

Six wolves were now revealed, all emerged from cover.

An impala is a powerful foe, capable of shattering bone with a kick, or impaling with the male's curved horn.

The wolves hunted as a pack, their numbers countering the strength of the prey. Their strategy was to force a chase, and a fleeing animal is unable to use its horns.

The herd moved as one, but only for a moment. Powerful rear legs were pistons, driving the antelope forward, accelerating as fast as any human vehicle. They then broke formation, darting in odd directions, this way, that, away, extend, escape.

The wolves moved as one, but with a keen mind honed by experience. Aalwyn twittered to her flanks —Kurkbos and Koorsboom—to spread out and envelop most of the remaining impala. Their method kept some of their prey from escaping, and they concentrated on this group. Another twitter and the flanks closed back in. The pack picked up speed and closed the distance.

The impala knew they would not all be killed. The most healthy and robust amongst them kicked powerfully forward with a pronk that carried each antelope into the air, and several body lengths forward.

Aalwyn's mind worked on this display, analyzing the vigor of the pronk, and ignored the strongest of them. These would be more work to bring down than the weaker members of the herd. The movements were also meant to confuse, and so she blocked out one candidate after another. "Isolate the slow group ahead!"

Kurkbos took the lead, and probed three antelope to one side of the herd. More impala escaped, and these were allowed. The fewer the prey, the easier they were to track and anticipate.

This slower group of impala were the only ones remaining, and it became a battle of attrition and speed. The impala all bucked forth, willing themselves to be the quicker one. A million years of evolution whittled away all unnecessary weight and crafted pure machines.

The wolves pushed forward to match their speed, but did not close the remaining distance. The same million years of evolution assembled a hunter of pure stamina, untiring, with muscles capable of churning for several kilometers before a hint of fatigue.

In the antelope, the adrenaline flowed freely, any bursts of speed were used up, and the one impala that remained was unable to outdistance the wolves. Every effort made, every muscle fiber worked to the limits of their performance, and the impala could only just keep the pace.

As Kurkbos slowed, Olienhout took the lead, so one would always stay on the impala's tail, allowing no rest.

Chance would now be all that remained between the teeth and the meat, chance that a lion would interrupt, or a body of water would be encountered. The nostrils of the impala flared, wildly searching for a way out.

The miombo woodland presented no barrier, no thorny brush that the impala could put between it and its hunter. There was no scent of a lake or river. The running space ahead appeared to stretch to infinity, wide open with no safety in sight.

A nip on its backside. The impala hammered the ground harder, but this panic burst only depleted its reserves quicker. Another nip, and a bite with jaws gripping the hide. It struggled free, but only as several more bites landed, and the impala knew it was over. The surging of adrenaline ceased, the heart beat erratically, the overwhelming exhaustion blunted the pain. Darkness took the beast as its belly was laid open, viscera yanked through the opening, and the blood loss stilled the heart forever.

Koorsboom ate his fill with the rest, a quiet feast with furtive glances to the surrounding brush for interrupting scavengers. He stepped away from the carcass, running a tongue over his chops. Leaving the meal behind him, he wandered a short distance to a clearing at the edge of the miombo wood. He did not realize how close they had drifted to the southwestern edge of the wild. The mountain to the north was not visible at this distance. He gazed across a field to see a bare patch of earth. He did not recognize this as a square, but its straight edges were unmistakably human in construction. He examined the details, his tail swishing back and forth. Standing on his hind legs for a moment, he was able to make out a structure in the distance. All four paws returning to the ground, he continued to watch.

A human walked into view, carrying an object. A large bag, slung over his shoulder. He set it down, opened it, and began spreading something on the soil.

An animal joined his side. Koorsboom did not know this was called a dog, but he did know it was a relation of his. Four legs, claws and jaws of similar form, ears to listen, a pair of eyes to hunt. Its coat was a patchwork of white and brown, different altogether from his, but there were enough similarities to be uncanny to him.

The dog was suddenly looking straight toward him. The wind had shifted, and carried his wolf scent in that direction. A bark.

Koorsboom instinctively crouched, ears flat, unsure of whether this meant a threat. He continued to watch while the human completed his task, and lugged the bag back to a structure. The dog had not altered its gaze, and let loose another bark.

He crept back to the kill, considering this creature, and whether they would someday meet.

Chapter 5

Lazing about in the sun, the wolves blended into the grasses that were slowly turning brown with the winter. The pups, bloated with impala meat from the morning hunt, were to all appearances dead. Only the occasional deep breath and a sigh of contentment were signs of life. The sun hung directly overhead, burning down on the wolves, who did not bother to seek shade. To one edge of the clearing under the fever tree, a heavily gnawed impala leg glistened. It was still recognizable, though denuded of muscle, and only the tendon insertion points remained. The knee joint was intact, and the hoof lay forgotten.

A cautious sniff from a narrow muzzle nearly invisible in the grass. The black-backed jackal peered around, and edged closer to the impala leg. The sleeping pack did not escape its notice. The jaws closed on the bone with a barely audible click, but that was all it took.

Kamassi was on her feet with the slight noise, and a warbling alarm bark erupted from within. The rest of the pack was galvanized, and gave chase. The jackal shot into the undergrowth and was away.

"Bloody *dief*." Kurkbos muttered. "He will steal from us once too often." He returned to the scratching he had made to reveal the cool earth beneath and lay down.

Koorsboom and Olienhout huddled together, though not for the cold. "Have you given thought to it?"

"Yes, Koorsboom. The time is coming." She reached back to bite off a tick. "Aalwyn knows we will be leaving soon."

"Did you inform her?"

"Of course not. She seemed to know already." She stretched her forelegs before her. "Little escapes her notice."

"I wonder what she has foreseen." Koorsboom sounded far away. "Care to join me on patrol?"

"I will come with you." Kurkbos lapped his muzzle. "Perhaps we will find the jackal den. Then you will see what our teeth can do."

The three left the fever tree behind, and trotted into the veld. Their noses were held high, and as they moved, scents of the trail were taken in.

Track of hyena—but no scat, and no scent marking. The scavenger had passed this way long ago.

Deep wheel rut—no smell of petrol or exhaust, nor the smoking sticks humans held in their mouths. People had not been there for a few months.

A white splat of vulture droppings.

Deep pounding of eland tracks. The heavy antelope were on the run, but not recently. The herd had likely moved on some time ago.

Wolf track—upon further inspection, the musk was of Kurkbos. The pack had returned this way several days ago.

Light scents reached them, blown upon the wind, suggesting a distant herd of wildebeest, and a grouping of waterbuck that was following the receding shores of Lake Urema.

The ever-present coo of the cape turtle dove greeted them with a gently rolling *Kuk-KOORR-ru Kuk-KOORR-ru* with no harsh alarm call. No danger nearby. No lion prints found, not here.

The wolves were attuned to the subtle language of the savanna, and listened to the news it had to offer. Hundreds of species left scent marking and spoor that told a story. What had moved through, whether they did so in fear, and what threats were faced. They continued their leisurely but steady pace, covering twenty kilometers without the slightest sign of tiring.

"Treacherous is the scent that reaches us, Olienhout." The wolves slowed, and their muscles tensed. Gradually a signal reached them as the winds began to shift, the sickly rich odor of decay. These mixed with another smell, that of fire, though not of plant material. When grasses burn, the straw scent is a dry one. This was a wet and dirty sort of burn, and only oil and machines could produce the bitter reek.

"What is the danger?" Olienhout's twitter was a faded whisper.

"It has passed... and yet remains before us." Kurkbos shook his head, as though realizing that was unhelpful.

The reek grew stronger, and they could hear the squawk of vultures. The brush became denser and mopane scrub became a stand of mopane forest. The trees towered overhead, the canopies still laden with leaves that were a kaleidoscope of autumn colors. Greens faded to yellows and light reds, the leaves in the shape of butterfly wings. The grey, deeply fissured trunks terminated in higher branches that stretched into V-shapes, as though each tree had arms held high in celebration. Turpentine scent was thick on the floor of the wood, released by the leaves crushed and decomposing underfoot. This did not conceal the scent of death, however, which grew as the wolves emerged from the edge of the forest.

"*Bliksem.*" Koorsboom uttered, as the clearing before them revealed a dead rhinoceros and her calf. Lappet-faced vultures were standing by, having performed their task of ripping open the thick hide. Three hyenas were working in the belly, pulling out entrails far enough to tear off manageable pieces. One vulture had buried its head in the calf's eye socket, worrying free what nutrition lay within. What caused the wolves to pause, however, was the man.

He stood within sight of the carcasses, though mostly enveloped in the shadow of mopane trees. Clad in nondescript khaki/green clothes with no identification, he seemed to be anyone and no one. Ranger, poacher, policeman, *tsotsi*. He removed the dying ember of a cigarette from his mouth, and drew another from a pack in his breast pocket emblazoned with DANGER: SMOKING CAN KILL YOU. He lit this with the still burning butt, which he tossed onto the rhino carcass. He did not speak.

"Withdraw at once." Kurkbos backed into the shadow of the mopane wood, and they filed slowly away. "There are more of those humans about. Or at least there were." The smell of smoke was heavy in the air to their sensitive noses, the cordite of gunfire faded but lingering.

"There is only that human now." Olienhout looked back to see the man standing like a statue, his face periodically glowing when he drew on his cigarette.

For the first time, he raised his right hand, and it held an assault rifle.

"Make haste, you fools!" Kurkbos cried, and the wolves quickly vanished.

The man continued to stare at the rhino corpses. The scavengers ignored him. Traces of smoke lazily drifted overhead. After this cigarette was finished, he ground it out under a heavy boot and walked quietly back to a dirt path. A white *bakkie* was tucked into acacia bushes. The 'Toyota Hilux' logo was mostly worn away, now unrecognizable. The wheels were bare, the doors of the truck crusted with dirt. One of the rear-view mirrors were broken off. He sat in the driver's seat and closed the door with an awkward bang, as though the door needed convincing to remain closed. One hand turned the key in the ignition while the other stowed the rifle, safety lever on, behind his seat.

* * *

"These are fresh, beyond doubt." Kurkbos sniffed the wolf prints on the ground. "The reek of urine is all over."

"Several different types, variant in size, some deeper than others." Olienhout sniffed about, disappearing in and back out of acacia scrub as she searched.

"The musk resembles that *oke* we encountered." Koorsboom nodded. "Ratel." He grunted to himself. "He must have great confidence to take the name of a honey badger."

Kurkbos did not respond, seeming to be lost in thought.

Olienhout ran to them, chirping as she loped. "Ratel's prints are accompanied by a different set — similar size. Fair to say his mate runs with him. What name did she have?"

"Did he mention one?" Koorsboom peered at the tracks.

"Varkoor." Kurkbos sounded like an echo, hollow and distant. Staring at the prints, he breathed heavily.

"What ails you?" Koorsboom prodded him with his nose, but the alpha seemed frozen to the spot. "Come, Olienhout, perhaps we can find a duiker to feed the pups." They bounded off into the brush ahead.

Kurkbos did not move, still staring at the ground, breathing heavily.

Four toes, central blot of a pad, no dewclaw.

Deeply impressed upon the ground.

Surrounded with copious defecation and urine markings, a bold scent impossible to miss.

Chapter 6

Frenzied splashing drew the attention of crocodiles a short distance downriver. Their entry to the water was almost imperceptible from a distance, a flicker of the eyes toward the source of disturbance, and they slid beneath the ripples. Any sign of panic would be promising to the lords of the river.

The dominant male croc weighed over a ton, but once underwater, he moved with surprising speed. Leather clad arms waved their way through the murk, eyes closed beneath double membranes to the opaque waters. Their ability to sense vibration was all they required.

An impala, a yearling, was now in the deepest midpoint of the river, legs bucking to swim the breadth. Only the head was above water, bobbing up and down as the muscles powered a body that was not designed for submersion. The slender mouth was open, gasping for air with the effort. Elongated ears flicked as it swam, irritated by the cool of the water.

"Bloody *bliksem*." Koorsboom grunted at the fleeing antelope. Olienhout, Kurkbos, and the yearlings were at his side. "Come quickly." He dashed off and the rest of the hunting party was close behind.

"It would be just as well to let it go. The crocodiles will make short work of it." Kurkbos eyed the water with anxiety as elongated shapes coasted towards their prey.

"It is nearly across." He sprinted at the highest speed he could manage down the riverbank, around a bend to a broadening of the waterway. The flow became more languid here, and exposed sand banks where silt deposited. Koorsboom turned sharply and bounded onto the soft sands. A young crocodile was sunning there, and remained still as the wild dog pack bounded past. The wolves wasted no time reaching the far bank, more rigid than the sands, anchored by grasses that were able to gain a foothold with the receding of the rivers.

"We have little time." Koorsboom shot along the edge of the water, paws occasionally sinking into muck, but losing no speed.

"There it is." Olienhout had kept the pace, but now powered forward. She bore down on the prone form of an impala, at rest after hastening across the river. Its head was on the ground, fatigued from its close escape from the crocodiles that lingered in the cool waters. The wolves closed in.

Exhausted from a long run and desperate swim, the impala was unable to get to its feet before being seized.

Olienhout at first held its snout, but saw no fight in its eyes, only resignation, awaiting release. The impala was spent, and there was no pain in death. She dove underneath and tore the belly open. Kurkbos was next to arrive and promptly ripped the heart out by the roots.

Kamassi and Besembossie took hold of a limb each, and Branddoring came in time to dismember the kill.

The *Dwalen* savored their meal.

"As ticks in the fur—there they are." Kurkbos stopped his feast to approach the jackals that had shadowed them. "What say you!" His high-pitched twitter became a reverberating bark.

The jackals tensed, and began to take a few steps back.

"Must we make a second kill this day?"

The jackals looked at one another, as though understanding the threat, and vanished into the brush.

Kurkbos returned to the impala.

Kamassi had eaten her fill, and was scampering about the corpse with a dismembered leg in her jaws. She murmured around the mouthful.

"Yes, Kamassi, I am sure Aalwyn would be glad of the fresh meat."

The hunt had taken them closer to a rocky escarpment that formed part of the shoulders of the great mountain distant. The river was continuous through the year, fed by the fresh rainfall of the wet season. Monsoon clouds laden with warm water from the Indian Ocean broke upon the higher elevations. Much of the water remained on the mountain, held by soil anchored by montane forest, and the porous rock beneath. This would be gradually released through the dry season for the wild of Gorongosa below.

Once the wolves had completed their feast, the jackal pair left their place of hiding and gnawed what remained of the meat and offal.

The *Dwalen* padded away from the rocky grounds, further down the elevated savanna toward the grass plains that held their den. Further from the river, the earth became more arid again, and the trees reverted back to drought-tolerant species. Scant shade was provided by the tangled canopy of common corkwood, and occasional groupings of winter thorn acacia. These stands of deciduous trees were just developing mature leaves as the dry season began to take hold, and would lose them with the beginning of the rains. Flowering plants took advantage of this, growing well in the summer sun despite being underneath the tree, and sheltered in the winter.

"Those tracks again." Kurkbos sniffed the ground. "The Selous pack patrols here as well." He raised his head, looking about from one horizon to the other. "The prints were made this morning." Raised in alarm, his twitter was louder than he intended.

"Then we must not delay." Olienhout lapped Koorsboom's muzzle. "The pups await."

Their path led them down into a sloping grassy plain, marked by termite hills. The large structures stood as high as their shoulder and dotted the plain. The drier grasses became a deeper green around the termite colonies, raised edifices of sculpted earth. Older colonies had fallen into ruin, and were reclaimed by vegetation that grew riot, supporting small trees and shrubs.

Olienhout, in the lead, watched one of the termite mounds serving as a perch for a goshawk. The grey plumage of the raptor contrasted with the nondescript brown of the mound. It eyed the wolves, knowing there was no true threat, but maintained vigilance nonetheless.

Olienhout stopped dead, suddenly recognizing death in the grass—a snake. It lay still in ambush for prey, but now raised itself a meter high off the ground, and spread its hood in warning. Olienhout stopped, but was standing too close already. Every muscle locked, to be a statue, the only defense against a quick striking cobra—but this was not enough.

Olive grey coloration along the back, yellow belly with black stripes!

Her mind screamed to her in a warning blast of information, and she averted her head with as little movement as possible—just as drips of fluid spattered her ear and neck. Eyes were held shut hard enough to cause her face to quiver. She waited.

And waited.

"It is gone."

Olienhout opened her eyes to see the Mozambique spitting cobra slithering through the browned grasses toward the greenery of a termite mound. She shook her head, and continued to shake, tossing away any venom that still lingered.

"If not for that, so long ago." Her muscles were sore, not from the long hunt, but from the moment of fright that brought her life down to the seconds.

"What do you mean?" Koorsboom moved to lap her muzzle, but she withdrew, fearing some venom remained.

"A half mention by my mother, so many seasons ago, when I was but a pup. She spoke of the snakes that carry venom, but one particular type that could throw it, and leave you blind for life. Helpless in a land that conceals our enemies. If not for a half-remembered remark. So long ago."

Koorsboom touched noses with her, and her eyes fluttered as though waking from a dream. "One never can tell what moment will be the crucial one, in a lifetime laden with such moments. An errant step, a cobra hidden, or a neglected lion track." He brushed alongside her fur, the contact electric to him. "Come, my *bokkie*. The pups are eager for our return."

Chapter 7

"Is this part of a general move to the south?" Venter held the radio antenna aloft, a handle under a crossbar connecting two parallel metal antennae in the shape of an H. She turned her body, arm and head rigid, in a slow circle until there was an audible 'beep' from the receiver. "Still fairly weak, but in that direction." She held the antenna still. "Move to the other side of that stand of tamboti wood?"

Marais nodded.

The antenna was placed in the bed of the Land Rover and they drove off carefully overland. With the end of the rainy season, the roads and grasslands were less hostile to four-wheel drive vehicles, though care was still required.

"I do wonder if this pack will break up. Most recent count seventeen individuals, strong alphas. That is fairly large." Venter held tightly onto her door as the wheels bounced over the rough ground, seeming to find every single warthog hole.

"No way of knowing, really." Marais shifted into third gear briefly before returning to second gear, the terrain too violently uneven to allow any real velocity. "Packs do not get so large today, but several decades ago they numbered twenty, thirty. So nobody really knows the behavior of a natural population since they barely exist anymore."

The Land Rover powered through the thick brush. Pale white acacia thorns squealed against the metal body as they chipped away paint.

"Hectic. Like driving high speed through a knife drawer." She laughed, and Marais could not help but smirk as he struggled with the steering wheel.

They drove on for the next hour, which was a fairly short distance as the vehicle lurched over the grasses. As they rounded the edge of a stand of tamboti trees, the younger ranger gestured to the driver to stop. She stepped out with the antenna in hand. Her slow circle stopped short, and she pulled a pair of binoculars out of a pocket. Abruptly she tossed the antenna in the back and jumped into the passenger seat. "Straight ahead, less than a kilometer."

Before long they were within sight of an entire pack of wild dogs, resting along the side of a well-worn driving track. The engine idled for a moment, and was stopped.

"Spend the whole day driving all over this *kak*, and here they are lounging on a road." Marais took notes, scribbling on a sheet of paper. In one hand he held a binder of plastic-covered sheets with photos of wild dogs taken in Gorongosa. He traced a finger over coat patterns while he observed the reclining wolves. After several minutes, he closed the binder. "Seventeen, all accounted for."

"No division yet, no deaths, no immigrants. Where are the alphas?" She admired the resting pack.

"Those two big *okes* just there." Marais pointed a meaty finger at two sleeping figures. One raised her head, as though summoned.

Varkoor stared at the rangers, and sensing no threat, laid her head back down.

"She's a big girl, no mistake."

Marais tapped his reference photo sheet. "I was expecting attrition. Though I am more than happy to be wrong."

"A testament to the power of the alphas, perhaps." Venter took her own notes. "Their hunt was attacked by lions, what, a week ago?"

Marais nodded. "They got away, and abandoned their kill." He grunted to himself. "Probably the only reason they all escaped was the wildebeest left behind."

"So they are moving south to get away from the press of the lions."

39

"And the hyena clans. Lots of carcass theft between them."

She thumbed through another binder, stopping on a page with multiple stickers, each dated. "This big pack here. They are pushing against the southern pack, the one that..." She paused for a moment. "Did they really kill a lion last year?"

"Not sure if it was them. All I can say is the radio collar on that *bliksem* was found in one place, the leg in another. Never found the head. *Something* ate him. And when the body was discovered, the smell of wolf was everywhere."

"That has never been observed. You should consider writing it up for a journal."

Marais did not answer her. He seemed lost in thought, looking at the pack before him, sunning on the road. He rubbed his ruined hand with the other, his face grimacing. "The young ones from that southern pack... yes, we must tag them both when the Tick is ready to go." He nodded to himself.

"Why? One may be enough."

"Yes, both." He continued to nod.

Sonja Venter did not argue further. In their short time working together, she had learned that when Marais had made up his mind, he stopped paying attention to other people altogether.

* * *

Four paws were in the air, and a torrent of muddy water went flying with the splash. As Koorsboom righted himself, he stood deep in the pond, up to the shoulders. His ears were erect, tongue was lolled out, and he stood on hind legs to attack. Descending upon his target, he knocked Olienhout over into the water.

"Do you pay no heed to your surroundings, *domkop?*" Olienhout nimbly stepped from the pond onto the bank, shaking what moisture she could from her black, white, and gold coat.

"I am on the hunt, my *bokkie.*" He leapt from the pond, onto the bank, and pushed her back into the water. Kamassi, Besembossie, Blackthorn, and Branddoring all splashed circles around her, deaf to her protests.

Kurkbos sat on the bank observing the melee, keeping watch over the surrounding savanna.

"Do you fear getting wet?" Koorsboom yipped happily to him.

"Only if it comes with crocodiles." Kurkbos muttered.

The wolves ignored him, sensing somehow nothing malevolent was under the surface. After they tired of the play, the wolves left the water and continued their patrol. They padded quickly, seeming in no hurry while covering ground at a rapid pace. Heads were held up, ears swiveling to detect errant noises, eyes peering through the scrub. On occasion heads were dipped toward the ground to sniff, parsing out the signals left by herbivore and carnivore alike. Urine, feces, scent marking were catalogued, creating a mental map of the region and the animals that passed through, some recent, some long ago. Ancient dung middens were given minimal notice. Fresh markings were examined. If quite fresh, one could tell the mood of the animal, traces of contentment or fear lingering.

"Hold here." Kurkbos sniffed the earth. "The *Selous*."

The rest of the *Dwalen* tensed.

Nostrils flared as he took in the scent. The others began sniffing the ground. Olienhout was first to nod to him.

They left their previous path, having found another. Now prints appeared in the sandy soil.

"These tracks were made this day." Koorsboom's twitter was barely a whisper. The joy of the morning had vanished.

"I have another set of prints here." Olienhout's voice rose above the sound of the murmuring wind. "And they are in the other direction."

The wolves at once stopped and pulled in together. Ears strained to listen for danger, and eyes were on alert, looking all over.

"Steady on." Koorsboom was no longer remaining quiet. "There will be no ambush."

Just above the tufts of drying grasses, large dish-like ears bobbed. They were joined by another set.

Emerging from the prairie grass, two wolves regarded the *Dwalen* with suspicion.

"Are you alone, then?" Koorsboom warbled quietly to the two visitors, but his teeth were bared and ears were folding back.

"We are." The strange wolf was dark, mostly black with the gold and white coloration only in traces. "Laeveldvy, you may call me." He stood staring, his expression fixed and blank. His companion said nothing.

"A mighty tree you are named for. My mother spoke of the Lowveld fig. Wherever they stand, they do so as tall and proud as the mountain."

The dark wolf did not answer him.

"Koorsboom is the name given to me."

"A small and delicate tree." Laeveldvy grunted, the pauses between words now inhabited by a steady growl. "And now you hunt the lands with this *oke?*" He gestured toward Kurkbos, who was now moving closer to the visitor.

"Indeed. He is our alpha."

"Alpha?" Laeveldvy raised a brow, and Kurkbos stood as tall as his shoulders could muster.

"Are you from that *Selous* pack?" Koorsboom peered at Laeveldvy.

The dark wolf gazed over the rest of the wolves before him, blinking away the dust from his eyes, ignoring the question. "I abhor violence between fellow wolves." He glared at Kurkbos. "As your 'alpha' can attest, I am alone in that regard."

"And Varkoor intends to fight us for a land as wide as the very horizon?" Kurkbos met his glare. "This place is one of plenty. We need not embrace conflict."

"The order is not mine to give, *broeder.*"

"We are brothers still, Laeveldvy." Kurkbos stepped closer to him. "I left our pack to find a land of my own." He paced about the open clearing. "The rains have brought renewed life to this place. The grasses flow like an ocean unbound, and the trees seem to beckon to a limitless bounty of prey. The impala and waterbuck number as seeds on the wind." He closed his eyes and took a breath. "Hunters like us belong here, under the great

Mountain." Opening his eyes, he gestured towards Mount Gorongosa, looming distantly. "And you are welcome to join us."

Laeveldvy had not changed his stare, a look devoid of affect. "The richness of this veld has not escaped my notice. Nor that of the lions that thrive. The hyenas that have laid claims of their own." He suddenly appeared very tired. "Mighty though the *Selous* may be, we are under threat. We were driven from our home, far to the north, by humans. They took away the antelope and replaced them with fences. Southward across the seasons was our journey, and ever there were the fences. That or arid pans with no hunting. Any promising grounds rife with antelope, there would be humans, and their thunder to strike us down. Ever southward across drying lands." He chuckled to himself. "After such a *trek*, I was of a mind to leave, as were others. In a way, you brought us to this place, below the mountain, by leaving."

"How so?"

"We followed you. Varkoor suspected you were onto something promising. And so you were." He looked around himself, as though seeing wild acacia for the first time. "So strange to discover a land so rich that has not already been taken by humans." He sighed. "And yet, there was no peace. We were not the only creature of serrated tooth to find this paradise. Lion and hyena alike. They sweep down like a wind from the north, leaving us to flee to an ever marginal existence." He looked to the east, where a glint of metal caught his eye. Far away, he could see a human clad in khaki holding an instrument in the air. "I suspect they have brought this pestilence upon us."

Kurkbos canted his head to the side. "What ever do you mean?"

"I observed one of their—*things*—transporting a lion." He shook his head. "Beyond any reckoning."

"The lion prides are burgeoning, then?" Kurkbos' voice was uneven.

"So it would seem. As I say, the order is not mine to give." His haggard eyes, hazel in color but lacking the animation of a younger wolf, fixed upon Koorsboom. "We shall press you."

Kurkbos took a step toward the dark wolf. "My *broeder*—"

"I only hope I am not the one who must kill you." Laeveldvy nodded his head toward the *Dwalen*, and he and his companion turned to leave.

Long after they departed, Kurkbos finally spoke.

"Aalwyn was right. Our time for wandering is at hand." He looked to the others. "We hunt before returning to the den." He was concerned about feeding the pups, but also welcomed the chance to delay bringing this news to his mate.

* * *

The brown Land Rover roared its way along the dirt track. Abruptly, it was halted with a slight squawk of brakes. Johan Marais held up one of his broad hands to shade his eyes, searching the brush near the path.

"Difficult to track that smaller pack—the one with the two young alphas in training." Sonja Venter scribbled in her journal while the vehicle was stopped. "We must tag the true alpha female as soon as we can."

Marais had left the vehicle and walked over to a thorn bush. He leaned into the sedge and the entire bush began shaking, leaves scattering.

"Have you named it yet?" She frowned, wondering what he was doing.

"Named what?" The bush shook twice more, then stopped.

"The smaller pack."

"Reluctant to name something so fragile." Marais walked back toward the Land Rover with a length of wire in hand, a large loop with a tangle at the end where it had been secured to a tree. His thick arms bent the wire into smaller knots and tossed the snare into the rear of the vehicle. "So close to being chased off, struck by disease, or destroyed."

"They will find a way."

"We shall see." Marais glanced at his watch. "We need to get moving if we are to reach the village by sundown."

"They should be ready for us. I had food and supplies delivered this morning." She grinned. "Word is traveling fast now that we are hosting these gatherings."

"Free food buys a lot of happiness." He grunted.

"Hopefully, what we are getting is trust."

Marais returned to the driver's seat and the Land Rover made its way south, away from the wolf encounter. Once the wheels came to a dirt road, the going was far easier. Though still jostled by the occasional rock, the vehicle was able to ease into a higher gear and cover more ground.

"The wild dogs—are we calling this three packs, now?" Venter put a boot up on the dashboard.

"Three. Though the two smaller packs are very much at risk."

"Three, then. All are showing good evasion behavior from the lion prides."

Marais grimaced as they struck a boulder, and righted the steering wheel without slowing. "The imported lions brought some good genetic variety. And now they multiply. The tourists should be happy about that. Though they are making life hard for the wolves."

"Will the wild dogs abandon the park, then?"

Marais glanced, but did not answer. "We shall see."

Two hours dragged by, and the Land Rover approached the edge of Gorongosa's southern border. Marais looked sharply over to his right and slowed the vehicle. He continued to look right, and gestured to the younger ranger with his left index finger.

Venter looked at the mutilated hand, feeling some sympathetic pain in her own. Reaching behind her seat, she retrieved an assault rifle and handed it over.

Marais hefted the wood and steel AK-47, removing the clip and checking it before slapping it in place. He pulled back the charging handle, and a single bullet was ready to fire.

"Would you prefer a proper hunting rifle?"

Marais looked at her for a moment. "This is better. It is not fully automatic, so there is good control. It can be immersed in mud or be used to pound a nail home and still work perfectly fine. Also, the bullets cost less than bread here." He exited the Land Rover and walked fifteen paces before crouching.

Before him was an impala herd, paying no attention to the vehicle or the person. The antelope were accustomed to tourists and vehicles, and had not seen hunters of any kind here. The closest male antelope, horns held proudly aloft, pulled leaves from a low-growing acacia shrub. Incisors removed the leaves, and rear molars ground them into a fine paste. With a swallow, the food disappeared. After a moment, a bolus of food came back up its throat, and the impala resumed chewing its cud.

Marais took aim and fired once. The sound of the shot faded across the savanna, and before it was silent again, the rest of the herd had fled. He strode to the prone form of the animal, a single hole in its side just behind the front shoulder. No sign of life or suffering.

Soon they were on the move again, with the impala in the rear. Within the hour, they were out of the park and in a village. Marais parked, and Venter jogged over to speak to two men in Portuguese. She gestured to the rear of the vehicle, and two young men, no older than seventeen, hefted the impala out.

"Who is preparing the feast?" Marais was new to this work detail.

"Those two kids."

"Do they know what they are doing?"

She laughed. "Those boys learned how to dress an antelope before we learned how to ride a bike. They could get a job at a professional butcher in the big cities of Europe." She beamed at them as they set to work, slicing the hide away and working on the ribs.

"I must give you credit, Ms. Venter." Marais scratched his head before replacing his hat. "You have not been here long, but you meet and move people quickly."

"The people living on the edges of nature reserves tend to be seen as a problem."

"That snare I removed earlier was likely placed by someone from this village." He eyed the people nearby with suspicion.

She waved to the boys as they neatly removed the impala's hide in a perfect sheet. "I want them to be partners."

As the sun set, the impala meat was roasted on the *braai*, the rich smoke drawing in every person in the village. The women prepared beans and greens in pots by the fire, and men told stories of past hunting triumphs. An earthenware pot containing an opaque beer brewed from maize was passed around, and Marais shared it with the men. Sonja Venter chatted with some of the people of the village. As they spoke, she brought out color photographs of various carnivores and passed these from person to person.

When the photos of African Wild Dogs appeared, the men pointed and shouted at them. Marais nodded, and calmly spoke of the Painted wolves, their wild ways, and the gentle manner they had with one another. Some of the men told stories of their own, about how children were devoured whole by entire packs. Marais frowned and glared at the ground.

Venter only smiled and spoke of how no Painted wolf had ever attacked a person, not with a hundred years of observation. The men only shook their heads, unconvinced.

She gestured towards the edge of the village where a wall of tangled, cracked acacia branches stood taller than the shoulders of the men. The barrier was of sticks woven carefully together, the wood tough but flexible. Smaller branches were interspersed between the thicker ones, making the wall difficult to penetrate by sight. The thorns of the acacia made the wall painful to touch or attempt to climb. The men nodded amongst themselves as she admired the craftsmanship of the thorned walls.

"The *kraal* has been working well. No cattle have been killed as long as they are herded in nightly." She gestured to the cattle *kraals* and continued to speak Portuguese to them.

"The wild dogs should pose little threat to their cattle." Marais took an impala shank from the *braai*. "These are more useful against the lions and leopards."

Marais spoke to them of the wild dogs, and gestured with his hands. The men of the village shook their heads. Marais smiled at Venter with a shrug. "Even if the cattle are protected, they are concerned about personal safety." He slowly opened and closed his mutilated hand. With the other, he gnawed impala meat off the bone.

"I am planning to visit the next village over in a week." She took a cup of beer offered by one of the women with a smile. *"Obrigado."*

"These banquets were a good idea, Ms. Venter." He swallowed a mouthful of the meat, enjoying the gamey flavor. "The education posters seem more welcome when they come with food."

"If the park resources are shared, the people have reason to care about the park."

Marais glanced at her, but said nothing.

They took their leave, with much shaking of hands, the departing friendly words taking every bit as long as the feast itself.

By the time they were headed back into Gorongosa across its southern border, the world was utterly black.

"You think the wild dog packs are headed this way?"

Marais nodded.

"What are the odds they will call you instead of shooting them all?"

"Fifty—fifty at best." He shrugged.

"Always worth a try." Venter peered into the darkness, searching for glowing eyes.

* * *

As night fell, the wolves returned from a successful hunt. They loped back to the den, Aalwyn, and the pups. Bellies distended with meat were emptied, and the pups gorged themselves on the winnings. Each hunter stepped toward the anxious pups, their pug-like faces looking up expectantly. Each pup in turn dined upon impala meat, and one after the next they retired, immobilized by the feast. Aalwyn watched each of the hunters, and saw they made subservient gestures to their chief, but none would look her in the eye.

Kurkbos lay by her side, also curiously silent.

"You encountered the *Selous* pack."

"Yes. One of them." He ran his claws over the ground before him, disturbing a small beetle that scurried off.

"Varkoor?"

"No... one of the older hunters. Our time here grows short."

"It is early to move the pups. We need more time." Aalwyn stretched her forelimbs before her and pondered this.

"Death threats from lions... these are expected. From other wolves... " His voice trailed off. "*Ag,* it happens when the land is scarce. From a wolf I once ran with, however..." He sighed, and rested his muzzle on his forepaws.

"We will make forays daily with the pups. They must adapt."

"This Varkoor." Kurkbos turned to look into her eyes for the first time since the morning. "She will come straight after you. She knows." He turned away, and the sunset reflected against his eyes. "The way to disperse a pack is to strike at the alpha. She can be fearsome to those not under her protection."

"We found this home, Kurkbos. We shall find another." Aalwyn lapped his muzzle, her voice even and sonorous, and managed a calm in his heart. She rested her head while two of the languorous pups tugged at a bit of discarded hide. It was not long before she could hear gentle snoring from her mate.

She issued a light twitter, and Koorsboom padded over lightly, moving around the pups engaged in a tugging war.

"Yes, mother?"

"Tomorrow we must start moving the pups. Short bursts at first, to accustom them to travel. After midday we patrol far to the south. You and me. *Verstaan jy?*"

He nodded. "I understand." He left her side to doze next to Olienhout. They would all need rest. He had seen that look before in his mother's eyes.

Chapter 8

The acrid smell of gunpowder remained in the morning air, the heavy scent of metal lingering long after the shooting ceased. The endless ringing in the ears carried on, ignored by the men who worked their harvest.

"Augusto!" One of the men gestured, tossing over a phone.

He plugged one ear with a finger, still struggling to hear the person at the other end of the line. He spoke into the phone in urgent Portuguese. "Yes, twenty minutes. We are at these coordinates." He read off numbers from a GPS unit and hung up the phone.

"We need to hurry—twenty minutes!" Augusto ran over to one of his men, now struggling with his machete to start the skinning. He took his own knife and worked to separate the hide from the deeper tissues. An entire herd of zebra lay motionless, brilliant black and white stripes now stained with blood. Working with expert hands, he ran the incision down the belly, down each leg. Then with caution, he worked the blade along the hide separating it centimeter by centimeter from the subcutaneous layer.

He stopped to shout at the man working the other half of the zebra hide. "No - the knife must be next to the skin, otherwise you punch through it!" He clucked his tongue, knowing the price for this hide will be less with the flaw.

"Just lay them out. Do not stack them until they dry!" He directed his men, and watched as rocks were placed on each of the skins to keep them stationary. The winds tousled the grasses around them, and brought to the hunters the sound of an engine.

The revving was of another vehicle, but one far more scrupulously maintained than the one parked by the carcasses. As the Land Rover drove into view, bouncing over the rough ground, Augusto marveled at how it managed to look clean despite the unrelenting dust, dirt, and occasional rain of the veld. It pulled up next to him and the engine was cut.

"Augusto—how many?" A man stepped from the vehicle, planting a black boot on the ground. He was wearing a canvas uniform shirt and pants, both a deep solid green. His head was topped with a black beret.

"Thirty-seven."

"I needed forty zebra skins." His hands were clasped behind him, chin up as he surveyed the other poachers with an imperious glare. "I needed them now."

"I will have the rest in three days."

"We will be to the north three days from now, in no position to fetch the skins from you." The man in the black beret snorted at Augusto, brushing unseen dirt from the green shirt.

"I will bring them all to you. Where will you be?"

"Raiding the hospital, so you must be there waiting." He took a metal hip flask from his pocket and upended it.

"What is worth taking from a hospital?"

"Cars, drugs, and target practice."

"Target practice?" Augusto glanced at one of his men. "On what?"

He adjusted his beret. "Whoever runs the slowest." He upended his flask again. "Did your men learn to shoot since we took the last shipment?" He laughed, though Augusto did not laugh with him. Everything the man in green said seemed in jest, but he meant every word of it.

"The hides are just there." He indicated the field, littered with stripped carcasses. "They need time to dry."

"Bring them all that morning then, at least forty. If the shooting has stopped, you are too late." He put away his flask and opened the door to the Land Rover. "I need you to be on time. A very important man will be there."

Augusto nodded in deference. "Yes, colonel."

* * *

The sun hung overhead, and bore down on the field with searing intensity. Winters in Gorongosa were mild, and during the day the heat and humidity could be oppressive.

The dirty white Toyota Hilux crawled along a dirt road, a head hanging out the driver side window. The rear cargo area was empty apart from a few dirty blankets. The face was twisted into a scowl as eyes scanned the roadside. He stopped the *bakkie* suddenly, reversing, and peered at the gravel as a portion of it was scattered into the grass. The depressions on the grass were barely visible, but he was able to follow it. Before long, he no longer needed to follow tire tracks, as the carnage ahead was visible. The flies were as thick as smoke from a burning building.

After parking, he stalked into the killing field, lighting a cigarette. The dead zebra were scattered across the plain, laying where they were shot. The mutilated bodies were concealed with cut brush, delaying their discovery by vultures. Hyenas, however, had found these treasures, and several were present, each working on their own carcass.

The dried skins had already been taken away. The man stood with arms crossed as the black flies filled the air with an unceasing dirge.

Once he finished his cigarette, he returned to the *bakkie*, started the engine, and steered back towards the dirt road. He noticed two wolves standing together, looking at him from under the green crown of a lavender feverberry tree. The normally lush tree had lost some of its leaves for the brief winter. The wolves seemed to be observing him as much as the valley.

His hand drifted behind his seat to the assault rifle for a moment, reassured by its presence. The vehicle trundled off the grasses and toward the dirt path. For the rest of the day, he uttered no words.

The man did not speak. He never spoke.

* * *

"Why?" Koorsboom glared at the field just below them, the zebra bodies unrecognizable even without the curtain of flies. He noticed the man in the field.

"Is there ever a reason for these creatures?" Aalwyn gestured to him. "Best to slip away, lest this human add our bodies to the field."

They slipped under the feverberry trees as the white *bakkie* moved off. The wolves continued south, loping through the pasture of herringbone grass. A herd of impala was startled momentarily, dozens of black marble-like eyes fixed upon the two predators until they were out of sight. The threat passed, and they resumed grazing on what would be the last good grass of the year.

From under a stand of Giraffe-thorn acacia, two jackals watched them depart. The male and female pair continued past them, scenting the dead zebra on the wind.

Tamboti wood trees gave way to a plain of mud and grass, a vast flatland that was until the month previous flooded. Green shoots stood tall to catch the sunlight above the waterline.

Water remained standing in temporary ponds, some still inhabited by small crocodiles. As the land dried, they would flee eastward to Lake Urema. The cormorants, herons, and kingfishers had already made this move, leaving behind grass seed eating birds and the small raptors that hunted the plains. Waterbuck, forever tied to permanent water sources, moved closer to the lake along rivers that threaded down from the great Mountain to the north.

Koorsboom and Aalwyn watched from the bank as a flock of white storks drank from the river, milling about, wings spread wide to sun themselves. Soon, they would depart on their migrations in search of other rain-drenched lands. A troop of baboons held station on the opposite side of the river, ever watchful against carnivores. A hulking male sat on his haunches while scratching his side, yawning wide to reveal his fangs to all who watched. Younger troop members stepped cautiously to the water's edge, and looking up and down the clear waterway, barked to the others. Once declared free of crocodiles, the rest came down to drink at leisure. Aalwyn stepped along the upper bank of the river, giving the deadly baboons a wide berth before crossing the cool waters.

South of the river the lands dried further, and trees once again appeared. Singular small trees appeared, low shrubs and acacia, followed by stands of miombo forest. Aalwyn called them to a halt within the shadows. She sniffed the ground. "Essenhout has been this way." Another sniff. "But not today."

Koorsboom watched as a warthog browsed close by. A white beard was buried in the drying grass as it grazed on its knees. It started momentarily when the wolves came close, then resumed feeding, sensing no threat. A sable, solitary where it browsed amid palm shrubs, also ignored them. Somehow, they knew the wolves as hunters of intent, rather than opportunists like lions. Should a lion happen upon a prey animal, it will kill even if completely sated, the body left to rot unless gnawed upon later. If the wolves planned a hunt, they would have known the instant they appeared.

"Newer tracks. She is closer now."

The wolves followed a trail, scent marking in a vast web that made up their territory. The strength of the scent grew more intense.

"*Who dares enter my domain?*" A warbling alarm bark reached the two, and Koorsboom tensed.

"*Ag*, Essenhout, you startled me." Aalwyn padded up to her sister, and they lapped muzzles in greeting. "You nearly were in for a *klap*. How fares your clan?"

"They are well, but the news of the veld worries me."

"You read the veld correctly. There is trouble afoot—and the *Selous* pack is moving south."

Essenhout sat and scratched behind her ear. "Whatever for? The whole of the north is theirs for the taking."

Koorsboom padded up to them. "It is true—the warning comes from the *Selous* directly. They are being pushed from their territory by an expanding lion population."

"I wonder how long we have." Essenhout's tail swished one way, then the next.

"Time enough. This wild place is quite large. I suspect it will take the season for them to be pushed into our territory. That distance will allow us room to prepare." Aalwyn looked toward the distant trees.

Essenhout sighed. "So it goes." She looked around her. "Walk with me."

They padded further south, and the miombo forest parted, yielding to a stand of fever trees. The bark appeared to glow with the burning sun. Under the sparse leafy crowns, a small group of Painted wolves rested. "This has been good hunting land. I was hoping to den soon... and now this." She sat, and breathed deeply. Though born only a year before Aalwyn, her shoulders hunched as though she were considerably older. "My hunts have pushed south, where the wild lands cease and give way to farms. And there are so many farms."

"Cattle?"

"Cattle, and crops. In the dry season, the humans place long skeletons of metal along the fields that spew *water*, of all things, and the wet season is renewed for only that bit of land." She shook her head, dislodging biting flies. "There are dogs, and there is anger. The humans spotted us on their farm, and we could hear the thunder as we fled."

"Were any of you harmed?"

"No—we were too quick for them to kill us so easily. The south is a dangerous place. Do you remember our *trek* here?"

Aalwyn nodded. "A lifetime ago, it would seem."

"These farms cover the land to the south. And to the west, montane forest where we would have difficulty finding prey larger than a monkey." She grunted. "I remember we passed through those forests on the way here. Scarce game, but we were overjoyed just to find the wild once again."

"There is nothing for it. We must make way."

Essenhout allowed a faint smile to cross her muzzle as she watched the yearlings play under the fever trees. "I always saw these trees as sanctuaries. As though we had fences of our own, ones that could protect us from danger. Where we could hunt antelope for season after season, and our kind would range to the very horizon."

"Perhaps we could find a way to persist on the edges of the wild." Aalwyn nudged Koorsboom. "We have survived worse."

"I tire of the *dwaal*. I do not wish to wander ever further." Essenhout sounded far away.

"Our packs could reunite, until this season of ill promise passes us."

Essenhout lapped her sister's muzzle again. "I take my leave of you. This bears consideration—once yielded, hunting grounds will not come under our control again."

"We shall hunt together again soon." Aalwyn held her face close to her sister's. "A path shall be revealed."

Koorsboom watched Essenhout retire with her pack under the fever trees.

"We continue to the south. This is where the *Dwalen* shall begin the *trek* anew." Aalwyn stared at the ground before her.

"Shall we run the pups again this evening?"

"Yes. We must work them harder if they are to be ready to move."

"The great Lake to the east may be of use to us." Koorsboom gazed at the fever trees nearby.

"Where there is water, there will be lions." Aalwyn looked toward the sun, descending toward the mountain range to the west. "And lions' command of the night is absolute."

Chapter 9

Long shadows cast by a rising sun hid a dead sentry. The heavy skull, lying against a baobab root, directed its empty sockets to the bare branches overhead. The jaw hung slack, long since stripped of connective tissue, giving the appearance of a scream rendered silent. The faded white of bone looked as though it had come to rest a thousand years before, but like any other part of the earth was in decay. The large nasal cavity once held the sensitive tools of a fearsome hunter. Two fangs several centimeters in length were rooted in the upper jaw, and with the shearing back teeth, revealed this skull belonged to a carnivore. Long since departed was the bold mane, the swishing tail, golden coat of fur, and the guttural roar that issued a challenge to the veld.

The lion was dead, and yet this clearing was alive. There was a scent to this place, carrying long and far, pungent of urine and musk from regular visitation by a Painted wolf. Distantly the sentinel mountain of Gorongosa wavered behind the faded clouds, ever watchful over the valley.

The visitor who marked this place stood as silent as the remains of the lion. His fur was wiry and coarse, rough-hewn like the savanna that sustained him. Smoky hazel eyes examined the skull, as though suspicious of resurrection.

"Were you ever, indeed, my enemy?" Koorsboom remembered that terrible day, a lifetime ago.

"Lions are well suited to the role of enemy."

Koorsboom tensed. "I will never become accustomed to your stealth, Olienhout." He turned to the other wolf, and lapped her muzzle. "You followed me, all this way?"

"This, and the last time you held vigil here." She sniffed the air. "Did you mark it this time?"

"Every time."

"Your mother will not speak of it to me."

"The wound is deep and unhealing." He lay down, resting his head on his forepaws. "As it ever will be." He sounded far away, his voice subdued and hollow. A pause, and several breaths were taken. "Long ago, when we lived on the great River far to the west, this lion hunted down and killed my father." His chest heaved with labored breathing. "And then he moved on to my brothers and sisters. One after the next. The entire litter, apart from me, taken between cruel jaws." The breeze tousled dried leaves on the acacia trees that ringed the clearing. "Our great journey brought us here. Somehow, he tracked us." He shook his head. "Aalwyn told me that humans were bringing animals here. Numbers beyond reckoning of waterbuck, impala, sable... and lions. Perhaps he was among them."

Olienhout began looking around her, as though sensing that they were being watched.

"My mentor... my new father... was hunted down next. He defended our litter of pups, to the very last." He turned to meet Olienhout's eyes. "It was Aalwyn who struck the lethal blow."

She padded away, and saw a vulture observing them from a distance. Moving with a bounding hop, the large bird edged closer.

"Why do you return here, Koorsboom?"

He shook his head. *"Ek weet nie.* There is no way to explain the need to mark this place. One must watch and remember."

"You seem troubled for a wolf so well-fed."

"Perhaps some paranoia is healthy." He watched the lion skull carefully.

"The complacent and happy wolf is the one ambushed by the lion." She lapped his muzzle, and he was cheered by this. "You share my mistrust of happiness."

"There is something else." His brow furrowed. "Fear pervades me, from my waking eyes to disturbed sleep."

"The *Selous* pack? The threat they represent is a grave one."

"No, something more." He peered at the ground between his paws. A column of ants crisscrossed his pawprint, carrying whatever to wherever, all beyond his knowledge. A single step would crush them, yet they knew nothing of the danger. He stared at this, through this. "A malevolence treads our paths. And now it envelops you, my love."

She stood closer to him, pressing her body to his. "Even caution can be heedless when excessive. Brood if you must, but only over that which you control. And so much is beyond the reach of our claws."

"A world entire is beyond us. Smoke and metal, fences and thunder." He closed his eyes with a soft moan. "I despair that we shall find no wild left to inhabit." He opened his eyes, wet and mired with pain. "And our pups will be doomed from birth."

Olienhout held her head next to his. Their fur brushed together. "Nothing of our lives is promised. Our mothers protect us, and our fathers hunt for us, only to be massacred for their troubles. The savanna promises nothing in abundance other than death, and we survive in spite of it." She rubbed her jaw on his shoulders. "I only hope that you doom my life with one litter after the next of fat, mischievous pups." She prodded him with her nose until he turned to meet her gaze. "That is what I demand of my mate."

He lapped her muzzle in kind, drinking in her scent and relishing the sensation of her fur. "We shall find a way, then." He nodded. "And we shall do so under the watch of human eyes."

They were on their paws, and he turned south to return to the den.

"So soon?" Olienhout had not moved.

"What have you in mind?"

"East before we return south again. Let us see if there is news of the *Selous* pack. And a kill, if at all possible."

***

On the *miombo* wood edge, a duiker nosed through the vegetation. Sniffing, it took one leaf after the next from the sedge, grinding them to a fine paste with the flat molars. The sensitive nose could detect the drying of the season. Food would not be so easy to come by in the months ahead. Moving away from the shade of the trees, it nosed the ground. Tubers could be detected below the surface here. The grey antelope, no larger than a dog, filed this information away for later.

Movement amid the grass. The duiker froze. The motion was tiny, and just below its snout. The duiker moved its nose closer, paused, and speared what was below with a sudden sharp stab. It pulled back a small field mouse, crushed in its teeth. The movement was instinctive, and now that it had hold of its prey, the duiker took its measure of this new food source. Closing further, the savor of blood overwhelmed its sense of taste. Recoiling for a moment, it continued to chew and grind up the remainder. Flavors of iron and meat were something it would remember always, a source of nutrient during desperate times.

Crash crash crash. The unusual meal had distracted the duiker, and the brush separated to reveal two Painted wolves. They looked at the duiker, and it looked back, utterly frozen. The mind strained for a method of escape, and there was none. Anchored, it hoped in vain to be invisible.

"What ever is it doing?" Olienhout twittered. The antelope facing them was small and alone.

"Is there a herd defending it?" That it continued to face them, motion-less, suggested to them a danger to the chase.

Koorsboom tensed, and began a dash toward the duiker.

Instinct took over once again, the duiker's muscles coiled, and its hind legs powered into a sprint.

Koorsboom relaxed, any sense of danger gone now that his jaws were in reach of a fleeing haunch. He lunged, and locked his jaws on a hip, pulling his body forth and out of reach of any potentially crippling hind kicks. Olienhout gripped the neck, then the snout. Koorsboom released his hold and ripped the belly open. The viscera were torn free in seconds, and the blood loss was immediate and catastrophic. The life drained from its eyes as quickly, and the hunters set to pulling the body apart.

"The sun has begun its descent. We need not patrol further." Olienhout gulped down muscle and organ at haste.

"Perhaps a foray further to the east before we return." They consumed their fill, and rested for a moment.

Their bellies hung low with meat as they began a tireless lope home. Traversing the *miombo* wood, they emerged from the other side to an open savanna. The waving green and drying grasses were dotted with Giraffe-thorn Acacia and Sand-olive brush.

"Your scent is familiar." Koorsboom sniffed a track. Central pad with four toes, claw marks, no dew claw present. "This wolf is *Selous.*"

"There are more over here." She sniffed the ground. "I find no pups or yearlings, only adults." She loped over the sand, around the green canopy of a jacketplum tree. The air around the tree was sweet, the scent of jam from browsed and crushed leaves. "Several scrabble marks over here. There was a chase."

"What made them run, I wonder?" Investigating the vast grounds yielded no new information, just the tracks of wolves moving in haste. The tall grasses of the savanna wavered in the breeze. Nearby, a dung midden from an elephant swarmed with dung beetles at harvest. A small gang of banded mongoose took up a position next to the pile, one standing at attention with eyes fixed on the wolves. The rest, comfortable under the watch of the lookout, rooted through the droppings for the beetles.

They continued to pad back south, the sandy soils returning to clay. Olienhout sniffed along the bank of a small river. "This runs back toward the den. I recognize the scent of this water." She looked up to see Koorsboom staring at the ground. Joining his side, she could see he was troubled.

"Lions." He looked down at a print, far larger than that of a wolf. The wide splay of the central pad and toes was unmistakable. Either of them could sit comfortably in the print. Moisture was still seeping into the depression.

Thud thud thud thud

"RUN!" Her high twitter galvanized them both.

Koorsboom and Olienhout reared into a dead run, and suddenly the air around them was alive with lion. Hot breath on their flanks, a labored breathing, a sound of a dark rumbling like thunder, with the storm right behind them.

Koorsboom could feel Olienhout next to him, and she could sense his presence. Their legs were pistons on the clay ground, every claw rooted to grasp for every centimeter to escape the terror behind them. The grunting sounded closer, and Olienhout could feel a sharp wind over her back. The wide swipe of the lion was capable of shattering bone, but missed its mark. The wolves pumped their muscles to the very limit, matching each other's strides, corners, and evasions. Each of their lives were reduced to the moments, and what they learned of each other's thoughts and habits over the past year were crushed down to the essence. Olienhout was a bullet of black, white, and gold, and Koorsboom was her mirror. A sharp turn around a tree, and he matched her movement. A drive into thornbush, and they clattered through as one.

Together they could sense the lion behind them slowing, stride after stride. The grunting and rumbling from the lion's throat faded into the sounds of the savanna. The wolves continued their sprint for another kilometer before they slowed in kind, and turned to look. Empty veld filled them with relief.

"Did you see him?" Koorsboom panted.

"No." Her chest heaved. "Nor did I need to." She looked around her, to the edge of another *miombo* forest distant, to the bare ground with scant grass and groupings of still-green Ananza bush. Many of the leaves had been nibbled off. The ground all around the tree was covered with scattered seeds and the rinds of fruit, discarded at the end of summer. "Some of this is looking familiar." They pressed south.

"*Selous* tracks again." Koorsboom reported. The prints were all over the soil, streaming into the grasses. "None too deep. It would seem the chase was over by this point."

"Now we know why they were in such haste." The sun casted longer shadows. "The days grow short, as does our path." They continued in silence.

The *KOO KOO, ku-ku KOO-koo* of a red eyed dove brought evening to the veld. Their path wound through tangled acacia sedge and over rivulets long since dried out. Before long they were loping underneath the glowing branches of fever trees, and then back to the den.

"A disturbing sign, that." Olienhout lapped his muzzle as they made their way back to the den, and the pups that were already outside awaiting the precious meat.

"Lions in ambush always are."

"No, Koorsboom. The distance."

The pups mobbed them, and began licking her chops. This prompted the regurgitation of nearly all she had consumed. Koorsboom did the same for the pups begging him.

"We covered a great deal of ground today."

"Not as much as you would think." Olienhout backed away from the feast set upon by the ravenous young. "We ventured into the *Selous* territory, and all signs indicated they were gone. It was on our return that we were attacked." She twittered to Aalwyn, who trotted over. "The lions have already moved south. And the *Selous* are sweeping down ahead of them."

* * *

The black mane shook with the winds of the evening, and a tail swished about behind. The male placed one broad paw before the next, surveying the savanna before him. Three lionesses followed him, casting glances about their new territory. They trusted him with their lives, and the lives of the cubs that were on the way.

The enormous snout of the lion dipped to the ground, pulling in air, and the scents of those who passed this way. Scattered wolf tracks crisscrossed the sandy soil. *Snuff.* His muzzle wrinkled, as though detecting something noxious. Wolf urine and musk were apparent here, as they had been for the season. He unleashed a steady rumble to the lionesses, who returned his rumble. He squatted, and released a quick but voluminous spray of urine over the tracks. He continued to work on these scent markings, taking his time. The lionesses raked the ground with their hind paws. Any hint of wolf musk was muted, erased from the earth. The scent of lion filled the air, and the existence of wolves in this area became a fading story, soon to be forgotten.

Chapter 10

The silent man was running low on cigarettes. While this was not a tremendous bother to him, it meant that a whole day had passed and he found no sign of those who skinned the zebra. He lit the last one on the smoldering butt, and stubbed this out in the car ashtray.

Rough terrain somehow did not stop the dirty white Toyota from traversing the land. Bloodshot eyes scanned the horizon, looking for heavy vehicles, fresh tire ruts on wet ground, plumes of smoke. A glance at the ground before him, then back to the distance.

The dirt road came to a washout. The way forward was a muddy quagmire that would trap any vehicle, even a *bakkie*. He rapidly studied the nile grass next to the road, and steered off the roadside. The vehicle lumbered across the grass and on to drier ground. Acacia brush thorns skittered along the car as he traversed back to the road, and he accelerated once again.

Hours passed, and he did not find the men who shot the zebra herd. Eventually, he gave up and returned to where the zebra corpses rotted in the sun. With a sigh, he stopped, and shifted to park.

The *bakkie* contained all his belongings in the world. The assault rifle, a coffee tin filled with ammunition, a few changes of clothing, a jar of peanut butter, cell phone, and a GPS unit. He reached for this, and opened his phone.

After a moment, a voice answered on the line.

He acknowledged the voice with a grunt, and read the coordinates on the GPS. "Poaching kill. Thirty-seven zebra." The voice asked if he would wait. He grunted again, and disconnected the call.

He laid the phone and GPS on the passenger seat, next to an ID. This was a cheaply made piece of laminated paper with a print of his photo and the words "GUARDA – RANGER". He finished his cigarette. His spartan existence was reflected in his barren manner of speech. He found speaking a waste of time, and most objects a waste in general. No friends or family cluttered his life, only acquaintances, personal and professional. What money passed through his hands was converted to fuel: the polluted gasoline from petrol stations, biltong, cigarettes. He lived in the Toyota Hilux, spending almost no time in the house he once owned just outside of Beira. Eventually, he had sold this as well.

As he waited, he checked the assault rifle, running a hand along the oiled metal body and wooden stock. His thick, black fingers were calloused from a lifetime of acacia thorn scars and vehicle repairs. Any clothing apart from khakis had been discarded long ago, and he disregarded the use of body armor. Weapons of choice for the poacher are assault rifles or rocket propelled grenades, against which kevlar provided little more shielding than the cotton shirt he wore.

* * *

"*Bliksem.*" Kurkbos growled, prompting the rest of the pack to raise their heads. The adults looked to him, then in the direction of his glare. The pups, now above ground, stopped their play, dropping all their toys and quietly awaited further instruction.

Two jackals stared back, seeming unaware of the alarm they caused.

"Get them in the den." A low, gruff buzz was all that was needed to make the pups vanish into the deep burrow.

Aalwyn stepped towards the jackals, and noticed one of them dipped their head, and it came up chewing.

Kurkbos bayed to the others, and four wolves sprinted off towards the jackals. As quickly, the diminutive predators darted into the brush. Ducking under low hanging acacia thorn, the male and female jackal pair evaded the wolf pack.

"Spread out—we may yet encircle them." Kurkbos did not slow his lope, sniffing the ground as he inhaled his breaths. Ahead, bundles of leafy branches bent and snapped back as each of the jackals made their way through the dense sedge.

"This is edged by open veld—we can surround them!" Koorsboom's excitement was palpable as he rounded the edges of acacia and *Combretum* shrub. The others swung around as well, and took up station at four points surrounding the thicket, waiting for a move from the jackals.

"They came too close to the den." Kurkbos was nearly frothing at the edges of his mouth. "If we can just kill one of them."

Olienhout paced back and forth on her edge of the brush. "Were they threatening us?"

"That close to home... the threat need not be spoken." Kurkbos glared at her, his anger flaring with every heave of his chest.

A White-backed vulture, wheeling above in a thermal, dropped to a nearby branch to watch. His dark-edged wings were held wide for a minute, then folded in. His long, snake-like neck craned back and forth looking for a carcass, then relaxed in wait.

Olienhout peered at the vulture for a moment before resuming her pacing. She sniffed at the branches. "I scent no enemies here."

"Keep on your guard." Kurkbos kept his fangs bared, ready to bury them in anything that tried to get past.

Another vulture joined the first, landing close by on the dead tree that was their perch.

"We are not alone here, Kurkbos." Olienhout looked up, seeing a few additional vultures whirling above them.

"Stay on task, young one." He uttered a rattling growl.

A rustling noise was audible. Kurkbos tensed, and he twittered to Olienhout to get ready. They converged as the rustling became louder.

Dried leaves scraped against twig and thorned branch.

"I have you now." Kurkbos dipped his head, jaws parted.

A black, gold, and white form dashed out of the brush, and shook its head and fur free of thorns and brambles. "They are not here." Koorsboom twittered to them.

"You cretin—" Kurkbos snapped his jaws at the young wolf. "You had your orders, fool." He bayed to the others with a brief hoo-call, a low-pitched *HROOOO!* aimed at the ground. The last of the party appeared. "We must get back to the den." He glared at Koorsboom. "This idiot may have let them escape—and they may have returned to a now lightly defended home."

The wolves padded the kilometer back to the den, no words spoken between them other than the grumbling of Kurkbos.

They met Aalwyn within sight of the den, and Kurkbos gestured to the rest to return to the pups.

"No danger here, then?" Kurkbos clawed the soil before him.

"All is quiet." Aalwyn stepped around him. "What disturbs you so?"

"My pups were put in harm's way today." He growled, almost to himself. "Those jackals bide their time, until they can exploit either the stupidity or laziness of our pack."

"What happened out there?"

He explained the attempt to surround the jackals. "Koorsboom did not deign to keep his station. They will get close to us once too often."

"They were not after the pups."

"*Kak*—they were standing, where we stand now, looking right at them, licking their chops in anticipation."

"They were after this." She gestured to her feet. An impala limb was there, the hide and part of the muscle gnawed upon.

"That means nothing."

"I agree that jackals can be a danger, should the pups be left unattended. For now, I feel there are far greater risks out there."

"Do not disregard them, Aalwyn, or my pups will be made to suffer."

She did not answer him, turning back toward the den. She lay down by

Koorsboom and Olienhout, who pretended to be resting.

"You have angered your alpha today, my son."

"You have my apology, mother." Koorsboom kept his eyes closed. "I have no excuse."

"However you do have a reason." She folded one forepaw over the other. "Why did you leave your assigned spot?"

"There was no sign of them." He opened his eyes, still looking down at the grass before him. "I had neither scent nor track to follow. We did not have them surrounded as we thought. Rather than waste further time, I felt it best to remove doubt, and I searched through the brush for them."

Aalwyn nodded her head, lost in thought. "Tomorrow we hunt—pay no further mind to this." She left them and joined Kurkbos, who lapped the face of a pup who had stumbled into a mud puddle.

"We must take the hunting party to the jackals. We end this threat before another sunset passes." Kurkbos prodded the pup with his snout. The pup blinked its eyes free of dirt, its pug face elated at the attention.

"Are you quite sure this is necessary?"

"Yes." He watched the pups, a storm behind his eyes.

"The time is better spent preparing them to move. Our time here grows short indeed."

"This must be done first. Consider it, Aalwyn. We will be leaving this den, roving for new hunting grounds. There will be no place for them to run. Jackals are not dim creatures. They will wait for us to leave sanctuary." Another lick. "And they will kill them in the night."

Aalwyn did not speak, laying down to rest after the long day. She looked back to the edge of the brush where the jackals had been gnawing upon their scraps.

* * *

"Thirty-seven." The man in the deep green canvas uniform shook his head.

"I have the other three here. They are just finished drying." Augusto motioned to his men, and they trotted over with three additional zebra hides.

Two more rifle shots cracked, the echo resounding off white brick walls. The hospital was laid out in a series of separate long buildings connected by concrete paths. Four men in dark green ran down a paved path between two cream brick buildings, the clomping of their boots echoing off the hard walls. Two stopped, pointed at the sign marked RADIOLOGIA, then in the direction of the surgical theatre. They rattled the door handle, then smashed the glass with the stocks of their rifles. Once they went inside, there were more sounds of breaking glass, and the sharp staccato reports of gunshots.

"And you were not followed?" He scratched his head beneath the black beret.

"We saw a ranger, but he did not see us." Augusto shifted nervously.

"If you saw him, he probably saw something. The rangers of Gorongosa are getting better training and equipment." He screwed off the cap of his flask and upended it.

"Nobody tracked us out of the park."

More shots, more breaking glass, and a sharp scream from a woman startled Augusto.

"Here." The colonel did not seem to hear the scream as he tossed a roll of cash to the poacher. "I pay you the rest when you have the horns."

"We have some horns as well."

The colonels' eyes widened, and he promptly screwed the cap back onto his flask.

Augusto pointed to the back of his large truck, the white paint covered by mud halfway up the doors.

"Good." He grinned.

Two men kicked open the door to the surgical theatre, each holding bags fashioned from starched white blankets. As they stomped their way toward the colonel, small boxes containing medications tumbled out of the edges of the bags.

The colonel shouted orders to the men, and they dumped the contents of their blankets in the rear of their own transport truck. They hustled over to the rear of Augusto's truck. The colonel clapped happily.

Five white horns were hefted, one at a time, toward the colonel.

"Well done. Leave them here, on the ground." They were lined up before the commander. He thumbed off a thick wad of *meticais* and handed it to Augusto. "He will be happy with this."

Augusto pocketed the money, wondering how much more this special visitor paid the colonel.

Another soldier clad in dark green with a black beret stomped toward the men, holding a radio. He strode past three men tossing patient records onto a blazing bonfire, black wisps of burned paper wafting into the air. He saluted the colonel.

The colonel bent closer, and they muttered to each other. Another salute, and the soldier strode off past a faded sign marked DEPARTAMENTO DE PEDIATRIA. He directed several other soldiers looting the ward, and fired a shot just over the head of a woman running from the building, carrying a limp child in her arms. She vanished into shadows cast by trees just outside the hospital grounds.

"He is coming now." The colonel straightened his black beret.

"Who is this man?" Augusto looked about, then down at his own filthy shirt.

"He is the money man." His deep voice rose as he spoke the words. "He exports to Thailand and Vietnam."

A Range Rover rounded the corner of a far building, along a drive. Dust stirred behind it, but the vehicle itself shined, without a speck of dust obscuring its brilliant blue color. The tires thudded as it left the drive and went over a sidewalk, throwing gravel as it went between the departments of the hospital. The wide body took up most of the walkway between the hospital wards, and entered the open courtyard where the men stood next to the horns. Two soldiers carrying boxes filled with medical equipment quickly moved aside before the Range Rover zoomed past them.

"He wanted to meet you." The colonel stood a bit straighter, before intoning toward Augusto: "Impress him."

Augusto took a step back as the Range Rover skidded to an abrupt halt less than a meter from where he stood. The windscreen and glass were tinted, and it was impossible to see inside.

The driver side door opened, and a man stepped to the ground, his crocodile leather shoes striking the concrete with a *whap*. Standing up, he looked at the colonel and Augusto with an utterly blank expression. Slamming the door shut, he strode toward them.

"Is this Augusto?" His nasal voice was as flat as his countenance. The rest of his form was clad in a white suit of nondescript fabric that shimmered as the breeze fluttered through it.

"Yes." Augusto spoke haltingly.

"I did not ask you." The man's voice was clipped, mechanical, as though he spoke to livestock.

"Yes, sir." The colonel beamed, holding out his hand to shake. It was not taken.

The man in white snapped his fingers, pointing toward the horns lined up on the concrete.

Four soldiers quickly picked up the horns and moved it to the rear of the blue Range Rover.

"On a blanket." The tone of his voice was even, but insistent. The horns were loaded, and the boot of the vehicle closed with a click.

"I need a steady supply of horn. My last man was arrested."

Augusto looked back at him, as the man in white was silent.

"Are you stupid?"

Augusto shook his head. "No, sir."

"Can you supply horn?"

"How much?" Augusto stammered. "Sir."

"However much I need." His face seemed to be made of stone. "Number?"

Augusto rattled off the digits of his phone number.

The man in white did not respond.

"Do you need to write—"

"No."

"What is your number?"

"I call you."

Augusto remained quiet, marveling at the way the fabric of the man's suit moved, like tendrils of smoke from a campfire. He had not seen silk clothing before.

"Colonel." The soldier with the radio strode up to his commander and saluted again. "Radio chatter from the rangers."

"About us?" The colonel looked nervously toward the man in white, then back to the soldier. "Do they know we are here?"

"Yes, and they have a description of his truck." The soldier pointed at Augusto.

"So you cannot supply me." His voice was still flat, but louder. The change was subtle, but raised the hairs on the back of Augusto's neck nonetheless.

"No, no. This will be fine." The colonel put his hands up, as though calming a fight. "The rangers get close to our men sometimes." He gave a nod to them. "We just need to take care of a few of them."

"Keep them under control." The man in white turned back toward the blue Range Rover. "There are always more rangers, breeding like rabbits."

Augusto gave the colonel a confused look. The colonel gave a subtle shake of his head.

The radio squawked again, and the soldier listened to it away from the other men. He returned to the colonel's side.

"Sir, they have called in the local police."

"So what?" The money man smirked, betraying the first sign of emotion. He pulled a wad of *meticais* from his pocket, thumbing off several bills.

"The police around here *might* take a bribe." The colonel muttered. "The rangers will not."

"Those horns will really cost you if you are caught with them, and when the police arrive, they will make sure the rangers are here to arrest you."

Augusto looked toward the colonel. "That road is the only way back toward Maputo."

The man in white glowered, and put the money back in one pocket. He lifted the edge of his shirt, revealing a gleaming chrome pistol. "We go back into Gorongosa."

The colonel nodded. "We can take the dirt road around and leave via another gate."

"Will the rangers find us more easily?" Augusto eyed the pistol.

"I hope they do." The man in white gave a thin smile. He strode back to his shining blue vehicle, opening the driver side door. *Bang.* The engine turned over and the Range Rover reversed, showering the men with dust and gravel.

The colonel gave an order to the soldier with the radio, and made a circle with his forefinger in the air. The rest of the men in dark green uniform clomped back toward the transport truck, each carrying a load of drugs, equipment, papers, and a large bag filled with gauze bandages. The heavy engine of their truck rattled to life.

"Follow us, and be quick. That man drives like a maniac."

"Who was he?" Augusto looked at the colonel, who took another swig from his flask as he opened the passenger side door of the truck.

"Nattapong Buatoom."

Chapter 11

Bathing the savanna with pale blue light, the full moon hung high in the sky. The katydids nattered, and the occasional bird call from a nightjar pierced the evening. Branches of Giraffe-thorn acacia were tousled by the wind, thorns rattling past one another.

A bull elephant stood under the tall arbor of an ancient acacia, stepping cautiously toward a female. She waited, and after a few more steps they were face to face, tusks knocking together. She touched his face with her trunk, the caress tracing along his head past two scarred bullet wounds before his broad ear. He pressed his head against hers. She pushed back, and their trunks became entwined. She opened her eyes and looked toward the moon, fat and luminous. She pulled back from her courtship display, and with a nervous snort made her way further into a grove of acacia trees. He did not chase her, looking into the sky with understanding.

A zebra stallion snorted his anxiety into the night. He made a circle around his harem, glaring across the wavering grasses. The females under his watch stamped, quick to bolt with the slightest noise. A nearby throng of impala glanced about constantly as they grazed on the grass. Even a slight change in the direction of the breeze was enough to startle them, with stamping and an alarm cough.

Lumbering out of the thicket at the edge of the plain, a white rhino swept knots of grass into its wide mouth, grinding the foliage. It stopped, listening, funnel ears inclining one way, then another, alert. A sniff. Fear was in the air. The rhino's vision was very poor, but it could perceive the bright light from above. With a frustrated grunt, it turned about and hustled back into a dense thicket.

Peering down from the high branches of an Apple-leaf tree, a leopard surveyed the sprawling plains below. It was time to hunt, but the hunter was not eager to move about on a well-lit night. He eased down the branch, down the trunk with a quick hop, and hastened into opaque thornbushes. He looked up to the sky, and knew the time had come for the Poacher's Moon.

Herds scattered at the sound of a car engine. The blue Range Rover tore along the dirt road, followed closely by a heavy truck. As it passed, the high pitch of the engines dropped, and faded. Animals either crouched in the brush or ran further from the road, escaping into heavy scrub.

Rocks crumbled under the tires of the heavy truck, and the engine gunned harder when encountering mud or inclines. When the two vehicles roared past a motion sensor, a camera whirred and focused on the moving vehicles. Far away, phones began ringing.

* * *

"They are moving along the access road." Two rangers hurried out to their vehicle, a beige Land Rover with a black snorkel snaking up from the engine along the passenger door. "Our patrol missed them."

"Where did the patrol go?"

"On the way to the hospital to catch the poachers where the rebel army was looting." As they opened the doors, a white Toyota Hilux crawled up to them. The silent man gripped the wheel, acknowledging the rangers in the Land Rover with a glance.

They regarded the man with a nod, and he drove past them.

"He will take the gravel path and rejoin the road." The ranger closed the driver side door with a bang.

"And cut them off?" The other ranger closed the passenger door.

"Or kill them before we get there."

76

The engine turned over, and with a shift, wheels spun and the rangers pulled onto the dirt path. They quickly caught up to the dirty white Toyota, and after a kilometer, a hand jutted out of the window and waved to them. The Toyota shot off to the side, bumping down a gravel trail.

"I hate the moonlight." The ranger shifted into a higher gear and powered forth, eventually joining the access road.

* * *

The blue Range Rover pulled off the dirt road next to a shack. The small structure blended into the environment with its nondescript brown paint, standing next to a snarl of thornbrush. Nattapong Buatoom parked the Range Rover next to the shack and stepped out. The night breeze stirred his white suit, undulating silk shining in the pale blue light. He looked up to the moon, and an alien smile crossed his face.

The heavy truck slowed to a stop on the dirt road, and then reversed behind the shack. Once it was out of view, the colonel walked out with one of his soldiers, still monitoring the radio. He stomped out to meet the man in white.

"Looks like only one vehicle is coming after us. They are coming up this road, from where we got into the park."

"They are expecting us to eventually go back along the same road."

"Well." The colonel pointed to the moon. "They are expecting us to be hunting rhino and elephant."

"They are right about the hunting." Buatoom gave a nod, and the colonel and several of his men clomped off into the nearby bushes, and crouched low.

* * *

"Up ahead."

The beige Land Rover slowed as they rounded a bend, the high grasses parting to reveal the blue Range Rover.

"What is he doing?" The ranger in the passenger seat squinted.

"Looks like he has a rhino horn." The other ranger pulled up near the Range Rover, and ignited a spotlight, training it before them.

Buatoom was lit up by the beam, his white suit rendering it even brighter, in contrast to the grey color of the horn standing on the ground next to him, his hand holding onto the sharp end.

The rangers left their Land Rover, and approached the man in white. Each pointed a rifle in his direction, and one ranger slid back the charging handle, chambering a bullet.

"Drop the horn, and put your hands in the air." One ranger put the stock to his shoulder, peering down the sight.

Buatoom did not put his hands up. The smile never left his face.

"Do you want to die here?" The other ranger flicked the safety off his rifle.

"Do you?" A deep voice boomed behind them. "Turn and I cut you in half, my friend." The colonel stepped closer toward the rangers.

The other soldiers seemed to materialize out of nowhere as they left the grasses, each brandishing their Kalashnikov rifles.

"Drop them." Buatoom continued smiling, and pointed to the rangers.

Two rifles clattered to the ground, the sound dampened by the dried grasses. The rangers held their hands in the air.

The soldiers stood at the ready.

The colonel scratched his head underneath his black beret. "Well, what do you want to do with—"

A shot cracked open the night, and the soldiers all flinched at the bright flash. Buatoom held his gleaming chrome pistol in one hand, smoke emanating from the barrel. The body of the ranger fell back on the ground, a red hole where his left eye once was.

The other ranger gasped in a panic and opened his mouth to speak.

Four more shots from the chrome pistol silenced him, and his body crumpled to the ground.

"Put the horn back in the Range Rover." Buatoom gestured to one of the soldiers with the pistol, and then toward his vehicle. The man in dark green uniform nearly saluted him before doing as he commanded.

Buatoom handed a camera to the colonel, and nodded to him.

"Be sure to get the moon in the shot." He held the chrome pistol up, and pointed it at the colonel, smoke still drifting out of the barrel.

The colonel laughed heartily, his shoulders shaking up and down along with his belly, and he steadied himself to take the picture.

* * *

KA... KA KA KA KA

Shots echoed across the savanna.

The man slowed to a stop and stood out of the driver seat of his *bakkie*, one boot on the road. Only the night sounds of insects.

He slammed the door, gunned the engine to life, and pressed on the pedal. The dirty Toyota spun its wheels, spraying mud for a moment before finding purchase, and it sped forward on the rough terrain. He quickly found the road, and drove as quickly as the vehicle's ailing suspension would allow.

He drove on, toward the sound of the gunfire. The dirt road made his progress painfully slow. The moon lazily traced its way across the sky. No other sounds came to him other than the rattling of his engine and a tinny love song in Portuguese emitted by the dying radio. He switched this off. His thick fingers gripped the wheel, eyes boring into the road ahead.

He strained, listening for further sounds of shots, or another engine, but nothing came to him.

The *bakkie* reached the access road, and gravel sprayed as he accelerated down it. Within the hour, he rounded a bend to find the ranger's beige

Land Rover with the black snorkel. The Toyota skidded to a halt, and he grabbed his rifle and was on foot in seconds. The vehicle stood with its doors ajar, bed empty of equipment. The driver side door was open, an emblem with a black and white design of a lion head, with the words PARQUE NACIONAL DA GORONGOSA around it.

Two men lay on the ground on the other side of the Land Rover, closer to the shack that stood by the road. Blood pooled beneath them. Both wore the khaki uniform of the park ranger.

He stared at the bodies for a moment. He pawed his shirt pocket for a pack of cigarettes that was not there. After a long exhale, he walked back to his car. The clearing had a robust, hollow silence, as though a storm had just departed.

The phone and GPS were used once more, and the information he relayed was just as brief. There was no show of grief for the men, one of whom he had known since childhood. There was no outburst of anger. Ebony eyes bored into the ground between his boots. They did not move, not wavering for a second, even as an hour passed before more rangers arrived. When they did, he did not respond to them, or acknowledge their presence.

He did not speak. He never spoke.

Chapter 12

With dawn, a leopard crept toward a Giraffe-thorn acacia, glancing about. With a pause, he hunched his shoulders, leapt toward the trunk, and crawled up, claws squeaking as they dug into the bark. Quickly reaching a high branch, he laid one forepaw over the other, and rested his head. Stomach gurgling, he was resigned to a day of hunger as he slept after a fruitless night.

Elephants strolled in silence through the *miombo* woodland, browsing on what leaves remained on the trees. Restless during the bright darkness, they paused to relax in the forest. The matriarch surveyed her herd, and considered going down to the waterhole in the daylight. Day was always safer here.

Herds of waterbuck were already at their pool, drinking their fill of water and snorting to one another in greeting. Impala gingerly returned to the savanna, glad the night of the Poacher's Moon was over. Grazing resumed for all the plant-eaters of the bushveld. It would stop for nothing.

The rising din of an engine set the nerves of the herds on edge, but only for a moment. The beige Land Rover, marked with the emblem of Gorongosa, crested the ridge and zipped along the dirt road leaving a cloud of dust behind it. The appearance of the ranger's vehicle was not what they recognized, but the pitch of the engine.

The two humans sat in glum quiet as the Land Rover bounced them about.

The maimed hand of Marais was on the wheel, tightly gripped. Between the sounds of the engine straining and rocks underneath the tires, Venter could hear his teeth grinding.

Orange washed over them, revealing the beauty of the veld as the road bent to the east. The chill of night evaporated. They had departed for the den of the *Dwalen* well before sunrise. She looked toward the driver, and cleared her throat.

"I saw the patrols getting started this morning. I thought they would take the day off."

"Never." He grunted. "This morning, right on time, like any other day." He took his left hand off the wheel and massaged it. "One of the men. His widow was here overnight." He clucked his tongue and paused, looking up to the sun visor and holding his breath before continuing. "She volunteered to take his place until someone else could." He drummed his fingers absently on the dashboard.

The fever tree came into view. Three, then four sets of dish ears were bouncing about above the grass tips.

"Why?"

"Their land, their home." The air whistled through his nose as he fumed. "The rangers take pride in defending their home from these—" He hissed through his clenched teeth. "—*people*."

"Some poachers are just making a living for their families." She spoke this quietly.

Marais remained mute for a minute before responding. "Do not say that in earshot of a ranger. They know many of the poachers, and the drug money their work provides." He exhaled, and seemed to calm. "Recruited villagers make pocket change for what they kill. Those driving the trade, bringing in all the money, creating the markets in southeast Asia, all at the cost of slaughtered animals, and slaughtered people." His fists tightened on the wheel. "The slave traders and colonists never left. They just changed jobs."

The Land Rover slowed to a stop, and the parking brake clicked into place.

"They got away, I had heard."

Marais did not answer, grinding his teeth as he exited the vehicle.

"And that the poachers were rebels."

"Rebels." Marais snarled. "That would imply an ethos. They looted a hospital, shot some of the staff, one of the patients." He picked up a rucksack from the rear seat. "They were the same monsters that destroyed Gorongosa decades ago, while destroying everything they could across the country. They never stopped stealing and destroying. Even they no longer pretend to have a reason."

"There was another man with them." She retrieved her own gear, and a pair of binoculars. "A witness at the hospital thought he was from overseas."

Marais stared at the ground.

Venter continued to set up equipment, and pulled the cover off an elaborate remote control drone.

"It was *him*."

"What was that?" She looked up toward Marais, who was still staring at the dirt between his feet.

"It must have been *him*." He breathed heavily, his face turning red, hands gripped into fists of concrete.

"Who?"

Marais breathed heavily, closing his eyes until he calmed down and eventually answered her. "Nothing." He looked up toward the fever tree.

"*Ag*, we are too late." She looked up to see five wolves bounding away from the den at high speed.

"Never mind. The alpha female has stayed behind with a yearling. We can still test the drone to make sure it does not spook them."

Venter checked the battery and cables underneath the drone, some hanging out of a custom-built housing.

"Are the police investigating?"

"If they want to." Marais continued watching the den, glassing the field. "Some get paid to look away, others are dedicated against the corruption the poachers cultivate." He tilted his head one way, then the other with an audible crack. "Life goes on."

"Did you know the rangers?"

He glared at the field ahead. Eventually, he cleared his throat and spoke. "I know all of them."

"I asked about taking up a collection for the families." She coughed. "From our European Union partners."

Marais, staring at nothing, nodded.

"Rangers seem to deal with death like it is nothing." Venter murmured.

"They have had a lot of practice."

* * *

The hunting party returned after an hour, and even at a distance Aalwyn could see that none of them were stained with blood.

"Hyenas." Kurkbos greeted her. "They were a skulking shadow."

"Did you lose them before returning here?"

Kurkbos nodded. "They can throttle their own meat if they are hungry." Kurkbos slumped to the ground, and the pups clambered over him. One pawed his muzzle, and wondered why his face was an impassive mask. "Did they do well with their small *trek*?" Another climbed on his back, attacking his shoulder with needle-sharp teeth.

"Very well." Aalwyn nosed one of the pups with her snout. "Their endurance is improving. They can move with speed now."

Kurkbos stalked away without comment.

"He seemed easily frustrated today." Olienhout noted to Aalwyn. "He kept on about 'parasites'."

Aalwyn padded over to her mate and lapped his muzzle.

"I will lead the evening hunt." She purred as one of the pups reared up on hind legs and batted at her nose.

"Are you sure?" Kurkbos shook his head, and the pup perched on his head tumbled off into a heap.

"Quite. Fresh meat is what I long for after so much time in the den." She lapped his muzzle again before walking away.

"I shall be your valiant defense." Kurkbos glared at the pup who he had shrugged off. The pup mewled, shaking his black and white fur free of dirt before pouncing again on his father's snout.

* * *

The setting sun lit the western horizon, a dull red leaving the Giraffe-thorn acacia and Apple-leaf trees in silhouette.

"They are back." Venter's voice was lowered.

Marais took the binoculars and watched. Several bouncing forms were inbound. This time, their black, gold, and white fur was obscured by crimson. Two clashed just before entering camp, each rearing on hind legs, batting at one another with their forepaws, jaws wide, teeth almost clicking together before they returned to the ground. One still had their forepaws on the other's back.

"The alpha female... and that other female that acts like an alpha."

"They are not fighting, are they?"

"No." He smiled. "They are excited. Triumphant from the kill." He motioned to Venter, who brought out the remote again.

The wolves strode into the encampment and regurgitated ropes of meat for the pups. The rangers could hear their excited yipping even at a distance.

"Let us see how it works for these *okes*."

The quadcopter drone sat still for a moment, a blinking red bulb the only sign of activity, until suddenly the rotors spun, and it quickly lifted off.

Sonja Venter adjusted the sticks on the remote, and the drone tilted forward, lifted higher off the ground, and drifted toward the den. Within a minute it hovered over the wolves. The wind picked up, rocking the quadcopter, but with adjustment she kept it relatively steady.

"See any problems?"

"If they even notice the drone, they do not seem to show any signs of it." Marais continued to watch them through the binoculars. The pups had consumed most of the meat that had hit the ground, and were sniffing about for scraps. Two found a segment of meat and tendon, and each grabbed an end, pulling until it separated, and each pup tumbled onto their backs.

"I think we can bring it back." He nodded to Venter, and the drone turned lazily around and hovered closer. As it landed, she picked up the unit and switched it off. She then folded up the flat of cardboard from a beer case that was used as the landing pad.

"That is unusual."

She looked up to see two wolves leading the pups away from the den.

"Another test run." He lowered his binoculars.

"Right after eating?"

"Usually the pups flop over and sleep after feeding." He scratched his unruly hair and replaced the wide brimmed hat on his head. "The alpha wants to give them a workout before it gets too dark."

"Then we need to tag them. They will be on the move soon."

"Right." Marais put away his binoculars, replacing the protective caps over the lenses. "We unpack the Ticks tonight, then. We will not tag them tomorrow, though."

"No. The funerals." Venter muttered.

Johan massaged the scar on his left hand, and they continued to pack up as the sun drew closer to the western horizon.

The drive back was hushed, the thrum of the engine the only sound.

Chapter 13

The bull tied to the stake suspected something was going to happen.

Twice it reached the limit of its rope attempting to walk on this grass field where it had been left. The bell around its neck rattled, and it strained against the length of rope for a moment. Then it returned closer to where the stake was secured to the ground. There was a distant tent erected on the field, canvas of white and blue stripes, with ropes holding it down despite the wind. The fabric strained against the ropes as air whistled through. There was a fire burning, but it did not seem out of control, isolated to a brick circle. Logs had been cut, some left in a pile where the fire smoldered, more stacked close.

He realized he was far away from the cattle pen where he and his fellow cattle were kept. He still held the rich scent of their bodies and dung in his sensitive nose. No other cattle were near him now, however.

He had been taken on the grass outside his cattle pen before, but usually with other cows and bulls to graze, and always accompanied by men holding sticks. Not this time.

Humans had gathered nearby in large numbers, far more than he could count, and there was much noise, and wailing. They had formed a crowd that ambled away from where the tent was located, further down the hill into an area with another fence. There were several markers of wood standing within that fenced area. If it was a farm, nothing grew there.

Only the lonely markers jutted from the ground.

After the humans crowded into that area, the bull could see two large boxes carried amongst the humans. After a great deal of time, the boxes then seemed to disappear into holes dug in the earth. The humans appeared to shovel dirt onto the ground. More time passed, and the humans slowly made their way in the direction of the tent, and toward him.

The bull stomped, and snorted, but knew he could do little else but wait.

One man, speaking softly, carried some sweet-smelling grass, and held it up to the bull's mouth. He sniffed, and was nervous, but took a mouthful and began crunching this between his teeth.

He did not feel the sharp blade slip between the vertebrae of his neck, but suddenly he was on the ground, and felt nothing.

Not exactly nothing. He felt as though his entire body had slipped into icy waters, and it took his breath away. It stunned him, and the grass, forgotten, fell out of his mouth in a wet wad. He wanted to breathe, but could not. His heavy head was sitting on the dry earth, and he did not remember falling. This faded, and the field before him seemed to pull away, while he inhaled the scent of the grass.

The scent of grass, and a memory of long ago. A calf, still awkward on four legs, bathed in the scent of his mother, now bounding about in the darkness.

* * *

The feast went on all afternoon, and the air was filled with smoke and the scent of roasted beef. More than two hundred people were seated under the tent, some milling about outside, and around the fire. They dined from plates heaped with hunks of meat, beans and gima, a white mash of dried and boiled corn. Under the tent, it was dense with chatter.

Sonja Venter felt awkward as she carried a plate and fork, looking for a place to sit. She finally found Johan Marais in the crowd. The man seemed shrunken despite his hulking form. He spoke softly to a woman dressed in black. He bowed his head, put something in her hand, and embraced her. The ranger walked away, rubbing his eyes, and made his way toward the tent. He sat down at a table next to Venter and two other rangers joined them. Each of them picked at their food without eating much.

A man she had not seen before was circulating through the tables. Dressed in clean, crisp khakis, his eyes were obscured by dark sunglasses. Upon spotting Marais, he carefully eased his way through the crowd. He extended a hand.

"You are Johan Marais?"

Marais nodded, his mustache unable to conceal the frown he wore all morning.

"Zhou Yu." The handshake was brief, the ranger appeared deflated. "Gorongosa's partner in China."

"Yes, of course. It has been a while." Marais attempted a smile, but it was unconvincing.

"I was given the news this morning." Yu's smile was friendly, but tone of his voice was edged with anger. "I am very sorry to hear about this." The muscles in his jaw spasmed for a moment, sending a ripple across his face. "We will be waiting for information on the poacher. He needs to be sorry as well."

"As soon as we have something, our rangers will be in touch." Marais gave him a nod.

"May I have your card?" Venter raised her voice to be heard.

"Of course." He fished out a white business card and handed it to her. "Where can I find the families?" Yu glanced about.

Marais got up and led him through the crowd to another table, where the extended families of the murdered rangers had gathered. When he returned to his meal, he seemed even more dejected.

"That was kind of him to come." Venter attempted to whisper to Marais, but with the din of conversations, it still came out as a shout.

"A good friend to have for a conservationist. Yu is a thorn in the side of anyone in Beijing who is in the wild animal trade." He resumed picking at his food.

"Blocking supply or reducing demand?"

"He works on both. Yu has a passion for the ethics of conservation, but his interests are also practical." Marais swallowed his gima. "He believes, and I agree, that wet markets where wild animals are slaughtered will be the drivers for pandemics that will crush the global economy."

The wind pulled at the flaps of the tent while the rangers stared glumly at the food.

"Everyone here seems to know each other." She looked at the neighboring tables.

"The local village. Some of the rangers come from there. They grow up and study especially to become rangers."

Men and women spoke loudly, telling stories from years gone by, memories of the two men. There was laughing, with a touch of bitterness. Many of the guests had not seen each other for years. Promises were made to meet in happier times. Children ran about the field, while boys kicked around a football.

Nearby, the brick circle still contained a fire, though it was now down to red coals. Iron grates sat over the fire, and cooking pots that had simmered the gima and beans were now cooling on the grass.

Marais stood, giving the others a nod. He left the feast behind, and walked back to the graveyard where his two friends were buried.

A man stood in the graveyard still, a statue. Until Marais took the long walk to his side, he seemed at a distance to be a tall grave marker.

"Razak."

"Johan." The silent man took Marais's large pale hand in one equally large, carved from ebony. The muscles of his arm writhed under scarred dark skin. His eyes were glaring onyx surrounded by white and red, bloodshot from sleepless nights. The dirty white Toyota was parked further from the cemetery, peeking out from behind a thicket. He absently fished in a pocket for cigarettes, but then put them back in his pocket.

"Are you well?"

Razak did not respond, other than pulling a tablet from a rucksack. He had borrowed this from one of the other rangers. Turning it on, he thumbed through a series of images until he came to a somewhat grainy photo taken at night. He showed it to Marais.

It was of a man, dressed in a white silk outfit, face clenched, black hair tousled by the wind. He held a chrome pistol that was pointed at the camera, which looked directly down its barrel. The full moon beamed over his shoulder. In the middle distance was a blue Range Rover, the license plate obscured by grass, and an equipment shack.

In the lower left-hand corner of the photo was a boot on the ground, lying on its side, and the lower part of a leg, wearing the beige khaki of a ranger.

Marais's jaw closed with an audible clack, and he heaved a deep breath. The two men glared at the photo, and each other.

He gripped Razak's shoulder and gave a nod.

Razak returned his gesture, then turned back to look at the grave.

* * *

The Cathedral of Maputo stood tall in the center of the great port city, an ivory spire that gleamed in the sun. Although the colonial structure had aged, and the paint flaked, it remained striking in a city filled with white buildings. Apartment blocks and business offices dating back over a century flanked brand new hotels built during Mozambique's economic recovery. A sprawling market in the downtown area was prowled by hawkers and tourists, acres of land filled with curios. Acrylic paintings hung from lines, carved masks were spread out on sheets, and shelves held small figurines of animals carved from wood or malachite. One stall contained wood carved from tree branches, tall as the humans who browsed them, turning and twisted spikes painted bright riots of color in yellows, blues, and reds. Another vast market held tomatoes, squash, onions, mangoes, and piles of spice dust.

The skyline of old dilapidated apartments and bright new condominiums was broken by tall construction cranes leaning over skeletal new buildings like still herons. Horns honked as cars made their way along streets, adding their exhaust to the humid air.

Across the bay on a barrier island, a small restaurant sat on the beach, a brick structure with dark thatch roofing. White plastic tables and chairs dotted the beach just outside the restaurant, looking back toward the Maputo skyline as the sun set behind it. Fishing and transport boats drifted across the bay. The restaurant was empty with the exception of two men. One wore the blue coveralls of a worker, stained with fuel oil and grease, black hands calloused with decades of work. The other wore an immaculate white suit, his hands soft and delicate.

"The shipping container is loaded?" Silk wavered with the wind, in contrast with a stony face devoid of emotion.

"Yes, sir."

"And the customs documentation?"

"All items identified as 'Souvenirs'."

"Freight invoice, Duty exemption..."

"All taken care of."

"Half now, half on arrival." Buatoom handed him a briefcase filled with *meticais*.

"Yes, sir." He took the case, resisting the urge to open it in front of the stern man. His eyes drifted down to the chrome pistol on his hip, peeking out when the breeze lifted the shirt of his suit. "Your cabin is prepared, sir."

"Good." His eyes were dead, as though the work of a taxidermist. Buatoom walked away without another word or greeting, toward the rubber Zodiac boat parked on the beach. A man seated inside waved at him, got out, and worked to push it as far out into the surf as he could while allowing the man in white to board without getting his shoes wet.

Within minutes, the craft roared out into the bay toward a giant cargo ship. The surface was loaded with multicolored metal cargo containers, stacked impossibly high and appearing ready to topple with the slightest wave. The broad white pilot bridge stood over the stacks of yellow, red, and green boxes.

The trip out to the cargo ship was brief, and the rubber Zodiac slowed until it was alongside the cargo ship, and the man in white was brought on board with a sling. The greatest care was taken.

"Mister Buatoom." A hand was extended. It was not taken.

"How long?"

"We will dock in Bangkok in twenty days."

"Where are the containers?"

"Center deck."

Buatoom was led to a nondescript red shipping container, the standard size of two and a half meters square at the end, and more than twelve meters long, enough for three cars to park inside.

"This one and the one next to it." The worker pointed at both containers, stopping in front of one of them. He gripped two handles to open the door, pulling up, and over, swinging it open. He stepped aside, averting his eyes. He knew better than to glance within at the contents.

Buatoom pushed the door aside with a metallic whinge, and a thin smile crossed his face.

In one corner was a stack of dried hides of zebra, sable, and kudu, separated by dry blankets. In another was a stack of wooden crates, each filled with the brown scales of pangolin, thousands of them.

The rest of the container was filled with horn. Varying sizes of rhino horn, neatly stacked together to save space. Neither the ceiling or the walls of the shipping container could be seen beyond the rhino horns.

The other container held the same.

Steel whined as the doors were closed, the bar locked in place.

Chapter 14

The small devices appeared for all the world like traps. A set of ten lay in wait upon styrofoam, jaws agape. Four razor edged teeth lay splayed open like metallic flowers with a central barbed needle in place of the stamen on each of the devices. The reverse side of each were smooth and opaque with the grey of gunmetal. Lined in two rows of five, they sat, waiting. The tray rested between the rangers in the cab of the brown Land Rover.

"This weather is nice, eh?" Sonja Venter patted her knees in the passenger seat. "Approaching winter, and just a little heat. Not sure if I could take the summer again. The hot, the wet is *kak*. Like walking constantly into a naked fat man."

"Happen to you often?" Marais guzzled his coffee.

She looked toward him, beginning to smile, but this faded. He continued to stare through the windshield at the road ahead, his stony expression unchanged.

She coughed. "So... is noon the best part of the day for this?" Her long black hair fluttered in the wind coursing through the open window.

"That is when the wild dogs are resting. Some prefer first thing in the morning, but then you risk interfering with the morning hunt."

"Has it been twenty years for you?"

"Working with wild dogs?" Marais flexed his hand, and gripped the wheel again. "*Ja*, twenty years."

"Well, this Tick, it could make tracking them a great deal easier."

"I would not bet on a single one of those pieces of junk working by the end of the day."

"A bottle of *Kanonkop* that you are wrong."

He did not speak for a while. He seemed exhausted. Eventually, as the den pulled into view before them, he gave a long sigh. "Done."

The Land Rover was parked on a grassy plain far from any road. They walked closer, one carrying the styrofoam tray and a remote, the other holding a medium sized quadcopter drone and a coffee. They had rehearsed for hours, and needed not speak further. Their voices could alarm the Painted wolf pack resting at the den.

Marais held up a hand, and their slow, careful walk was halted. The drone was set carefully on the ground. The remote was checked, batteries in place, and the unit was switched on. Half of the control panel of the remote had been sawn off, and a panel had been bolted to the rest. The soldered wiring snaked between the open hole in the remote and the panel, which had a set of ten buttons. Marais carefully took each dull metallic unit and snapped them into a custom-built housing on the bottom of the quadcopter chassis. When finished, the drone had a series of chrome flower blooms in two rows of five underneath. It was set down on a patch of bare dirt, and a small switch at the base of the motor was turned on. With a nudge of the joystick, the quadcopter whirred into life and ascended quietly into the air. As it hovered, it emitted a buzz no louder than a bumblebee.

Venter now had a sheen of sweat covering her sharp features despite the mild temperature. She piloted the drone toward the den, carefully noting its response to each movement of the stick. Marais laid a computer tablet before her, and shielded the screen as best he could from the sun.

"Linked." Marais whispered as he looked at the screen, which morphed into a dizzying view of constantly shifting dirt and grass.

The breeze was barely perceptible, which made the drone easier to pilot. It whirred slowly toward a fever tree, where several Painted wolves lazed in the sun nearby. Gradually, with subtle motions of the stick, the drone was positioned just above the pack. On the tablet screen, the prone figure of a wolf drifted into view.

"Close... close... mark."

She pressed the first button, and the first grey unit dropped.

Each Tick was weighted with a lithium battery that caused them to fall jaws down. On contact, the jaws sprung shut tightly, biting through fur and skin, and pulling the barbed needle home. Kurkbos immediately started, identified the source of the pain, and began scratching the spot with his hind leg. The Tick was quickly dislodged.

The drone drifted to another target, and the second Tick was released. It clamped down on the flesh above Aalwyn's right shoulder, and despite her attempts to scratch with a hind leg, or crane her head around to bite, it was out of her reach. She turned over onto her back, and scissored her body back and forth on loose rocks, and the second Tick was pulled free of the fur.

The third unit failed to drop. The fourth and fifth dropped simultaneously, one of which attached to Kurkbos successfully. He ignored this bite, preferring to sleep through it. The downdraft of air stirred his fur gently.

Each Tick was carefully deployed, though over half of them were immediately dislodged or destroyed.

"Last one, *meisie*."

Venter chewed a fingernail. Each Tick had cost over seven thousand euros to produce. She centered the drone over a wolf. On the tablet, it was in the crosshairs.

"Move a bit to the left—a little—mark."

The last unit plummeted, striking its target between the scapulae, the razor jaws biting deep, and needle buried in fur and skin. Koorsboom awoke, wondering for the moment why the rest of the pack was aroused and thoroughly annoyed. He was on his paws, and lapped the muzzle of Olienhout. "Awaken, love. There is much to be done."

The wolves greeted one another, with lapping of muzzles, brushing of bodies, gestures between dominant and subservient. Kamassi greeted Aalwyn, her tongue rolled and head held below that of the alpha, with deep whining. Besembossie and Kurkbos lapped muzzles, and he stood on hind legs for a moment to box her roughly. Olienhout twittered to Blackthorn, rubbing her head along her pack-mate, and ran in a circle.

The rangers crept back to their Land Rover after retrieving the drone. The equipment was placed in the back, and Marais tapped the tablet.

"How many Ticks are functioning?" Venter could not hide her anxiety.

"Seven of them." A few more taps. "Four are not moving. They were picked off or failed to adhere." He rubbed his mangled hand, pressing his thumb where the middle finger once sat.

"Well, they are off to hunt." She looked up at the glare of the midday sun. "Not a great time of day, eh?"

Marais did not answer, staring at the three blips as they moved off.

* * *

The pack loped along the floodplain, now a flat of herringbone grass dotted with acacia trees. The sun burned overhead, and the land below drank in the warmth. Antelope and carnivore alike were in the shade, resting. The only thing on the move was a small troop of guineafowl browsing for seeds. Soft *kek kek kek* sounds were uttered as they meandered, hidden within tall grass.

"Why would we hunt now?" Olienhout groused, her brow furrowed in the glare.

"Any time is good for the hunt." Kurkbos kept focused on the plains ahead.

The rest of the pack did not speak, their tongues panting with the heat and effort. They slowed the pace below a towering Apple-leaf tree, though some of the leaves were gone and the shade was reduced.

"Pulling down a beast under the glare of the sun doubles the fight." Blackthorn lay down despite Kurkbos's attempts to encourage them. In the end, they resigned to rest until evening, at the base of the twisted white tree.

The time drifted by, and the sun lazily dragged itself across the sky. The *Kuk-KOORR-ru Kuk-KOORR-ru* purr of a turtle dove was the only sound, that and the gradual scrape of grass blade against blade.

Kurkbos was on his paws.

Blackthorn looked up, and about. Koorsboom did the same.

"Is a danger upon us?" Olienhout padded to him.

Kurkbos did not answer, and walked away, out of the shadow of the Apple-leaf tree. He sniffed the air. Sniffed the ground, and the air again. He whirled around and bounded to them. "They are close." He padded off, the rest of the pack close behind him.

Their path threaded through a random dotting of Knob-thorn acacia trees, and through a rut where a river flowed in the wet season. A Kori bustard ambled along the edge of the dry river bed, its tan plumage edged by a white and black speckled patch, blending with the semi-dried grass. It paused as the wolf pack passed, and resumed its browsing when sure there would be no attack.

A short search was fruitless, the yearlings chirping to Kurkbos adding to his frustration.

"What is it?"

"Is the danger closer?"

"What are we tracking?"

Kurkbos growled to them, and retired once again to the Apple-leaf tree. He looked up at the twisted hulking branches, resembling arms held towards the sky, an appeal for rain.

"We return to the den." He abruptly was up and away, and the wolves followed him, one at a time.

They retraced their steps, along a gully and through a small stand of fan palms.

Kamassi bounded up next to Kurkbos. "How do you know what to hunt?"

He grumbled, but after she prodded him with her nose, he answered. "You do not know until you find it. As we range far across our territory, we test, one herd after the next. If there is a weakness, whether in one or in the herd dynamic, we exploit with all speed." He slowed his pace and began sniffing. "There it is again, but stronger this time."

The rest of the pack waited quietly in vain for him to explain.

"You are mine." He bounded off, and the rest looked at one another before following.

A short run through a tangle of sedge brought them to a stand of wild pear trees. The small deciduous trees had shed their leaves for the winter, the rough grey-brown bark naked to the sun.

"A den." Koorsboom twittered, and his ears went flat. "Just there, at the base of that tree."

Kurkbos was next to the hole in a flash, nosing at the raised edge around a hole too small for even his lanky form. The dirt was heaped up over the top, and it resembled a funnel. He paused, and lowered his head to the opening.

"There are pups inside." As he spoke, his voice just above a whisper, the subdued mewling of young reached him. "Several of them." He left the opening and paced about. After a moment, he returned to the opening. "Koorsboom."

"What are you considering, Kurkbos?"

"Can you fit through this?"

"Barely." He tilted his head to the side in consideration. "Even if so, there is a danger of becoming trapped."

Kurkbos growled to himself. He clawed the ridge around the opening, and the dirt was the consistency of concrete. "What do you mean?"

"A twisting burrow. These can run deep, so my father said."

Kurkbos looked around them, then back to the hole. "We wait."

The sun continued to slowly grind across the sky. Shadows cast by the empty wild pear branches became spindly fingers reaching far into the grass clearing by the trees. The grunting honk of an Egyptian goose broke the quiet that hung over the wolf pack. Another honk answered it, then more honks traded between the male and female geese as they flapped overhead. The breeze picked up and stirred the grass, producing a low hiss that rolled with the waving grass. Crickets sawed, and the rising and falling *kookuRUkuru-koo* of a laughing dove became a steady call to greet the evening.

"We must leave before we are taken by the nightfall." Olienhout whispered to Kurkbos.

He glared at her, but did not answer.

"There will be no moonlight to provide warning of enemies in the dark."

He gave a low sigh. "They are not coming back to their den." He padded to the opening, but did not hear any further low-pitched murmurs from the pups within. Scanning the grasses, he muttered to himself. "This haven, however, has not been abandoned." He twittered to the rest, and they were on their way to their own den under the glowing arbor of the fever trees. Now that the sun was dropping quickly to the horizon to the west, they moved quickly.

As the white of Kamassi's tail tip vanished in the wavering grass, two jackals looked on, glanced to each other, and sprinted to the den. The small opening into hardened earth was indeed narrow and twisting, designed to deny any larger predators. With practiced haste, their lean bodies threaded the needle and disappeared within.

* * *

The pug faces of the pups seemed set in permanent frowns despite their joy of seeing the vast world outside the den. Eight black and white furry shapes bounded about the clearing, bouncing off one another, leaping over tree roots, yipping with excitement. One climbed over a root to bat another pup in the face with little paws.

"*Ag*, shame." Aalwyn watched them play, but kept her eyes on the periphery of the clearing for danger. She sniffed the air, detecting a trace of gasoline and human in the air, but this was a remnant from yesterday. The wind shifted, and she stood, noting the faint smell of wolf musk in the air.

"The hunting party returns."

Soon, the wolves of the *Dwalen* loped into view, with Kurkbos bringing up the rear. She greeted him with much licking of muzzles, but she frowned when this did not bring forth any meat.

"Did the hunt go poorly?"

"We encountered nothing worth the effort." He padded off to nudge one of the pups away from her toy. She whined upon seeing him, and began prodding his snout for food as well.

"Koorsboom." She greeted her son. "What news of the veld?"

"We made little effort at prey, mother, what with the strange time to commence a hunt. We have never ventured out in the middle of the day. Even as it came to evening, Kurkbos did not wish to tear his attention from his new obsession." He twittered to Olienhout, who joined them. "This was a day for the jackals, it seems."

"Yes, we spent most of the time awaiting them at their den."

Aalwyn sat, glared at the dirt before her, then at Kurkbos, then back to the dirt. "Do not speak further of this."

They nodded, and left to play with the pups. Koorsboom batted one of the most energetic of the pups, prompting the young one to scrabble up his face and sit on his shoulders, gnawing an ear. Olienhout chirped happily as she licked clean another pup.

Aalwyn watched the pups playing with the adults and yearlings, each pup constantly demanding attention. The young took up toys from the morning kill, a bit of hide for one, a remnant of hoof for another. Small jaws seized these trophies and paraded them around with pride. If the prize was worthy, other pups would charge and try to take control of it, until the thing was forgotten.

"Ag, shame." She smiled to herself as the black and white balls of fur scampered about. Her smile left when her gaze crossed Kurkbos, who stared intently in the distance, beyond the edge of the clearing.

* * *

"Three Ticks surviving." Sonja Venter adjusted her broad-brimmed hat. "You owe me a *Kanonkop*." Her notes from the day filled page after page, tracking the movement of the pixels over a topographic map. Her free hand drifted over toward an open bottle of red wine, feeling blindly before gripping the neck. She poured the dark red fluid into a ready tin cup, the first drops missing to splash on the ground.

Marais packed up the tablet as they watched the wolves rest by the den.

"This pinotage is a fine vintage." She looked toward Marais, who quietly packed his gear. "This is still good news. We just collect the dead Ticks when the pack departs and figure out why they did not work."

"You bring wine on all of your field surveys?" He set his bag in the Land Rover.

"*'n Boer maak 'n plan.*" She laughed. "On this occasion, yes. I have two more bottles of Spier in my bag." She lifted the cup in a silent toast and drank. "Imagine. An end to the days when we need to dart animals in order to track them." She stood, shading her eyes as she looked toward the den. "Is wild dog mortality from darting about the same here as it is in the Kruger?"

"I do not know." Marais had fetched his binoculars, and was now watching the pack mill about the den.

"How many wild dogs have been darted here?"

"If I make up a number, will you stop talking?"

She closed her mouth, and returned to packing up the gear. After stowing her notes in a rucksack, and securing the tarp over the drone, she slowly sidled up to Marais, and looked in the direction of his binoculars.

Aalwyn trotted away from the den, leading the pups on a patrol once again.

"We will need to dart her for a tracking collar." She said cautiously, eyeing him for a reaction. "She is not carrying a Tick."

Marais sighed.

"She is a beauty, *né?*"

Marais nodded, in spite of himself. "More sedative is coming in a few days."

Venter took a long pause before her next question.

"Who was that man at the graveyard?"

"Ranger." He lowered his binoculars.

"He did not look like one of the rangers."

Marais looked at the sunset. "We camp here tonight."

"*Ag*, man. I was hoping for something more substantial than peanut butter tonight."

"Change of plans." He handed her a paper bag from behind the driver seat. The brown paper was greasy over the bottom half. The rich scent of coriander and beef drifted out of the opening.

"Thanks." She took a piece of solid biltong and with her teeth ripped off a small hunk and chewed.

"We need to go on the road for a few days, and there is little time to drive back to the station, then drive back out here." He pulled out a blanket. "In the morning after some data collection we need to drive far south, so you will need your rest."

"As though I will get sleep out here." Venter grumbled as she retrieved a hiker tent from the rear. "You snore like a hippo."

The tent was deployed, and even as they were quickly enveloped by the dark, the structure was up in a few minutes. A tarp underneath kept the damp of ground from the tent, and another draped over the top would repel any rain.

"A pack of wild dogs was spotted east of Gonarezhou." Marais consulted a map with a flashlight.

"Good news, eh?"

"They were spotted multiple times near a farm." The light of day had melted into complete darkness, and his torch was blinding.

"Any livestock killed?"

"No, but the farmer is ready to *strip his moer*." Marais rolled his jacket up as a pillow and punched it once, laying down on it in the rear of the Land Rover. "He is demanding immediate removal of the entire pack. He was angry to begin with, but got really pissed when the ranger on the phone asked about how the wolves were doing, their health, and so on."

"Farmers require some diplomacy, and they need to feel like you care more about their farm than wild animals." Venter folded up her own jacket and hat as a pillow. "*Dankie* for the tent. I did not think to bring camping equipment. I am grateful you packed one for this contingency."

"*'n Boer maak 'n plan.*"

She smiled.

"The farmer said he would just shoot them and hung up on the ranger from Gonarezhou. They called me for help since they were getting nowhere with the man. The Zinave and Banhine parks do not want wolves there." He rubbed his eyes. "I am not sure even Gorongosa wants more wolves imported. There is always the fear that wolves will kill everything and chase away all the herds. I keep telling them that never happens, they always hunt over a huge area to avoid depleting local herds. Old habits die hard."

"We could drive down tonight. I would like to talk to the farmer, if possible."

"No, we can watch this pack come morning to get more data." His large body heaved under the blanket with a resigned sigh.

"You sound tired."

"When you realize the thing you spent a life researching is going to be extinct within that lifetime, every single day gets tiring."

"I have not worked with wild dogs for very long, but I have learned that the work requires patience." Venter smiled to herself. "You must be like a wild dog. Speed is important, but not so important as stamina."

"If you say so." Marais exhaled.

"Nothing of conservation work ever seems to go right. People are hostile to wild dogs, there is no habitat left, they are impossible to find over hundreds of kilometers. You deal with it, days at a time, seasons at a time. Somehow they find a way to survive, despite what people do to them." She smiled in the darkness. "You may live to see the return of the wolf to its natural range."

"I do not want to live longer than absolutely necessary."

She listened for some indication that he said this in jest, but nothing came.

Within a few minutes, the snoring began. Venter dug into her pockets and pulled out earplugs. Though this would also muffle the sound of a lion sniffing about their tent, she feared this far less than what the snoring would become as the night wore on.

* * *

Aalwyn watched the vehicle in the distance, sniffing the air, and the faint hint of gasoline that came with it. The humans were staying put for the night, but did not seem to be a threat.

In the dark, the pups tired of their playing, and the adults and yearlings settled down to rest. They all huddled together in the black, under a sky crystalline with stars.

Aalwyn closed her eyes, a chill wind once again greeting her, probing her body gently, never allowing her to rest entirely in peace.

Chapter 15

Darkest night, the moon low in the sky and obscured by clouds.

The men were clustered around small campfires, the flickering light barely illuminating the leaf-strewn ground beyond their backs. Their dark green uniforms and leather boots were nearly invisible. Several such groups were scattered in the forest, and the wisps of smoke rising from the fires would have been barely noticeable in daylight, let alone the black of nightfall.

Brachystegia trees towered over the camp, smooth, grey-barked trunks vaulting high over the men below. Branches meandered outwards in jagged directions, resembling a lightning strike going upwards into the sky. The feathery, bluish green leaves rustled in the breeze, cool in these higher elevations. The sprawling shoulders of the great Mountain had hidden these rebels for many years.

A stream of cool water ran past the men squatting around the fires, snaking down from the Mountain, on its inexorable journey toward the distant Lake Urema and the ocean beyond.

Voices muttered, loosened by beer, the empties collecting just beyond the fires. The clink of glass intermingled with shuffling of black boots on the ground as they rested, the occasional high rising laugh punctuated by the clunk of a rifle on a rock or tree.

The cargo truck was parked nearby, now emptied of its horns, but still laden with plenty of stolen hospital drugs, cash, and equipment.

The wind stirred the leaves, bringing a hiss across the forest. A distant baboon barked an alarm. No other sounds rose above these.

One of the men raised his voice, and the rest hushed. He stood, listening in the darkness. There were no other sounds from nearby animals. Frowning, he looked about, and trotted quickly over to the truck.

The front grille lay open. The soldier rounded the front of the vehicle, unslinging the rifle from his shoulder. Hearing a crunch under his boots, he peered down to see he had stepped on a tangle of cables and parts tossed onto the ground. As his eyes adjusted to the gloom beyond the fires, he could just make out what was probably a distributor sitting uselessly on the ground.

He opened the door to the truck to find one of the other soldiers seated inside, slumped over the steering wheel. A cigarette smoldered next to him on the seat. A small ring of black had spread across the fabric. Pulling the man over, he could tell the throat had been cut, the raw flesh stark and red even in the dim light.

Stumbling back, he tripped over another body, nearly invisible in the night. Thumping to the ground, he looked to his side and saw the doll-like eyes of his fellow soldier. Throat slashed open, dark blood had cascaded over his chest. A broad roll of *meticais*, the size of a fist, was stuffed into his open mouth.

He shouted, and the alarm was raised, voices clattering, rifles banging against rock and tree again with no further easy laughter. The din quieted gradually, and the men searched around their camp, further away from the fires. Men in pairs spread out, rifles held up, darting through the tangle of *Brachystegia* trees. Gun barrels pushed aside leafed branches, eyes peering into shadows of shadows.

A shout, given by one of the men, drew the soldiers back toward the encampment. The dim flickering lights caused their silhouettes to dance against the smooth grey bark of the trees that looked down on them. Not far from the campfires the soldiers gathered together, looking down at the ground.

A stream burbled past a boot print in the mud. More boot prints led away from that stream, and stopped next to the lifeless body of the colonel. He lay on his back, mouth wide in a soundless scream. The ribbed horn of an impala was buried in his neck. Blood covered his dark green uniform. The beret was missing.

One soldier melted into the darkness, still clutching his rifle in fear. Another followed him. And another.

Silence enveloped the camp, as another hiss moved through the high leaves of the trees above.

Chapter 16

The nocturnal creatures made their way back to their burrows, from katydids to rodents, finding no safety without the darkness. Lesser bushbabies sprang along branches to return to their leafy nests, their stomachs filled with the night's hunting of insects and tree sap. A giant Eagle owl glided silently over the plain back to the nest, folding vast wings of brown and white plumage shut to rest during daylight hours.

Diurnal hunters opened their eyes to prepare for the day. Kurkbos was among them, awakening with a long stretch of the forepaws and an arch of the back. Blinking away the sleep, he slowly resumed his thoughts of the previous day. And with that, his brow furrowed.

"Right. Koorsboom!"

He padded over.

"I am *gatvol* of those jackals. We go today to drive them altogether from our veld, or—"

"Aalwyn has already set out to do so."

Kurkbos merely stared back.

"She left before first light."

"And has she returned?" Kurkbos spoke quietly.

"Due perhaps by midday."

He issued a sigh. "Very well. We wait for her return."

"She needed all of us to do so." Koorsboom scratched behind his ear.

"Shall we run the pups again?" Olienhout bounded up to Koorsboom.

"Short runs this morning." Koorsboom peered at the periphery of the denning area, despite knowing his mother would not be back so soon. "We must be ready to move."

Kurkbos joined the others, and sat patiently as a pup gnawed on his tail. He seethed in quiet, knowing better than to speak his mind. The pup continued to gnaw his way up the tail.

* * *

Several pixels lit up, remained lit for a moment, and winked out at once. After half an hour, they did so again. The tablet otherwise showed the static image of Gorongosa savanna from the air. The lurching of the Land Rover over the dirt road made it difficult to focus on this.

"Three of those were still on the move yesterday. Most of the rest seem to still be working despite failing to attach." Sonja Venter was still effusive about the project. The clipped tone of her Afrikaans accent reminded Marais of a wild dog.

"Once they are on the move permanently, we can retrieve the rest. Even the dead ones should be easy to find."

"At least we know there was no problem with deployment. The software worked with no issues that I could see." She stowed the tablet in her rucksack.

The road evened out after joining with another track, one heavily travelled by the rangers. The air was still relatively cool, the sun just beginning to peek through the trees.

"How will the talk go with the Gonarezhou farmer, do you think?"

"I phoned him this morning." Marais gripped the wheel. "He told me he was cleaning his rifle."

"Did you offer reimbursement?"

"He did not care about getting paid for killed livestock." He rubbed his maimed hand again. "Farming has been in his family for generations. And when a carnivore kills your livestock, you defend them. It is personal."

"Wild dogs are not personal about it."

"No point in arguing that, Venter. Tradition trumps all—including science, data, and anything you hold dear. The most we can hope for is that either his sons are more open minded, or he sells to a conglomerate that goes along with conservation for PR purposes."

The younger ranger looked off to the side, scratching her chin. "I wonder where they could be moved."

Marais sighed. "I have no idea. Even for the wolves in Gorongosa, they seem to be migrating south, and back out of the park entirely. We are in for a busy winter and spring with all the complaints coming our way. Unless..."

"What?"

"The complaints about wild dogs stop altogether. As the farmers deal with it themselves."

The younger ranger waved a hand. "Defeatist. The teaching takes time to work. Will we have time to make some education stops?"

"Yes. Do you have your posters?"

"Posters and handouts." She checked the box behind her seat.

"Two large farms will agree to take on Malinois guard dogs. We will need to visit them monthly to sort out any behavioral and health problems." He looked over to the younger ranger. "I am not sure if they will do well here, let alone do the work necessary." He watched the road.

"I would like to make stops at some of the small, poorer farms around the villages." Venter rubbed her eyes, regretting not packing any instant coffee. "We need to convince people that it is cheaper to build *kraals* than shoot whatever leopard or lion finds their livestock. Hopefully we can offer reimbursement only for the farms that build the *kraals* to protect the herds at night."

"These educational stops will not have much of an impact unless you keep hammering away at it." Marais looked at her. "How long are you planning on being here?"

"Well, the Tick monitoring can be extended for a while yet before I need to write it up. My commitment here remains open-ended."

The dirt ruts met a wider road, and the Land Rover picked up speed.

"Maybe Dyk's farm could take some of the wild dogs." She eyed her companion.

Marais looked at her as though she suggested the circus.

"Worth a try. He expressed an interest last time we spoke."

"What on earth for?"

"It sounds as though we have no options. The wolves are running low on space. And no local wildlife parks are taking them. Besides, Dyk thinks they could be educational—"

"He has been selling cheetahs to the Saudi royal family."

"That's just a rumor. Besides, he wants to do more education—"

"And qualify for government grants." Marais sighed. "He has no interest in anything but cash."

"If you can make money while doing conservation—" Her finger was in the air when she was interrupted.

"By *compromising* conservation. That's the problem. Not the profit. Even private hunting reserves can do good conservation work, at least those that know the science and work responsibly. Dyk does neither." He drummed the steering wheel as he swung around a pile of rhino dung. "He works with poachers as well."

"I thought he was acquitted in court."

"Acquitted in a provincial court. The judge was from Musina, and had a history with the poacher." Marais closed his eyes. "Never mind, forget I brought it up." He rubbed his hand again. "Long road ahead."

* * *

Phosphorescent green bark glowed in the morning light. The soft surface of the fever tree was an uneven array of ovals resembling thumbprints pressed into clay as it was shaped by greater forces. This tree lay on its side, the red meat of the wood torn open and branches sprawled over the ground. The elephant that had pushed the great tree over had stripped the now lowered branches of leaves. Ants still crisscrossed the trunk on their way down to the roots, still intact and buried fast in the ground.

Aalwyn sniffed this, marveling at the power required to topple such an edifice. She sniffed the ground, allowing not a single track, dropping, or other spoor to escape her notice.

The brush rustled nearby, and she tensed for a moment. Emerging was the black form of a Ground hornbill, stepping carefully along the ground. Dark eyes were nestled in the bright red flesh of its face and throat. It gave Aalwyn a glance, their eyes level. The tall bird felt no threat from her, and continued to peer at the ground between grass stalks for prey. With a lunge, it stabbed a sharp bill into a grass tussock. Standing tall again, it held the broken body of a field mouse.

Aalwyn padded on into the savanna, marking the position of trees, rocks, and any other point of reference. The sun climbed higher in the sky, and the temperature rose.

Buzzing of flies drew her attention, and she loped closer to a towering baobab tree. The broad trunk was greater around than an elephant, and the heavy branches lifted the sky on its broad shoulders. Not far from the gnarled base of the baobab lay the decaying remains of a wildebeest.

She looked around with great caution, sniffing the air. No signs of danger. She trotted closer, and could see very little remained other than a dried rib cage and tendons. The flies still deposited their eggs and beetles searched for the smallest fragments of nutriment.

On the ground, she found what she was looking for. Central pad, four toes, each with a claw. Slender, like their owners. The tracks of a jackal.

* * *

Stretching endlessly across the plains, a tar ribbon wound its way south. Cars and heavy trucks roared down this artery of industry, reeking of gasoline and smoke. Even as it brought vast numbers of people great distances, the edges of the road slowly crumbled under the wear of weather, rain, and the steady creeping invasion of grass. Maintained by seasonal road crews, the highway continued to exist, but only just.

The beige Land Rover sped down the road with the rest of the irregular traffic, slowing to swerve around the occasional pothole. Johan Marais turned the wheel, guiding the dusty tires over another gaping wound in the asphalt.

"*Sies, man*, watch out for the kid!" Sonja Venter pointed to a boy, no more than five, in the road.

"Nobody needs to watch out for him." Marais slowed as he approached, and the boy stepped aside. He upturned a bucket, dropping his load of dirt into a pothole. As the Land Rover passed him, Marais dropped a folded bill into his hand.

"You get him on the way back."

She watched in the rearview mirror as the boy brought another bucket of dirt to the pothole, where he waited.

"Fixing the road. He will dump more sand into the hole when another car approaches."

"For tips?" She turned forward again.

"Drivers can afford it."

The Land Rover coasted, slowing before turning down a nondescript dirt road. There were no sign markers indicating the destination. Shortly, this road came to a gate. Marais hopped out and unwound a length of wire from the gate, opening it. He got back in and pulled forward.

"What are you going to say?" Venter jumped out to close the gate.

"Do not shoot the wild dogs."

Metal banged against metal, and she got back into the passenger seat. "From what you said, he seemed to have already made up his mind." The engine revved and they proceeded up the dirt road, leaving a rising cloud of light brown dust behind them. Brush and grass swept past as they entered the farm. Crops of maize and beans stood as dried stalks after the harvest, the rest of the land given over to grass and the cattle it feeds.

The farm house emerged from behind a hill as the vehicle rattled down the track. It was a simple brick structure, windows covered with metal bars, and a tin roof that burned in the sun. Two men hacked at brush with panga knives, and they ignored their approach.

From the front door stepped a man dressed in overalls, a light blue long sleeved shirt. His light brown skin was covered with sweat, and he mopped his brow with a cloth while walking out to meet the Land Rover.

Marais was out the moment the vehicle ground to a halt, his large frame seeming to cover the distance between them in a single stride.

"Manuel Daviz." Hands clasped in greeting. "It is good to meet you. I thank you for taking the time to talk."

"No need to thank me. I am taking no more time for this problem." He ambled over to his own *bakkie*, and hefted a hunting rifle from the rear bed. *"Vamos!"*

The two men walked over with their panga knives, eyeing the visitors with suspicion.

"I thought we could talk about this."

"I have had enough of talking." He opened the breech, and blew into it. "You rangers do not care about people, only your stupid animals."

"Daviz, look." Marais clenched his hands into fists. "There are ways of dealing with this without shooting them all."

"Yes, there is. Waiting for them to kill my cattle, and *then* shooting them all."

"There are damned few of them left." His teeth were grinding, even as he spoke. "We need them alive."

"I do not." The farmer closed the breech of the rifle, and held it tightly. The barrel was drifting vaguely in Marais's direction, and Daviz's sweaty face became stone. The panga knives caught the sun, held at the ready in eager hands. No sound was heard other than the razz of crickets.

"You will need help tracking the dogs, *né?*" A lighter, friendlier voice.

Marais turned around to glare at Venter, who was calmly walking toward Daviz and his two farmhands.

"These wild dogs, they know just how to hide, and when to run." Her clipped Afrikaans accent sounded oddly chipper. "And they can run, fast and far, more than fifty kilometers a day if they must."

"I can find them on my farm." Daviz shifted the rifle in his hands. "I know every centimeter of it." He rested the stock of the rifle on the ground.

"So do they." She smiled, and held a hand up to shade her eyes, and looked into the sun. "And they have a talent for knowing when danger is coming."

"You are offering to help me shoot them?" Daviz cocked his head to the side.

"I will help you deal with this problem however you see fit." She held out one hand to shake Daviz's, the other holding the strap of the rucksack on her back. "Sonja Venter. I work with this *oke*."

"Yeah." Daviz peered at him expectantly. "So we are off, if you want to show me where you think they will be."

"*Ja, ja*." She looked around at the farm house and the distant cattle, grazing absently on the dried grass. "How long has this farm been in your family?"

"Three generations."

"Three?" Her eyes bugged open, and she unslung her rucksack. She set it on the ground, with a clink of glass. "You must have learned the grounds as a little one, eh?" She held her hand level with the ground at her hip.

The workmen eyed the sack.

"My father and mother kept this place through the bad times." He looked at the cattle with a slow nod. "The civil war, they killed nearly all of our animals."

"*Ja, ja*. Even now, times are hard for farmers everywhere." Venter unzipped her bag. "Big companies want to buy out the little guy. The buyer for crops and livestock sets the price." She pulled a bottle from her bag, and twisted off the foil cap with a squeak and a light crack. "It is hectic. Farmers here attacked by rebels, pushed out by corruption. Farm murders in South Africa while the police look the other way. Everyone seems to forget they feed the world, *né?*" She handed a tin cup to Daviz and poured the wine. As the rich red splashed in, the farmer's arm visibly relaxed, and a smile crept onto his face.

"Everyone forgets." Daviz swirled the wine in the cup. "Everyone thinks the food just grows in the stores." He took a swig, and his brow went up. "Mmm." He nodded his approval.

"Do you mind if I?" She took out another cup, and when the farmer indicated agreement, she poured her own. "My father still farms. Has land in Mpumalanga."

"Cattle?" Daviz took another drink.

"Impala."

"Low yield."

"Not so bad." Venter took a drink as well. "Demand for game meat is not as high, but farming them is more sustainable." She thought for a moment. "Less water, less maintenance, they do less damage to the land."

"Less money."

"True. But the *cost* is less." Venter swallowed her wine. "His theory is, if he keeps the cost down — and impala breeds well on good land — then he worries less about the bank and debts." She noticed the bottom of Daviz's cup was visible, and kept it hidden with another pour from the bottle. "The lean times are weathered less painfully."

"We get by fair enough with cattle. But we are still prisoners of the market."

"Price of beef goes up and down, but the cost of feed, supplies, and medicine never seem to go anywhere but up." She smiled, with sadness in her eyes.

"Why is that?"

"Not enough farmers become president."

Daviz looked at both of the rangers for a moment, and the three shared a laugh. The rifle had been placed back into the bed of the truck.

* * *

Aalwyn padded through thick *Combretum* brush, her large ears trained forward, listening. The leaves were still plentiful on the branches, which obscured her vision. So far, only the rustling of leaves and the flit of a sparrow reached her. She emerged from the snarl of shrubs.

Her hazel eyes peered about, and fixed upon a dry earthen mound. Trotting closer, she could discern a small hole near the base of one of the trees. Looking around, she detected no other movement. Even close to the denning hole, the ground hard as stone, she could barely scent any sign of the jackal pups. Another sniff. The scent of Koorsboom was still on the ground from their recent foray.

She looked around, awaiting a charge from one of the jackals in defense of the den, but none came. Retiring to the higher grass, she watched the sun make its lazy circle across the sky.

Nothing for it but to wait.

* * *

The sun was setting when the beige Land Rover pulled into the small town outside Gorongosa. The thick brush seemed to retreat to allow space for metal and brick structures, with interspersed small houses of thatch and mud. A heavy truck stacked high with freshly cut trees roared past on the curve of blacktop past the spaza shops. People hawking their wares, pineapples, vegetables, and clothing were packing up for the evening.

Marais parked the Land Rover before a tin roofed structure, inside of which the marimba music blaring could be heard over singing and shouting voices. He recognized a few of the voices as rangers from the park.

His large hands held the steering wheel as the engine rattled to a stop. He was silent for a moment, and sighed before speaking for the first time since they had left Daviz's farm.

"Venter. Well done."

"It seemed promising, when we left." She beamed.

"*Ja*, well, no, it was good. A team from Gonarezhou is coming with a chopper to start the darting." He sighed. "We needed him to delay long enough to allow us to cobble together a plan." He clapped a hand on her shoulder, and the young woman could not help but wince.

"I am not sure I am up for a drink after all that wine before a long drive." She held her eyes open with considerable effort.

"Well, I am. *Kom, meisie.*"

The two rangers walked toward the entrance to the pub, and the sounds of laughter and raucous stories grew louder. Inside, men leaned on wood counters holding onto bottles of beer. The sound of a guitar strumming with drums beating poured forth from a speaker, and it was a wonder the people could hear one another. Marais took one hand after another in greeting, enveloping those hands and gripping them with hearty shaking. He put a finger in the air and made a circle, eyeing the bartender, and clapping a fist to his chest. A minute later a dozen bottles were planted on the counter. Marais left a small stack of *meticais* in payment. A steel opener expertly removed the caps from each, and a fountain of foam covered the red and yellow label marked IMPALA on one of the bottles.

"Johan."

The deep, sonorous voice somehow could be heard over the racket, and the rangers turned toward the source.

Stalking toward the rangers at the bar was a man in plainclothes, face devoid of emotion. He fished for his cigarettes in a breast pocket. He did not wear the ranger uniform at the moment, but he did not need to. All conversation throughout the pub ceased, the marimba music now sounding strangely hollow.

"Razak." Johan Marais clasped his hand.

He did not speak, simply nodding toward Sonja Venter and the other rangers. They nodded back, unnerved by the silent ranger's presence.

Razak reached behind him, pulling an object from his waistband and he planted this on the countertop next to a bottle of Impala beer, still foaming. With another nod, he turned and disappeared again into the shadows beyond the entrance of the pub.

"What is that?" Venter stared at the folded bit of cloth he left behind.

Marais picked up the folded cloth. Opening it, he saw a hip flask, metal shining with reflected light from the pub. The cloth, once he turned it over, was a black beret. On the front was the insignia of a colonel.

"He was in the cemetery, the day of the funerals." She stared at the beret. "Who is he?"

Marais nodded gravely to the other rangers present, and they stared at the beret.

"A hunter."

* * *

The carcass of the impala lay prone in the twilight, its abdominal cavity hollowed, congealed blood pooled underneath. It still moved, with a sudden shudder, and stopped as more tissue was pulled free. The fluid-drenched head of a spotted hyena emerged from behind the exposed ribcage, heavy jaws working on the muscle that it tore loose. A swallow, and he gave a furtive look about. He worked to bring down the antelope, and was loathe to lose his prize. The grassy clearing was without cover, save a small lavender feverberry bush. He buried his head again inside the impala.

A golden head peeked from behind the bush. Large pointed ears were directed toward the impala, now shuddering again with the work underway inside. Keen eyes rimmed in black were set above a narrow muzzle, and the rest of the reddish-brown body stepped away from the bush. Its back was a flat stripe resembling a cape of silvered black, ending in a bushy black tail. A barely audible woof was given, and the jackal's mate emerged from the other side. They shared a look, and set to work.

One crouched in the grass, its ears barely detectable above the wavering dried blades.

The other trotted toward the dead impala, making no effort to hide.

A rattling growl, and a head encased in blood rose from the body cavity. He issued a slight giggle. The jackal held its position. Dripping saliva, the hyena dipped low.

The male jackal sprinted to the impala and tugged a leg.

With shocking speed, the hyena was away from the carcass with teeth bared. A louder giggle was given as a warning.

The Black-backed jackal withdrew a few meters.

Returning to the feed, the hyena barely got its teeth around the tenderloin before it sensed movement. Looking up, he saw the jackal had quietly set to work on the hip, and nearly scissored free the hind leg. A high, cackling giggle echoed across the field, and the hyena was on the chase. The powerful forelegs churned the large body forward, while the lithe jackal easily outpaced its enemy.

The impala was left unguarded. The female sprinted to the body and cut free the rest of the hind leg. She left this, taking several mouthfuls of tenderloin and pelvic muscle, rich in protein, before she sensed the hyena was returning to the kill.

The male continued to harass the hyena, while the female took more food. When they had their fill, the hind leg left with them. Running separately, they took care to keep any scavengers from giving chase.

A short jaunt across the veld, and the jackals rejoined at the mouth of the den. The hind leg was dropped to the ground for a moment as they greeted one another. The female began nibbling tenderly on her mate's ear, moving slowly down to the face. She opened her eyes to see him returning her gaze, one they would share for the rest of their lives.

He began to nibble her face as well, then stopped. A movement in the *Combretum* shrub not far from the den was apparent. He gave a woof of alarm, and she whirled about to face the threat. As she saw a larger predator emerge from the leaves and shadow, she backed toward the hole with a high foxlike cackle.

Aalwyn made no effort to hide, shaking her body to rid herself of the chill. Her ears were erect, her body relaxed. She gave off no scent of hostility.

"Why do you follow us?" Aalwyn spoke slowly and with care. She had never attempted to talk with jackals before, and did not know what to expect.

The jackals looked at one another, and the female continued to back towards the den. She eyed the hind leg, gave a low rumble, and the male took hold of it. He tensed, preparing to be attacked for the prize.

Aalwyn made no motion, still no hint of any ill intent. "Why do you follow my pack?"

The male backed to the den, dropping the hind leg into the hole, and darted into the opening. Inside there was a symphony of warbling and mewling as the pups recognized the feast, then nothing as the male bid them to be quiet.

"Why do you follow my pack?" She patiently repeated herself, slowly and clearly.

A stuttering woof followed, and the female jackal remained tensed and low to the ground. She woofed further, and eventually Aalwyn began to understand the crude common language between them.

"*Urrhh Guhhrrmmm...*"

Aalwyn waited patiently, though she could feel the time slipping by her.

"*Guhhhrmmmm... Meaat.*"

"The meat of our kill?"

The jackal raised her brow, and her woofing became quicker, though more difficult to understand.

"*Meeeaaaaat hrooff grullllll wull... wullllff.*"

"You do not attack our pups?"

The jackal emitted coarse growls, which Aalwyn interpreted as a negative.

She turned to leave, but the woofing continued.

"*Ehhhhrrrrrhoofff Truuhhhhh Hyooooo.*"

She dipped her head, an almost subservient gesture she hoped would be interpreted as somewhat friendly.

"*Wullllffff Reeeahhrrr. Vuhhhlllulfff Hreaaaahhrrr.*"

Aalwyn paused, a gnawing in her stomach becoming apparent.

The jackal repeated her words.

Aalwyn took a breath as her heart stopped.

"*Wullffffff Hreearrrhr Naa. Komm voorr Hyoo.*"

She darted into the brush, and returned to her den with the greatest speed she could muster.

"*Wolves here now... they are coming for you...*"

Chapter 17

Black, white, and gold flashed in darkness, between shadow and grass impossible to track. Aalwyn scythed through the brush and continued a flat run as though on the hunt. Her lean body arced over a low growing acacia shrub, and her sprint swung around the Apple-leaf tree that indicated the way back to the den. She ran to the very limit of her stamina, her muscles aching with the work.

The fever trees were ahead, and the wolves lazed underneath, preparing for sleep.

"Koorsboom! Olienhout!" She slid to a stop.

The pack mobilized around her, pups bounding over after dropping their toys.

"We move now. We live under the fever tree no longer."

Kurkbos lapped her muzzle, but she did not return the gesture.

"The time of the *Dwalen* has come."

* * *

The pack was underway within minutes, their mutual greetings muted with anxiety. A White-backed vulture perched on a fallen tree viewed this with mild interest. As the pups departed with the rest of the group, the scavenger took to wing, sensing there would be no more leftovers here.

Aalwyn took the lead, with Koorsboom and Olienhout by her side. The yearlings Kamassi, Besembossie, Branddoring, and Blackthorn grouped in the middle, nervous and excited in equal measure about discovering new lands to the south. Kurkbos brought up the rear, herding together the eight pups as they bounded behind the pack. Each time a pup stopped to investigate some mysterious plant or insect, he nosed their rump back in motion. Each wolf followed those in the lead, the terminal white of the tail able to signal their position in tall grasses. Even then, sometimes the white of tail disappeared, and it was a guess as to what way forward was best.

The pups whimpered, glancing about with fear in the dim light.

"Koorsboom—take the lead, and do not slow." Aalwyn trotted around the group of yearlings, and found the pups unattended. She began to release a growl as Kurkbos emerged from the brush, one of the pups in his jaws.

"*Onderrd Awff*" He spoke around the body of the pup, gently grasped by the hip. The pup wiggled his legs happily at the free ride. Kurkbos set him down amid the rest. "They keep wandering off. They are not ready for this."

"There was little choice. The warning was clear enough." Aalwyn spoke over her shoulder, pushing ahead.

Kurkbos arched his brow as he licked his chops, the taste of musk in his mouth. "You could understand them?"

"Some hunters share enough of our language." She peered into the scant light offered by the moon above, and could make out white tail tips above the grass.

"Even lions?"

"Yes." Aalwyn's voice hollowed, as it did when talk turned to the past.

Kurkbos spoke haltingly. "Hu—humans?"

"Of course not." She snuffed. "They are as foreign in speech as the wildebeest."

They kept a quick pace as the night wore on, passing through wet savanna. Their path slowed as they reached a wide artery of blue water cutting through the veld. The bank rose above the river on both sides, and was lined with dense brush. Ripples played across the surface, blue upon black, a shudder from the depths.

"Strange, that. The land changes just the other side of this river." Koorsboom muttered.

"Humans control the far side." Olienhout joined his side. They could see two women in colorful dress, barely visible in the moonlight. Small thatched huts stood close to the river itself, and the rest of their view was of the maize fields that stretched further from the riverfront.

"What are those plants?"

"I am not sure." Aalwyn intoned. "But the plants are theirs to command."

"Do they move when ordered?" Kamassi's quizzical expression brought a smile to Aalwyn's eyes.

"No, dear, the plants remain rooted. The people *place* them, intentionally, though it is not clear why." She sniffed the high bank, and the water just below. "The fading rains have left the river at a lower level." She examined the river in both directions. "But not low enough." Another sniff to the air. "We will need to cross this." The wolves looked up and down the waterway, but saw no shallow point or bridge.

"Can we splash through it?" Blackthorn reared on hind legs, ready to dive in.

"Crocodiles. Best not to chance it."

As though on cue, a log surfaced mid river and slowly floated toward their bank. The log took on life as a pair of eyes opened, took notice of the wolves, and dipped beneath the waves again.

Aalwyn loped to the east, looking about for rocks or sand bars as signs of crossing points. In the dark, it was impossible to tell the depth of the river.

"Careful, my love." Kurkbos indicated the ground before him with his nose. "Wolf tracks. And not ones I recognize."

Aalwyn took a sniff, and regarded the paw prints in breathless silence.

"There is nothing for it." Aalwyn grumbled in frustration. "We must rest now, and wait for morning light."

The pups and yearlings seemed relieved at her announcement, and the adults began digging into the earth to make shallow depressions for the pups. Koorsboom joined them, flinging small clumps of mud behind him. The pups were herded into the scratchings, where the adults would keep them warm. Aalwyn peered at the edge of the nearby forest.

And we must hope they do not find us in the night.

***

Daylight erupted in the east, and the *Dwalen* was already on the move. The pups mewled for more rest after their short sleep, exhausted from their desperate flight in the dark. The adults continued the search for safe passage across the Pungwe river which formed the southern border of Gorongosa. The grass up to the river was a rich green, and became dense further from the water, until it stopped at thick deciduous and tangled palm brush a small distance away.

"Where are we going, mother?" One of the pups murmured.

"I know not where we are headed, young one."

Kurkbos prodded the pup with his snout. "Have you chosen names for them, yet?"

Aalwyn smiled at Koorsboom. "We shall wait out the season. As we must." As she watched her pups, her smile faded.

"You are apprehensive." Koorsboom scratched his ear.

"Out in the open, protecting these pups will be a constant struggle." She shook her head to repel the flies. "More than this... we have lost something today. The wild was filled with promise." She eyed the river with regret. "And now we wander once again, leaving behind all we have gained."

Besembossie padded over. "There are more wolf tracks over here. We are not the only ones to have come this way."

Aalwyn sat, frowning at the river. The water was still blue here, rather than the muddy brown that could indicate water shallow enough to cross.

A high twitter reached her ears, and she spun about, the gnawing sensation in her stomach now overtaken by a steady fall.

"You have been warned, Aalwyn." A hulking wolf sprinted out of the brush and slowed. One at a time, wolves emerged from the wavering palm shrubs that lined the river. The pack fanned out, at once outnumbering and outflanking their quarry on either side.

The *Dwalen* was caught off guard, each wolf glancing about wildly, and seeing only more of the larger pack facing them. Each of the *Selous* wild dogs were tensed, rounded ears directed toward their enemies.

Varkoor stalked closer with confidence. At her side was Ratel, dark fur marked with flecks of gold and white. A single eye glared at Aalwyn, the other clouded and blind, yet still filled with anger. His muzzle parted and revealed jaws of white so striking against his black coloration.

Aalwyn stepped carefully toward the alpha female who addressed her. "Indeed you have, and we have taken leave of the veld."

"Varkoor does not believe those lies so easily." She snarled, her muzzle wrinkled, drool dripping on the ground she walked upon. "Were you so eager to make way, we would not have been able to find you." Her shoulders were higher and broader than Aalwyn's, rippling with muscle. Her fangs bared, ears folded back against a threat.

Another dark wolf walked behind her, smaller than Ratel, but similarly colored.

Koorsboom ruff-barked to him. "Laeveldvy—surely you do not intend to attack us?"

He did not answer, dipping his head beneath that of Varkoor.

Aalwyn hissed at him. "*Bly stil*, you fool." She took a step back. "This is between the alphas—and us alone."

The wall of the *Selous* pack closed around them, a barrier of lithe and powerful figures, while the river was to their backs.

"We can still flee..." Kurkbos chirped, his voice cracking with fear. "I can take the pups."

"They would drown in the river or feed the crocodiles. Down to the last pup." She closed her eyes and clenched her jaw. "There is no escaping this." She took a step forward once more.

Varkoor gave a sinister grin. "And now you embrace my wrath?" She released a warbling alarm bark that caused her entire pack to tense, the ears of each wolf folding back in preparation.

"Koorsboom—when I am dead, you take the pups with Olienhout and protect them." Aalwyn took another step forward.

"Mother—you can run, and—"

"There is nowhere to run for me, my son." She lowered her head. "My death will reassure them we pose no further threat as our pack fragments. So be it." Without warning, she shot forward and sank her fangs into Varkoor's shoulder.

The attack surprised Varkoor, but she absorbed the blow and bit back in kind. Wrenching herself from Aalwyn's grasp, she whirled about and laid her opponent's shoulder wide open, and stepped back with a snarl.

Aalwyn's wound throbbed, seeping blood, her head held low, eyes narrowed into hateful shards. She pounced, but Varkoor sidestepped her, delivering another bite to her side. Leaping onto her back, Varkoor ripped an ear to shreds, and buried her jaws in the base of Aalwyn's neck before being thrown off.

Aalwyn rolled upright, but only just, working hard to balance, and stay on her feet. Her eyes struggled to focus.

Kurkbos raked the earth with a claw, and moved towards the melee.

Four *Selous* wolves mirrored him. Each glared at Kurkbos, willing the wolf to stay put.

Aalwyn gasped, her wounds spilling blood. The grass was pattered with red, and the two matriarchs circled one another. Varkoor lunged and missed, withdrawing before Aalwyn could connect. Snarling, a steady hiss, the sound of the *Dwalen* alpha breathing heavily.

Downriver, a herd of elephants left the dense green of the bank, splashing into the river. The two wolf packs paused to glance in their direction. The ten grey mountains moved swiftly, stepping down into the river with the lightest splash imaginable for such behemoths. They waded across to plunder the rich maize from the nearby farm. A low buzz accompanied them, rising slowly as the elephant herd set foot on the far bank. Within minutes all ten were out of the water, and were tearing into the field, hoovering up the crop.

The pups shrank against the ground, looking into the air as a helicopter roared overhead, the ear-shattering metallic grind bringing alarm to all below. The rampaging grey shapes in the field released a trumpet, then another, and they left the field behind to escape deeper into the farms.

As the helicopter followed, the *whupwhupwhup* faded, leaving the wolf packs on the riverbank shaken.

Aalwyn wavered on her paws, and regarded her adversary. Her jaw hung open, a streamer of drool hanging on the ground, mixed with blood. She sank onto her side, eyes closing.

Varkoor stood steady, head down, prepared for her next strike. Her only wound was a light one by her shoulder. She spoke in a ruff-bark meant for all of her adversaries. "When next you receive a death threat, you *run as though a lion is upon you.*" Her voice lowered. "As for you... my litter will mark your remains." She lifted a lip as she spoke, and her hind legs coiled.

A flurry of black, white, and gold struck her, and Varkoor rolled past Aalwyn, writhing on the ground with a high-pitched peal of cackling.

Teeth flashed and claws dug into the ground, and Varkoor pulled herself from the attack.

"Who dares come between me and my land?"

The other wolf was upright, teeth on display, and eyes wild with fury.

"The land is yours... Essenhout shall bury you in it!" She unleashed a sharp cry and threw herself at the *Selous* alpha, with no plan, no angle, and utterly no mercy. The whirling ball of fur rolled over and one wolf managed to stand just as the other knocked her back over, never leaving the grass, covered with blood.

Essenhout paused only for a breath, and lunged again, missing Varkoor's wounded shoulder. She leapt again, jaws wide, giving the alpha no chance to prepare for her attack, and left a stream of blood dripping from the larger wolf's side.

Varkoor withdrew for a moment, and was chambered for the next attack. When Essenhout leapt at her again, Varkoor dove underneath her and closed her jaws on a hind leg. Biting down, a sickening wet snap left the riverbank in silence.

Essenhout fell to her side, writhing in pain. She tried in vain to stand, and immediately collapsed, her hind leg dangling uselessly.

Varkoor stepped back towards Ratel, who lapped her muzzle and wounds. They looked over to see Essenhout's small pack, standing outside the bloody circle, unsure of what to do.

One of them walked to Essenhout, ignoring the twittering from the *Selous*. Rukato lapped Essenhout's open mouth, and prodded her with his snout. "On your feet... I beg you." The old bullet wound gave him the appearance of perpetually grinning, though his face was creased with worry.

"It is over, Rukato." Essenhout breathed heavily.

Varkoor panted, her eyes wild with anger. She padded laboriously back toward the rest of her pack.

"The fight has left her." Essenhout flailed again on her feet, slumping onto her side. "There is only the *trek* ahead for us now." She managed a smile despite her agony.

Aalwyn raised herself on her forepaws with great effort, opening her eyes. Slowly she realized what had happened.

"Whether by our teeth or those of the crocodile..." Varkoor breathed heavily. "... you will not live on this side of the river." Her large frame swayed, but each member of her pack carefully stooped and bowed lower still. She led the way, one paw after the next, into the brush, followed by the rest of the *Selous*. The fan palms swayed as the wolves pushed by. Soon none were in sight, but every wolf on the bank knew they were being watched.

Aalwyn knelt by her sister, using all her strength to stay upright. "We must flee—they will not give us long."

Koorsboom touched noses with her. "Ever taut, my *Dwalen*. I will find a way across." He and the yearlings were off.

"Where is..." Essenhout took a deep breath, the searing pain of her broken leg clamping her eyes shut. "... my *Droom?*"

"The rest of your pack is here. They await your command." Aalwyn whispered.

Awkward and hesitant, her pack-mates looked to the distant brush, the riverbank, the rest of the *Dwalen*. One began to wander down the bank toward the water.

Aalwyn twittered to Kurkbos. "Collect them. They know not what to do with their alpha fallen." She tried this in a whisper, hoping her sister would not hear.

He chased after the other wolves, drawing them back.

"Fallen, have I?" Essenhout opened her eyes again. "You could not fell me with the stomp of an elephant." She stood once again, and fell again, her mind failing to understand her injury.

"We will bring you with us." Aalwyn managed a half-smile. "A family once again."

Her sister nodded.

Koorsboom bounded up to them. "Found a sand bar just there, by a sharp bend in the river. The languid water slows enough to allow us passage."

Aalwyn issued twitters to the *Dwalen*. "All of you with me. Kurkbos—mind the pups do not get lost or stumble into the deep." The wolves started down the river. They could feel dozens of eyes watching them, willing them to run, ready to kill if the escape was not quick enough.

Koorsboom lapped Essenhout's muzzle.

"It is time. I can help you." Aalwyn gripped her side in her jaws, beckoning her onto her paws. The two walked alongside her, slowly, one paw before the next, on the wet ground, leaving behind the blood shed upon the grass. Each step, Essenhout whimpered, unable to swallow entirely her torment. Each limping step nearly led her to collapse on the ground.

"Stay up, my sister. If you fall... you will not live out this day."

Step. Another step. Limp.

Wavering, not falling.

Step.

Another step.

Aalwyn looked over her shoulder and saw Varkoor peering out from under a palm tree. There was no joy or victory in her eyes. Only resolve was there, the meager triumph of simply living another day.

Each step was a bitter fight, and Essenhout growled in a constant dirge.

They crossed the river by the sand bar, and rested within a few meters of the river edge. There they remained through the day, and Aalwyn tended to her sister. Night took them, rolling over the land like a wave that crested and crashed down, allowing none to take a breath.

"Must we rest so close to the water? Crocodiles and hippos are likely to come this way in the darkness." Koorsboom eyed the river with concern.

"We cannot go further today, my son." She lay next to her sister, already asleep. "Our vigil has begun."

Chapter 18

A light drizzle woke the pack, a cold sheen of moisture on every surface. The tangled thicket the wolves lay within was alive with the tapping of water on leaf. Water may be precious, but every animal in the veld feels miserable when drenched in it.

Aalwyn nudged Essenhout with her snout. She continued to snore.

"Koorsboom—you and I will patrol." Close by, the sounds of people talking. "Though I fear we have far to go to find safety."

Some of the pups had begun to arouse, and so she slipped away quietly. They wound through the palm leaves under the sheltering canopies of wild custard apple trees, branches long since robbed of their sweet fruit. Her slender muzzle parted the leaves, then shrank back into them.

"We are on the edge of a farm." Her ruff-bark was muted. "And the humans run about like ants."

Women busied themselves with hoisting armfuls of maize stalks into bundles, others dragging them away. Most of them had dark skin, wearing old, worn-through clothing. One was dressed smartly, clad in khakis. He stood next to a pale-skinned man, wearing what appeared to be the same khakis. They spoke to a farmer, and there was much pointing and excitement. Sharp words were spoken by the man in the tattered garments, and he made a gesture to suggest a gun, taking aim, and shooting.

"They know we are here..." Aalwyn gasped. The gesture of the person meant nothing to her, but the scent of anger poured from the humans. She returned to the rest of the pack. "On your feet, whether able or not. We have little time."

The pale skinned man and dark-skinned man in khakis shook the hand of the farmer, promising to do something about the elephant raids. The farmer appeared happy about this, gesturing to the now razed fields. During the night, a single herd had consumed an entire year's worth of maize.

The men turned and exclaimed, pointing, shouting, in fear. A column of wild dogs sprinted from the brush at the river's edge, adults and pups bounding forward as though on a hunt. The two rangers pointed as well, though their shouting was with delight. They gesticulated wildly to the farmers, especially to those who already had their guns in hand.

Aalwyn loped ahead, waiting and waiting for the shots that would cut them down. She wheeled about, looking down the line of wolves moving too slowly for her anxiety to bear. She nudged each, lapping their muzzles, each lick encouraging them to move more quickly. The pups responded by darting off in random directions, corralled back to the line by the yearlings. She stole glances to the humans, mostly standing and watching, pointing. Two held long sticks in their hands, but none opened fire.

"Kurkbos! Move the pups along, with all haste!"

With a wary eye on the men with the sticks, Aalwyn nosed Essenhout along with the rest of the pack, though concealed by thicker foliage. She did not want them to know her sister was so severely injured.

The pack loped in fits and starts through the ruined maize field, bewildered by the fields bare of vegetation and the straight rows and lines of the farmland. Aalwyn worked her way to the rear. Rukato escorted Essenhout forward, as she concentrated on every small step.

"Mother, I do not think they will attack." Koorsboom kept looking over to the humans. "Though I am loathe to guess, I cannot but think they are *enjoying* this."

"Think if you must, but move." She trotted alongside, lapping Essenhout's muzzle. "Sister, how do you fare?"

She opened her rolling eyes. "Ready for the fight."

* * *

Further from the river, the land was drier, the grasses sparser, and the vegetation less lush. The topography was still dominated by farms, but with rocky areas breaking up the villages with land impossible to cultivate. Aalwyn took in the view from a rock outcrop overlooking the Pungwe river with farms below her. Rukato remained by his mate's side, staring, waiting. When she twitched with a dream, he started, prepared for whatever he needed to do.

"Kurkbos—how are the pups?"

"None the worse, though they need the hunt quite badly."

She peered at the gravel between her claws. Ants passed this way and that, carrying small food parcels. "For the first time in my life... I know not what to do."

"One paw after the next." Kurkbos began to twitter and lick the mouths and palates of the closest yearlings, bidding them to begin the hunt. Koorsboom and Olienhout joined in, wolves leaping about and chirping with excitement, running in circles. Before long, they were gone. The quiet resumed, broken only by a distant *hwee - kow kow kow* of a pair of fish eagles.

Aalwyn lay next to her sister. "Do you recall our hunts on the great river to the west?"

Essenhout rested on her side. "A lifetime hence. The good lands, filled with antelope, pronking from sunrise to set." She moved her ruined leg to scratch off a tick, and the explosion of sudden pain stopped the movement dead, her jaws clenched shut. After a few minutes of heavy breathing, she continued. "Grootboom taught me much about the hunt." She waited. "I should not have mentioned his name."

"There is no reason to hold your tongue, dear. We have all lost." Aalwyn looked up to a martial eagle soaring. She issued a sharp growl, and the pups scrambled about looking for a den that was not there. They settled for an anvil-shaped boulder that provided a sloping roof.

"Death was denied once, by his doing." She opened her eyes and struggled onto a foreleg. "We were on the hunt. A duiker was ours, all within a jaw length. He bid me to halt just before the kill." A faint smile crossed her face. "A black mamba made that kill. A single step more and it would have me." She looked up at the martial eagle still riding a thermal. "Always, it is the single step. Any one of us could make it."

Aalwyn sniffed the injured rear leg. The fracture was surrounded with swelling, but there was no sign of gangrene. "Essenhout... on the riverbank. I—"

"Who knew I would ever become an alpha." Essenhout interrupted, managing a grin. "Never did I expect to have such good fortune." She batted her ear with a forepaw. "Time enough to command a pack, my *Droom*, such as it was."

Aalwyn smiled. "Yes, my sister." She ignored her own throbbing ear, torn during the fight. She craned her head over to lick the wounds she could reach. "The litters you shall have will do well under your tutelage."

Essenhout looked at her, head canted to the side for a moment, confused. She lay back, closed her eyes, and rested.

Rukato lay by her side, as a statue.

* * *

The hunt returned, and the bellies of the hunters did not hang low. The pups lapped the muzzles of the hunters to beg the food, and some meat came forth, but very little. The yearlings that made up the *Droom* milled about, unsure of what to do next. Aalwyn padded over to them, and offered to take them on a hunt as well. They left, taking Olienhout with them, ever hopeful.

Their return in the evening was somewhat more profitable, and yielded some meat for the pups, and for the yearlings. Essenhout declined anything, preferring to sleep. Rukato at first sniffed her, prodded her to eat, but eventually stopped. He begged for a small amount of food for himself, and slept.

The next two days passed in this way, with failed hunts, hunger among

136

the pups and adults, and their camp bordered by the anxiety of what was to come.

Chapter 19

Hazel eyes peered into the brush, suspicious of every bit of shade. The large dish-like ears swiveled, striving to detect the signs of an enemy. The wind carried no musk scent, nor sound of territorial lion call.

"Forward." Kurkbos padded from under the monkey-orange tree, and the others followed him. The Pungwe river was left behind them as the wolves ventured back into Gorongosa.

"This wild is all things to us, is it not?" Koorsboom kept his voice low, wary of attracting attention.

"How so?"

"When we first came to this land of lush veld and the rains, we sacrificed all to stay here. It became a place of healing. My mother's first litter—every last pup survived."

Kurkbos nodded to himself.

"It has now become a place of fear, and cruel loss." Koorsboom looked across the ground for tracks. "And now the lush bushveld is denied to us. Every shadow and leaf could obscure a wolf that will bring death to us all." A fluttering White-winged widowbird startled him as it flapped away, showing off its black and white plumage. "It seems we are destined to have a poorer portion."

"If we make a kill." Rukato joined them, having brought forth the straggler yearlings. "Even if we do that, the victory is bittersweet." He shared a glance with Kurkbos. "The richest meal in exile becomes dust in our teeth." Shaking his head to dislodge the flies, he grunted. "And now Essenhout..." His grim-set eyes examined the gravel.

"This hunt is worth the risk until we find reliable hunting grounds for the pups." Kurkbos brought his nose closer to the ground. "Impala—this way!"

They picked up speed, and Kurkbos twittered to the yearlings to move more quickly. Kamassi and Branddoring ran ahead to get a closer look.

Through tangled scrub the wolves padded, ears folded flat, heads held low. There was a careful bounce to their step, hurried, yet cautious about creating too much noise.

Over a slight rise, the thicket parted near the base of a Red-leafed fig tree, perched on exposed rock. The roots spread over the grey stone, biting into the surface, splitting it gradually over the last century. In the shadow of the tree, the wolves peered at the impala herd before them.

Kamassi joined them, and stepped on a dry fallen branch with an audible snap.

Hoofbeats erupted immediately as the herd took flight. Kurkbos sprinted forward.

"Kamassi—you spooked the herd. To the coursing with us all!" Probing the herd, they watched the males pronk away. Shortly, they singled out an older male too fatigued to put on a show for the carnivores. After less than a kilometer, it was dragged down and ripped in half.

The wolves tucked in, opening the hide and gulping down, each nearly a third of their weight in meat. The return across the Pungwe river was a walk, the extra weight welcome, but slowing them down.

"Will you flee elsewhere, Rukato?"

"I have given it no thought." He stared at the ground before him as they padded onward. "Before finding Essenhout, I wandered alone for one season after the next. For a time, as I made my way east from the wild across scattered farmland, I thought I was the last wolf alive." He gave a weak smile. "Before finding this wild place, I hunted alongside jackals. Could you imagine such a thing?"

"No, I cannot." Kurkbos eyed this wolf, still a stranger to him.

"I thought, for a time, that this was how the last wolf would die. One hunt after the next, sharing meager company with jackals, until I could hunt no more. And that would be the final appearance on this earth of the Painted wolf." His jaws parted slightly as he panted, and the old bullet wound seemed to part as well. The light red color of the healing tissue appeared to writhe as he walked.

The river came into view, the familiar sand bar emerging from the water as the Pungwe slowed around a bend, widened, and deposited silt from the distant mountains. The wolves picked their way through the farm under cover of twilight, and found Aalwyn at camp with the pups, scent markers placed around the perimeter.

The pups eagerly greeted the hunters, and the regurgitated meat spent no time on the ground. The yearlings shared their food, and Aalwyn begged her ration.

Rukato nudged Essenhout, who only returned his gaze without a word. She did not beg for food. Retiring, he walked over to another female from the *Droom* pack, and shared his kill with her.

* * *

Aalwyn raised her head, taking in several things at once. The pups were safe. The rest of the wolves were sleeping.

A man stood near the pack. He had a backpack on, and appeared to be traveling.

She issued a ruff-bark. The wolves were awake at once, and on edge. The man backed away, his hands extended outward, palms toward the wolves. No weapon was pointed, but they were not aware this meant no malice was intended.

"We must move."

The pack slowly worked its way further south, and found itself on the verge of a low plateau overlooking grasslands. No fences were present, and a small herd of impala was visible on the horizon.

Off with an excited twitter, Koorsboom, Olienhout, Kurkbos, and then the rest of the wolves were after them, eager to hunt again.

"Is this a new Wild?" Koorsboom managed to lap Olienhout's muzzle while at a dead run.

"Every place we go shall *become* wild!" She matched his speed, and took the lead for all of them.

Before long, the herd was within reach. Rather than attempting stealth, the wolves pressed through with their sprint, and overcame a sick impala before it had a chance to escape. The pack surrounded the carcass, white curved tails up in the air, high chirps and whines the only sound as they consumed their fill. Within several minutes, nothing remained save bones, entrails, liver, and bits of hide. A decapitated antelope head stared at the sun.

The two packs settled to rest nearby as a figure emerged from the brush. Essenhout, limping along, finally had caught up to them. Rukato rushed over to share food, but she ignored him. Hobbling over to the impala kill, she sniffed its remains, and sat down with her sister.

Aalwyn licked her mouth, but she did not respond with anything more than a low moan.

"We hunt again with the night. You can eat then, if able."

Essenhout did not return her look, only peering at the distant grasslands where an impala trotted.

* * *

As evening descended, the wolves rallied again for the hunt. Kurkbos sprinted about with the pups, struggling in vain to tire them out, and leave them behind. Twice he moved away, only to drag them back, sometimes within his jaws, to the camp.

Aalwyn lapped her sister's muzzle, bidding her to join them. "The pain is great, but you must stay with us. That impala herd was a small one, and has already moved off."

Essenhout scratched the dirt with a forepaw.

"Very well. I will wrench free a foreleg and bring it back for you."

That evening, the wolves made a kill, though it was soon stolen by hyenas roving south from Gorongosa.

Dejected, Aalwyn returned to Essenhout to offer what little measure of meat there was. She pointed her snout at the ground and left it there. As Aalwyn rested next to her sister, she looked across the grass where Rukato sat. He rested side by side with another female from the *Droom* pack, eyes closed and at peace.

Chapter 20

The next few days brought the entire group to move further south. A scouting patrol found an impala herd a few kilometers away, and still on the move. The wolf packs were forced to move with it. The pups were kept in line by Kamassi and Kurkbos. The yearlings moved as one, making too much noise for any hunting party. Rukato and Aalwyn were in the rear. Every now and then, as they padded after their packs, they looked behind them at Essenhout, who hobbled along one excruciating step after the next. Aalwyn and Rukato hoo-called when she was out of sight, and waited for her.

***

Aalwyn left the next animal they killed, and hoo-called as dawn glimmered upon the savanna. Lowering her jaw to the ground, she released a low, sonorous *WHOOOO! WHOOOO!* that traveled for several kilometers.

This time, Rukato did not join her in the call.

Few shreds of meat remained on the newly killed antelope as Essenhout came into view. She did not meet anyone's glance. Her broken hind leg dragged, each hop with her good hind leg met with a wince. Her shoulder wound was bleeding again, either from a stumble or from the wound failing to heal properly.

She lay down far from the rest of the pack, and rested her head on her forepaws.

Aalwyn padded over and lay by her side. So many words rolled through her mind. Memories from the Savute marsh, the Chobe riverfront, and their long *trek* across Zimbabwe and Mozambique boiled within, but she could give voice to none of them.

There was nothing she could ask. There was no way to lessen her pain. Every kind word in her mind felt callous by the time it reached her tongue. Gratitude for her life, saved on the riverbank, became thoughtless. Appreciation for the mutual hunting forays that helped her family became heartless. Fond thoughts of the past became poisonous. Every breath became an accusation, a fang inserted in her heart leaking venom. Hours passed this way, Aalwyn ready to speak, but unable to so much as stammer.

The west became a brazier of orange as the day crept by. A yearling sprang up and began yittering to the others, attempting to rouse the pack with a late afternoon hunting rally. A few of the other young wolves began twittering as well. The adults stood, taking awkward glances about them. Kurkbos lapped the muzzle of Blackthorn, while Koorsboom and Olienhout began to exchange greetings and box each other. The gestures of the rally became muted as the wolves looked to Aalwyn, still rooted to her sister's side. They milled about uneasily. Stomachs of the pups growled.

Essenhout emitted an almost inaudible groan. "Go."

Aalwyn was on her paws immediately, though she felt a burning shame with her eagerness to go to her pack. They shared a brief glance, and Essenhout's gaze returned to the ground before her.

Aalwyn felt a wave of nausea pass over her. After so many escapes from danger, her impotence now gnawed a hole through her stomach. She had no choice. Wolves must wander. Those who cannot must be left behind.

As Aalwyn stared at the ground, she sensed movement. Essenhout was on her feet again, stepping gradually away from the rest of the pack, toward the edge of their clearing. The grass where she had lain was still compacted. Her scent was present, but fading.

Stumbling, each footfall a misery, she made her way toward the *Combretum* shrubs that bordered the wide circular grass clearing where the two packs were preparing to depart for the hunt. As the light dimmed, her lurching figure edged away from Aalwyn, and the white tip of her tail gradually disappeared behind a fold of leaves as the branches swayed shut behind her.

Aalwyn stayed a mute witness, regretting every word she wished to say, but could not bring herself to utter. Behind the veil of the thicket, there was only silence.

Farewell, my sister.

Chapter 21

With morning, the pack was preparing to rally. Koorsboom and Olienhout shared their greetings, and Kurkbos called for another foray to the south. The packs were up with the dawn, greeting one another. The rally was a disorganized rabble. Wolves lapped one another's muzzles, but with no clear hierarchy, the rally broke down. It was no longer clear who was a leader, who was subservient, and the bonds of the packs were lost in the noise.

The hunt started in chaos, as the yearlings struck out to search for an impala with a near constant buzz of twittering noise. The rest of the adults followed, bivouacking the pups along. The group broke in half, and half again with no real plan in mind. The groups disintegrated, and the wolves each took off to chase prey individually. Kurkbos and Aalwyn struggled to keep the pups together, and she bid them to stay put.

"Call them all back. This has gone far enough."

After two hours of hoo-calls, the wolves all wandered back with nothing to show for the morning. Even as they gathered, most milled about, aimless, with no real apparent desire to return to the hunt.

She waited until the excitement calmed, and for the yearlings to silence their yapping.

"The time has come to divide the pack. The *Dwalen* and the *Droom* must be reforged."

The yearlings from the *Droom* looked at one another, unsure of what to say.

"You will come with me. As yearlings, you lack discipline. You need leadership to survive the dry season."

They looked at one another, and haltingly they came to her side.

"Essenhout is dead." She choked on the word, biting down on the howl of grief within. "I owe my life to her, and will keep you safe."

Rukato sat, his head hanging low, appearing lost. "Where shall I go?"

"You have no alpha. And now is not the time to seek one. You may remain with me until you have found your way again." She looked over to her oldest son. "Olienhout and Koorsboom—you shall be the ones to lead your pack." She took a deep breath. "And to leave."

The young wolves shared a glance. "Our *trek* begins anew?" Koorsboom lapped his mate's muzzle.

"It began when you fought a lion, and held your ground." Aalwyn beamed at him with pride. "And your journey led you here from far away, Olienhout. You are resolute as a mountain, and I have yet to know a finer hunter. More than equal to the task."

"Kamassi, Besembossie, and Branddoring can join us. They have proved to be quite keen." Olienhout held her head high.

"Very well. Blackthorn stays with me." She gestured to the young wolf, who rubbed his muzzle aside his mother's. "You still have much to learn, young one."

The wolves rejoined one another, now separated into two groups. Lapping of muzzles and excited twittering passed between them, bonds crafted and reformed. Olienhout stood on hind legs to box the young wolves now under her command. Besembossie rose to meet her, quickly thrown off balance by her batting forepaws, and fell to the ground in a heap. Branddoring whined as she threw her paws on Koorsboom's back, and jumped over him to embrace Olienhout, muzzle alongside muzzle.

Aalwyn and Rukato drowned in the yelping sea of yearlings that joined them. She rose from beneath two squirming bodies only to be brought down by a third that gripped her neck from behind.

"Off me, you silly oaf." She held the young wild dog's foreleg in her jaws and pulled him over to the ground. Watching the pups and yearlings together, she thought of Essenhout, and felt an aching emptiness within.

Koorsboom padded away from his newly cast pack to join his mother's side. Brushing along her fur, he twittered to her.

"We have come so far."

"And you have far to go." Aalwyn spoke almost in a whisper.

"I miss her already." Koorsboom whimpered.

"As do I." She sighed. "All of our lives, across the world one paw at a time. We were always together."

"The veld will not allow time for us to mourn." He ran a pink tongue with black spots up the side of her head.

"Indeed, my son."

"You will never leave my mind."

"Never forget the lessons your fathers taught you." Aalwyn intoned.

"Nor those of my dangerous mother." His hazel eyes met hers, burning with the rising sun. "Our tracks will cross again."

"And those of our pups, which will number as great as blades of grass."

Koorsboom and Olienhout stood apart from the *Dwalen*, as Aalwyn watched. Kamassi, Besembossie, and Branddoring scampered back and forth, giving parting words to brothers and sisters. Koorsboom did not, sharing the quiet regard of his mother as though a conversation between them had never, and would never cease.

Olienhout batted Kamassi's ears, and lapped her open mouth. *"Welkom* to my pack." The younger wolves held their heads low to her, and the submissive gesture was accepted.

"Farewell, Aalwyn." Olienhout twittered toward the other matriarch. "We will be strong together."

The two packs separated across the clearing. The round grass field could be crossed in minutes, but hours would pass before the packs left one another's sight.

Chapter 22

THE VILLAGE

Every day of survival is a victory on the way to defeat.

A scent of slow death hung over the savanna like a pallor, at once intriguing and repellent to the nose of a wolf. Koorsboom steeled himself for attack, or to flee from whatever enemy the smell promised, but none were present. At least, none he could perceive.

Dry bushveld sprawled before him, *Combretum* shrub and acacia thorn brush dotting the fields of dried grasses. In the midst of this formerly wild place was a gathering of huts, walls of sculpted mud and roof of grass thatch. Between some of the huts, the earth was cultivated in roughly square fields of maize, beans, and squash. Cattle and goats wandered everywhere. And amid these, there were people.

The pack had ventured further south from Gorongosa, far from any major cities, but even the deeply rural areas were occupied by humans. Months had passed since the *Dwalen* parted ways, and it was now February, well into the season of the hot summer rains. In years past, the clouds would gather and burst, with intense deluges that would abruptly end, day after day. This year, the rains did not come. The land grew dry, and in places resembled cracked pottery. The grasses turned yellow and the trees shed leaves burned by the sun, but these wild plants maintained their hold on hostile land. Crops, however, withered and died. Above it all was the burning sun, scowling upon its anvil.

The heat brought the pungent scent of garbage to Koorsboom's nose where he lay low in the desiccated grasses. He chanced to move closer to investigate this strange new thing.

The rubbish pile was on the edge of the village. Rotting food piled upon...

Odd translucent green and brown shapes covered with designs piled upon...

Crushed paper boxes with more designs piled upon...

Black plastic and white plastic ghostlike things that shimmered and wavered in the breeze piled upon...

Other objects he could not begin to identify. The sharp reek of spoiled beer residue mixed with decomposing food and plant material, and the wolf snuffed at the insult.

Bong.

Steel upon steel echoed, an unmistakably human sound. His heart quickened, though he was growing used to these unnatural noises.

Staying hidden, he watched the people who wandered into view with avid curiosity. Washed cooking pots lay gleaming in the sun. A figure walked from a faded red plastic basin filled with suds, leaving a pot with the others to dry on the grass. Her head was wrapped with a colored cloth that matched her red-maroon-white splotched dress. As he watched, she continued to move metal pots from one basin to the next and then to the ground for reasons that were beyond him.

The men looked different, wearing less colorful clothing. They seemed to do two things: escort cattle or be seated on the ground holding a bottle. When they did the former, they carried the weapons. He had come to recognize the sticks that could create thunder.

Nearby, a Lappet-faced Vulture observed Koorsboom with disinterest. It suspected correctly there was no hunt underway, and so there was no point following him. After deciding this, a few flaps from its broad black wings took it away to rejoin its mate. On a distant rock *koppie*, it sat on its biennial egg. They hoped this pack would be successful, aiding in the feeding of their chick, and of the many chicks to come over the fifty years the vultures would remain a couple.

Koorsboom crept away to return to a higher perch, and the smell was more familiar from up there, the subtle inflections of the wild. The rocky rise above the village stretched away into *miombo* woodland that was edged with thorn thickets. Below, the people busied themselves with inexplicable tasks.

"How fare the people of the village?"

Koorsboom flinched, annoyed at once again allowing Olienhout to approach him without detection. "Are the rest ready to depart?"

"Not until later. It is too hot to hunt." She looked up to the orange disk above, hanging heavily over them. She lay next to Koorsboom.

"Their activity is mystifying." He watched a group of children kicking a large ball consisting of clear tape and plastic. Back and forth it was knocked about foot to foot, to head, to another foot, rarely hitting the ground. "They remind me of pups." One man walked with a stick, muttering something as he directed a handful of cattle into a grass field. Other women ambled about, carrying large objects on their heads, tubs of food, cans of water. A few men were passed out on the ground, rousing to drink from bottles. One child kicked the tape ball into a wash basin with a splash, prompting much fussing by the adult. "Blackthorn always beheld these creatures with terror. They seem amiable enough."

"We have yet to disturb their food supply."

"Nor will we ever." He scratched loose a tick with his hind leg, and lowered himself again in the grasses. "Blackthorn was fanatical on that rule, to never hunt their animals."

"I am not sure killing their cattle would be necessary to provoke them."

Koorsboom nodded. "I witnessed a pack of humans slaughtering a herd of elephants once." His face was an austere mask. "Strange they would commit such an atrocity. They seem at times so at peace."

"Beware of these mercurial creatures. And I am not certain what to think of *them*."

A knot of domesticated dogs galloped into view, rummaging through the rubbish pile. One gripped a bone, and was promptly deprived of it by another dog. These two fought bitterly as a third escaped with the prize.

He snuffed again. "They are no match for us, my *bokkie*."

"Open conflict is not what worries me." The dogs continued to fight, fur eroded in places with open sores, their ribs straining against the skin. Some drooled continuously.

"Shall we return to our own kind?"

"*Met plesier.* There is nothing I enjoy more." Olienhout stood to leave, her belly hanging low, teats prominent and ready for the litter to come.

"Soon, my love?" Koorsboom brushed against her muzzle.

She only returned his gaze with a smile. On her paws, she moved swiftly despite her protruding abdomen. Her pregnancy was close to term.

They loped back to the den, a short distance into the *miombo* forest. Tall zebrawood trees vaulted over the wolves with wide branching canopies that dwarfed everything below. The rich green gathered the rays of the sun, leaving the floor of the forest dim and muted. Beetles ruffled through the leaf litter and fragments of seed pods discarded the season previous.

A penetrating *kong-kong-koweet* reached Koorsboom's dish-like ears, though the bushshrike that made the call was never seen. It could be heard daily, greeting the wolves around the abandoned porcupine den where they made their home.

The yearlings were on their paws as the two returned. Kamassi padded up to Olienhout, her head dipped beneath her alpha's, licking her muzzle. The gesture was happily returned, and Kamassi whirled upon Branddoring, reared onto hind legs to box her with forepaws before being pulled into a heap. Besembossie pounced on top of Kamassi, mock biting with her jaws open against the other's mouth. Kamassi would have none of this, rearing up on her hind legs to push over her sister. Branddoring ended up on the bottom as usual when they played, making a show of blocking with her forepaws, waiting until the tussle was over. Tongues lolled out in the heat, white tipped tails wagging in slow swishing waves back and forth.

They were embraced by the familiar savanna, though the occasional human noise intruded. An errant bang of metal, the bark of dog, and a remote echo of sharp thunder.

Chapter 23

Olienhout sniffed in the darkness, detecting no sign of damp or disease. The earth was dry, the interior of the den dusty and cool. Little noise penetrated this far underground, and her sensitive ears could just detect the shuffling of burrowing rodents somewhere in the walls. She crept along one side of the den, a large sprawling affair several meters long and three meters below the surface. Her footfalls were silent and careful, her hazel eyes peering into the dim chamber.

Along the wall, she found something foreign. Gripping it in her jaws, she plucked the object from where it was embedded in the wall of clay and dirt. The length of her forepaw, each end was sharp as a hypodermic needle, brilliant in black and white coloration. She brought the porcupine quill to the surface and dropped it outside the den.

Nearby her mate was fast asleep. Koorsboom did not seem to hear the quill clatter on the ground, but he uttered a whimper. His paws twitched as he lay on his side. A low ruff-bark issued from his muzzle.

"It is time." Olienhout watched him.

Koorsboom jerked, then awoke, looking up to his mate. His eyes took a moment to focus.

"Strange, that." He rolled onto his stomach and stretched his forepaws before him. "The dreams I have had here."

"Of what did you dream?"

"Our pack ventured far into the veld through thicket and forest, hunting where we pleased, lording over the land. I could not savor our success, however. There was an insidious enemy at work."

She studied his face, handsome but troubled.

"I was being eaten, very slowly, day after day, by a rat." He seemed to turn to stone. "It would take its due, day after day, mouthful after mouthful." He shook his head and was quiet, until he realized she waited for him to finish. "My insides were taken, bite after bite, eventually consuming me from the inside out." He clawed the ground. "I would each day hunt to feed myself, and my parasite, and I did nothing to stop it."

Olienhout lapped his muzzle, and he brightened. "The hunt beckons."

"Right." He twittered to the yearlings, who awoke instantly, and after shaking off their sleep, began the rally in earnest. Each wolf greeted the other with effusive lapping of muzzles and an excited whining of joy for what the day would bring.

The five departed the den clearing, the light of the sun just reaching into the zebrawood forest with tentative fingers. Pairs of rounded ears bobbed up and down over the grass tips as they loped through the forest at a brisk but leisurely pace. A Golden-breasted bunting fluttered over them, coming to a rest on a tree branch. Stark brown and white stripes covered its head resembling a racing helmet. It viewed the wolves with mild interest before fluttering on.

Leaving the forest behind, they trotted through a grassland with the odd mountain acacia tree and thornbrush thicket.

"Just past the *koppie*, we shall see if fortune favors us." Olienhout gestured with her slender chin, showing no sign of the weight she carried. She could feel the movement of all eight pups, these precious lives.

In single file, they took a wide circle around a granite monolith that stood in the vast field. The bald dome of the rock was not large enough to be a mountain, but stood high over the surrounding lands, resistant to the erosion that worked on this savanna over the past several million years.

On one edge of the *koppie*, a squat acacia shrub stood, anchored to what seemed bare rock. Roots curled into crevasses, having found soil even here to exploit. Atop the shrub was a large nest of sticks and broken branches, haphazard in appearance but tightly woven together to create a structure that would last a decade. The Lappet-faced vulture couple were perched on the nest tending to their egg, taking notice of the carnivores that stole across their hunting grounds.

"Ever taut—the wind is shifting, and the impala are not far." Olienhout's nose was in the air. Her ears folded back, head went down, body tensed and hovered closer to the ground. The rest followed suit, and prepared to study their prey. Kamassi took the lead.

Their path brought them around the *koppie* to a grouping of Lowveld fig trees.

"Just ahead." Koorsboom indicated.

The herd was a dozen strong, and were grouped by the fig trees. Heads were held high, peering about, ears erect and scanning for any sign of danger.

"There is more than impala casting about a watchful eye." Olienhout crouched lower in the grass, not slowing her creep.

Baboons were gathered, though they kept closer to the pale grey-barked trees, relishing the shade under the verdant leaf crowns. The fruit was gathered by the primates, each fig lifted to their mouths as they watched the horizon.

"I have not seen baboons this close before. Are they dangerous?" Branddoring looked on with curiosity.

"They defend their troop with claw and fang, either able to open your throat with a single lethal strike." Koorsboom was almost on his belly as he placed one paw before the next. "That, however, is not their greatest weapon."

Branddoring looked at the ground. "Are they quite clever?"

Koorsboom smiled in the way only dogs can smile. "Spot on. Much like us, they attack and defend as one. And they suffer no threats to their young."

"Perhaps this is too dangerous?"

Olienhout showed her white fangs in a macabre grin. "We shall find a way to close this chase, no matter the adversary."

* * *

BOGGOM BOGGOM BOGGOM!

Baboons sprinted for the nearest trees, claws easily gripping the rough bark, shaggy grey bodies shimmying up into the broad branches. Each baboon that reached safety joined in to the alarm bark.

BOGGOM BOGGOM BOGGOM!

The last baboon was a mother, tending to her baby. She paused only for a moment to scoop her young onto her back, where it held on in fear. She reached safety in moments, and the barking ceased.

Four wolves padded around the base of the tree, looking up at the primates in the branches.

"What are we to do if they counterattack?" Besembossie chirped.

"Pounce on it!" Kamassi twittered excitedly, her tail wagging in wide, slow sweeps.

"Do not be daft. You run, and do so quickly." Olienhout sternly warned. "Now we shall see what the herd does."

The impala herd, startled by the unnerving screams from the baboon troop, initially bolted, but stopped, each one noticing the wolves had gathered around the fig trees. Some of the impala had released gruff growls of their own, but did not run away. The soil was rich here with fallen figs, and the grass grew in a riot of green on the droppings left by generations of antelope that visited this place. They would not give up a food source so easily.

One impala cautiously took a mouthful of leaf from a bush. Another followed its lead. The chewing resumed. The impala herd as a whole settled down, but with a wary eye on the wolf pack that held station under the fig tree.

A high-pitched whinny from the other direction caused the impala to startle, look about in a panic, entirely too late to run from the wolf that tore out of the grass. Koorsboom selected one of the impala and sprinted to it. The antelope turned to escape, but he was already upon it, and jaws like a vice gripped its side.

The rest of the pack mobbed it after his signal, and the impala was dismembered in less than a minute.

"I have a name for us, if I may be so bold." Koorsboom spoke around the mouthful of haunch muscle as he swallowed it whole.

"And that would be?" Olienhout bolted down most of the tenderloin herself, relishing the rich flesh.

"*Gambiet.* It suits this place, midway between the wild and the human."

"As well as the risk we take." Besembossie pulled hide from the impala's side in a sheet. "Everything we do here is a gambit of some sort."

"Very well." Olienhout took the heart, swallowing it in large pieces. "*Gambiet* it is. Time will tell if it was a worthy one."

* * *

Besembossie led the way back toward the den with a bouncing lope. Branddoring followed closely, gripping an impala hind leg in her jaws.

"Did you not have enough to eat for this hunt?" Besembossie eyed her sister's belly, as close to the ground as her own.

"Indeed I have, but this is a good habit to develop." Branddoring muttered around the leg in her mouth, hoof bobbing as though waving at her companion. "When Olienhout is sequestered, she will appreciate the fresh meat." Her fur coloration was striking, whorls of gold and black, flanks marked by white diamonds.

Besembossie considered this, eyeing the flopping hoof.

"We are nearing the human village." Kamassi sprinted up to them, turning about. "There is a new scent in the air."

"New? With so many bizarre smells from that place it is a wonder you can discern a unique one." Besembossie raised her snout to the air to sample. "You are right."

The leg of the impala thumped to the ground. Branddoring stopped, and glared ahead. Her sisters peered before them and saw the source of her concern. Dish-like ears flattened back against skulls, and each body crouched, at the ready to attack. Besembossie issued a ruff-bark.

Standing a hundred meters away was a brown dog. It lacked the bullet nose of a jackal, and had a nondescript coat of fur marked with mange that had none of the beauty of a Painted wolf. It was unmistakably canine, however, with the bearing and scent of a dog.

"Shall we kill him?" Koorsboom's voice acquired a graveled edge. He took a step forward, ears flat and head held low. Lips parted to reveal white knives.

"Do not waste your time." Olienhout twittered to her pack. "Be certain, though, that it does not follow us."

Kamassi and Besembossie charged, their wiry bodies rapidly closing the distance.

The brown dog gave out a yelp and fled the savanna in the direction of the village. The two young wolves slowed, and watched the dog escape. It showed no sign of turning, or attempting to track them.

"Back to the den." Olienhout resumed her pace, belly hanging lower than the rest, swaying as she walked. Kamassi and Besembossie followed her, tongues hanging out, panting.

"I can patrol around our den." Branddoring stooped to pick up the impala leg. "They might try to find us."

Koorsboom pondered this, staring at where the dog was standing. He scented no malice in the air, no aggressive behavior, and no sign of attempting to hunt on the part of that animal. Even so, he continued to stare in the direction of the village, and the source of those odd sounds of work and industry. Metal, wood, and speech, sounds equally incomprehensible and echoing through the day, reached into the wild.

Chapter 24

Wheeling in the endless blue above, dark figures glided effortlessly. From the ground they appeared tiny, like the winged seeds of trees that flutter spinning to the grasses below. Capable of soaring on thermals for hours, the vultures slowly grew larger as they lost altitude. Canting their wings slightly, they allowed a loss of lift, sinking from the sky.

As one approached for a landing, the broad wings were spread as widely as possible, each feather angled to slow the descent. Legs extended to air brake as much as possible before striking the ground with a bounce. Black wings with beige edging folded shut. An angular head with a bare pink face glanced about. Amber eyes glared imperiously as it surveyed the area.

Halting steps with clawed feet brought it closer to a prone figure on the ground, lying on its side. In silence the white-headed vulture regarded the body of a carnivore. Rounded ears, lanky limbs, and a coat of gold, black, and white swirls left little doubt as to what the creature was.

The Painted wolf took a deep breath.

Wings extended wide again as the vulture retreated several steps, orange beak opened at the unexpected movement.

The chest rose, the ribs standing out in starvation for the wolf. And it fell, with a long exhale. Lids parted to reveal hazel eyes that were glazed over, unseeing.

The vulture folded its wings again. For an adversary this dangerous, it would not do to try to kill it. Given its apparent starvation, the wait would likely be short.

A rustling in the brush to the rear caused the raptor to open its wings again, and take to the air. The wait would be longer than it thought. As it angled its wings to catch the wind and soar higher, it saw five more Painted wolves enter the clearing. To its surprise, the prone wolf eventually took to its feet.

Rising higher still, the vulture continued the search elsewhere.

* * *

"Are you hurt?" Koorsboom approached the stranger.

For some time, he did not speak. Heaving, his mouth gaped, sounds of a rusty engine issuing forth.

"He may have the Sickness." Kamassi uttered. She was unsure what this truly meant, but Aalwyn had warned her of it long ago.

"No, not this one." Olienhout peered at the wolf. He was quite old, with thinned fur that was bald in a few places on his flanks, his skin dry and clinging to his bones. This aside, he did not seem off balance, nor had any of the secretions that suggested illness. "He is weak. And has been alone for some time."

"Who are you?" Koorsboom inquired.

"His paw is broken!" Besembossie gasped.

For the first time, they noticed he was balancing on three legs.

"Hyena." His voice was slight, but startled them all. His bird-like twitter croaked from a dry throat.

"From where do you hail, Hyena?" Branddoring wondered.

He croaked again, eyes shut, in a sound that resembled a cough, but became a ghost of a laugh.

"Mitseeri." He opened his eyes again, and hobbled closer to Branddoring. "My name, borne of a red-leafed tree that sheltered my mother." He dipped his head toward Olienhout in a gesture of submission. "A hyena is something else entirely." He glanced toward his ruined foot, then back toward Branddoring. A glint in his eye made her retreat several steps.

"Were you attacked?" Koorsboom sniffed him, and glanced at one of his hind legs, held off the ground. The lower part of the limb was crooked, the pads of the paw twisted inward. It would bear no weight.

"That is so. A clan fell upon me." Mitseeri coughed again, and hobbled forward, holding his injured rear leg off the ground. "I gave them several wounds in exchange." His choking laugh returned, before fading into the silence.

"Passing through?" Koorsboom sounded chipper.

"Passing indeed." Mitseeri lay down again with a grunt. "Though I am unaware if I am bound for another world soon."

"Should we not drive him away?" Besembossie whispered to Olienhout. "He is on our territory."

"He is no threat to us." Olienhout peered at him. "And a pack as small as ours can benefit from an additional set of jaws."

"If he survives long enough to reach the den." Besembossie said, though she regretted giving voice to the thought.

"I shall finish any journey I undertake, young wolf." Mitseeri shut his eyes. "Particularly the final one." He lay down again, visibly exhausted. The old predator returned to sleep, snoring gently.

"Come, my *Gambiet*." Olienhout rasped. The others followed, leaving Mitseeri behind. From a distance, he did not seem to breathe at all.

* * *

Rustling in the brush, branches breaking. Light footfalls.

Mitseeri barely stirred, until a scent reached him. Despite his severe dehydration, he began to salivate. As he raised his head, a fountain of meat and blood plopped onto the ground beside him.

"As you can see, any journey is worth the ending." Olienhout studied the old wolf.

He acknowledged the gift with a humble nod, and began to take small bites. Before long, he gulped mouthfuls, and stood again. He seemed to grow in size before them, exhaling with contentment, and gave them a cautious smile.

"I owe you—"

"Nothing." Olienhout interrupted. "For the Pack, there are no debts." She turned to leave, and the other four filed after her. With little hesitation, Mitseeri joined them in an awkward lope.

Their path carried them from the great grass plain under the granite *koppie* to the shadows of the zebrawood forest. Paws stepped quietly on the leaf litter.

"Were you injured in the village?" Koorsboom indicated one of Mitseeri's forelegs. It was shortened slightly, a sign of an ancient healed fracture.

"No, not this one nearby." He grunted with the effort. "Given my poor agility, I would not chance going near humans." He sighed. His fur was mostly white and gold, with crescents of black amid bald patches. "Since the winter season the dead is all that kept me alive." His voice was hollow despite its higher pitch. "I am unsure what use you will have for me."

They neared the abandoned porcupine den, smelling for now only of dry earth. Soon this would change.

"A wolf living alone is a desperate one." Olienhout intoned. "There is only the Pack." As she trotted, she brushed alongside Mitseeri, reassuring him. "For us all."

Chapter 25

"They are coming, my love."

The morning had passed without a successful hunt. The *Gambiet* pack rested in the high of the day, the sun directly overhead threatening to burn through the zebrawood trees. Somewhere amid the branches a loud *cuck-ook-oooo* was released by a mourning dove.

Koorsboom rolled onto his belly and stood, padding over to Olienhout, lapping her muzzle tenderly.

Her abdomen wracked with pain, she descended into the den, crawling along the loose dirt down into the cool earth. In utter darkness the nausea washed over her. She held onto the residual food in her stomach, knowing she would need the strength it would provide.

She breathed heavily, snuffing a cloud of dust before her snout as she lay on her side. The pain would be borne in near silence.

On the surface, the rest of the pack lay on the ground resting in the heat, but none slept. Kamassi, Besembossie and Branddoring lay awake listening. They felt every spasm that struck Olienhout.

Branddoring sat up, gazing toward the den hole. She thought she heard a moan, and stood fast. But the wolf heard nothing. She lay back down, but every muscle was taut as a bow string. She glanced over toward Mitseeri, who rested apart from the rest of the *Gambiet*.

He lay on his side, barely moving. A slight rise of the chest, and an exhale.

164

Otherwise he seemed dead. The deformed hind leg twitched.

Branddoring's eyes drifted from the old wolf to Kamassi, who was already meeting her gaze. They shared a doubtful glance before returning to rest.

A loud *cuck-ook-oooo* broke the calm again, causing the rest of the pack to startle momentarily.

Koorsboom stood and padded over to Mitseeri, who roused himself.

"See to the den. Allow none to approach."

"Are you... certain?" Kamassi whispered to Koorsboom.

The old wolf blinked away the sleep from his eyes, and gave a nod. He took position nearby, hobbling into place.

"Certainty is not to be found on the veld." Koorsboom gave a grin to the younger wolf. Kamassi shook her head.

Koorsboom leapt toward Besembossie, prodding her with his snout. Twitters erupted from the two as they began scampering around the den site, brushing against one another, lapping muzzles and chirping excitedly. Kamassi and Branddoring joined, rolled tongues and bounced about, chattering as the hunting rally began in earnest. Quickly, Koorsboom led them away through the zebrawood.

One last glance was given in the direction of Mitseeri.

He met the glance with steel, brow furrowed in a stolid glare as he stood before the den, a faded statue.

* * *

Towering a meter over the surrounding dirt, the termite mound was imposing, particularly as it was crafted by creatures a centimeter in length. The walls of mud and termite saliva baked in the sun were rendered as hard as concrete. Great power was required to breach this defense, but that power was brought to bear.

Foreclaws like crowbars dug into the walls and wrenched them loose, opening a fist-size hole in the mound. Another dig by the claw, and an entire army was laid bare. A long sticky tongue darted in and out, in and out, flicking rapidly, shooting down passageways and taking dozens of termites with each shot. The piglike snout was held a slight distance from the exposed honeycomb of tunnels to avoid the grasping pincers wielded by the defending army. The stout legs were perched on the walls of the mound, skin thick enough to ignore termite reprisals. A powerful kangaroo-like tail gave it balance as it fed. Engrossed in its labor, the aardvark leaned in, suddenly discovering that larvae were now being returned by the tongue. It penetrated deeper into the catacombs for the protein-rich prize.

Elongated tubular ears listened for threats, but the discovery of the larvae-filled chamber distracted the animal.

Snap

The aardvark whirled about, its sandy brown fur rustled by the wind. It faced, unusually, an African wild dog. Normally the two never meet, but the aardvark was forced to forage during the day for the meager offerings left by the drought.

Koorsboom regarded this odd creature. He examined its husky body, long tail, and then its powerful forelegs terminating in menacing claws. Deciding this would not be a useful fight to engage, he watched it leave. The large mammal scurried off with a surprising burst of speed. Koorsboom followed it at a distance. Once it turned, annoyed at the attention, but continued on its path. Before long, it dove into a hole.

A wild dog hole.

Koorsboom crouched, expecting wolves to burst forth, but nothing happened. Small flies gathered around the entranceway. The wolf sniffed, scenting no musk of his kind. It occurred to him those powerful claws were meant for digging such a hole.

"So this is where many of our dens originate." He grunted, some satisfaction at a mystery solved. He loped off, continuing his search.

He padded along a worn path, dotted with impala dung in various stages of desiccation. Soon enough he found Kamassi sniffing a more fragrant pile.

"Not an hour hence." She flashed fangs of white. They loped away together.

* * *

Flies had only begun to gather on the impala carcass as the four Painted wolves left it behind. The hide had been torn open, bowels spilled on the ground with a shallow pool of coagulated blood. The meat and some of the internal organs had been stripped away. Koorsboom turned and boxed Besembossie, twittering to the others as they returned to Olienhout.

Hurry... Hurry...

Thumping back into the shade of the zebrawood, they listened for signs of danger. As they approached the former porcupine home, they did not see the older wolf.

"Did he abandon us already, then?" Besembossie called out.

"It would not be the first time." Koorsboom rasped. "Sometimes new migrants leave a group if they have misgivings." He grunted to himself, his heart beating faster.

Coo-coo... Coo-coo... A cuckoo called overhead.

Koorsboom hurried the others, the entryway to the underground den in sight.

"All is well."

The four ground to a halt, their claws digging into the dirt. Koorsboom crouched at the sound of the voice.

"None approached." Mitseeri limped forth from the brush, head held high. "Olienhout's nursery remains pristine."

Koorsboom shook his head for a moment, and lapped his muzzle. Mitseeri dipped his head low.

He gestured to the old wolf, and dove into the den.

"*Welkom.*" Olienhout intoned in the darkness.

Koorsboom edged forward and she lapped his muzzle, prompting him to regurgitate the meat from the kill. She consumed this avidly, sighing her relief.

In the darkness, he saw nothing. Then, two shining stars as she opened her eyes.

"It has begun."

***

The rest of the *Gambiet* clustered around the den. Koorsboom padded up to the opening, but stopped himself from entering.

A low moan emerged from the dank hole.

He sniffed, and wanted to enter, but could not. The moan burst with a punctuated *HRAA!* that descended again into a muttering growl. He lay down, resting his head on forepaws.

Olienhout took a stone in her mouth, chewing it between grunts to deaden the rippling pains that coursed through her pelvis. Pawing the dirt, she whined, a plaintive call to nobody. This she would bear alone.

The panging moved further down, and she sat up. Olienhout took a deep breath. Reaching between her legs, she pushed to the verge the first of her pups. With the gentlest touch, she pulled the young from her birth canal, and bit through the umbilical cord. She licked the face first, the mouth, the eyes, and the snout, freeing the airway of secretions. The pup, blind and helpless, issued a snuffling mewl. She licked it clean and placed it by her side. It reached with forepaws, kicked with hind paws, and upon locating his mother's fur, became quiet.

Olienhout lifted away the next pup. Free of its cord, it was cleaned thoroughly, and snuffed its approval. Each pup was birthed with throbbing spasms, and laid carefully by the others after being cleaned with her tongue. Each held their heads up, straining to see with eyes that were sealed behind immature lids. Sniffing, learning, the pups came to understand this scent that made up the entire world was mother, and that she was their safety.

Eight bodies squirmed in the dim light. Mouths opened, tongues tasting the air. Ultrasonic whimpers sounded. As they strained in their search, Olienhout positioned them next to her belly, and one pup after the next found a teat and began to suckle. As the rich, warm milk flowed into their tiny bodies, two new concepts entered their minds: food that powers the body, and love that powers all.

* * *

Koorsboom sat at the opening, and the low, subtle calls from the den reached his ears. He thought of Blackthorn, his second father, and how he described the feelings of a new parent. An overwhelming fear that threatens to consume one with panic. A drowning love that blocks out all else.

He bounded off, searching through the brush, sniffing the dirt carefully. Around a tussock of grass, he detected something of interest. He stepped with care, and found himself face to face with a scrub hare. Pouncing, he broke the neck with a practiced bite, ripped open the hide, and consumed every scrap of meat and organ he could tear away from the bones.

Bounding back to the den, he pulled himself down the hole, creeping as he would into the den of a lion. In the darkness, his eyes adjusted and he saw the outline of Olienhout. At her belly were eight tiny figures, the size of small birds, suckling with unified need.

He did not speak, only sidling up to Olienhout and regurgitating his kill. With a dipped head in deference, he backed out of the den. Before he was out of sight, she raised her weary head and returned his gesture with a smile, exposing white of fang.

Back in the light, he took a deep breath. He felt a strange new pride spilling out of him, as though he had grown immeasurably in size. He and Olienhout were just over two years old, though they did not think in terms of years. Looking out into the zebrawood forest, his eyes searched the darkness as the night consumed the savanna whole. Within the shadows he found the wood filled with danger and wonder.

Closing his eyes, he felt the presence of his mother, further to the north on the edge of Gorongosa.

Underneath the broad crown of a bushwillow tree, Aalwyn closed her eyes as well, and searched the night for her son.

Together, they were joined by their ancestors, ghostly figures from an instinctive memory. Generations of wild dogs as one listened to the rhythms of the savanna. As long as they ran the veld as a pack, going from strength to strength, they may just live for generations more.

Aalwyn exhaled a long sigh. She felt in her heart that the season of the wolf was coming to an end.

But the time we have shall be mighty indeed.

Chapter 26

"Another one gone." Marais took notes, GPS coordinates written as barely legible numbers.

"Well, that was bound to happen. Still have the Tick intact on the alpha male, though." Venter took notes of her own, processing the hundreds of data points they had already harvested.

The two sat in a small pub on the periphery of Gorongosa park. Other than the bar minded by a man dressed in khakis, there was no roof, every table sat under the open sky. Venter and Marais occupied one of the larger tables, their notes weighted down against the wind with rocks. A few of the other tables were occupied by travelers to the park. Each of them wore the expected khakis, including two nearby donning safari hats that continually threatened to blow away.

Marais continued writing. "So they are just to the south of the park. They will be more difficult to track." He tapped his pencil on the paper, lost in thought. "The one I wanted most. Just disappeared."

"Poacher activity looks to be on a downtrend in Gorongosa." She read from a report. "The patrols have been increasingly effective. Fewer firefights at the very least, and this past two weeks, the rangers report no contacts."

"I suspect that is related to the loss of rebel support." Marais wore a barely suppressed grin.

"Was that the work of that... ranger?"

"Razak." He glanced at her. "He struck the shepherd."

She cleared her throat, unsure how to wade into that discussion. "The Painted dogs have scattered as well."

"We may get more complaints now." He scratched at a scrabble of beard.

Venter nodded. She played with a length of wire they had removed from a bush, the snare intended to kill wildlife. "The snare count has plummeted in the northern half of the park."

"I suspect they are easier to find in the south. The periphery will be filled with them." He resumed his notes.

"The rangers could move their patrols south to try to catch incursions."

"They cannot patrol all of the villages. That will only make the people more hostile." Marais rubbed his hand, setting down his pencil. "We must be careful, *meisie*."

"After we are done today I will spend some time visiting the villages." Venter put down the wire after having bent it in the vague shape of an animal. "You might be surprised what you can learn if you bring a case of *bier*."

"We may need the information." He sounded very tired. "Buatoom will be back at some point."

"The one who murdered the rangers." Venter glared into the distance.

"They were not the first. And they will not be the last."

"Why would he take such a chance?" She furrowed her brow.

"Working around the halfhearted China bans on ivory or horn likely needed his personal involvement to guarantee a shipment." He underlined what he was writing and closed his notebook with a *whap*. "He has been seen before going on his own poaching runs. Posting photos of his conquests. And of his guns."

"Marketing for his rich customers?"

"He also enjoys it." Marais's voice took on a low growl.

"Murders or poaching?"

"To a psychopath, nothing else on Earth is really alive. It is all the same to him."

The two tourists at the adjacent table were looking in their direction, listening to the conversation.

She awkwardly picked up the wire and continued twisting it. After a few minutes of quiet, she hazarded a question.

"Gorongosa has not had the poaching activity that most other parks have suffered. Think our luck is running out?"

"Between RENAMO rebel activity and the poachers, the activity can always pick up. The Asian markets have an insatiable demand for horn, pangolin scales, whatever is rare and on the verge of extinction."

"Traditional medicine."

"Medicine." He scoffed. "Rhino horn is just a way to show off wealth. Powdered horn is eaten at parties for the elite. A way to impress the rest of the herd that you have cash to burn."

"Education may turn this around." She consolidated piles of notes under fewer rocks. "Misguided as it may be to eat wildlife to cure cancer, people do consume less when aware of the sheer industrial scale of the slaughter."

"It will not matter." Marais stared into the street at nothing. "I genuinely need to ask what the point of this job is." The pencil turned round and round in his hand. "People are getting poorer, and they do not benefit from most national parks, at least not as much as they should. So they push. Hunting interests could make more money shooting all the animals—within a single financial quarter—than we can on tourism. So they push. Nobody gets that wild reserves can make any wildlife-based business—even raising antelope livestock or hunting safaris—more sustainable. Nobody cares."

Venter took a breath, feeling a fight coming on.

"The tourism industry cares." She saw Marais roll his eyes. "And the people all around us. They want to see Africa in the wild. Preserved from a time before colonization. The land is a part of their culture. They value this, especially if the tourism economy is coupled to theirs."

"They care about money, which the poachers sprinkle out after a massacre."

"We can do better than they can." She was not sure whether to continue responding. This was more than he had spoken in weeks.

"Poachers like Buatoom will always give out more cash to the people who protect them."

"People are not as simple as that. The Social Contract is what matters here." The wire animal in her hands acquired four legs.

"The 'Social Contract.'" Marais spoke this with evident sarcasm. "Is essential to humanity, not the human." Marais tapped the table with his pencil. "The human takes every advance for granted, and as soon as there is a benefit from a thing, we shirk efforts to sustain that thing. Clean air, the absence of war, environment, conservation. Even science is regarded with suspicion. The very things that make our world livable are what the average person regards with contempt."

"The rural Mozambican farmer is not to blame for that." She sat back, arms folded.

"In every country, science is undermined and disregarded. The ignorant achieve public office, and their accounts in the Caymans are filled from the public till."

"Right." She remained still as he vented.

"Tourists travel to Virunga in Rwanda to see the mountain gorilla. Meanwhile oil companies fund rebels to slaughter those gorillas and the rangers who protect them to destroy public interest in the park." He eyed her with a sinister glare. "That happened here, you know. Back in the 1970s. This place was an abattoir. RENAMO killed everything bigger than a field mouse. All for money. People cannot see past the next mouthful, business cannot see past the next shareholder meeting."

Venter nodded. She considered that he had probably been waiting for some time for an audience.

"People like Dyk, with their trophy hunting." He grunted. "Killing off what little is left."

"There are trophy hunters here?" One of the tourists, a woman, was leaning in their direction. An accent of greater London rang clearly.

"No, not in Gorongosa." Venter cheerfully answered. She spoke more slowly than usual, ensuring her Afrikaans accent was intelligible.

"Though you can find them everywhere else." Marais grumbled.

"Well, glad the animals have a sanctuary here." The woman answered.

"Yes, we enjoy being here." The man chimed in, holding her hand, indicating her spouse. With the other he left a small stack of *meticais* behind to cover the cost of the drinks and food that littered their table.

"Tell your friends—and ask the guides about the conservation projects here!" Venter smiled widely, more than Marais thought was possible.

The tourists were on their feet, holding their hats down on their heads.

"Best of luck." The man waved. "Hope this works out despite the hunters."

"Nasty people." The woman shook her head. "We met one in Johannesburg, bragging about killing a lion." Her teeth were showing as she grimaced. "All of those people should be shot."

Sonja Venter stopped smiling. She seemed to consider several responses, but was quiet as the couple walked away.

"That sort of thing is unlikely to change minds." She muttered, disappointed at her silence.

"What would?" Marais had begun assembling his papers, merging them into a single stack topped with several rocks. "Trophy hunters hunt to show off. They do not care if anything survives long term."

"Perhaps their children would." She mused. "If the craft of hunting is important to them, they may care if a species is available for their children to hunt."

He smirked. "They will just shoot something else." He bunched the papers together, putting down his pencil. "Between the hunters, the poachers, and the superstitious *okes* who think rhino horn cures cancer, these animals do not have long to live."

"Well, Johan, it seems the elephant population is rising here, unlike most other parks in Mozambique where poachers are out of control." She adjusted the wire figure in her hands, holding it up. The animal had two large rounded ears. "And we have Painted wolves here. An incredible expansion of their territory."

Marais sat back, appearing deflated. "Those two young wild dogs that disappeared. That was the Tick we needed most. How many months ago did it drop off our screen?"

Venter shrugged. "Last we saw was on the southern border of Gorongosa. It lasted long enough for us to get some movement data." He sighed. "The company that made the Ticks might lose its investor. They called this a pretty expensive failure, with only the one Tick left functional. The CEO blamed me."

Marais waved it off. "Not even a weak signal from the young dog?"

"No—and a search of the area around the southern border found no further data points from the Tick. That device died like the others."

"There is something special about those two." Marais reached for his pencil again. He seemed to have forgotten repeating that phrase.

"I have some news there." She shielded her head. "Dyk messaged a lot of people this week—he wants as many wild dogs as we can dart for his farm."

The pencil was snapped in two, both halves sailing harmlessly over her head.

* * *

Five Painted wolves relaxed in the hot afternoon in the zebrawood forest. Kamassi lay with her head on her forepaws, stirring in the heat only to pounce on Branddoring whenever she attempted to move. Each time she got up to adjust her position, Kamassi pressed down on her body with forepaws, mock biting her muzzle. Besembossie lay on her side next to a tree root, rubbing her back against it to crush a biting insect. Mitseeri watched them, taking in their movements, their reactions. The periphery of the den had the detritus of hunts scattered about: a bone, an odd piece of hide, a worn wildebeest foreleg.

Koorsboom lay by the hole, listening to the high-pitched whimpers of his eight pups within. With each sound he prepared to move, to fetch, to do something, but no response from him was required.

On his back between his shoulders, the gunmetal grey Tick remained lodged in his fur and skin, and emitted its pulse.

* * *

Augusto thumbed through the stack of paper. The bills, brightly colored in green, purple, and blue were emblazoned with the face of a politician, some with cape buffalo or kudu. The corners sported numbers like 1000 or 200000. A small stack was counted out and placed in an outstretched hand.

"What happened to the colonel?" One poacher had fear in his eyes.

"Killed. Maybe by his own men." Augusto continued counting.

"I heard the rangers killed him." The other poacher held out his empty hand.

Augusto met his gaze, but did not respond to him, other than handing over another small stack.

"Is that why we are staying away from Gorongosa?"

"Just being careful, hunting other parks." Augusto busied himself with counting the rest. "We are on our own."

"When do we hunt again, Augusto?"

"Soon. The boss needs more horns." He thumbed through the stack, counting out another pile. "Lots more."

Chapter 27

Heat rose off a flat surface baked hard as cement. It could be mistaken for cement if not for the ragged stalks of maize that rose from that surface, pale tan roasting to a darker shade. Nobody tended the fields, other than rodents scrabbling for what little nutriment was left. The sky was devoid of cloud, and there was no promise of rain to come.

Koorsboom set a paw on the ruined field, withdrawing it, and placing it again. Every unfamiliar sign of humanity produced in him an anxiety. He snuffed, and walked across the field, ignoring the warning inside him.

"Should we not join the others on the veld?" Branddoring's voice rose, her twitter descending into a lower ruff-bark. "What do you hope to accomplish with this?"

"We shall see." He sniffed the ground, and looked about. No humans in sight. A fan-palm shaded the ground in one corner of the field, but the rest was open, naked, bare dirt. Straight branches had been whittled smooth into stakes and set into the ground. Thin wires crossed between the stakes horizontally, and also vertically somehow, creating a thin fence. He wondered what this kept out. He leapt over the fence with ease. "Not us, evidently."

"What?" Branddoring sniffed the fence.

"*Niks.* Just a thought to myself." He padded across to the fence on the far side, a ragged and leaning wood barrier that seemed ready to collapse.

On the other side was a rubbish pile. Garbage and plastic were heaped as tall as a lion's shoulder. Half of the pile was smoldering, smoke rising from the heap. Beyond this was a house, the wall of pale mud, uneven and cracked in places. This rose to a thatch roof that appeared to have flat metal beneath it. The grass thatch was also ragged, with holes in places, hanging over past where the wall supported the roof. More vertical poles held up the roof overhang. A string between two of the poles was festooned with clothing.

"There may be food in those rubbish piles. This could be of use in desperate times." Koorsboom glanced about.

"This is incautious." Branddoring whispered.

"Agreed." Koorsboom leapt back over the fence, and padded away with the young wolf.

"One could say the placement of our den is incautious." Branddoring glanced about fretfully.

"I cannot argue with that." Koorsboom muttered. "My mother spoke of this, the disappearance of the wild." He stopped and looked about, at the now distant field of dead maize, the footpath the people used, a discarded glass bottle. "In the seasons to come, this may be all that is left for us."

"We were borne at a terrible time." Branddoring gazed longingly at the veld further from the village.

"So it would seem." Koorsboom lapped her muzzle in reassurance. "Go, join the others. I will be behind you."

The yearling sprinted off, clearly relieved to depart.

Koorsboom continued to investigate the periphery of the human habitation, the straight lines of the building, the obscure purpose of the fencing. Listening, he could hear distant movements of people, muttering cryptic messages to one another. He wondered if, given enough time, there could be some way to crudely understand their communication.

A figure further off shuffled into view before the young wolf knew it was there. Koorsboom looked up to see a woman standing in the shade of an acacia tree. She was old, stooped in her posture, and held a walking stick in one hand. Her colorful wrap was faded with splotches of red. Dark markings were etched upon her face, sweeping thick lines ending in sharp corners and a zigzag across her cheek. She seemed to look at the wolf, and through him.

Koorsboom bounded off toward the distant grasslands.

The woman's eyes followed him, in a penetrating stare.

* * *

Vultures wheeled above, a storm cloud above a roiling tempest of scavengers. Within sight of the granite dome, a body fast became a focus of attention.

"What could have killed an elephant here?" Koorsboom eyed the giant grey body, obviously an adult. Lappet-faced vultures stood idly by, waiting for their chance to probe the carcass later when the other scavengers cleared. Several hyenas tugged at the thick leathery skin, after several powerful pulls ripping free a section of hide. Buried under the hide, tails and hind legs were the only parts of the hyenas that were visible. Muscular jaws gripped, pulling free organs and viscera, and gulping them down. One and another emerged again to breathe and look about for enemies before resuming the feed. Each hyena head and long neck were soaked with crimson, only their short hindparts revealing their black-spotted coat. Heads dove in again and again, pulling out organs within reach. The matriarch hyena paused to grip the hide again and pull it further open. This was to expose more meat for the feeding, but the effort backfired.

Nearly a hundred vultures now advanced and closed in a circle around the carcass. Razor sharp beaks pecked at the vulnerable hindparts of the hyenas, nipping the genitals. Each hyena whirled about after a stab, teeth bared, facing a hostile audience. Quickly the hyenas abandoned their feast, and the belly disappeared under a boiling mass of dirty white and black feathers.

The hyenas moved to the other side of the elephant, starting over on the difficult work of tearing open a new hole in the dead animal.

The belly was filled with delights for the birds, and one white-backed vulture pushed in ahead of the others. Deeper were the rich intestines, and the raptor attacked this, packing its belly full.

More vultures of various species and marabou storks landed, hopping toward the elephant to take advantage. As soon as the hyenas opened a new hole and took a share of the bounty, the vultures began to pressure them and eventually crowded them out. Nonetheless, each of the hyenas left the carcass behind, filled to bursting with a third of their weight in carrion.

Black-backed jackals tucked into the exposed flesh. They concentrated on the elephant's head, its face a ruin, the tusks gone without a trace. Two heavy tire ruts led away from the killing field, toward the village. Spent cigarettes were scattered around the head where it rested on the hard ground.

The vultures continued to riot, pushing ever harder into the carcass. The daring vulture that wriggled its way into the elephant now found itself trapped, unable to thrash its way back out of the wound. Biting struck all around it, again and again, taking away chunks of elephant flesh. The relentless pressure brought with it the probing beaks, now stabbing the bird and ripping away feathers. The vulture, unable to cry out, was consumed alive as the scavengers worked in a frenzy.

The wolves watched, unnerved.

Koorsboom backed away from the site, and the other wolves followed wordlessly. The scavenging would continue for days.

"Be wary, all of you." Kamassi intoned.

"Of what?" Branddoring glanced about her.

"A creature larger than an elephant." Kamassi peered through the brush.

"I suspect I know the killer." Koorsboom stated grimly. "And it is much smaller than an elephant."

* * *

"Closer, Besembossie—press the attack!" Koorsboom pealed.

She bounded closer, lunging for the flank of the impala before her. Her teeth clicked just behind the haunch on empty air. Panting, her pace flagged.

The impala drifted to the side, away from the young wolf, gaining distance.

"Kamassi—close the chase." Koorsboom nodded to her.

Kamassi accelerated from the rear and closed in. Cycling which wolf was in the lead kept a fresh hunter up front at all times. This allowed a pack to tire a target even after several kilometers of pursuit.

The impala pronked over a thicket and continued its flight. Its hooves were hammers upon the dry ground.

Darting under the thorns of the acacia thicket, Kamassi dashed in a burst of speed, and locked her jaws on the hip of the impala. Slowing her pace, she became an anchor, and the impala finally collapsed in utter exhaustion. Dying as it fell, the impala was only dimly aware of the outcome.

The wolves clustered around the body after ripping open the abdomen, heads down, hind ends up with tails curved in the air, waving as they tore loose meat from the corpse. Muffled whines and twitters were the only sound.

The Lappet-faced vulture alighted from the *koppie*, and began to descend on the kill.

"We have little time." Besembossie glanced up as the shadow of the bird passed over them.

"This impala herd has been bountiful." Koorsboom spoke between gulping down chunks of heart muscle. "We must hunt elsewhere soon." He dove in again, tearing aside the liver to reach the muscle behind.

"To avoid dispersing the herd?" Branddoring asked.

Koorsboom grinned in her direction.

"I noticed spoor of reedbuck just before this hunt began." Kamassi gulped down blood.

"Towards the den?" Koorsboom's fur was slicked with red.

"Not far from the village."

* * *

Padding back to the zebrawood, the pack took a narrow, ragged path through the brush. The ground had been worn by hooves and paws over the seasons, footfalls beyond counting. The dirt was bare, the width of a small antelope. Off this game path, the grass grew somewhat longer, though stunted compared to the brush further away. The grazers and browsers kept the surrounding foliage trimmed.

"Here, Koorsboom." Kamassi indicated prints in the softer ground to one side in the path. Twin wedge-shaped marks, rounded on one end, sharp on the other, were pressed into the soil. "Reedbuck."

"Well spotted." He sniffed. "Not a day hence." He glanced about him, and at the declining sun approaching the horizon. "We track them at dawn."

The path bottlenecked as it passed through a hole in an acacia thicket. The branches arched overhead, festooned with white thorns and green leaves.

Branddoring abruptly stopped at the verge.

"What is it—is there a danger?" Besembossie's ears flattened against her skull.

Branddoring did not speak. She raised a forepaw, but it was restrained. Her black and white splotched limb lifted against an iron wire. She sniffed it, and looked up and to the sides of the yawning hole in the acacia shrub.

"Part of the vegetation is most unnatural." Branddoring spat this out, repelled by the strange object.

"Your eyes are sharp as a vulture's." Koorsboom studied the circular wire, held in place with twine against insubstantial branches, and secured to the trunk of a nearby tree. "Blackthorn spoke of these. Cruel things meant to throttle one to death, and leave the corpse to rot."

"To what end?" Besembossie recoiled.

"To eat, perhaps? Unless you are a hyena, however, you will not be able to eat the meat of the dead lying in the sun for day after day." Koorsboom frowned. "Perhaps these are crafted from an impulse more malevolent."

Kamassi looked to him and to the wire.

"To destroy those of the wild." Koorsboom barely spoke above a whisper.

"Are you reconsidering living so close to these creatures?" Besembossie's voice was laced with venom.

Koorsboom did not respond for some time. Staring at the earth along the path, and the snare hovering in space upon the game path, he breathed heavily.

"Remember this place." He indicated the wire, and moved off to the side of the path, trotting through the brush toward the den.

The younger wolves followed him, moving with great care, afraid to disturb the leaves and the thorns lest they take hold of them on their way past. Besembossie took the lead, her lean body bouncing as it weaved through the grass and sedge. The rest were close behind, white tail tips in the air.

Koorsboom glanced back one last time at the snare, poised, ready for the next victim. It would remain ready for days, weeks, and months to come.

The sun glinted off its metal edge, a wink at the predator that narrowly escaped its embrace.

Chapter 28

Brilliant yellow birds patrolled the ground in search of grass, selecting carefully the longest stalks. Hundreds of them were scattered throughout the village. One discovered an unlikely green shoot, long and fibrous, growing from the earth close to a pile of rubbish. Clipping it free, the bird examined the grass stem, dark red eyes scrutinizing its girth and weight from within a black mask of feathers. Satisfied, it gripped the prize and darted off, olive-brown wings edged with yellow carrying it to a tree. There stood a kidney-shaped nest of woven grass secured to a thin branch. This nest was mostly green, the village weaver bird having an expert eye for strong, fresh grass stalks. Built on the terminal tip of the branch, the nest hung precariously, bobbing as the dozen other birds in their nests on the same branch moved about. The chirping was chaotic, erupting from several hundred nests that filled every available spot on the acacia tree. Other trees around the village were laden with weaver nests as well, but the best location was near the rubbish pile, and the discarded food within.

The village weaver bird perched beside his home and carefully threaded the fiber between adjacent sticks that formed the frame of the nest. Hanging upside down, the weaver peered about. Finding no other weavers preparing to ransack the nest, nor any tree snakes conducting an invasion, it flew off to find another grass stalk.

The sun was already just above the horizon, barely visible under the tree canopies. The hole entry was dark, smelling of earth and the wet-dog musk of a Painted wolf. Koorsboom lay there, listening. Every few minutes, he could discern a nearly subsonic whine.

"I wish you well in the hunt." Olienhout intoned from the darkness.

Koorsboom understood. He began prodding Besembossie and Kamassi, and with twittering and muzzle lapping, the hunting rally was underway.

"We are hoping for a substantial kill today." Koorsboom lapped the snout of the old wolf as well.

"I seem to have burdened you at the worst time." Mitseeri looked on with a rueful smile. "You already need so much meat to provide your matriarch."

"On the contrary, Mitseeri." Koorsboom reared on his hind legs to box him, though the older wolf was unable to match him. "It is fortunate to have a sentry. Even if you were unable to guard them all, we would provide for you." He lightly gripped the other's snout with his jaws for a moment. "There is only the Pack."

Mitseeri dipped his head in deference. "I shall take to task any who approach."

***

As the sun climbed in the sky, the wolves sped their pace. Tongues were out, panting, ears erect, listening for activity. White tail tips were in the air, and their bodies bounced as they crossed the savanna in search. Koorsboom surveyed the ground, seeing no sign of the tracks.

"Divide the hunt—each of you drift away. Call out if you find what we seek." Koorsboom nodded to the others, and each wolf disappeared into the brush. They sniffed the ground, the air, each tree they passed. Signs of the feed were not in sight.

An hour passed, and the sun began to burn the ground.

Branddoring suddenly stopped, and went back to examine a bush. A short herb, squat against the ground, wavered in the breeze. Several of the leaves appeared to have been cut or pulled away. She sniffed the ground beyond this, and noticed blade after blade of grass chewed short. She inhaled sharply, and examined the soil amid the brush.

Twin wedge tracks of the reedbuck.

She twittered loudly, and the sound echoed across the plains.

The others converged upon her signal, and the group resumed their pace.

"More tracks here." Koorsboom twittered to the others. "And more." He snuffed, and the others followed him closely. The paired wedge tracks appeared fresh.

They crested a rise under a towering Apple-leaf tree, its thick trunk holding aloft branches laden with greenery. Within the shadows, they could see the savanna open before them.

"I have you."

Two reedbucks grazed tender shoots of green grass that stood in a shock near a termite mound.

The four wolves made no attempt to hide, instantly breaking into a sprint. Missiles of black, gold, and white burned across the plain, and the reedbuck detected their approach. A sharp whistle from one, and both were in flight.

Lean and muscular antelope powered across the grasslands, followed by the slender carnivores. Hooves hammered the ground, a staccato beat that reverberated across the veld.

Pawfalls made no sounds, claws scrabbling on the ground to buy every centimeter.

Snort—snort—

"We are gaining!" Branddoring pealed.

The reedbuck abruptly changed course, splitting up, and angling back toward the Apple-leaf tree. The wolves paused before resuming their chase.

"Branddoring and Kamassi—follow the ewe!" Koorsboom called.

"The buck is mine!" Besembossie flashed white of teeth, gulping air in the chase. Koorsboom grinned at her resolve.

The buck leapt deftly over a thicket and continued its course, across the open grasses under the granite *koppie*. Thunder followed it with every fall of a hoof.

"We are upon it!" Besembossie cried.

Koorsboom took the lead, allowing her to reserve her power.

Shaggy tan fur was covered with a layer of dust, the hide rolling as the muscles beneath were worked to the limit. The reedbuck sprinted in desperation. Black ribbed curved horns rocked back and forth as the antelope powered its way across the savanna, verging on the zebrawood forest.

Koorsboom twittered loudly, and Besembossie did the same, calling out to the other wolves to join their likely catch. He was within striking distance when the reedbuck emitted another harsh whistle and turned sharply. It slowed, but threw off Koorsboom for a moment. Hooves pounded toward the village.

"Close the chase, Besembossie!"

The antelope whipped past a thatch dwelling, ducking around a dilap-idated brick structure. The mud bricks had fallen apart in the last rainy season with no repair. Up a path of dirt hardened by generations of feet and past a fig tree, and the reedbuck left the confines of the village.

Further away signs of the wild returned, with acacia and clumps of milkberry trees.

Jaws clenched the flank of the reedbuck and brought it down beyond the stand of milkberry, their densely clustered green leaves flitting in the breeze. As their prey hit the ground, Koorsboom released hoo-calls to the others.

Besembossie held the buck still with a vice grip upon its side while Koorsboom ripped open the belly and spilled out the intestines. These were yanked free, and the gush of blood stilled the animal forever.

Hoo-hoo Hoo-hoo

The call sounded vaguely metallic, as though blown through a culvert, and echoed across the veld.

Bottomless throats swept up kilograms of muscle and organ. Shortly Kamassi and Branddoring joined them, and all four rooted deeply into the carcass to strip away every particle of meat from rib and hip. Hide was torn from the prey in a sheet, blood was guzzled greedily. By the time they were finished, a skeleton was nearly glistening in the sun, and four wolves stood coated in blood.

"We can return to the den along the edge of the village." Koorsboom shook some of the gore from his coat. His rounded ears were erect and listening for noise from the humans. "They lie between us and home."

The four bounded within sight of a thatch structure and found another carcass. Koorsboom paused.

"Did you kill anything on your way to us?" He wondered out loud.

"No, that I would have remembered." Kamassi laughed.

The dead animal was cattle, a heavy and muscular bull, dark coat spotted with blood. Its heavy head lay on its side, a pair of horns extending straight out from that head, curved at the tips. The enormous body shuddered.

"Still alive?" Besembossie mused.

A blood-soaked head poked up from behind the dead steer. It barked toward the wolves.

"It is one of their... things." Koorsboom padded closer.

Five more heads popped up behind the corpse, and all began barking.

Koorsboom took a step back, and looked about. He was not expecting a challenge. There seemed to be no other carnivores in the vicinity. No jackals, no lions, and certainly no hyena. Somehow, these dogs managed to bring down a full-grown bull.

The six dogs stepped away from their kill, growling.

Four wolves stood poised. Ears folded back, heads lowered, resembling bullets within their chambers.

"Withdraw, my *Gambiet*."

"Why, Koorsboom?" Kamassi glanced to him.

"We want nothing to do with their animals." His jaws were bared. "We will not consume their cattle."

"These dogs can be seen off with little difficulty." Branddoring took a step forward.

"There is a danger in hunting the cattle they keep. Make no mistake."

Kamassi took a step back, glaring at the dogs, each covered in blood.

The yearlings crept away, as the dogs continued snarling behind their kill.

Koorsboom remained where he was, waiting to ensure none followed them back to the den. He wondered for a moment whether they would attack, when abruptly all six of them lurched away from the bull, and scampered off.

As though a finger snap had rendered them vapor, they melted into the grass, dove under rubbish, vanished behind structures.

The young Painted wolf stood alone.

"So much for that hazard." Koorsboom snuffed. He glanced at the partially devoured carcass.

"HAH!"

He crouched, and turned to see three people standing there. They had walked around a crumbled brick structure to see what disturbance caused their dogs to bark. Looking from the Painted wolf to the dead bull, their faces twisted with anger. They were joined by a fourth. The old woman with the dark facial markings. On sighting Koorsboom, her mouth hung open and she began chattering to the other humans.

One held up a stick and began to jog toward him.

Koorsboom fled into the savanna, leaving behind the carcass, the dogs, and the angry village. Though far away before the shouting began, Koorsboom thought he could hear them even as he reached the zebrawood forest.

Padding to the entrance of the den hole, he found Olienhout waiting. The yearlings had each regurgitated fountains of meat and blood which she had lapped up with vigor. She sighed with contentment.

Branddoring deposited some meat for Mitseeri who bowed gratefully as he lapped it up. Some of the meat was kept by the hunters.

"Quiet has remained over the den?" Koorsboom greeted the old wolf.

"As though in a desert."

Koorsboom chortled. He glanced back in the direction of the village.

"We encountered several of their dogs as we came this way. They had apparently killed one of their own cattle."

"Hmm. I have pondered whether they ate something other than garbage." Mitseeri grunted. "They managed to kill one of their large pets?"

"Indeed." Koorsboom's brow furrowed. "They ran away, certainly no threat to us."

"Did the people see you?"

"They saw me, alone."

"Near the kill?"

"Yes." As Koorsboom answered him, he felt a strange hollow in his stomach. Looking toward the den hole, he noticed Olienhout had already descended to continue suckling the pups. "I do wonder if a new danger is upon us."

Chapter 29

Ki Kerrik, Ki kerrik

A nondescript bird stepped through the shade of the savanna on the eastern edge of the zebrawood. The broken light made it barely visible, its streaked coloration with dark brown vermiculations breaking up its profile. The crested francolin froze for a moment, watching.

The wild dog was near enough to be a threat. It seemed an unlikely enemy, but one can never be too careful on the savanna. It darted into the brush, disappointing the carnivore.

"You will never catch one of those sedge birds." Koorsboom muttered.

"The hunting has been lean." Besembossie still stared where the francolin had stood. "It has been a few days since we took the reedbuck."

"Even that impala herd has departed." Kamassi grumbled. "Olienhout needs meat badly."

"Indeed." Koorsboom shook his head. He knew his mate had become disappointed. Since their kill near the village, scrub hares had made up the bulk of their prey.

"There has been thunder in the days since then." Besembossie glanced for a moment at the sky. "Thunder, without a storm cloud above."

"Carrion from that wildebeest the day previous." Branddoring grimaced.

"The meat was foul, but perhaps we should return to it?"

"Stronger stomachs than ours will already have dealt with that carcass." Koorsboom thought for a moment. "Disturbing, that."

"What?" Besembossie flicked an ear to ward off a biting fly.

"That wildebeest was killed, but not by the wild." He considered this. "The body was opened up, but there was something strange about it. The wounds were... not from teeth." He was not sure how to express this, that the animal had been slit open and the cut lines were straight, rather than the hurried rips and tears one would expect of a hyena or lion. "Humans killed it."

They padded further into the bush in search. From a nearby rock a hadeda ibis took flight as the morning sun began its walk across the sky.

HA-DA! HA-DA!

"Did we drive the impala herd away?" Branddoring glanced about.

"I doubt that. We—"

CRACK!

The report broke through the dawn, causing the wolves to crouch, and several birds to take flight from the nearest acacia tree.

"That was close to us." Koorsboom surveyed the horizon in that direction. "Impala."

Distant, a small group of impala were on the run. Springing bodies all leapt in the same direction. Their speed was remarkable from this distance. Each pronk carried the graceful antelope high and far, leaping far ahead of the hunters pursuing them. Koorsboom wondered for a moment how they ever managed to catch them.

Two of the impala fell, one after the other.

CRACK! CRACK!

Another fell, and a third shot echoed across the veld.

From behind a faraway rock outcropping several people strode in the direction of the fallen antelope. They carried some equipment that allowed two of them to carry away a single body.

Koorsboom snuffed at the sight. "I knew it was not our doing."

* * *

The warm morning gave way to the relentless heat of the day, and the rising buzz of cicadas. The wolves paused under a Giraffe-thorn acacia tree, which scowled down on them with a dozen pairs of eyes from a vervet monkey troop. The largest male had a stern grey face under a white band across the forehead. As the pack moved on, the male gave a calling squawk, but did not come down from the tree until the wolves were out of sight.

"There is that black pathway again." Kamassi could see the busy road in the distance. It was coated in tar, and in the baking heat it gave off a noxious smell.

"Is that the same road we crossed on our *trek* south?" Besembossie's ears swiveled.

"It likely is." Koorsboom stopped. "I was hoping to find another herd subsisting on this land." He grunted. "The wild is eaten away."

"What do you mean 'eaten'?" Branddoring did not share Koorsboom's penchant for abstraction.

"Taken, by these humans. Not all at once, like a lion at a feast, but by innumerable mouths like rodents. Ever hungry, and never resting."

"I do not follow you. Humans are eating the ground?"

"Never mind my rambling." He lapped the yearling's muzzle. "The place from which we came were level rolling lands, farms everywhere. Perhaps it is time we pressed south."

As the pack loped back along the same route, they passed the vervet monkey clan, again leaping to safety within the same tree.

"The hunting has been sporadic, Koorsboom." Kamassi sidled up to him. "The pups are becoming more quiet. Have you noticed?"

"I have. This veld is testing us. The meager resources on offer may push us still further south."

"How does the alpha know where to settle?" Kamassi inquired.

"Do you hope to ascend to the position of alpha?" Koorsboom gave a grin, fangs on display.

"As you have, yes."

"Perhaps I err in sharing this secret with you, but we do not know." He smiled to himself. "We are on the same journey of discovery you are. And we guess, as best we can."

"Even Aalwyn?"

"Even our greatest matriarch. One never knows where home shall be. Not until you stalk the land will you discover its riches. Not until you fight will you know your adversary, or know yourself. And not until you succeed in bringing pups to the veld will you find your quality as a leader." Koorsboom bumped her. "Every moment a negotiation."

"Every moment." Kamassi loped ahead to scout their path.

* * *

"The high of the day is a poor time to hunt." Koorsboom squinted at the sun, and back down to the dusty plain before him. It shimmered in the heat.

"We could rest." Branddoring squatted under a bush that afforded a small amount of shade.

"Tracks!" Kamassi twittered excitedly. She sniffed at twin markings on the soil, sharp on one end, rounded on the other, small in size.

"Impala." Koorsboom glanced about for more. He found them in a staggered line, forehoof and hind hoof markings indicating a walk. Except one hind hoof was misplaced relative to the other.

"And it is injured." He took off at a run.

Before long, they found the impala, limping and alone. There was no chase. The wolves surrounded the ram and dragged him down, horns clattering to the ground.

"He was bleeding from his flank before we took him." Kamassi ripped open the abdomen.

"A human wound, I suspect." He eyed the hole where it entered the hide just over the hip.

They lost no time dismembering the corpse and stripping it clean of all but the bones, hide, and intestines. Branddoring took a hind leg in her jaws for the return journey. Koorsboom took the other.

* * *

Olienhout scarfed down the meat before it hit the floor of the den, ravenous in her appetite. She took a share from each of the hunters.

Gasping between bites, she bid Koorsboom to stay after the others had parted.

"What news of the veld?"

"Strange tidings from the world." Koorsboom did not lay down, knowing that he was not welcome so close to the pups. "The humans are roving about, and striking down anything of the wild. We saw some fall to their thunder this morning. On the veld, we have seen bodies left to molder." He looked at the hind legs left behind for her to gnaw on. "Why we would see so many dead at once is beyond my understanding."

"It is because of us." Olienhout spoke at a calm, even whisper. She glanced at the eight pups suckling. Their black and white fur made them nearly invisible in the dark. "It may only be a matter of time before they find us."

"It is too early to move."

"Feed my pups well, my love. And they will be ready when they must be."

Chapter 30

"Would you honor me with a place in the hunt?"

Koorsboom looked from Mitseeri to the other wolves. Kamassi and Branddoring could only respond with a shrug.

"Are you well enough to run?" Koorsboom searched the old wolf's face.

"Always." His high-pitched twitter had a plaintive edge to it.

Koorsboom ducked his head into the den hole for a moment, muttering to Olienhout. His hind end was in the air, the tail at first down, then up, and waved. He backed out and shook the dirt from his fur.

"Right, you shall join us for the *jag*. Follow our lead." He pounced on Branddoring, and she rose on her hind legs to box him with forepaws. Kamassi bumped against Besembossie and lapped her muzzle, and the hunting rally was underway.

Mitseeri managed to join in, hobbling about and greeting each of the wolves for the first time. The effect was electric, and he seemed years younger than his appearance. His ruined hind leg ceased to matter as he matched the others in vigor, the sheer joy of returning to the Pack.

"To the veld, you bliksems!" Mitseeri screamed. His jaw hung slack, slaver dripping upon the ground. "The *bloedrivier* awaits." His hazel eyes glittered darkly.

The wolves left the zebrawood in a flurry of gold, black, and white, bounding for the bright dawn of the savanna.

* * *

"The tracks are aging." Mitseeri sniffed the ground. He peered across the waving grasses dotted with the occasional acacia and wild date palm. "You were not wrong about the thunder." He stood tall, no longer wavering on his three legs. His faded coat seemed to shimmer despite the bald patches on his sides and back. His ears swiveled, listening for news carried on the drifting winds.

The rest of the pack milled about.

"For what are we waiting?" Kamassi wondered.

"Patience." Branddoring examined the older wolf. "I rather think he is accustomed to a visual survey, given his injuries." She looked to Mitseeri, who eventually turned his head to give her a smile.

Another minute passed, and he remained a statue. Flies buzzed, alighting on him, and he did not notice.

Abruptly he crouched.

"Forth." He spoke, and was off like a shot.

Koorsboom twittered to the yearlings, and they were close behind. The old wolf still struggled to keep a swift pace, but he powered his way across the grasses, spine arching and flexing to maximize his speed. Claws stabbed the ground, lean legs pistons propelling the wolves across the dusty land. Nearly a kilometer was crossed before Besembossie detected a sign of their quarry.

"Distress call!" She twittered, and the others assented. "So faint—how did he hear that?"

"A suggestion in the wind." Mitseeri huffed as he bounded. "The seasons past have provided instruction." His mouth hung open, fangs exposed.

The wolves assumed an attack posture, heads low, ears flat against their bullet shaped skulls, bodies held toward the ground. Five pairs of hazel eyes peered through the brush, seeking their target.

Thorned bushes parted, and the wolves found an impala female, sprawled on the ground. It was dying, a round hole punched into its shoulder, shattering the bones underneath. Blood had long since dried on its hide, cascaded down its breast and on the ground along the great distance it covered to reach this place. Black globe eyes barely glimpsed their surroundings. A hoof kicked slightly, perhaps responding to some sign that the end was finally near.

"Its rest has come." Mitseeri pronounced as he took hold of the abdomen. The five tore the beast open. Its blood splashed on the ground, which took up the moisture greedily.

As the wolves gorged themselves on the meat and offal, Koorsboom kept glancing at the bullet wound. Even after the carcass had been dismembered, and the body no longer recognizable, he continued to ponder the meaning of the fatal wound.

* * *

Skeletal remains, hide, a length of intestine, and a head was all that remained of the impala. The wolves had spotted the resident Lappet-faced vulture gliding down from its thermal, knowing more scavengers were to follow.

"Though the matriarch beckons, I might suggest." Mitseeri mused.

"What have you in mind, *Oom Mitseeri?*" Kamassi padded to him and playfully took hold of his snout in her jaws. During the feed she had pestered him as to how he knew where to find the impala, but he was unable to elaborate.

"How many impala have been left for you?" He shook himself free of the flies that were attracted to the blood that soaked his fur.

"Left?" Branddoring asked. Kamassi jumped on her back, her forepaws hanging over her spine.

"For dead."

Koorsboom considered this. "This... and one other, thus far."

"There are more beyond them, surely." Mitseeri turned to glance at the rest. "Our search has hardly been exhaustive."

Koorsboom felt a hot and loose sensation in his bowels. His jaw hung open, his breaths ragged as they passed through his teeth. Beating heart, driving blood, throbbing as it passed through his system, every limb on edge.

"They are slaughtering them all." Koorsboom gasped.

"What is to come?" Branddoring wondered.

"With these humans... death." Mitseeri appeared serene. "When it shall arrive, we know not." He stared at the ground. "It shall come, in one form or another."

"What is their intention?" Koorsboom shook his head, visions in his mind distracting him.

Mitseeri laughed, in the way only wolves can laugh, jaw agape and twittering. He hobbled toward Kamassi, and lapped her muzzle. "A veld too far, my wolf." He managed to box her, upright on a single hind leg before returning to the ground. "One hunt, one day at a time."

"This old one is tiresome." Besembossie whispered to Koorsboom.

"And what do you suggest?" Koorsboom peered at the old wolf, the sun rising to its apex above.

"That we survey the bushveld, Koorsboom." He nodded, satisfied with his own proclamation. "Perhaps this day has not been one of good fortune." He sighed, a vague, sad exhale. "I shall warn Olienhout." With a nod, Mitseeri began to lope for the den. After their circuitous route, he departed directly for the zebrawood.

The yearlings looked to Koorsboom for orders. He hesitated, wondering what the day would bring.

"Spread out, across the savanna." He stepped forward, placing a four-toed paw upon a rock. "Run. Search, and find. There shall be no hunt." He sucked air through his fangs. "For the hunt may yet be against us."

* * *

As the sun descended, its orange fire burned against the western horizon. Mitseeri lay staring at the den hole. He listened for any sign that his service was needed, but heard none. He continued to rest as the twilight approached.

He alighted on his paws and padded to the hole. He hesitated at the verge.

"Pardon my discourtesy, but the *jagters* approach." He glanced aside, his jaws bared. He moved away. The first of the hunters had returned.

Koorsboom padded toward the den hole, thrusting himself inside to regurgitate the bulk of the meat he had consumed. He scrabbled back out, glancing about, regarding Mitseeri.

"All quiet?"

The old wolf nodded his head and smiled.

They both heard the approach of hunter's paws.

Kamassi entered the zebrawood, exhausted. She stumbled to the den hole and regurgitated the impala meat. She fell to her side, panting.

Within the hour Besembossie and Branddoring returned, leaving their bounty at Olienhout's feet. They each rested, heaving after their runs alone.

"What news of the veld?" He reclined where the yearlings lay. "What have you seen?"

"That old wolf is canny." Besembossie grumbled. "He seemed to know what was underway."

"Assume the worst, and you will not often be wrong." Mitseeri flopped down next to them.

"I saw bodies." Kamassi gasped. "Torn apart."

"As have I." Branddoring shook her head. "Two that I could find." She seethed. "They did not seem to be taken... harvested." She struggled to explain that the carcasses were not butchered. No meat had been removed. "The bodies were left to rot."

"It defies explanation." Koorsboom rested his jaw on the ground. He snuffed, his nostrils stirring the dust before him.

"As does any task these creatures do." Mitseeri lay on his side. His hind leg stuck out into the air, the muscles atrophied, the paw contracted. "What I do know is... when the inexplicable occurs, the Pack must run."

"The pups are not ready." Koorsboom noted gruffly.

Mitseeri nodded. "Then one must prepare as best one can." He grimaced. "The most difficult task, however, is yet to be performed."

"Which is?" Branddoring huffed.

"Explaining this to the one whom must decide all." Mitseeri stared at Koorsboom.

He stared at the ground, nodding his agreement. He padded to the den hole.

"My love." Koorsboom muttered.

"Danger is upon us." Olienhout's voice resonated in the black. "And the humans mobilize."

"Yes." He felt oddly ashamed of not having to elaborate.

"One of your hunts strayed too close to the humans."

He had nothing to say.

"My pups require more time." Her voice was edged, a surface that would not be breached. "May your hunts be more discreet."

Koorsboom alighted and returned to the yearlings. "We hunt at dawn. Likely we will scavenge the dead that was noted." He stared at the ground.

"I had thought we were careful." Kamassi asked.

"Not as careful as she." Koorsboom intoned. He lay down again. "None are as cautious as a mother." He took hold of a stone in his teeth. "Would that I understood this a season past." He struck the gravel with a paw. "Would that I understood *anything as a father.*"

Kamassi and Besembossie watched him quietly.

"There will be no running. Not from what we face." Koorsboom rasped. He nodded to the older wolf, and the yearlings around him. "We see this through, however it ends."

Branddoring moved closer to Mitseeri, touching noses with him.

"We owe you a debt of this warning." She peered into his eyes, the expected color of hazel, but faded with age.

"There is no debt. Not for those who serve the good of the Pack." Mitseeri gave a deferential nod. *"Ons vir jou."* He gave a weary smile, white of teeth exposed.

"What do you mean by that?"

"We for thee." He sounded far away. "Purpose must be as one with their kind."

Branddoring lunged at his snout, and he reacted with confusion. Lapping his muzzle, she reassured him. She admired his faded eyes. *So long this old one has been away from the closeness of wolves. And here he is, moments away from these paws.*

He responded with a jaw grip on her paw, lightly, not enough to draw blood. Enough to feel pressure.

She smiled at this, and seized his paw as well in her mouth.

They regarded one another as night descended on the world, and the calls of cicadas rose with the dusk. Nightjars took flight with their chatter, embroidering the darkness with their calls, along with Spotted eagle owl *hoos*, scops owl *krrrups*, and the ubiquitous *good lord deliver us* of the Fiery-necked nightjar.

The indigo horizon faded into black, the day never to return.

Chapter 31

Late morning had come and gone, and Olienhout noted its passing.

Eight pups suckled, growing quickly on the rich milk she provided. When they did not feed, they slept, calling their ultrasonic whimper when they awakened. In the darkness she felt their need, and their growing strength. The large chamber, dug out in a season past by a porcupine, felt smaller each day. Few sounds penetrated this deep into the ground, though she could hear the *Kuk-coorrr-uk* of the Cape turtle dove nested in the tree just outside.

Four wolves had come to the den, regurgitating undigested meat in large amounts, the most that each could carry. Olienhout took up all she could stomach, passing it on to the pups in her milk. In the Pack, the pups eat first and foremost.

Koorsboom was last to arrive of the hunters. His take was left on the floor of the den.

"Carrion." She did not phrase this as a question as she began eating Koorsboom's share.

"Yes." He panted. "Did Mitseeri tell you?"

"He did not need to." She swallowed. "You have all brought back more than one would expect of a single kill. Unless our small *jagter* band has been taking down eland."

"Indeed." Koorsboom peered into the gloom at the pups as they wriggled against her slender body. "We have found many dead across the landscape."

"The humans you had hoped to understand remain elusive to you." She gave a wry smile, teeth unsheathed in the dim light.

"I suspect they always will." He began to back out of the den.

"Learn quickly." She gave an effusive twitter.

"Your sense of humor can be macabre at times." He snuffed, a puff of dust erupting before his snout. "I must be away. The dead shall not remain still for long." He shuffled back out of the den, blocking the light from above for a moment before it returned. The sounds of twittering above as the hunting rally began again was muted.

"Make haste for the downed." Koorsboom's voice was low but urgent.

Paws struck ground, and faded quickly into the distance.

* * *

Koorsboom thrust his lean body through thornbrush thickets and low bushwillow trees, pressing on despite the sun being at its apex.

"You torment me, but I know not why." He gazed at the burnished orange globe above. He loped on.

Before he reached the clearing of the red bushwillow where he found a dead wildebeest the day previous, he could see the cause was hopeless.

High above, dark figures wheeled in the sky, broad wingspan gliding gently down toward the earth below where the dead could be found. As they approached the ground, they joined a more raucous assembly, with numerous vultures present. White-backed vultures held forth, brown and black wings folded, waiting for a turn at the carcass. Lappet-faced vultures dominated the kill, their bulk shrouded in black plumage, naked red heads glaring imperiously at the others. They attacked the hide of the wildebeest, gulping down what they could before the press of the crowd intensified. Cackling of hyena announced the arrival of another wave of scavengers.

Koorsboom turned and left. He began a patrol, roughly circular from here, around where the den was located. Eventually, he found another dead impala, and began to fight the vultures for a share.

* * *

Night was falling as the wolves returned to Olienhout. Outside, a square-tailed nightjar began its prolonged churring.

The hunters were less productive, with each of them regurgitating their meat at the opening of the den, but in reduced amounts.

Koorsboom appeared at the entry.

"We resume the hunt at dawn." The grim set of his jaw spoke on his behalf.

"I expect nothing less." Olienhout intoned.

He moved to depart.

"Stay."

Koorsboom shifted his glance back towards her, and relaxed for a moment. He never felt at ease in the den, even in the entryway.

"Death is upon your brow this day." She winced as one of the larger pups latched onto a teat. "It is upon us all."

Koorsboom did not know what to say.

"Every meal you provide to your heirs gives them life for a day at a time, staving off the darkness. The Pack is a bulwark against Death, and repels its attentions to the last." She adjusted herself on the ground. "And in our fight against Death, we send so many lives its way."

Koorsboom smiled to himself, apparent even in the gloom. "My second father mentioned that once to me. On a hunting plain, he stated it, as though to someone else, long ago. *'Death comes to us all... and when it comes for Blackthorn, it will know my name.'*"

"Indeed. One cannot hope for more. And so there shall be life, amidst it all." She lay her head down to her side, resigned. "Whether the fight availed us will remain unknown. Perhaps to others after our passing."

"*Ek verstaan.*" Koorsboom nodded, and took his leave.

He padded to the other wolves, the yearlings who panted in their exhaustion after seeking out the carcasses of the day, and Mitseeri who returned his gaze with uncertainty.

"On the morrow, we shall find what is living." He glared out toward the fading sunset. "Should there be anything left."

Chapter 32

The hunting rally was muted, the whines and twittering of their greetings seemed muffled. Enthusiasm was shown only by Mitseeri, glad to depart the den for a greater excursion. The five left the zebrawood grove.

"We need a wide patrol, the most expansive we have undertaken." Koorsboom set his jaw.

"A way shall be had." Mitseeri bowed. *"My kreet,* as a Painted wolf."

"A better creed is not to be found." Koorsboom smiled. "Mitseeri, see to their safety." He indicated Kamassi and Branddoring. "Besembossie, with me." The two parties split, going further east and west than they had since settling the den.

Oo-krroooo, oo-krroooo, coo-coo called a mourning dove, its greeting to the dawn.

* * *

The savanna was enveloped in a yellow glow, and the temperature was still relatively cool from the night. Nocturnal animals such as pangolins and genets had already retreated to the shadows. Katydids quieted, and the morning calls of birds began.

"One would have expected antelope to be quite active." Mitseeri mused. He surveyed the veld from a rise that enabled the wolves to see over the low treetops of acacias.

"Perhaps we will see more as we move further from that village." Branddoring ventured.

"Or we will see another bloody village." Kamassi grumbled.

The three weaved through feverberry and willow shrubs, woody thickets that were nearly impenetrable. The ground was dry beneath their feet, all the moisture having been pumped out by the trees around them. The desiccated grasses withered in the sun, the blades whispering as their fur brushed past.

As they went around one barrier of sedge, they found open grasses devoid of grazers.

Mitseeri nosed Branddoring. "Take heart, young one. The next kill is just there."

"Just where?" She stood on hind legs for a moment, peering across the veld, then back down to all fours as her bounding continued.

"A manner of speech." He chuckled to himself. "For a Painted wolf, everything is 'just there', arriving 'just now', even if it is beyond the horizon."

She lapped his muzzle tenderly.

"I am glad of your good humor." Branddoring beamed. "We face an uncertain time."

"Is there another kind?" He closed his eyes and faced the sun above.

"Are you quite well with your injury?"

"I would be of lesser use in a hunt, I am afraid." He looked back to his hind leg. "Between this and age, I would have difficulty coursing a tortoise."

Kamassi hurried ahead to a dense wall of thornbrush, pushing her way under branches, and through the wooden obstruction with snapping and breaking of twigs. On the other side, she viewed another empty grass field. Mitseeri and Branddoring soon joined her.

"Onward." Mitseeri smiled gently. "The next field, replete with prey, is just there."

* * *

The carcass of the hare was torn apart, mangled beyond recognition by the larger hunter. Koorsboom made expert work of scissoring away the available meat, nodding to Besembossie for her to take a turn.

"Little bounty there for Olienhout." She smacked and swallowed.

"Indeed." He resumed a tireless lope across the uneven veld, Besembossie close behind. Kilometers passed with little effort, and even less sign of prey.

They left paw prints on a dry stream bed, the hard ground covered with dust. Each print had four toes, the middle two fused at the base, over a triangular foot pad. Four claw imprints were pressed into the dirt above each toe. These marked their path, down a rocky slope and back up from the dry gully onto a grass plain.

The grasses were dried, and in many areas worn away. Signs of an older farming plot remained on the landscape. Sections of weathered wood chopped from thornbrush had been used to form a rude fence, bordering a broad field where the soil had been tilled. A mud house had been built further away from the stream, now with walls collapsed, thatch roofing gone, all nearly reclaimed by one of the periodic floods that occur in the wet season. The land where grass had been stripped away by tilling and cattle grazing had since eroded, leaving naked dirt baked in the sun. Rills were carved across this by runoff rainfall, expanding into gullies until they reached the stream itself. Abandoned at least a year ago, the earth was now unusable for any crops, and even the hardiest weeds would have difficulty gaining purchase.

Claws clicked on the gravel as they passed this, the ruins of the mud house and a broken hoe sniffed briefly by Besembossie as they pressed on.

"Where are we bound?" She peered as far as she could, seeing only more sedge.

"A wide arc around our home forest. From there, we see what lies beyond our usual hunting range." They paused in the shade beneath a Lowveld milkberry. Green leaves festooned the branches in terminal rosettes, now bare of the edible fruit.

"Inconceivable they wreaked such havoc in a short time." Besembossie shook her head as she lay in the high grass.

"Killing every animal for a day's run in all directions?" He snuffed. "The thunder that reached our ears may have been a sign of their work." He glared at the ground before him. "Blackthorn told me of far more extravagant destruction by these creatures." He growled darkly. "And I have seen them work. I watched, and remembered."

"The desire to ask why you embarked upon this venture returns, only to recede as I remember your answer. And again, it returns. A vulture circling within my mind." Besembossie laid her head upon the ground and closed her eyes.

Koorsboom stared at her for some time, unable to rest. Glancing up through the branches of a milkberry tree, he could see the sun hanging high in the sky as the leaves waved in the breeze. His gaze shifted to ants, busily moving about along a scent trail. The heavily armored insects trundled along a path, passing one another along the way, some of them carrying the fruits of their expedition.

Would that I had such confidence in purpose.

Koorsboom allowed an hour to pass before rousing Besembossie to continue their patrol.

* * *

"Shall we chase him off?" Kamassi twittered.

"Or will he chase us?" Branddoring chirped happily.

The hulking beast before them bared powerful conical fangs, its black muzzle wrinkled in anger. Rounded ears were angled back, shaggy yellow mane standing on end. The Spotted hyena hunched its powerful fore shoulders, one paw raised, as though deciding whether to attack.

"Take heed—this enemy can kill you both." Mitseeri had lost his jovial twitter on encountering the scavenger. "It is a male, and so less aggressive. Do not, however, doubt its power."

The hyena's legs were encased in a thin layer of mud, its paws planted on the edge of what remained of a wallow. Mostly dried, the former waterhole retained just enough moisture to be a sticky trap. In the middle of that wallow lay a wildebeest on its side, two of its limbs submerged entirely. The other two struggled in vain to pull away, hooves striking the mud with a splat. Groaning its distress, it was stuck fast.

"What say you, hyena?" Mitseeri's voice lowered. His ears flattened, and his head lowered, lips pulled back in a rictus grin. "Will you join this wildebeest in death?"

It withdrew a step, heavy jaws still agape, forepaw again planted on the ground. He looked at the two yearlings, both standing back.

"Your kind will not have an opportunity to lock teeth on *me* again." Mitseeri ruff-barked, and bounded closer. Though he tottered on three limbs on the uneven ground, his jaws were as sure as a mountain range.

The hyena backed further away, moving along where the mud ran deeper. Its hind parts were tucked in closer to the ground, protecting its vulnerable genitals. He emitted a harsh giggle, a sign of anxiety.

"Stay clear of his bite." Mitseeri charged, causing the hyena to bumble backwards into the mire, then lope further away, cackling the entire time. Kamassi and Branddoring joined in, harrying him away.

"Run for the sunset!" Branddoring flattened her ears, ragged breaths in between twitters to her pack mates. She moved to plant a vicious bite on the hyena's flank, but he turned about quickly, forcing her to cautiously retreat a step.

Mitseeri hobbled as best he could into the wallow, and this became deeper as he approached the trapped antelope, sinking in with each step. Carefully he crept toward the prey, approaching from behind. Peering over the wildebeest's shoulder, he gave a wary eye to Kamassi and Branddoring.

The hooves free of the mud spasmed, ready to kick through bone.

Mitseeri leaned over the wildebeest's body, his forepaws planted on the ribs. He took hold of the belly and ripped it open with two lunges. Blood spilled into the thick brown muck, and the kicks of the animal weakened, then ceased.

"Eat, and do so quickly." Mitseeri glanced about, seeing the hyena was still alone, hovering nearby with its mouth wide open, panting.

As the three wolves moved in to take their measure of the meat, they could hear the hyena approach. The *schloorp* of each step made stealth impossible.

Mitseeri grunted, turning about to provide the yearlings with some protection as they fed. This was a challenge, however, as the hyena could quickly extricate itself from the solid edge of the wallow, dance around to the other side on harder ground, and move in closer.

"Stuck, *jou bliksem!*" Mitseeri raged. He fell over, pulling his good hind leg out of the mud and with great effort righting himself. He glared at the hyena. "There may be a better option."

The hyena skulked closer.

"Hold off, the both of you." He gestured to the wolves. "Do not attempt to intimidate him further. He is welcome here."

"Are you mad?" Kamassi was aghast.

"I see your intent." Branddoring smiled. She dipped her head subtly toward the hyena.

He moved closer, the yellow mane no longer standing on end. His spotted coat was pattered with dirt.

Branddoring moved her mouth close to the exposed meat, watching their guest. Kamassi did the same, though with a look of confusion upon her face.

Mitseeri lowered his gaze, and rested his lower jaw on the open wound. He made no sound, gave no physical sign of aggression, and showed no sign of anger.

The hyena's rounded ears again stood erect, and he bared his jaws once more before gripping the hide of the wildebeest. Tugging once, then twice, he tore a section off in a sheet, exposing the meat. Watching the wolves for any hint of a trap, he then began ripping away flesh from the back.

"Resume eating, my *Gambiet.* With care."

"Do not hyenas normally summon their kind?" Kamassi reached in to take a mouthful of the rich loin muscles.

"He might have, if we kept fighting him off. They are canny, and serve the clan, but they also serve themselves." Mitseeri pulled aside the stomach and intestines, working to unroot the heart.

"He was attempting to eat all he could before any others arrived." Branddoring said, swallowing. "He is a subordinate male."

"The lowest of the low." Mitseeri chuckled to himself. "If he could not have his share, he would *whoop* the clan down upon us."

"I shall remember this tactic." Branddoring lapped his muzzle.

As the hour passed, the wolves and the hyena slowly dismembered the corpse and tore aside what hide they could, though movement was sluggish for all involved. When a hindquarter was separated, the hyena gave a high cackle and pulled this away from the wallow. Bounding off, he hid the limb in a thicket before returning.

"I am not sure if I can fit more meat." Kamassi withdrew, struggling to lug her hanging belly to dry ground.

"The matriarch awaits us." Branddoring shook herself, her fur obscured by mud and gore.

Mitseeri gave a slight nod to the hyena, who charged the carcass again, attacking it with gusto. Above, vultures descended on the scene. A distant *whoop* reached their ears.

"Quickly, now." Mitseeri began his awkward lope back to the den.

* * *

The sun declined in the sky, and birds began their territorial calls of the evening. Shadows began to grow long upon the ground, creeping across the landscape to join the coming nightfall.

"This *kak* trail was cursed." Besembossie grumbled.

"Not all hunts are bound for triumph." Koorsboom lapped her muzzle. "Though I do not dispute the notion of a curse." They padded closer toward their home within the zebrawood forest. As their paws struck a footpath, they saw the print of a human. Unlike their own, it was a large, angular pad, roughly semicircular in shape due to the arch of the foot. Five toe blots were above this.

"They have no claws." Besembossie noted.

"They do not need them." Koorsboom said dryly.

Their bodies no longer bounced with each step, each walking with greater caution. Ears flattened against their skulls, their form lowered closer to the ground as though stalking a kill. Another path crossed, and they moved with even greater stealth. The grasses were of medium height, though sparse in the dry weather, and provided scant cover. Wolf coloration did not blend with the pale fibers, and so they threaded between woody scrub to obscure their path. They had not encountered any dwellings, nor any structures that would guarantee the presence of a human.

"We must be close." The sedge grew less substantial, allowing glimpses through the wooden tangle.

The cry of a child was heard nearby, and their hearts froze for an instant. Koorsboom relaxed only slightly, glancing about.

"For concealment." He indicated a thicket of thornbrush. They peered past this, toward the first rude structures of the village they could see.

"Impossible." Besembossie gasped.

Mud huts were interspersed with small gardens of vegetable and the odd fruit tree. Chickens clucked within wired enclosures, and a goat *nyahh* called from where it was tied to a stake. A distant human tended to a fire, her colorful purple garment wrapped around her, hair secured under another purple scarf.

Their attention, however, was drawn to a reedbuck.

And another.

And an impala.

The wolves looked on, confused.

"Impossible, but there they are." Koorsboom shook his head.

Three antelope stood in a clearing in the middle of the village. They chewed mouthfuls of grass, endless chewing of those nearly indigestible fibers. When finished, each leaned down to take another helping from a pile of cut green grass that was provided for them.

"Why?" Besembossie's jaw was slack. "Why are they just standing there?"

Koorsboom said nothing, watching carefully.

"Why have they not been killed?" Her voice tailed off, consumed with wonder.

"They certainly have not escaped the notice of those humans." Koorsboom eyed a man striding past one of the animals. He did not seem to regard the impala, though the impala startled as his boots crunched upon the gravel when he passed. It tensed, then resumed grinding the grass in its mouth into a paste. As it grazed, the antelope gradually made a small circle around a steel stake hammered into the ground. From this small area it did not deviate.

"Distress. You can scent it on them from here." Koorsboom sniffed the air.

"On the antelope, or on the people?" She crouched.

"Everywhere." Koorsboom backed from the edge of the brush that shielded them. "We return to Olienhout."

***

"Inexplicable." Besembossie muttered to the others. She glanced at the den hole where Koorsboom conferred with his mate.

"Surely they were trapped there." Mitseeri pondered this strange news.

"We could not discern. However it happened, they did not move." Besembossie paced. "They attempted no escape."

"They will kill and eat them." Kamassi stated.

"Will? For what does one wait?" Branddoring lay down.

"They keep animals. This is not new." Mitseeri lay next to her. "Cattle and goats, dogs and chickens. Many are held in thrall."

"Antelope are not their pets." Koorsboom was bounding to them. "This is unexpected, though not relevant." He lapped Besembossie's muzzle. "Well done today. It was an arduous patrol. Olienhout is pleased you managed to take the wildebeest." He gave a nod to Mitseeri.

"For our matriarch." He lay down with some effort, fatigued by the run.

"She does not wish us to court danger by going near the village again." Koorsboom peered at the ground before him.

Dusk crept into the wood, marked by the call of a fiery-necked nightjar.

Whir-whrrr-whhhrrrrr!

"Another patrol upon sunrise?" Branddoring lapped Mitseeri's muzzle.

"To the Earth's edge." He gave a smile, exposing white of fang. "From the highest mountain tarn to the endless water. The mother of our pups shall be fed." He glanced in the direction of the village.

"All else is nothing."

Chapter 33

Scattered clouds wandered across the sky, evanescent wisps that gradually dissipated into nothing. Burning down from overhead, the sun seemed as lazy as the land below. Winding its way from one horizon to the other, it was in no hurry.

"The high of the day." Kamassi lay in the highest grass the patrol could find. The hunters of the *Gambiet* had split up again. "Grasshoppers are all that are moving about."

"Olienhout's need is most pressing." Branddoring was laying on her belly, restless, ears swiveling about, listening to the veld about them. She could see little beyond the grass that surrounded them. "Two days have passed without a kill."

"We cannot consume what is not there." Kamassi heaved a deep breath in the heat.

"Perhaps there is prey within our vantage." Branddoring shook her head, dislodging a biting fly. "One can but rise and begin the hunt." Her paws twitched, claws upon the ground. She started for a moment, but stayed put after noting that Kamassi remained inert. She looked to Mitseeri, who lay sprawled under an acacia thornbush. She emitted a whine.

"You shall rise and see the same savanna that we found on arrival." Kamassi spoke slowly, as languorous as the day itself.

Branddoring pulled herself forward on her belly toward Mitseeri.

"Rest, my *kind.*" His lilting voice startled her.

"A child, am I?"

"Be grateful for being a yearling." He roused himself, and opened his eyes with effort. "You have survived thus far, in a world bitter towards the young." He parted his jaws, white fangs against black gingiva. "And you have many seasons to come, hewn by the veld into a fine hunter." His hazel eyes were wet, regarding her for some time in the silent midday.

"And many seasons to hunt by your side." Her tail swished one way, then the other, a flash of white amid the pale yellow of grass.

Mitseeri smiled again, and looked at the ground.

"Kamassi has enjoyed these forays as well." She looked toward her sister, who did not move or offer even a grunt in assent.

"You honor me with the attention." Mitseeri gave her a low nod. "And you have my service, such as it is." He lay back down, and closed his eyes without further comment.

"Your service is..." She glanced, and he did not respond. Kamassi was asleep as well. Branddoring lurched for a moment, the urge to move almost overwhelming, but she surrendered to fatigue. Two rounded ears fell back amid the grass tips, and quiet took the savanna again.

* * *

"*Bliksem.*"

Koorsboom glared at the empty plains before him. They sat on a rise that overlooked a wider grassland, interspersed with thornbrush and the odd acacia.

"I see no waterholes." Besembossie stood on hind legs for a moment before returning to all fours. "Would that not be a better choice for a patrol?"

"I am not certain where they are." Koorsboom grumbled. "This is new land to us all."

"I hope we are allowed enough time to learn it." Besembossie looked to him, hazel eyes searching.

He did not return her gaze.

She shook her head. Claws clicked as she walked across an outcropping of sandy brown rock that jutted from the ground. She sniffed among the large stones, thrusting her snout into the crevasses.

A yelp brought Koorsboom bounding closer, to find Besembossie crouched near a small boulder, breathing heavily. Shocks of grass grew here and there, hiding little. The contoured boulder held several ledges, worn by time, wind, and rain into folds that provided shelter to smaller animals. What drew her eye was a light brown snake with reddish blotches on the anterior half. Two light stripes ran along the head, one running from the tip of the snout to the base of the head, the other to the angle of the mouth. A tongue tasted the air, and the snake abruptly vanished, the nearly one-meter-long brown house snake slithering into a deeper rent in the stone to await a safer time to venture out.

Besembossie stood for some time before uttering an apology. "I failed, Koorsboom."

"You fail no test of the savanna." Koorsboom lapped her muzzle.

"Olienhout needed a kill. Of any kind." She stared at where the snake first moved, and distinguished its presence against the fawn-colored rock.

"She did not, however, need a dead member of the Pack." He glanced about for another danger. "There is a reason we hunt what we know. Our kind are well versed in how the impala and wildebeest move." He lapped her muzzle, and she reciprocated. "Some wolves can kill a zebra or an eland—possible if you know just how." He led her away from the rock, concerned about puff adders or spitting cobras. "Snakes, on the other hand, are altogether different from what we are accustomed. A move wrong, and we are down a hunter. And the pups who depend on us are lost."

"Caution, then." Besembossie set her jaw, snuffing her disappointment.

"There are few creatures we cannot kill. Though the exaction can be greater than we can bear."

"Should we have many more fruitless hunts, the pups shall die." She looked him in the eye. Her jaw hung open, her head shook once, and she continued padding into the veld beyond the rock outcropping.

Koorsboom watched her leave, tail in the air. Glancing up, he saw the sun begin its inexorable descent toward the horizon.

* * *

Koorsboom and Besembossie returned to the den at nightfall, in time to see Mitseeri, Kamassi, and Branddoring arriving. Each group looked to the other, hopeful for bloodstains or heavy bellies in the other party, only to see disappointment.

With a snuff, Koorsboom went to the den hole.

"There is no bounty from the veld, my love." He peered into utter blackness.

For a moment only silence hung in the air, then a faint mewling. Over this, Olienhout's sonorous voice responded.

"The moonlight beckons."

"We shall commence at once."

He backed out, and padded over to the rest of the pack. Mitseeri had already lay down to rest.

"Kamassi, Besembossie, Branddoring." He panted. "Are you at the ready for a run?"

"I am keen for the hunt." Branddoring's tail swished back and forth.

Kamassi leapt on Besembossie's back, forepaws hanging over her.

"The moon shall not be kept waiting." Besembossie looked up to her sister, and shrugged her off.

As the four wolves left the zebrawood, their black, gold, and white fur left the shadows and entered a silvered bushveld. The moon hung fat and full in the sky, bathing the land below in a pale glow.

"We shall find it tonight." Koorsboom rasped, his lope accelerating across the veld.

The yearlings sniffed the air, and looked about for spoor. In the night, hoofprints and broken branches, half-gnawed bush leaves or cut stalks of grass were more difficult to notice. Game trails, where herbivores had pounded the ground to bare dirt over years of movement, were the best sign of prey. Even these, however, failed to bring them to herds. No fresh tracks were apparent. Dung middens were weeks old and dried of scent.

"No lion prints, at least." Koorsboom grumbled. His eyes were wide, brow furrowed in desperation and anger.

"We can divide our search again." Branddoring suggested.

"Not in the night." He loped faster. "The risk is too great."

"Why did you not bring Mitseeri with you? He is eager to assist." Branddoring sped up next to him.

"He may slow our hunt." Koorsboom bared his fangs. "I do not doubt his valor." He glanced at her, then the ground. "Where we will likely find prey, however, I want him nowhere close."

The arc of their patrol rounded the northwest of the wood, an attempt to find trails that had escaped their notice in days previous. Finding nothing, the four drew closer to the den.

"Are we heading toward the grass plain with the granite *koppie*?" Kamassi wondered.

"Not that far." Koorsboom slowed his pace. He stopped for a moment to confer with the young wolves, speaking in a hushed twitter. When he finished, they each took a step back, a hush settling among them.

"Are you certain about this?" Besembossie gasped.

"As certain as the *koppie* that shall watch us." Koorsboom nodded to them all.

* * *

The only sound was a brief alarm bark, and the scuffling of bodies on the ground. A scrape of hoof against stone, a tinkle of iron chain, and then nothing. The three antelope stood near the periphery of the village, secured to the iron stakes embedded in the ground.

Koorsboom and the yearlings struck an impala at a flat run, one seizing the throat, the others gripping the body and slashing open the abdomen. The wolves held limbs fast and began to dismember the carcass, dead as it hit the ground.

As the intestines spilled out of the cavity and ruptured, they could hear activity further away in the village. A shuffle of cardboard, and a claw upon wood.

The first dog issued a bark.

"Our time is short." Koorsboom gulped down large pieces of meat torn from the pelvis and hip. The other three ripped away all they could, scarcely pausing to breathe.

Another bark, then another.

Branddoring pulled the hide from the flank, savagely wrenching loose the powerful muscles that gave the impala speed in life.

The barking from the dogs became a raucous wall of noise.

Besembossie and Kamassi severed the rest of the other hind leg, shredding the muscles of the hip and choking down what they could.

More claws upon rocks. Barking of various dogs, large and small, all bearing down upon them.

"We flee." Koorsboom twittered, and the other three were off as though fired from crossbows. Besembossie paused only to heft the hind leg of the impala in her jaws, and she sprinted after the others.

By the time the village dogs reached the carcass, the wolves were gone.

The scent of wolf musk hung in the air, but was quickly overwhelmed by the stench of the dogs as they fought bitterly over the remains. Growls became snarls as the dogs attacked one another, followed by the humans who came to the disturbance.

Clubs and garden implements rained blows down on the dogs, the snarling curdling to yelping as they fled back to their hiding places.

Two dogs lay lifeless next to the impala carcass.

The men holding the clubs were joined by an old woman, the etchings upon her face barely visible in the fading light from the moon above. They looked at the mutilated remains of the impala, and the dozens of tracks all around the site. The men pointed back toward the village, and the dogs that fled.

The woman walked well beyond the scene, past streaks of blood soaking into the ground, scattered entrails, and scraps of hide. Further on, she bent down, and peered at the earth.

Paired tracks were barely visible between blades of grass. It was impossible to tell how many individuals made them, as hard as the ground was in most places. Even so, in some spots a paw print was impressed upon dust. Triangular pads with claw marks above each toe. She called the men over, and pointed them out.

Unlike the tracks of the village dogs, these were larger in size. They led out toward the grass plains, over which the *koppie* shined in the silver night.

Chapter 34

"I ordered you not to hunt the village." Olienhout's eyes glowed in the darkness. The hazel of her iris appeared to darken to a crimson in the den. "Restraint is expected in an alpha, Koorsboom."

"We were desperate." Koorsboom lowered his head, contrite with questioning her.

Silence covered the den, the earthen walls absorbing all sound. His heartbeat resounded within his head.

"We shall soon know true desperation." Her voice acquired a deep growl. "They will come for us. Fire and thunder shall echo, day and night, through wood and veld, until every wolf is one with the earth beneath us." She stood, walking toward him. The gold, black, and white of her fur arose from the gloom. Stark white of fang was revealed as her jaws opened, and she released slaver onto the ground.

Koorsboom retreated a step, now laying on the dirt. His ears folded flat.

"You shall not disobey me again." Olienhout's ears lay flat in kind, head lowered, shaped as a bullet, chambered and ready.

"No."

"That was not a question." Her breath was hot and ragged, sounding as an engine worked to its limit. She moved closer, and her mate flinched for a moment. Instead of an attack, she lapped his muzzle tenderly.

His shame felt all the greater with the gesture.

"Now go. This error will be corrected." She stepped back toward her pups, lying down with great care. "Patrol now, short courses to find if they pursue with all haste. And if so, find where."

He backed out of the den.

"If we must run this night, the pups will not survive." Her voice was faint at the opening of the hole, but nonetheless shook him.

The yearlings and Mitseeri were waiting for him at the opening.

"You heard your matriarch." Koorsboom loped off through the zebra-wood. The others followed, fanning out across the forest as they reached the edge. Each wolf hesitated as they left the concealing shadows. A paw placed upon the loamy soil, now lit by harsh moonlight. Koorsboom took a deep breath and lurched forward, onto enemy ground.

* * *

Within the hour Kamassi bounded back into the vicinity of the den. She paused, looking about.

Eerie quiet pervaded. Even the calls of the nightjars were muted.

She poked her head down into the hole, and could hear mewling pups, and the measured breathing of Olienhout.

Her heart pounded. She sniffed around the clearing in the zebrawood, black snout examining the roots of the nearest tree for signs of a return. A muted whine rose in her throat, she was seized by a near uncontrollable desire to bound for the village to look for the others.

A broken branch distantly made her gasp. Rustling of leaf litter, and a claw on rock. Mitseeri hobbled forth to her, a gap in the arbor above catching the light color of his coat, faded gold and white with speckles of black. He limped more than usual, the extensive patrols taking their toll on him.

"I must speak to the alpha." He gave a long exhale, and thrust his front half into the den hole.

His paws scrabbled upon the hard earth, a dank smell greeting his nostrils. The entryway was narrow, and he felt immediately on edge. At the end of this, the den widened, into a larger chamber. He saw nothing, but felt a presence that seemed larger than the forest above.

"What news?" Olienhout rasped, her anger at this invasion of her pups' sanctuary apparent.

"Forgive my intrusion—we are safe."

A moment of silence.

"Explain."

"I managed to circle the village and approach where the impala was killed." He panted. "Next to the carcass were two of the dogs from the village. Their deaths were from human weapons." He paused for a moment to assemble his thoughts. "They were not throttled by jaws, nor opened by fangs. Sticks wielded in rage felled them both."

"Are you suggesting the humans believe their own dogs butchered the impala?"

"So it would seem. I swear, we have this one."

"Leave."

Mitseeri backed out as best he could, taking considerably longer than expected. He shook his fur free of the dirt once outside the den. Immediately he noticed Branddoring had returned. Faltering next to her, he lapped her muzzle, balancing on his three paws.

"Why so excited?" Branddoring laughed between tongue laps.

"Worried that you were in danger, young one." He attempted to lay down near her, but this became more of a crash, his ruined hind leg in the air. A long exhale, and he took a breath. "Olienhout is angry with us for this transgression. And she is in the right."

"Do we have time to move the pups?"

"That may not be expedient, as it happens." Mitseeri shared his news about the dogs.

Koorsboom and Besembossie were last to arrive. Besembossie flopped next to the others, resting on her side while Koorsboom went to the den to report.

"Did you hear?" Branddoring beamed. "We may be safe."

"Is that so?" Besembossie's four paws went into the air as she turned over to face her. "That seems good fortune."

Koorsboom loped into the clearing, regarding the others with a nod before diving briefly into the den hole.

"I doubt Olienhout will be so comforted." Besembossie spoke at nearly a whisper.

Koorsboom quickly extricated himself and padded over. He lay down and after a few deep breaths began to snore.

"What shall come next?" Branddoring pressed.

"Those who would answer know nothing." Koorsboom's voice creaked. He paused, still lying flat on his side as though deep in sleep. "The *Gambiet* must be at the ready."

"She was not reassured." Besembossie gave a sardonic smile.

"At the very least, they do not stalk us here this night." Branddoring chirped.

"Our patrol must continue. Though it leaves little time for the hunt." Koorsboom rasped. "The morning hence, at the ready. Ever taut."

"Ever stalwart." Mitseeri joined in. His twitter faded into the depth of night, consumed by the razzing of katydids and the call of nightjars.

Far off, the distant echo of a thunderclap. The calls of insect and bird alike ceased at once.

Within seconds, the incessant din of night shrieks and warbles resumed, the nocturnal conversation of the wild never interrupted for long.

Chapter 35

Dawn and the erupting sunrise had already taken the savanna before the wolves aroused from the severity of their fatigue.

Branddoring was first awake, and she rolled onto her paws and stretched, her head and forepaws low, hind end arched into the air. Padding to Mitseeri, she tongued his muzzle.

"My *droom* was interrupted." He opened his hazel eyes to glimpse the tree canopy above.

"I am sorry, Mitseeri."

"Do not be—it was a dreadful one, visions bizarre and bloody." He stood with some effort. "Worst of all—unavoidable." He returned her gesture.

"Will you join us in the hunt?" Her voice rose, tail wagged, jaw agape and eager for the day to come.

"I thank you for the invitation." He looked toward the den hole. "Security of the den, however, shall be my devotion."

The rest of the wolves aroused, and with their frantic twittering and yelping, the hunting rally commenced. Kamassi and Besembossie brushed past one another, leaping on and running around one, then the other, and Branddoring joined in, effusive licking and lapping of muzzles as one wolf greeted the next. Bonds reaffirmed, the *Gambiet* prepared to strike the savanna before them.

"Where shall the hunt take us?" Branddoring chirped, scampering before the rest.

Koorsboom hesitated at the edge of the grove.

The way forward, I know not.

***

Bu bu bu bu bu bu

A descending bubbly call broke the silence of the thicket, falling, then rising in cadence. A robust bird stalked the ground, just under half a meter in height, negotiating the dense brush. The White-browed coucal glanced about, its peering blood-red eyes seeking prey in the foliage. Rufous wings were marked by conspicuous cream streaks along the feathers closer to the head, the streaks resembling thorns across its nape and mantle. A broad tail was held high in the air, clawed talons striking the earth as it clambered off the ground and into brush. Stabbing a black bill behind a bushwillow leaf, it found a small lizard. Taking flight, the heavy Coucal seemed as gainly as a garbage truck, but took to the air nonetheless.

"We press on." Koorsboom set his jaw. He plunged through the *Combretum* shrub, just missing the Coucal as it departed. The three yearlings followed closely.

A tireless lope began for the Painted wolves. Their slender, splendid forms bounced from step to step, efficient in motion and time. Panting only slightly, their bodies had no difficulty with the hot climate. They passed an old termite mound, its sides hard as concrete. It was extinct for the past few seasons, its architects dead, their offspring departed to create other citadels on the savanna. One side of the mound was broken, a common corkwood having grown from a sapling to a mature tree with thick grey bark. Its trunk jutted from the periphery of the termite castle, clusters of green leaves on short branches giving some shade to the land beneath. To one side of the corkwood, the land sloped down into a yawning hole in the earth.

"Another den?" Besembossie broke her lope, drifting from their course to examine this new finding. She sniffed the opening, sensing it led to a chamber below.

"Aardvark hole." Koorsboom barely paused. "They dig them every-where."

Besembossie snuffed, rejoining the patrol.

"We use them, however, for our dens?" Branddoring twittered.

"We are not the only ones who adapt to their expert digging." He gave a nod. "Ever be on the lookout for such places. They can be a sanctuary when need be."

"When would we need a hole?" Kamassi wondered.

"Any thoughts?" He listened for the response.

"Lions?" Kamassi mused.

"Fire!" Branddoring howled.

"Those, and more." Koorsboom approved.

Their course took them across the veld as the sun reached its height. Even as the heat peaked upon the savanna, their pace did not flag.

"Tenacity." Branddoring twittered to her sisters. "That is what we see here."

"Obstinacy seems more like it." Kamassi laughed.

"Should we begin the arc back to the den?" Besembossie bayed to Koorsboom.

"No—we hunt until we kill. She needs the meat before we move the den." He did not turn to issue this directive, nor did he slow.

The four bounded across the veld, passing tangled sedge of bushwillow and towering Apple-leaf trees. Rolling up and down, sloping from one hill to the next, the uneven ground shielded them from the sight of enemies, but also concealed their prey. The land flashed past, rock outcroppings and dried gullies from long ago rains drawing their attention. Each wolf witnessed these features, cataloguing them in vast maps they crafted each day within their minds. Water courses and signs of predators deserved special notice, but ultimately each tree and stone had a place. Tracks of jackals were observed. Stored away were calls of songbirds that flitted across the grasses. Kilometer after kilometer passed beneath their paws, their relentless pace devoid of lassitude.

"Is that the same *koppie* that has greeted us in the past?" Branddoring twittered. She glanced up toward a solitary granite dome that towered over the surrounding veld. Its peak was bald, void of vegetation and gleaming in the sun.

"No, it is a different one." Koorsboom's voice was without tone.

Their path carried them across a road, ruts ground into the hard surface by heavy vehicles. Claws clattered across this and they disappeared again into the brush, thorn laden branches sweeping back into place as they passed.

They raced across ground that became wild and unmarked, fan palms waving with the wind. Eyes swept across the veld they traversed, searching for prey. Minds were focused upon their legacy, hidden in the den behind them.

In the distance, the sunlight reflected off a new feature. Besembossie was the first to spot it.

"Water!" Her twitter broke the quiet of their run, and when the rest agreed, their course centered upon it. They navigated a rockfall, down a dried run where past floods carved gullies in the landscape, now parched and sporting cracked mud plates. Paws left prints in soft soil, pads with claw tipped toe blots, pairs of them all the way to the waterhole.

"At the very least we are out of the reach of the humans in that village." Kamassi pealed.

"Perhaps within sight of another." Koorsboom cautioned. "We are never far from those creatures."

Their slender bodies powered across the veld toward the shimmering surface, silvered in the light.

"Prey is before us." Branddoring announced this with a muted twitter, but it sounded louder as the rest silenced, and dropped into hunting poise. Ears flattened against skulls, heads dropped, bodies crouched. Their pace slowed only slightly. Harsh breaths broke the calm.

"Pause here." Koorsboom physically blocked Kamassi and Branddoring from progressing.

"We shall take them." Kamassi eyed a large antelope standing near the pond. Grey fur covered his form, ribbed horns that curved back and up from his magnificent head announced the pride of his standing. "Their musk is apparent, even from here." She sniffed the air, the pungent scent pervading the air.

"Assurance is what we need." Koorsboom did not move another step in the direction of the waterhole. His head jerked slightly, indicating small figures in the trees above.

A black face, marked by sharp eyes and a white brow line, surveyed the area. Grizzled grey fur, long and coarse covered its body. A long dark-tipped tail hung beneath the vervet monkey, hands gripping the thin branches. Their alarm call was ever at the ready, custom fashioned for each different predator threat.

"That is problematic." Branddoring whispered.

"Indeed. We must allow no possibility for escape." Koorsboom eyed the veld beyond. "There are a few of them." More waterbuck appeared beyond the one first sighted. "The waterhole is large enough that crocodiles are possible."

"Waterbuck would flee into the water." Kamassi nodded, remembering a past encounter.

"Indeed. And considering this is waterbuck, I have little doubt this pond has been here for some time. Should we fail, they would stand within that pool, and wait forever for our departure." Koorsboom stopped his advance. The rest followed suit. He continued to watch the scene before him, ensconced in bushwillow shrub and shadow.

"Perhaps crocodiles are not present. If they were, would they not take the buck?" Branddoring wondered.

"Care to test that theory with your life?" Koorsboom smiled at her.

The waterbuck strode near the pond's edge. Short, rounded ears constantly flicked away insects beneath the curved, forward-swept horns. Shaggy grey fur occasionally rippled to ward off flies. There were at least three bulls established in this territory.

"They are young bulls. Look there—their length of horn." Koorsboom thought aloud.

The yearlings noted this, filing it away.

"Food abundance is limited." He surveyed the area, dried foliage in all directions away from the water source.

"That is obvious." Kamassi chuckled.

"Quite." Koorsboom regarded her. "With little food about, the herds tend to be small in size."

"We have one chance, then." Branddoring nodded. "They are clustered about that pond, and we must prevent them from dashing into it."

"And from their sentries noting our approach." Koorsboom eyed the vervet monkeys in the trees.

"Cover." Branddoring took a step forward. "Just there."

She indicated a rock formation adjacent to a bushwillow thicket. It would provide ample cover for their approach.

"A formidable hunter you have become." Koorsboom bumped against her.

* * *

Razzing of insects were the only sound of the day. Burning sun baked the rocks that surrounded the pool. The vervet monkeys lazed at the base of the small Governor's plum tree that stood near the waterhole. A few of their troop clung to branches above, reluctant to forage in the heat. One browsed the foliage of a bee sting bush, careful to avoid the thorns.

A waterbuck grazed further from the waterhole, having wandered from the more close-cropped grass that grew near the water's edge, preferring the lusher growth elsewhere. Gripping a shock of grass within its teeth, this was ripped free and chewed between powerful molars into a coarse paste. Eventually this was swallowed, later to be regurgitated for more chewing. The digestion of grass was a long-term process.

Arka arka arka arka

The chatter of a single vervet monkey broke the quiet of the early afternoon, soon joined by a cacophony of more calls from the troop. Stillness abruptly turned to a continuous din, and the waterbuck lurched from its peaceful eating to look about.

Four slender figures shot across the grasses toward the buck from behind a rocky rise, each clad in gold, black, and white fur, armed with white knives unsheathed for the hunt. In a heartbeat, they had closed within striking distance.

The waterbuck began its bound, its hind hooves planted on slippery grass, leaping for the cool waters. So close, the scent of still waters filled its nostrils. This mixed with the scent of rust and cinnamon as blood filled its airway, the veld suddenly upended, the grass where the sky once was, and the pool forever beyond reach.

"Quickly now." Koorsboom glanced about after the kill, and saw no enemies around them, and no vultures above.

The musk of the hide and meat did not deter them, skin ripped aside and every shred of flesh taken from the ribs and limbs, the rump stripped bare. The intestines were spilled aside, the heart unrooted. Koorsboom pulled what he could from the lining of the stomach. Very little was left behind other than bone, hide, liver and entrails.

Gasping, Koorsboom called to the yearlings.

"We return triumphant. Another day." As one they headed for the den.

* * *

The granite *koppie* peak sparkled in the early evening, reflecting the setting sun.

"Is there another kill nearby?" Branddoring looked up into the sky as she ran, looking expectantly at Koorsboom.

His gaze followed hers, blinking against the sun's glare. He noticed the broad wingspan of a lappet-faced vulture soaring high over the rock.

"I suspect not." He watched for a moment, panting in the declining heat. "No, it is rising." They resumed their pace. "Vultures may circle a carcass, when they are landing. This one here is rising, so his search is underway."

"The forest is close." Besembossie sounded relieved. They bounded forth, sides bulging with meat for the hungry pups waiting. The sun began its inexorable descent, shadows from trees pushed toward the distant horizon that awaited night.

Besembossie halted, sniffing the air.

"What is it?" Kamassi stopped as well, her ears swiveling to listen for danger.

"An odd scent reached me. Something that reminds one of that village." Besembossie's ears flattened against her skull as she uttered this, and she crouched low.

"We make for the den." Koorsboom twittered quietly. "Stay low, move with all haste."

The yearlings sprinted off, followed closely by Koorsboom. He paused in his run for a moment as he caught a strange smell in the air, which he recognized as the dank odor of human sweat.

His tail low, he was right behind the rest of his pack. They melted into the dim light of the wood.

Within the hour, a human walked across their path. His eyes upon the horizon, scanning the edge of each ridge, he trudged steadily. One step after the other. A rifle leaned on his shoulder, bouncing against his collarbone as he marched.

* * *

Koorsboom joined the panting yearlings at the den opening, where Olienhout awaited them. Once it held a porcupine. Now it held the love of his life, his pups, and his world entire. He stepped to her and they lapped one another's muzzles tenderly.

The meat of the hunt was shared with Olienhout, and they rested in the approaching cool of evening. Mitseeri emerged from the shadows to join them.

"There were no threats here." His cheerful chirp was a rasp of dehydration and fatigue.

Koorsboom brought up the bulk of the meat from the waterbuck kill.

Mitseeri merely bowed, and left eating nothing.

Olienhout glanced his way and consumed the lot, leaving nothing but a slight stain on the ground.

"Fretful are my thoughts about him." Olienhout watched as the white tip of his tail vanished in the dark.

"We all have reason to be concerned." Koorsboom whined.

Whir-whrrr-whhhrrrrr! The Fiery-necked nightjar called out.

"I sense the humans are on patrols of their own." Koorsboom lay down by the den opening.

"Their foul scent reached me on our return." Besembossie nodded.

Olienhout nodded. "You have done well, young ones." She looked to the rest. "You have all done well to provide under the burden of the village." She returned to the den, the white of her tail receding into the hole.

"Now we rest." Branddoring closed her eyes.

"Now you rest." Koorsboom lay down on the ground, though his head remained off the ground, ears twitching as they listened for the slightest extraneous noise above the calls of bird and insect.

Mitseeri returned from the darkness and lay down near the den, opposite from Koorsboom.

"Our vigil is unending." The old wolf turned to glance at him before resuming his survey of the wood.

Koorsboom nodded his agreement.

"Unto death."

Chapter 36

Gnaw gnaw gnaw

The fibrous ripping sounds seemed to open the dawn, so still was the morning. Pausing for a moment, the porcupine waited to listen for threats before continuing to strip away the bark of a young sapling tree in a clearing. Sharp teeth made short work of this, exposing the nutritious inner bark which was pried away.

A scent of dog in the air stopped its work, but only for a moment. The enormous rodent was on all four feet, back end carefully aimed at the source of the smell. The wolves bounded closer from thick brush, and halted when they sighted the porcupine.

Kamassi took one look down the quills, sharp as hypodermic needles, and backed away.

The porcupine stamped its feet, shaking its body, vibrating those quills in an unsettling rattle that made Kamassi retreat with greater speed. The porcupine held off in dashing backward with a deadly ram attack, content that its enemy had moved a safe distance away. With one more glance to the rear, it continued its work on ring-barking the small tree.

"Beyond your ability, young one?" Mitseeri smiled on the wolf.

"You hunt these?"

"Lions." He glanced at the hind end of the porcupine. "Lions cannot hunt these creatures. Any who do so can die upon their piercing attack." He prodded her with his snout.

"Quite right." Koorsboom crept up on them with little warning.

"If only we had such armaments." Branddoring beamed, imagining a back filled with quills.

"It makes mating considerably more difficult." Mitseeri chuckled.

They watched the porcupine work at a distance.

"Imagine. Eating plants, trees." Koorsboom mused.

"Elephants go further—before eating, they topple an entire tree, root and trunk, before consuming what they will." Mitseeri laughed. "It is fortunate we have no sightings of lions within our vantage here."

"Perhaps." Koorsboom glanced at the ground. "I am unsure how to give word to a thought."

"One word at a time."

"The lack of enemies here does not assuage me." Koorsboom paused. "A nemesis can be avoided, or even killed."

"I see." Mitseeri considered this.

"I sense a malevolence here that cannot be escaped." Koorsboom held his head up in the air, eyes closed, scenting the air.

"Humans." He nodded. "They never seem to be far away, no matter how far into the wild one lives."

"Something else." Gnats buzzed about Koorsboom's face, flicked aside with a shake of the head. "The wind. Claw through it, and it whips around you. Howl into the storm, and it sweeps past you, rendering your futile protests impotent and lost."

"Branddoring tells me you chose this place with intent."

"There is no running from them. Whether here, or another land, we must face them, and understand them." Koorsboom stared beyond the clearing. "A reckoning is imminent. For our kind." He swallowed hard. "For all kind."

Mitseeri attempted to lap Koorsboom's muzzle to reassure him, but the younger wolf may as well have been a statue.

Kamassi sniffed the air, prodding Koorsboom with her forepaw.

"Our patrol must begin with this dawn." Koorsboom shook his head, and lapped her muzzle tenderly.

"So it must." Mitseeri glanced through the treetops above, the zebra-wood offering a golden glow through their arbor. "As mine shall."

"There is no need for you to patrol."

"Are you certain?" Mitseeri sounded downcast.

"I worry." Koorsboom glanced at him.

"That I may bring attention on the den?"

Koorsboom could only look down, unable to voice his thoughts.

"Understood. I shall return to Olienhout." He took his leave with a bow. Turning with a few halting steps, Mitseeri hobbled away toward the den hole. His faded coat melted into the shade of the wood.

"He may be able to help." Kamassi muttered to him. "Despite his injuries."

"I worry that his yearning to aid the Pack is heedless." Koorsboom stared after his departure. "We ask too much of him."

* * *

In the shade of a corkwood tree, yellow eyes glared out at the surrounds. Golden fur marked with a regular pattern of black spots broke up its appearance in the dappled shade. The cheetah sat on his haunches, chest and abdomen heaving deep breaths. Jaws were open wide, gasping, exhausted from his run. As he panted in the heat, he looked down at the dead impala, sprawled on the ground, lifeless, head twisted into an unnatural direction. Blood covered the throat of the ram from the killing bite. Dragged into the shade, the corpse was hidden from the sharp vision of vultures above.

The cheetah paused its gulping of air to gnaw open the hide over the rump of the impala. In between deep breaths it took neat bites from the exposed muscle. Eventually he recovered his strength, and lay down next to the carcass. Powerful hind legs were drawn up beside the predator, and he began stripping away flesh from the rest of the rump before moving on to the rib cage and shoulders. Pulling open the abdomen, the liver and heart were eaten piece by gradual piece.

After eating his fill, the cheetah took his time, sides bulging. The predator lay on his side, digesting the best meal he had in weeks.

He rolled back onto his belly, ears pricked and listening with care. Twittering reached his ears, and he realized he was about to lose what little remained of the hunt.

"We should encounter him soon. The shredded bark from that tree we passed had his claw fragments embedded."

"Leopard or lion?" The excited chirp of Branddoring drew nearer.

"Neither. The tracks were tipped with claw marks. Only cheetah will leave those marks." Koorsboom's voice lowered.

The cheetah held his head lower, sensing he would need to run.

A ruff-bark confirmed his fears, and the cheetah locked eyes with Koorsboom. The other three wolves gathered behind him. A growl erupted among them.

Rising onto his paws, the cheetah slunk away, long tail rising in the air. His long, slender body weaved through the grasses, giving an inaudible hiss over his shoulder as he disappeared from sight.

"Leave nothing behind." The wolves dismembered the carcass, tearing away every fragment of meat.

* * *

In the midafternoon, four pairs of ears bounced just above the grass tips as the wolves bounded across the grasses under the granite *koppie*. The Lappet-faced vulture looked down upon them, studying their movements. Guessing they were returning from a hunt, the raptor spread its wings and took to the air in search of the remains.

"The meager bounty of the day will not sustain the pups." Besembossie mused. "We will need a sizable kill tomorrow or their hunger will worsen."

"So much effort is needed to feed another generation of hunters."

Kamassi shook her head.

"Imagine when they are weaned, and on return to the den they are expecting meat." Koorsboom laughed.

When the shot rang through the air, at first they did not realize what had happened. The yelp from Branddoring removed all doubt.

She fell to her side with a whine. The others stooped low, breathing rapidly. Ears folded flat against their skulls, hearts pounding.

Branddoring rolled onto her belly, shaking her head. Her eyes were wide with disbelief, and she craned her head around to look for the source of her pain.

"You are wounded." Koorsboom placed a forepaw on her back, and examined a furrow dug into her hide, piercing the flesh beneath. Her licked the wound, unsure of whether cleaning it with his tongue helped. It usually did.

"The thunder did this." Besembossie peered at the narrow and shallow laceration as blood began to well in its base. She glanced all around and saw no humans nearby.

"They must be coming from the village." Koorsboom did not stand, his ears still flat. "Everyone remain low." He lapped at her wound again, clearing clotted blood, noting the flow was ceasing. "Branddoring, when you are ready, we must make for the den."

She did not speak, only panting rapidly, eyes still wide and fearful. The rest of her fur remained pristine, swirls of gold and black throughout with sparking white spots on her side and flank.

"I am ready." Branddoring calmed herself, slowing her breathing, closing her hazel eyes and opening them again with a nod.

"The three of you will take a longer route. I shall expose myself to this creature. Stay low." Koorsboom growled. "Ready, my *Gambiet?*" Koorsboom growled, and closed his eyes for a moment.

If my judgment is wrong, forgive me, my love.

The rest crouched, paws planted firmly on the ground, tendons tight as bows strung for the hunt.

"Mark."

The three yearlings bounded off, ears flat, bodies low, keeping to lower elevations. Koorsboom took the other direction, from where the shot came.

He accelerated to a sprint faster than any car, his lean body worked to its full ability. The color of their fur made them difficult to spot, and at speed impossible to hit.

A shot rang out. Another.

The high whine of the bullets was above him, the sound strangely inconsequential, despite their deadly potential.

Another staccato crack, and a *whump* caused a clump of ground near him to jump in the air.

He crossed the field at a blinding pace. He looked to one side to see white tipped tails between grass clumps, barely visible, reaching the edge of the zebrawood.

Koorsboom soon reached the forest, weaving past the gnarled roots of their trunks.

He turned to look back, and spied a standing figure on the plain. Tall, straight as one of their fence posts, and unmoving. Dressed in dark clothing and a long-sleeved jacket, he was visible between the closer wavering stalks of grass still waving in the wind. Shading his eyes with a hand, he looked straight at Koorsboom.

The wolf knew how small the zebrawood grove was, and how long it would take the humans to search it.

"Bliksem."

***

Mitseeri knew there was trouble when Koorsboom dove into the denning hole nearly at a run. Kamassi and Besembossie padded about the entrance consumed with anxiety. The old wolf choked when he saw Branddoring return with a limp.

"What ever is wrong, my *kind*?" He lapped her muzzle.

"We must be on the move." She returned his gesture, wincing slightly.

"That wound is from one of them." A growl erupted in his throat as he glanced at her back.

"No matter—the pain subsides even as we speak." She bent low to regurgitate the small measure of meat consumed from the carcass taken from the cheetah.

Mitseeri stared at the meat offered to him, lying on the ground. His stomach gurgled, but he did not bend down to accept it. He glanced at the furrow on her back, the blood now a dark maroon color as it dried.

Koorsboom backed out of the den as Olienhout exploded from the opening. He padded to keep up with her as she reached the rest of the pack.

"You have been sighted too close to the den. There is no doubt, the time has come to move." Olienhout's voice was curt, and she did not bother with the usual greetings after a hunt. "We face an arduous *trek*. A danger against which the pups are not fortified."

"There must be a way." Branddoring yelped.

"Haste is our only hope."

Branddoring gave a nod in assent. Mitseeri indicated the meat he left for her on the ground. With reluctance, she consumed it all.

Olienhout ducked into the den, her hind end still outside, white tipped tail in the air like an exclamation point. She issued a deep whine, a low call that reverberated beneath them.

Following this was a sudden eruption of slight whines and whimpers from the earth. Thumping, padding, and more whimpers from below. Olienhout reversed out from the den, shaking dirt from her head and rounded ears. Striding forward, head held high, she was followed by eight rotund scampering bodies.

Each was clad in black and white fur, the gold that would eventually come with age yet to accent their hair. Each face was set with a pug frown, rounded ears erect and listening. Hazel eyes blinked open and shut, burning at the sudden flood of light from the world above. Each pup took short, halting steps forward, backward, unsure where to go.

Kamassi pounced on one of them, lavishing a licking tongue to clean off its sides and belly, effusive at finally being able to greet the pups from the den.

Besembossie and Branddoring readied themselves to take hold of their beloved pups as well when they were deterred by a growl from Olienhout.

"Stop—there is no time to spare." She glared at the pack. "We make for the edge of the wood." Olienhout looked up at the dimming sky. "This could not have come at a worse time."

She nosed the pups forward, her snout pushing each into staggering short steps. The young wolves whined, glancing about them. One after another reached for a teat, extending their snout upwards, some able to suckle for a moment before she moved forward.

"Very well, then, you greedy wolves." Olienhout smiled in spite of the danger. "Follow your meal." She walked forward, slowly at first, looking back to make sure her young were close behind.

One fat pup began to wander off, sniffing the ground near a discarded bone from an impala leg. Koorsboom prodded the pup to return to the forward movement of the *Gambiet*.

"It is just as well they have not been weaned." Besembossie mused.

"They have not been taken on runs." Olienhout sighed. "My mother took us on short jaunts once we left our den. Longer, then longer still. Eventually we were able to keep up with the adults as we drifted from hunt to hunt. So long ago, along the great river."

"I was born near that river as well." Koorsboom spoke quietly, almost to himself. "Before my pack, the *Dwalen*, embarked upon our great *trek*."

"The home range of my pack bordered yours." She chuckled. "I believe the hunters of our packs encountered one another. Once."

"Did your pack undertake a *trek* as well?" Besembossie wondered.

"No. We remained by the great river, though one day we were all struck with sleep, and some of us awoke in another world entirely."

"Our new world." Koorsboom was familiar with this story. "The end of our *trek*."

"Strange, our journey has been." Olienhout nosed a pup forward, and it stumbled on its short legs.

"As was ours. Across the thirstlands, through the dangers of farms, and escaping the claws of human capture. And finally, into the wild again." Koorsboom nudged two pups that stopped to playfight with each other. "How most of us survived it all defies belief."

Olienhout nodded. "I remember the tales." She looked down, herding one of the pups away from a particularly interesting leaf. "The threats you faced is a testament to your mother's cunning. Aalwyn is a force beyond any wolf alive."

Koorsboom smiled at her name. "She led us through dangers that would have destroyed entire packs."

"We must survive, and so must her pups." Olienhout nosed another little wolf forward that had stopped to sniff at a beetle. "Else her history, her prowess, her expertise dies with us." She glanced up through the branches of zebrawood as they wavered in the winds moving through the treetops.

"The wisdom of Aalwyn...Blackthorn...and now you...has been hard won. This is owed to the wolves long dead before our time. And those to come." Koorsboom smiled.

"Generations shall know her story."

"As they will yours." Koorsboom lapped her muzzle.

Olienhout did not lap his in kind. She stared at the path ahead, concentrating.

"They are not ready for the daylight." Kamassi looked around at pups as they stumbled. "They are so much smaller than I expected."

"They usually stay below ground until they are ready, and strong enough to move quickly when needed." Olienhout said flatly. "Should we encounter a jackal or hyena, even a single survivor would be a gift."

This hushed them all. A cracking ahead in the brush at the base of one tree caused Kamassi to jump, until they noticed Mitseeri limping toward them.

"No dangers before us, should our course not alter." His usually higher pitched voice was lower, on the verge of a rasp. "You wish to keep this passage short?"

"Within reason." She set her jaw grimly. "Shorter journey, the more likely it is the humans will entrap us. Longer, and we expose our *kinders* to hyenas or eagles."

Koorsboom looked up in terror. He had not considered an airborne attack. Remembering the size of martial eagles and harrier hawks, he bared his teeth, and his glances went from the pups to the sky and back.

"We happened upon aardvark dens during our patrols, Olienhout." Mitseeri tripped on a tree root and bumbled onto the ground. Alighting on his feet with effort, he continued. "Near an acacia thicket far beyond the *koppie.*"

"The one lorded over by that lappet-faced vulture?" Olienhout considered this. "A long enough way, I would think."

"Open skies, however." Koorsboom surveyed the air around them.

"That will do." Olienhout nodded.

"Are you certain, my love?" Koorsboom whined gently. He was consumed by visions of each pup being plucked into the clouds, speared on sharp talons.

"A peril that we can understand, to evade a peril we cannot."

At the edge of the wood they paused, facing east.

Eight rotund pups mewled as they stood in the shadows of the wolves around them. They gaped at the improbably titanic world that unfurled before them.

Distant echoes reached them, a rifle shot reverberating off tree and rock.

"*Trek voort.*"

* * *

Every rock was a near insurmountable obstacle that the pups struggled to climb. Each shock of grass was a jungle they got lost within. Short legs battled foliage that seemed designed to tug on them, weigh them down, hold them back. One pup stumbled into a thorn, nearly the length of its head, and the prick caused it to emit a sharp yelp. Herded back together, the eight kept wandering, separating, drifting between sticks and boulders.

It took the labors of the entire pack to keep them moving vaguely in the same direction.

And the sun did not slow for them.

A shadow caused Olienhout to unleash a deep growl, and the pups romped to her side, running headlong into her legs, or overshooting the mark and scooting back underneath her hanging belly.

The shadow passed over them, and continued onward.

"The vulture." She peered into the sky and could easily make out the broad wingspan of the Lappet-faced vulture that had left the *koppie* to investigate.

"Press on." She strolled forward, and the work of keeping the pups as close as possible resumed.

Stumbling over a gully, the pups tumbled into the now dry channel, and clambered up the other side.

"Keep clear of those boulders." Olienhout ruff-barked to Besembossie in the lead. "Puff adders may shelter near the rock."

Besembossie nodded, and stepped away from the stones leading up to a rock outcropping, and instead led the pack around through grasses.

Koorsboom glanced west, over his shoulder, to the broad orange curtain flaring on the horizon.

"We are not close to the new den." Mitseeri grumbled.

"Nor would we want to be." Olienhout twittered. She nosed the pups close together into another rain gully, broad enough for them to huddle together in the night. "We want as much distance as the veld will allow from those creatures."

The others clustered around the pups, with Olienhout in the center, laying in the depression with the pups. They slumped next to her to suckle, half of them falling asleep mid-feeding with exhaustion.

"Remarkable how far you brought them." Mitseeri smiled at Olienhout.

"Any task becomes easier when one is forced." She returned his smile, white teeth glinting in the twilight.

As the sun descended, the darkness crashed down upon the bushveld. So far from any urban centers, the blackness of night was near absolute without moonlight. Katydids began to razz, followed by the call of nightjars.

Mitseeri lay down further from the others. He winced as he reclined on his side.

"Are you injured?" Branddoring lapped his muzzle, finding him by scent.

"Only with age, young one." Mitseeri lapped her muzzle as well. "Sleep well."

"Why are you not closer to us?" She glanced back toward the pack, a stone's throw away.

"Are you certain you wish to know?"

"I am."

"Should a hyena or a lion creep upon us in the blackness, I shall be the first one they find."

"You can fight one off on your own?" Branddoring wondered.

Mitseeri did not answer. As the rising calls of the birds and insects created a curtain of noise, he lapped her muzzle once more.

"Sleep, while you are able. Should there be trouble, I shall call you to give the killing bite."

She prodded him with her snout before returning to Olienhout's side. Sleep came quickly to them all, but was interrupted time and again.

A nearby crack of brush.

An abrupt pause in the calls of cricket and katydid.

Soft calls from a scops owl, *krrrupp krrrupp krrrupp*.

The pack was aroused with each disturbance, but they gradually settled as these sounds continued well into the night.

Chapter 37

The rifle shot awakened them all at once, each wolf upon their paws, bodies low to the ground, ears flat. Echoing in fading crashes across the veld, the report faded into the silence as dawn crept onto the savanna.

"That was not far off." Olienhout remained crouched, slowly standing to her full height to survey the horizon.

"From whence we came." Mitseeri pronounced. He stared west, in the direction of the zebrawood grove.

"Not everyone was alarmed by that disturbance." Besembossie looked into the gully, smiling widely with her canines bared.

The eight pups remained fast asleep, snoring gently.

"*Ag, shame.*" Olienhout sighed. "If they were not so precious when awake, I would never arouse them from such a peaceful slumber."

With reluctance, she nosed each plump body, until with much whining they awoke and swiftly found a teat to suckle.

A rustling in the bushes nearby alerted them that Kamassi was on the hunt, and she promptly returned with a dead scrub hare. This dropped on Olienhout's forepaws, and the meat was quickly devoured.

The adults were on their feet, stomachs rumbling, snouts propelling the pups back onto their tiny paws. After surmounting the edge of the gully, the tiny wolves were herded together and moved further east.

"The aardvark hole is just there." Mitseeri indicated the savanna ahead.

"We know what you mean by 'just there'." Branddoring bumped against him. "A day? Or two perhaps?"

"But it is just—" Mitseeri finally caught on. "Very well, young wolf."

She opened her jaws and clamped down lightly on his snout, and he snuffed this away. She rose on hind legs to flail her forepaws boxing him. He was unable to stand on his hind leg, merely waving a forepaw back at her.

"Enough of that, you idle jackal." He managed to catch an attempt to bat his head and she fell to the ground. Lapping her muzzle, he indicated the trail ahead with a nod.

"The *Gambiet* needs you." His kind features became hardened as he regarded Branddoring.

She gave him a quizzical look before regaining her paws and trotting ahead to help recapture a pup that had become tangled in a thornbush. The trunk of the sickle bush sported branches that bore double compound leaves, each 'leaf' composed of many branches filled with hundreds of tiny green leaves, angled to catch the morning light. Branddoring thrust her snout through the curtain of leaflets and gripped the pup in her jaws, on the hip. The pup's feet waved in the air.

Deposited back on the earth, the little wolf resigned itself to trotting forward with mother.

"We should reach the aardvark den after the high of the day." Mitseeri regarded the rising sun, then the stumbling pups. "With good fortune."

The sun continued its rise, the heat gathering on the veld in sunbaked rocks and sands. Grass eagerly took up the rays, and each bush and flowering plant basked, storing resources for the coming season for seed and flower.

Winds stirred the grass tips, bringing a slight chill to the air.

Olienhout froze.

The rest followed suit, except the pups who continued to bump into rocks and plants that lay in their path.

"Smoke."

The rest sniffed the air.

"The smoke that moves." Olienhout spoke this as a half-whisper, and hunched down.

Koorsboom suddenly realized what this meant.

"Down, everyone." He crept ahead, herding the pups toward a larger clump of sickle bush. Kamassi and Besembossie helped, snouts corralling them toward safety.

Olienhout scanned the horizon that lay behind them, and bounded away from the rest of the pack.

"Strange, the acrid nature of that burning." Mitseeri loped beside her. "And the way they carry it in their mouths."

She remained silent. The two wolves stopped moving, watching the horizon, their large ears listening with the greatest care.

Further on the savanna, they watched a distant figure, walking upright. Two figures.

One appeared to have a glowing mouth for a moment as they took a drag on their cigarette. A third figure joined them from behind a tree. This one seemed to point at the ground, here and there, indicating a track.

They moved toward the wolves steadily.

Every member of the *Gambiet* held their breath. The pups mewling rose further and further above the quiet.

"I appreciate the way your pack has cared for me." Mitseeri balanced on his three legs as his weight shifted. "I was close to the end when we met."

Olienhout shared a glance with him.

"My ability to hunt was failing. Unable to run, unable to ambush. Carrion kept me alive as often as not." He inhaled the air, and nodded. "And then there was you." He lapped her muzzle.

"My hunters provide for the Pack." Olienhout touched noses with him. "And that you are."

He smiled to himself. "Indeed. There is only the Pack."

Across the veld, they watched the humans draw closer.

"They are clearly on our path." Mitseeri grunted.

"Staring into the rising sun." She stated this hopefully.

He glanced back with a doubtful shake of his head.

Olienhout looked over her shoulder at the wolves gathering in the brush.

"Then I am off." He leapt forth into a gully beneath a rock formation, and began to lope back toward the zebrawood. Within this depression, he could escape being seen by the men hunting them for dozens of meters. This depression grew shallower further on, and would no longer provide cover.

"Are you certain of this?" Olienhout ruff-barked to him.

"I can draw away their interest." He gave a smile, revealing white knives and black gingiva.

"Meet us at the aardvark den. You know where we are bound." She twittered to him urgently.

He closed his eyes for a moment, and took a deep breath. "I do." With a bow, he turned and left along the gully.

Olienhout watched him leave, loping with an awkward lurch.

"When my life depends upon it, I can only hope that I have your courage, my *vriend*." She turned to rejoin the *Gambiet*, as they weaved through the sickle bush and acacia shrub.

* * *

Mitseeri kept his nose in the air, scenting the enemy. The sharp odor of the cigarette came and went, varying with the wind, along with human sweat, and a sinister undercurrent of anger.

"You risk far too much."

He spasmed with terror at the sound before he calmed.

"Have you taken the paws of a lion?" Mitseeri turned.

Branddoring glared at him.

Mitseeri shook his head and turned back toward the grass veld. He stood next to an acacia tree, half hidden in shade. Rocks and termitaria dotted the savanna along with trees that could tolerate the arid environment. The roll of the land rose and fell.

"I am uncertain where the humans are. Now, at this time." Mitseeri continued to stare at everything, and nothing. "This vista is unrevealing. They could be behind us." He looked over at her.

"Come back to the *Gambiet.*"

"Return to your matriarch." Mitseeri shifted his gaze to the ground. "She will require your skills to bring those pups to age."

"She requires yours as well."

"And she has them." Mitseeri looked her in the eye.

"Come back to me."

Mitseeri turned again to see Branddoring, eyes wet and wide, searching for a way to convince him.

"I am fond of you as well, young wolf. I had hoped for more time to teach you the ways of the hunt." He touched noses with her. "Alas, the veld has its own sense of time. There is a reason they had come so close, despite our fleeing in the night." He grimaced. "We are not the only creatures who track their prey."

"You are hoping they track you." Branddoring uttered this as a gasp.

"I will ensure they do."

"How will you outrun them?" She batted his head with a forepaw.

"*'n Wildehond maak 'n plan.*" Mitseeri gave her a smile. "When without."

"You recall where the aardvark den lies?" Branddoring looked to him longingly.

"I do." He angled his snout into the air. Nostrils flared.

Cigarette smoke wafted their way.

"I shall undertake my last great *trek.*" Mitseeri gave a faint smile.

The young wolf stared at him, unable to think of an argument against this.

"Conceal yourself, fair Branddoring. Long after I lead them away." He loped off from under the shade of the acacia tree in the direction of the scent. His clawed paws left prints clearly in the dust.

Before he departed, he turned again.

"Thank your hunters for giving me this time above earth."

With a last flash of his teeth, he disappeared into the veld to the west.

* * *

The sun had crossed the sky, and had begun to set the west on fire. Hours had passed, and fatigue had set in.

The cigarette was reduced to the filter, dropped to the ground to continue smoldering. In the shade of the zebrawood, three men stalked around the clearing. They were out of breath from stalking a wild dog that had crossed their path. It was injured, but no less able to outrun them. The tracks were easily followed, four toes tipped with claw marks over a triangular pad. Inexperienced with this predator and its tracks, they could not tell a pack from a rogue, and so they assumed it was alone.

Within the zebrawood grove they found prints all around a denning hole, rank with wolf musk. Several bones were within sight, gnawed free of any flesh, along with lengths of hide and other remains of hunting. No doubt, they had found its home.

The humans muttered to one another, rough hands indicating the spoor of the wandering wolf all over the clearing.

One man got down on his knees to peer into the dark hole of the den. His nose wrinkled with the stink of wet dog. He stood again, nodding to the others.

As they debated whether to fetch a pickaxe or gasoline, a rising growl silenced them.

Gold, black, and white fur flashed from the hole, bounding forth on three legs as though he were a Painted wolf in his prime. With a snarl he charged off in the direction of the village.

All three men opened fire with their rifles.

One bullet whined into the air, a panicked shot discharged in terror. Another shot, also blasted in a paroxysm of fear, slashed through a man's knee, leaving him on the ground writhing in agony.

The last bullet struck Mitseeri on his side, going through one lung, then the other, before embedding in a rib. He stumbled and fell, his jaw grinding to a halt on the dust, gasping as his chest filled with blood. A cough, and his limbs spasmed. He looked up through the branches of the zebrawood.

This forest, his last home, and his last happiness. He thought of Olienhout and Koorsboom, hoping they escaped the reaving humans and their weapons. Wondering if they will survive this time, he recalled it did not matter.

There is only this day. And the hope that one finds a way to endure to the next.

His last thoughts he left for Branddoring, and a final run with the young wolf through endless grass fields, until they both collapsed, exhausted, together, always, laying close to the body of a fellow wolf. Lapping one another's muzzles, they slipped off to a sleep well earned, within the honor of the Pack.

* * *

"We are fortunate no aardvark was here." Koorsboom peered around the den, deep within the cool earth.

"With our occupation, none will return." Olienhout called to the pups, who sniffed around at the opening before tumbling down the meter long entryway. Each of the eight pups settled next to her abdomen and began to suckle.

Koorsboom sighed and began to ascend back to the world above.

"He will not be returning to us." Olienhout spoke this with reluctance.

Koorsboom stopped. After several deep breaths, he left. Darkness had taken the bushveld.

The rest of the *Gambiet* rested on the gravel-strewn earth outside the aardvark hole. Koorsboom padded over to Branddoring and tenderly lapped her muzzle. She continued to watch the blackness to the west. Eventually she gave a whine and was on her paws.

Kamassi got up to bring her back.

"Let her go." Koorsboom bid Kamassi to lay down where she was.

Branddoring stopped several paces away from the den. She lowered her muzzle to the ground and released several hoo-calls into the ground. The low, plaintive sound echoed across the savanna for kilometers, the hail reaching far across their world.

Branddoring continued the hoo-calls, summoning a treasured member back to the Pack, long into the night and the days after.

Chapter 38

A buttonquail hopped through short grasses browsing for insects and seeds, calling to its mate with a deep *hroom* call. A rustle in the grasses caused it to freeze for a moment, angling its head in search of the disturbance. The footfalls of the wolves compelled it to rush into the tussocks, its speckled brown and fawn plumage melting into the foliage. A paw landed where it had been standing a minute before, and was lifted out of view. The quail had no need to move, instinctively knowing it was invisible, and any hunt for it would be a waste of time.

"Further from the village, I am hopeful that the antelope will not have been annihilated." Koorsboom kept his gaze high as they bounded across the undulating grass plain.

"Unless another village nearby has done the same." Kamassi grumbled.

"Be not cynical, young one." Koorsboom stopped his pace, and the yearlings followed suit. "So much can hinder our chances, in this most unpredictable of places. From the exotic machinations of humans, to the mundane warthog holes that can shatter a foreleg on the run." He closed his eyes and brushed aside her snout. "Cynicism can cause one to lose sight of the joy and wonder of the world."

Branddoring emitted a sharp whine.

Koorsboom was quick to lap her muzzle to comfort her. She did not return the gesture.

"You are so young to learn about death." He prodded her with a wet nose. "It comes for us all in time, and follows no prospects we fashion."

"He still may be out there."

Koorsboom smiled at her.

"Mitseeri gave all for the pups, for the Pack. And for the *Gambiet* we shall sustain."

Branddoring could only whine gently, glancing back over her shoulder.

"He would have joined us if he were able." Koorsboom opened his jaws and closed them gently on her snout. "In the teaching he imparted you... he already has joined us."

Branddoring gazed at him, hazel eyes torn with sorrow.

"Do not keep the pups waiting." He bounded off, with Kamassi and Besembossie in tow. After a moment, Branddoring looked over her shoulder once again, resisting the urge to hoo-call into the ground. She turned and rejoined Koorsboom in their tireless lope.

* * *

"Besembossie—the point is yours." Koorsboom bowed.

The yearling padded forth, her hazel eyes peering across the veld. The uneven grounds flattened here, ideal coursing land. The wolves could feel the hunt coming. Kamassi, Koorsboom and Branddoring followed.

Padding from the *miombo* wood to an open savanna, dotted with the infrequent acacia tree, Besembossie found few hoof prints on the loose dirt. Knots of dried grass stood defiantly in the dry soil, as though a pantomime of vibrant life. They briskly made their way across the plain, the desiccated stalks towered over by tall *kniphofia* flowers. Called 'red-hot pokers', these were topped with a vivid red orange over yellow bloom, and caught her eye as little else did.

Besembossie took her eyes from the sharply colored flowers as they rounded a rocky outcropping to face a sable antelope. Standing as tall as a man at the shoulder, the stark black of its coat contrasted with the gentle brown of the surrounding oatgrass. Its white face was split down the center with a stripe of black, two ribbed horns curved up and over for a length as great as most of its height. The sable stood still as it regarded the wolves it faced.

Besembossie's ears folded back, and the rest did the same. Muscles rippled beneath wiry fur, but none present moved. The sable weighed running or charging, and unable to decide, it remained fixed to the spot. Its life, up until this moment in time, was forgotten, as was the adult bull's herd and calves.

Besembossie sprang toward the antelope, teeth bared, and her silent assault startled the bull more than any sound could. In a panic, it turned to flee, and quickly accelerated to match the pace of the wolves.

Kamassi raced forward to attempt a quick end to the chase. The antelope banked around a rise adorned with acacia brush. The wolves followed closely around to find ten other sable antelopes, cows and calves.

"Take the calf on the ground!" Besembossie released an excited twitter, and their path broke away from the black bull.

The rest of the herd turned tail and ran, but the calf on the ground did not. It lay, reddish-brown fur blending somewhat with the yellowish-brown of oatgrass. As the wolves bore down upon the calf, it began to struggle onto its feet. Lame from birth, it barely got onto its hooves before Kamassi swung round to grip the snout. The calf planted itself back down, resigned to its fate. Staring into the middle distance, it reacted little as Koorsboom ripped open the abdomen. The dead calf was dismembered quickly amongst the four wolf hunters. Meat and offal were packed away with blinding speed, made all the quicker by the lean hunting and the needs of the pups.

They sprinted soundlessly back to the den, drenched in blood and bellies hanging low.

As the hunters approached the new den, Olienhout emerged from the aardvark hole. The pups quickly followed her out.

"It is time." Olienhout pronounced to the hunters.

Koorsboom understood, and halted on his paws before the pups. He bent his head down and let loose a torrent of blood and gore from the sable kill.

It splashed upon the ground before the pups, who at first did not seem to comprehend.

After a moment, the scent of meat seemed to intrigue the pups. Then it excited them beyond measure. One pup bounded forward, in its fervor tumbling forward in a roll, then into a heap before the offering of meat. She dove in and began to gulp down a piece of muscle. The other seven pups descended on this at once, yipping in a curtain of noise that ended upon impact with the food. Each hoovered up meat and organ as though milk had never existed on Earth.

Kamassi and Besembossie kneeled to provide their own bounty, and as more meat struck the ground, the pups found themselves in a wonderland eternal. Quiet hung over the meal as the pups gobbled down the meat, followed by sharp yips between mouthfuls. Two pups found a hunk of meat too large to scarf down, and they proceeded to tug against one another. As the tenderloin muscle was pulled in half, their hind ends smacked into the dirt. Both pups realized this was a skill that will pay off for years to come.

The feeding frenzy continued until the pups had consumed all they could, eventually wandering in a daze, unable to even move. The pups were round to the point of immobility, their bellies bulging and scraping the dirt below them. Falling to the side, they snored like full grown hyenas.

"*Ag, shame.*" Olienhout sighed.

"We may chance another hunt this evening." Koorsboom spoke quietly, as though he were capable of waking well-fed pups. "The grounds are far better than those near the village. The humans back there truly killed everything that did not fly."

"We shall see." Olienhout watched her litter sleep in peace.

"We took an awful chance at this place." He lapped her muzzle.

"Therefore, the *Gambiet.*" She returned his gesture, touching noses. "Was it worth it?"

"It is always worth the venture. Even in disaster, we have learned well, for the generations to come."

Branddoring lay further from the others, resting in the afternoon.

"Are you well, my sister?" Kamassi lay by her side, lavishing her with an attentive tongue.

She did not answer, staring at a distant Giraffe-thorn acacia, bristling with thorns.

Kamassi watched her, thinking better of the questions in her mind.

"That one requires a close eye." Kamassi indicated one of the pups on the move.

Branddoring turned to see.

A pup, sides rounded to where any stumble would send it rolling, trotted toward a broom cluster fig tree.

"Where is she off to, then?" Branddoring was on her paws and padding after the young wolf.

"Adventurous one." Kamassi was right behind her.

The broad, spreading canopy of the tree was festooned with large, oval, dark green leaves. The heavy trunk was anchored by aggressive roots that expanded into the earth, capacious and drilling through rock if necessary to reach water below.

The pup padded with confidence under the fig tree, scrabbling over an enormous white root toward a dark figure.

Branddoring dashed forward to meet the pup, placing a forepaw before the young wolf blocking her path.

Perched on a tall boulder of granite near the fig tree was a bird, over half a meter in height. Eyes black as marble set in a pale pink face regarded the pup that approached. A sharp beak lowered slightly in the direction of the young wolf. Blackish brown feathers with paler brown margins fluttered in the breeze.

"What is that?" Kamassi hissed.

Branddoring ushered the pup back under the fig tree, reassuring her that the raptor before them was not food.

The hooded vulture peered down at them without apparent emotion. The wind continued to tousle its feathers, as it otherwise remained still as a statue, ever watchful.

Chapter 39

Whack

The hoe was raised overhead, the heavy iron wedged into a wooden handle, sharp edge glinting in the light. The woman's hands brought this down onto the dirt.

Whack

Raised again, and again, each time with the same outcome. A trench was forming under the attack of this implement.

Branddoring stared in wonder. The woman's dress was a vibrant purple, these dyed garments that were different shades upon different people. Further away a man hoisted a tool of his own, banging it for whatever reason on a wooden post while holding another piece of wood to it.

Tock tock tock tock

He stopped, and somehow the wood remained suspended in the air against the vertical column. He wiped his brow and moved to the next post of the fence.

As the pack expected, there was a village less than a day's run away. There would always be humans in relatively close proximity. Branddoring found herself drawn to the artificial sounds of their industry.

She had come closer to the homes, on this patrol and others since they parted. As Mitseeri crossed her mind she gave an involuntary whine. She had searched for his prints, the musk from his tracks, knowing there was nothing more to find. Despite her loss, she understood Koorsboom's fascination with these creatures.

A rustle in the brush nearby startled the wolf. The thornbush branches parted and a white dog emerged. Smaller than some of the village mutts they had seen, this dog had long white hair, matted with dirt and neglect. The dog sat, and reached forward with a hind leg, scratching its shoulder with long claws.

"You seem lost." Branddoring twittered.

The white dog moved closer, tail giving a slight wag. Hanging its pink tongue out as it panted in the morning, it padded toward the wolf. There was no scent of aggression or anger about this diminutive canine.

"And what have you been hunting for?"

The dog sniffed, and then snuffed loudly, startling Branddoring for a moment.

"Rubbish, no doubt." She laughed lightly at this. The scent of spoiled food and stale beer was on its fur.

The dog approached the Painted wolf, and touched noses with her, sniffing heavily all the while, as though unable to get enough olfactory information. Branddoring turned to leave, departing for the den further away on the open savanna.

The white dog watched her leave. Unleashing another sneeze, it snorted and coughed. Secretions dripped from its snout onto the ground.

* * *

Over the next week the rains had finally begun. At first furtive, they came to last an hour or two at a time. When they came, the ground that had dried as hard as concrete would be flooded, absorbing nothing, and the water would wash away in newly made rivers to more distant waterholes and ponds. The people of the village, cheered on by the local village weaver birds, tried to plow furrows to prepare for the farming, though the soil seemed as poor as before when the rains stopped and the surface water quickly dried away.

Further from the small village, impala browsed on bush leaves and shoots. Where the savanna offered thicker cover with trees, duikers fed on sedge foliage.

Hyenas were denned several kilometers away, and the alpha female was occupied with her two cubs. She lay on her side in the burrow, suckling the two brown forms. They greedily took their nutrition from the richest milk of any land animal. Soon they would be able to play with the older juveniles of the clan, though their suckling would continue until they were a year old. Eventually, their mother would begin the prolonged and traumatic process of weaning them from milk, sure to provoke frequent tantrums.

Further away, within an old aardvark hole, the Painted wolf pack rested after their morning hunt.

"This new den seems just the right distance away." Koorsboom remarked to Olienhout. "Still close enough should we wish to observe humans."

"I might have known you would still have an interest, despite what happened." Olienhout nudged one of the pups, still bloated from the morning meal. "You may have been right about this place. Hyenas notwithstanding."

"Any place without hyenas or vultures is diseased and forgettable." He grunted. "Imagine the savanna without scavengers, the bodies building up. There would be as much flies as air." He took a deep breath and exhaled. "The hunting here is ideal. And the pups seem to show that."

Their coloration was acquiring hints of gold as the pups matured, though they were still mostly black and white in color.

"I saw a honey badger!" Besembossie scampered into camp, coming to an abrupt halt that showered Koorsboom with small rocks.

"It was a cheetah cub, you mongrel." Kamassi trotted in at leisure. "They look like honey badgers to scare dogs like you."

"How dare you call me a dog!" Besembossie boxed Kamassi, who deftly sidestepped this and propped herself on Besembossie's back, forelegs resting on her shoulders.

"You belong in the village."

Besembossie tried to throw her off, but Kamassi stayed, holding her down.

"The both of you belong there." Branddoring taunted them. She lay down heavily, fatigued and out of breath.

There was an intolerable heat by midday, and no animal larger than a tsetse fly would be out of the shade. The wolves lazed, barely moving as they digested their meal. Only the flick of an ear or swish of tail gave a sign of life.

The sun drifted across the sky, and the heat relented in the afternoon. Sensing this, the wolves came back to life and rallied for the next hunt. Each wolf greeted the next, the rapid chirp of their call quickening as each readied for action. Pack mates walked side by side, tonguing one another's muzzles, ears flattened back. As though unable to contain themselves any further, the wolves struck out to the northwest. They ignored a nearby herd, as was their habit to avoid dispersing a reliable food source.

Onward, they found the bushveld growing thick and green with the rains. The wolves stopped at a water hole, diving in with raucous splashing. Koorsboom dipped his head in the pond, and brought it up, the muddy water cascading over his back. Besembossie gripped his tail in her mouth, and attempted to pull him down until Kamassi bowled her over in the water.

Koorsboom left the pond, and indicated a distant field with his black muzzle. Dirty water dripped from the ruff of fur around his neck. The green was dotted with a few animals moving on the grass between thickets. The rest of the pack followed his lead, and they descended into thicker scrub toward their prey. Padding lightly on quiet paws, they threaded in stealth through the *Combretum* sedge now dense and heavy with leaves.

"It will be difficult to coordinate any sort of hunt. We spread wide, and hope to flush an impala towards us." Much of their skills depended upon visual tracking. If their prey was invisible, it made a plan difficult to formulate and less likely to hold up very long.

The pack converged upon where the antelope were detected, and they saw nothing. Forward, a series of branches snapping identified at least one individual. The wolves darted forward to intercept, and quickly lost the impala. A sharp twitter from Koorsboom and they stopped. Still, unmoving, ears swiveled about to detect the slightest movement. Besembossie sniffed the air. Another crack close by and the wolves pounced, finding only Kamassi. They looked about, seeing nothing. The only sound was the incessant chirping of the weaver birds. They sounded agitated, likely from the presence of a hawk or snake raiding the nests.

"We lost it. Spread out, there may be more." Besembossie was above all patient, and did not allow a lost quarry to cause her concern. They crept through the impenetrable copse, cracking and snapping branches as they went. Green branches tugged at their fur, as though to ensnare them in a trap. Every several minutes, Koorsboom would issue a sharp signal, and each wolf would halt and await the odd sound that would betray the presence of prey. On this stop, a short series of cracks would resound as each wild dog halted. *Crackcrack... crackcrack...* A moment too long later, *Crack.* Besembossie leapt up over the brush toward the sound and nearly landed on an impala female. A fusillade of snaps and cracks then followed as the wolves surrounded the source, tearing through the brush and ignoring the lacerations of thorns.

"Surround it!" Koorsboom called in an agitated twitter. The impala attempted to pronk above the brush to escape, but was stopped midair by Besembossie's jaws closing on the rear leg. It crashed awkwardly to the ground, surrounded on the instant by wolves.

The pack had their fill, reducing the herbivore to bones and sinew. Here the thick brush now worked in their favor, shielding them visually from lion or hyena that could steal the kill. They departed for the den, with not a single scavenger harrying them.

"I am pleased with these hunting grounds. We could not have done better, Koorsboom." Kamassi ran a tongue along her chops.

Branddoring prodded Koorsboom with her blood-encrusted snout, pausing for a sneeze.

Besembossie bounded with an impala hind leg bouncing in her jaws.

On their return the pups exploded out of the den once again, now well aware of what the return of the pack promised.

Each of the triumphant hunters loosed torrents of gore and blood onto the ground, and the pups were there to intercept it. The dust scarcely absorbed the moisture of the meat. Their sides expanded outward, threatening to burst, or perhaps roll away. Kamassi caught one about to tumble off a root and licked the young wolf clean.

Branddoring nosed another fat pup over, lapping the young wolf's face with her tongue. Though she relished spending time with them, she tired quickly of this. She padded further from the group, breathing heavily, and lay down to sleep.

Besembossie dropped the intact impala leg, and Olienhout ripped into the flesh.

"The fresh meat is most welcome." She thanked Besembossie for her effort, lapping her muzzle.

Besembossie rolled on her back near Olienhout, whipping her body side to side as she scratched off ticks. "A most excellent day's hunting, Koorsboom." She sighed. "Odd, that."

"What?" He scratched his ear with a hind leg, still unable, months later, to have dislodged the opaque gray device between his shoulders.

"That hunt was more difficult than I anticipated."

"The thick brush only presented a challenge. One which we were more than equal to."

She shook her head, snuffing secretions from her sensitive nose. "My sense of smell... it is off today."

Chapter 40

Olienhout tended to the pups, growing fast, but still requiring constant supervision. Two of them played next to the hole of the den, their jaws open, teeth against teeth, jockeying for greater position. One eventually pushed the other one over onto its back. The victor looked to his mother for approval.

She nodded to him, and gave a long exhale.

"What is on your mind?" Koorsboom darkened her in his shadow.

"Do you not sense something wrong?"

"I cannot say I have. Our lives have been without ill omens since we moved further from the village."

She frowned. Within stirred a sensation. "Your dreams of late—what were they about?"

"Nothing out of the ordinary. Hunting, feeding the pups. One of an elephant herd—"

"Mine have been of fleeing. For our very lives."

"From what did we run?" Koorsboom's brow was furrowed.

"Something terrible. Faceless, nameless. A dread that had yet to achieve form."

"I worried about an ill-defined menace when we dwelled near the last village. I had thought we were clear of it."

"We must move the den, Koorsboom." She stared at him, her eyes wide and alert.

"We have detected no sign of lion, the hyenas leave us well enough alone—"

"That is not why." She had not altered her gaze. "An implacable foe that is descending on us." She looked lost. "It has already found our den."

"I scent no fear other than from you." He lapped her muzzle, but she did not respond.

She laid her head on her forepaws, then promptly stood up again. Her anxiety was palpable and seemed to spread across the area like an insidious fume. The pups began whining again, from hunger, but also with sympathy for the fear that washed off Olienhout, pervading the clearing. "They feel it too. Strange you do not."

He touched noses with her. "We are out of reach of the humans' thunder. It will not be long before these hills echo with the calls of our kind." He looked up to the nearby *miombo* trees that vaulted above them, the trunks waving gently to the winds far above. "We came far, you and I, from the great river to the west, to this place. Vast and inscrutable was the land of our birth. And the challenges we faced were many. Nonetheless, we found a way. We found one another, my *bokkie*."

Olienhout did not speak, still struggling to find a comfortable position.

"My mentor, Blackthorn, shared with me stories of giant packs of wolves, far greater than any we have seen, ranging across the bushveld." He sighed. "A long departed era, with lands empty of our kind. Our time shall come again."

"There are laws beyond our understanding." Olienhout's voice sounded hollow. "Yet ours is the void if we fail to adhere to laws we do not know. That is why you sought out this place, to be close to these humans, to their exotic ways."

Koorsboom chuckled to himself with a low chirping. "I am not sure such awareness is possible."

"Yet you felt the compulsion to try. And so we have established our mark on this savanna, so close to humankind." She shook off her anxiety. "We are bound to drink deeply these bitter waters."

He thought for a moment. "We must survive in the midst of these dangerous creatures. As enigmatic as they are, every animal of the savanna is destined to be in close proximity. They are everywhere, and there is no escaping them. Blackthorn predicted the wild would one day disappear entirely." He grunted. "Perhaps our fate is in sifting through the rubbish piles of villages."

Olienhout nodded. "You think the languor that pervades me is the oppressive shadow of humankind. Perhaps you are right."

Koorsboom turned to leave for the veld on patrol. He had learned to trust her instinct, as she was not often wrong.

As he departed, his nose dripped secretions on the ground.

Chapter 41

On the edge of the *miombo* wood, two figures were deep in shadow, as though barely a part of the material world. As the sun glinted through the trees from its rise in the east, their eyes reflected a brilliant bluish green like gemstone sapphires.

The leopards were lying next to one another, a rare occurrence. The female stood up, walked in a circle, its long tail undulating in a sine wave, then laying down roughly next to the male with a powerful nudge. He did not respond. After a few minutes, she stood again, walking around to his other side and shouldered against his rump. She then stood again and crouched before him. Finally taking the hint, he stood and straddled her from behind. Mating was very quick, taking seconds, and he gave a growl, gripping the back of her neck gently in his jaws. He released her, was up on his paws, and crept away, not to be seen again for months.

She rested, and as the sun continued to rise, the rays left her clearing and she was again enveloped in shade.

Further from the wood edge, the trees became a tangle of thornbrush, through which antelope browsed. Birds flitted from branch to branch, retrieving seeds from the ground.

Though the sedge moved four forms of gold, black, and white, cracking branches as they went. Olienhout, Kamassi, Branddoring and Koorsboom found themselves in another tangle of acacia thickets, wheeling about, straining to hear their prey. Kamassi was frustrated to no end.

"What is this *kak*? How have they evaded us?"

Straining to hear, they ceased moving. Nothing. No sound other than the slight scraping of thorn against branch, the ambient noises of the breeze. Each dish-like ear swiveled, willing into being the sounds that would bring them closer to a kill.

Nothing.

"You are not the only to have them escape your notice." Branddoring panted. She sneezed, loosing a ribbon of mucus onto the ground.

Kamassi loped away from the others, hoping to triangulate a whispered sound. Only the chatter of a southern black tit, *phee-cher-phee-cher*. The bird sang to Kamassi, or so it seemed, a small pitch-black form with striking white striped wings.

Nothing else.

"Well, bugger this." They each weaved their way out of the thicket to search elsewhere, stepping right past two impala standing still in the brush.

* * *

"Ready for the hunt, Branddoring?" Koorsboom lapped at the yearling's muzzle.

"I can stay behind with the pups."

Koorsboom looked aside at her. "When have you ever declined a hunt, or a fight of any kind?"

Branddoring entered the den. As her eyes adjusted to the gloom, the pups came into focus.

"Olienhout, I can mind the young ones if you wish to hunt today." She wheezed, and mucus dripped from her nose. "It has been a while since you had your meat fresh."

The alpha raised her head. "Not for me. Not today." She lowered her head again, and nuzzled a pup close to her snout. "I do not want to leave them."

"Does something worry you?" The yearling coughed.

Olienhout tugged one of the pups closer to her breast, and closed her eyes.

* * *

The next three days produced only one successful hunt, a victory only possible as the impala had already been captured by a snare. The meat was returned to the den. The pups had their fill, though Olienhout needed to encourage them to eat. The rest of the hunters rested.

Branddoring coughed on a constant basis, sleeping fitfully at best. She no longer hunted, but still was able to stay hydrated as the others brought her food. Each member of the pack lapped her muzzle lovingly, hoping to heal an unseen wound with their cares.

Chapter 42

The trees around them were silent sentries, their smooth grey bark rough in texture, reaching high over the den with wide canopies of bluish green leaves. The rain became a daily feature, pattering on the greenery above, and the leaf litter and earth below remained relatively dry. Soon the feathery leaves would be joined by creamy white flowers that produced copious amounts of pollen and nectar that would draw insect and bird alike.

On the ground, the wolves lay prone, fatigued more than usual in the spring heat. The flies found their biting and feeding on wolf blood uninterrupted, the predators scarcely moving.

The pups slept in the den, Olienhout next to them. The cool of the earth did not offer respite, as the pups languished with fevers. When last they were presented with meat, they ate only with difficulty. Their noses were congested and dripping, and eating made breathing considerable work. Their rest was broken by coughing.

Olienhout sensed dully that an enemy was upon them, but no longer bothered to rouse in search of an adversary.

* * *

In the evening, the hunters failed to rally.

Branddoring awoke, and quickly returned to fitful sleep.

Besembossie greeted Kamassi, and lapped secretions from her muzzle. She lapped hers in kind. With muted twittering, they moved on to licking clean each one of the pups, though with little of the enthusiasm they once had.

The pups were pleased with the attention, but rapidly returned to sleep.

Besembossie eventually tired and slumped to the ground again. Kamassi followed suit. Koorsboom tried to lick Branddoring's muzzle again to entice her to hunt, but the younger wolf did not respond.

They slept easily, no longer concerned with their hunger.

Chapter 43

The downpour hammered the savanna, water standing on the ground a few centimeters deep. This ran off into gullies and rivulets, draining into distant rivers and swamps, but enough seeped into the hard ground to bring life to the dry veld.

Corn finally sprouted green by the village, though the ears of corn would not develop fully. Grass shot up everywhere, an ubiquitous thick carpet that made even walking through the veld considerable work for any animal shorter than a kudu. Mosquitoes were everywhere, lazily buzzing about and finding their targets without fail. Birds of all types gorged themselves on the insect bounty. Impala, duiker, and eland grazed on the luxurious greenery, ripping away mouthfuls and swallowing even as they dipped their heads to the ground for more. Their fat reserves grew, recovering from the lean times of the drought.

The impala seemed to be everywhere at once, and could not get enough of the grass. A herd gathered on the edge of the *Brachystegia* woodland, sampling all they could. One strayed from the herd to try some of the new green leaves on the mountain acacia trees growing at the wood's edge. Reaching gingerly in between the thorns of the branches, it managed to take several without being impaled on the spines.

The impala was suddenly thrown onto the ground before it knew what hit it, breaking a rib as it fell. The leopard had ambushed with the skill of a master. Wasting no time, she gripped the throat before the impala could cry out. Dying in the stillness of morning, the limbs eventually stopped twitching.

Still holding it by the neck, the leopard hefted the impala several meters up the mountain acacia tree the antelope browsed upon. Raising the carcass would keep it out of reach of the Painted wolf pack that had recently taken up residence.

The leopard gazed over the surrounding veld from its elevated view, seeing no sign of the wolf pack.

She considered this, wondering when she had last seen them crossing her territory.

* * *

Koorsboom dragged himself away from the den, lapping the muzzles of the sleeping yearlings and his mate. None responded with anything more than a murmur.

Every step was a saga, and he could feel the long, thick grass dragging along his belly, thousands of hands reaching out to stop him from the hunt. Those hands began to beckon him back to his pack to rest.

Eventually he gave up, sniffing the air and finding no sign of prey. An impala standing at the edge of the clearing remained still, bewildered. It could not tell why the hunter was oblivious, but was not about to ask him. It leapt off with a clack of its hoof on a rock.

* * *

The days bled one into the next, the pack having lost the rhythm of sunrise hunt—rest—evening hunt—rest. Koorsboom was as dazed as the others, coughing, nose steadily dripping with congestion. Fever wracked his brain.

Resting outside the den, he raised his head to behold the sunset. Blurry as it was, he dimly realized the entire day had passed without any of them attempting to rally a hunting party. This troubled him, but only vaguely.

He looked over to see Branddoring on her belly, somehow hovering above the ground.

"Where are you going." Koorsboom thought for a moment. "What was your name?"

"Name." She murmured, seeming not to understand. She appeared to be floating before Koorsboom realized she was actually lying upon the ground.

"Of course." Koorsboom mused on this, and as his mind wandered, he forgot she was there.

His life became an abstraction, a thing he observed from a distance, like a fish eagle soaring high in the air. His memories fogged, things and places that may have belonged to someone else.

Chapter 44

Koorsboom stirred with the morning, and saw a great beast looming over him. It was black as twilight, mouth wide and filled with even darker fangs. Its hot breath washed over him.

He recoiled, his hind legs wheeling, and the dark figure vanished. His vision cleared and nothing was around him in the grass.

Slumping to the ground, exhausted with the effort, he busied himself with the important work of breathing.

Chapter 45

"I do hope you will be well without us."

Koorsboom aroused to a voice that filled the world around him. He looked up to dark skies with a black sun. It pulled heat from the earth below, and seemed to relieve his fevers.

"Branddoring?"

"The same." She smiled, revealing ivory teeth in that way only wolves can smile. "I thought perhaps we would try another hunt. One last time."

"There is more to teach this one, Koorsboom." An old wolf stepped next to her. "She shall be an alpha a few seasons hence."

"Mitseeri. You can manage the hunt?"

"Better than you, young wolf." Mitseeri growled, shifting his weight on four paws.

"Be one with the wind." Koorsboom attempted to stand, his aching muscles pulling him to the ground.

"Fear not, we shall return with a bounty that has no equal." Branddoring lapped his muzzle, turning with Mitseeri to lope onto the distant bushveld. She leapt about with an excited twitter, and he matched this, standing on both hind legs to box her with his forelegs. She returned the blows before they returned to the ground, bounding off to the far grasslands.

***

How long had it been since there was a hunt? It may have been days, perhaps weeks. It was all the same to the wolves.

Time no longer passed for Besembossie, who blearily regarded the morning sun through eyes thick with purulence. She rolled to one side, blinking and breathing heavily. She could barely be troubled to move as another attack of diarrhea hit her. The smell did not matter as none of them possessed that sense anymore.

Wolves can be ostracized if evidently sick, but none of them perceived this. Besembossie took it upon herself to leave.

Summoning her last reserves and focus, she raised herself on her paws, surveying the clearing. Koorsboom and Kamassi rested in the shade. Olienhout was below in the den with the pups. Or perhaps not, she could not tell. A white-backed vulture peered at them with increasing interest from a short distance away.

She padded further from the others, with no intention of returning. Day and night, she loped onward to the far veld beyond. In reality, she went a dozen meters, but it felt like a vast *trek* to another world. Collapsing on the ground, she did not react when the shadow of a vulture passed over her.

* * *

Olienhout shook awake, her hind leg spasming as though on the run from an enemy. Even beneath the ground in the den, she sensed that Besembossie was gone. This would have been devastating news at another time. Now, she let go and continued to breathe.

She felt no movement elsewhere in the den.

Chapter 46

Father, where are the antelope?

  Ever taut, my son... there are lions about.

Koorsboom looked to see his mentor, Blackthorn, sniffing his way through camp. The greyed wolf nosed the leaf litter before pausing. He looked up. His eyes were long gone, gored sockets swarming with maggots. A gaping wound in his side festered, unhealing. The old wolf opened his mouth to speak, but there were no soft tissues inside, no tongue projecting from the ruined jaw that dropped to the ground. He continued to walk, his steps no longer producing sound as he left the denning area.

We kill and eventually join the killed.

You will be hunted yourself, and one day you will join your father in death.

The voices roiled in his head, fever taking hold. He raised his head and across the clearing of the den in the shadow of the *miombo* forest he could see Kamassi awake.

  She was not awake, however. Her extremities twitched, convulsing, tongue hanging out of her mouth, eyes sightless. Her paws quivered, as though she were dreaming. Or perhaps he was dreaming.

His eyes closed, ignoring what must be another hallucination.

The first few illusions frightened him, and he remembered Olienhout's talk of terrible visions. He calmed over time as he learned to disregard these.

Seizures continued to strike Kamassi, coming in waves, the high fevers ravaging her brain.

Koorsboom lifted his head and dragged himself over to a clump of grass. He took a mouthful, chewing it before drifting off again to sleep.

Enjoy your dream, Kamassi. I hope you are catching enough impala to no longer feel hungry.

* * *

There was a pungent smell of death about the den, coming from the denning hole. It was emitted by a censor that was everywhere and nowhere. Even though he could no longer smell, he could feel it on his skin, stinging his eyes.

He looked up to the sun and saw night. Lifting his head and rolling onto his forepaws, his head spun about him.

So vivid, this. What shall come next?

He looked into the eyes of a leopard, the luminous greenish blue of its eyes almost convincing him that it was real. The heavy skull was covered in spots, short snout festooned with long whiskers, topped by short rounded ears. The spots became larger roundish splotches of black across its stout, muscular body, terminating in a long, swishing tail.

Koorsboom wondered, as his mind swam, what he would do if this were real. He decided it did not matter at this point. He laid his head down and watched as the leopard took hold of Kamassi's body by the neck and dragged her away. Off into the night, or possibly day. He could no longer tell the difference.

* * *

A mechanical sound, so close. Another symptom of the fever? Is there any reason to care?

Gravel crunching underfoot. Regular steps, like a machine, not an antelope hoof.

No, definitely not a hoof, their march is halting, stopping and starting to graze and watch for danger.

Though a lion might walk right into their denning area.

Koorsboom started in a panic at the thought, then discarded it as a lion is one thing he would never hear coming.

Two figures stared down at him. They were giraffes. For some reason they wore hats.

Shorter than giraffes. But wearing hats—this was beyond doubt. Their faces morphed into humanlike shapes.

Koorsboom closed his eyes, determined to reject these mirages that served only to remind him that life was coming to a close, his last failure upon them all.

* * *

"This one is bad off, eh?"

"He does not have long at this rate. Fetch me the shears."

Koorsboom could sense the men touching him, prodding his nearly unconscious form. His fur was cut short over his foreleg, and a needle was forced into the tissue.

"Nearly there... hand me that bottle."

Blood dripped out of the intravenous catheter now seated in his cephalic vein. A plastic tube was connected to this, and the other end was screwed into a bottle of saline. This was held aloft, and the red fluid that was oozing down the plastic tubing reversed and flowed back into the catheter and into Koorsboom.

"Ah, that's nice. Secure." The catheter was anchored in place with clear tape. Fluids dripped to a reservoir and down the tubing, providing rehydration.

"So what do you think, then?"

"Distemper." The human surveyed the clearing, hands on his hips. "The whole lot of them have been wiped out."

Chapter 47

SOUTH AFRICA

We have no place in this world.

Ever taut, young one. The dangers are legion here.

To whom do I speak?

Blackthorn, my son. You are alive, I can assure you. Nothing else, however, is promised. Alive, but no longer in the wild.

Humans have taken me? So be it.

I am pleased with you, Koorsboom.

And how has my failure, and the death of my pack pleased you?

You did not waste time questioning this new and strange turn. You have accepted your fate. Survival requires this resignation. But remain ever taut... nothing of your life so far has prepared you for this.

Koorsboom awoke with a start. The voice of his mentor faded, and he returned to his world of fevers and deceitful visions. His first sensation was that the fevers were now gone, leaving him with a brutal lingering headache. The sun was setting, into a faded evening.

He became dimly aware of a cage. The floor beneath him was hard packed dirt, sandy in color. His periphery consisted of chain link fence, twisted iron that enclosed him on all four sides. The bottom edge of the fence sank into the ground, and he guessed it was buried for some distance. If he had the energy to pace this enclosure, he would determine it was fifteen meters to a side. The center was occupied by a small Giraffe-thorn acacia tree that provided cover and shade.

"What sad place have I come to inhabit?"

The wind teased leaves off the ground, scraping against the iron links.

"Our new home."

Koorsboom jumped at the familiar voice, thinking it another hallucination. From around the tree walked Olienhout. She walked with hesitation, a slight limp from her weakened state. He noticed her nose had a hardened surface, a keratosis that was one of the long-term complications from distemper. The mark of a survivor.

She lay to rest by her mate, and they tongued one another's muzzles. She rested her head on his shoulders.

Koorsboom opened his mouth to speak, and found himself unable to ask, the words turning to ash in his mouth.

"All of them, Koorsboom." Olienhout rasped.

He felt an uncontrollable urge to pace, to search, to find. To hoo-call into the ground, a call that traversed kilometers across the wild to find the Pack. His pack.

He emitted a low whine that faded into the dusk.

* * *

They both awakened again at the same time. Night had fallen, their world lit from the full moon above. Everything appeared metallic in the pale blue

288

light.

Koorsboom raised his nose. "My sense of smell has returned."

"As has mine." She sniffed the air. "And we are surrounded by a bizarre mélange of scents indeed."

"The Sickness is passing. For us." He laid down his head, the melancholy weighing him down.

"Gather your strength, Koorsboom. What is past shall remain so—and I need you for what is to come." She continued to sniff the air. "I believe ours is not the only cage. I do not see far, our vision obscured by grass and scrub, but there are others here."

"Antelope." He sampled the air, muzzle parted, tasting it. "Impala, kudu. Eland, perhaps. There are others I cannot identify as yet."

"A ratel, of all things. The scent is strong." She shook her head. "Why—or rather how—anyone would trap a honey badger is a riddle without solution."

"Humans have captured the lot of us?" He cocked his head to the side. "For what purpose would they work to cage the entire wild?"

"That threat will come to us in time." She was on her paws, pacing the edge of the link fence. "There is something sinister at work here. The humans who have come to the fence—before you awoke—were rank with loathing towards us." She snorted. "And their clothing is covered with a myriad of animal scents. One of them was lion."

Chapter 48

Drive north from the steel and glass monuments to industry of Johannesburg along ribbons of tar, and one enters rural veld of tree and brush. The endless urban walls topped with barbed wire and electrified fence yield to scattered shops, gatherings of security complexes, and informal housing of tin shacks. These give way to the iron dust of the highveld, dotted with flame thorn acacia and velvet bushwillow, farms and spaza shops.

The roads wind from the vast northern suburbs between hills dotted with gated communities and concierge farms for tourists, and the occasional casino decorated as a faux-Tuscan villa. Amid these concerns lie informal settlements of sheet metal and cinderblock, crowded living spaces with mud tracks between them and a snarl of crisscrossed wires from electrical poles.

Past a dam holding back an expansive lake surrounded by companies catering to people on holiday, smaller cities sprawl, filled with industries rolling away from the outskirts of Pretoria. Further still away from the city of gold, the land is occupied by farms and freeholdings.

Private game lodges abound. Some have their own landing strips, ushering in travelers direct from Joburg's international airport, offering minimal contact with Africa and its people. Obscure properties advertise nothing, hidden behind high walls of concrete and electrified fence, providing those within discretion. An escape from the hustle and bustle of the city within thatched lodges offering a true African experience. Hiking, game viewing, birdwatching, team building. Perhaps even a chance to track game. Rifle fire is heard commonly enough that it is never paid any mind.

Along a road with a black surface, winding its way north, smaller dirt roads shoot off into indistinct bushveld. One such dirt road snaked far off into the bush, coated with gravel, but kept smooth enough for standard cars to traverse without leaving their suspension in tatters. Wandering around black monkey-orange and wild pear trees, the distance from the main road was far enough to promise seclusion, but not so much that a traveler would think they were lost. This terminated at a rusted fence adorned with the faded paint of a sign: WILDSPLAAS.

Also, another sign: PRIVAAT EIENDOM – GEEN TOEGANG – PRIVATE PROPERTY – NO ENTRY

The dirt road continued beyond the outer fence, opening up to various enclosures, some more robust than others. A small cage enclosed a pair of warthogs slumbering in a shallow scratching. A larger cage held two dozen lions, some pacing the perimeter, others lying about in utter boredom. The ground was covered with feces and scratch marks. Their fur was matted and encased in filth.

Within a smaller enclosure, a lioness was giving birth. She was ensconced in a thornbush, and felt comfortable in the solitude. While standing, she pushed each cub to the verge, and out onto the grass. Gnawing through the umbilical cord and cleaning each of fluids, she then stood again to bring the next cub into the world. Each birth, she noticed the cubs would disappear, though she was unable to see the human hands reach into the narrow enclosure and whisk away the newborns. When the last vanished before she could finish cleaning the birth fluids away with her broad pink tongue, she slumped to the ground, dejected. She would soon be able to ovulate, and birth more cubs for the farm.

Further from the lion pens, a concrete wall bordered an oval depression in the ground. This held a few large cut tree branches and a wooden structure that resembled a doghouse. From behind the house strode a powerful and confident ball of muscle clad in black fur and tough skin, a white stripe stretching from its small head to its broad body, and bushy tail. It was the size of a small dog, but had the presence of a far larger creature.

The honey badger bounced as it walked, emitting a grunt as it considered its predicament. The small head looked left, then right, noticing a new large branch in its home. Fresh cut from a fig tree, it was over half the length of the depression that imprisoned it.

Sharp claws dug into the branch, and despite being twice the height of a human and far heavier, it maneuvered the branch easily with tugs and pulls, bringing one end over the edge of the concrete wall. Resuming its bouncy gait, the badger ascended the branch. It gave another dismissive grunt atop the concrete wall and ambled off into the bushveld to raid a nearby farm.

It cast a glance at the last enclosure it passed, snuffing loudly. The honey badger had no regard for the carnivores within, two sleeping African wild dogs. Nothing worried a honey badger, especially two wild dogs that appeared sick and starved.

It trundled off into the veld as evening descended on the game farm.

***

Morning brought the sun rising over the hills and high wild seringa trees. The first rays opened the eyes of Koorsboom, who raised his head, fighting away the residual headache that plagued him. As he watched, a honey badger jogged past him, face slick with honey and studded with a few dead bees. He momentarily worried of attack, but remembered the fence that separated them.

The badger left his sight, and he could hear a tree branch sliding against concrete in the near distance, and thudding to the earth.

Men's voices. At first faint, then coming closer.

"See now, it was not this *oke*, eh?" Clipped tones, a man speaking to nobody. "I am staring at him just now, and he has not left his home. Somebody else is at your bees." The man was coming closer, and he rounded a stand of high grass and acacia shrub. He was before the wild dog pen now. He lowered his hand, and it held a device. So he spoke to the device, maybe. Koorsboom was bewildered by this, as he was with this new place.

This man was dressed in light brown khaki pants and shirt, his balding head pink under the burning sun. His hands were on his hips, and he regarded the wolves with a nod. He whistled.

Two other men joined him, clad in blue overalls. They trudged heavily, and did not often make eye contact with the man in khaki or with the wolves.

"See how they do with the chicken, eh?" His hands stayed on his hips as the workers in blue overalls lugged over a white bucket. As they drew closer, one of the men wrinkled his nose.

"*Yoh*, these things stink." The other worker murmured his agreement.

One reached into the bucket and produced a strange bird of white feathers and a red hole where a head was expected. With a heave, he tossed it up and over the top of the fence, and it landed with a thump on the ground beside Koorsboom. Before he realized she was there, Olienhout was on it, gripping the bird in her jaws.

"Koorsboom?" She spoke around a mouthful of feathers, sounding muffled.

He suddenly remembered his stomach, and it exploded within him, a rumbling with a gush of fluid that became a boring ache. He seized the other half of the chicken and they pulled it apart. A cloud of feathers burst around them, and they gulped down every scrap.

"They are recovering nice, eh?" His hands left his hips to stretch.

"Yebo, *baas*." The workers carried their bucket away.

"Right." The khaki man kept nodding to himself. "The rabies vaccine, now."

The two workers returned with a tray containing two foil-wrapped lumps. These were opened, revealing small cubes of compressed raw beef. They approached the chain link fence, and before the wild dogs approached, they fed one cube through an opening.

Olienhout trotted over and took it in her mouth, and with a smack of her jaws, it was gone.

Koorsboom looked toward her, and back to the fence. He moved closer to the fence, now noticing the other cube was deposited on his side. He took the beef with his teeth, and with a slight flip, it dropped down his throat. The fluid packet filled with rabies vaccine dissolved in his stomach.

"What are they doing?" Koorsboom's mind swam with puzzlement.

"Does it matter, if one cannot change their fate?" Olienhout tired of pacing around the tree and lay down.

Koorsboom did the same, resting against the acacia tree at its root. The gunmetal grey of the Tick clicked against the hard bark. Periodically, it sent its signal.

Chapter 49

One heavy hand opened, upturned, holding a thick wad of multicolored bills.

Another hand took hold of it, thousands of *meticais.* The money vanished into a deep pocket. The two hands then shook, a deal sealed.

"You are certain?" Marais said, his clipped Afrikaans accent having some difficulty with Portuguese.

"Not of the day, but sometime in the autumn he will need to make a delivery to Maputo."

"Augusto has not been around here for some time." Marais stroked the stubble on his chin, his eyes narrowed.

"The game reserves he has been using are nearly empty of white rhino. Gorongosa is too dangerous for him to hunt. He needs to expand to meet the demand." The man speaking to Marais wore jeans and a white shirt, adorned with gold necklaces.

"And will you be running the horns with him?"

"Yes—but I have your word that the arrest would not involve me."

Marais nodded, trying to avoid the migraine that was creeping from behind his eyes.

"So he is moving to exporting now? Is that why he is going to Maputo?"

"Augusto will not be alone."

"Who is coming?" He forgot his headache for the moment.

The poacher looked at the ground, and then behind him, despite knowing nobody stood in the grass clearing amid the palm trees.

"Somebody important?" Marais raised his voice.

"I need more money."

"Depends on who it is."

"Nattapong Buatoom."

Marais sucked air through his teeth, and his face darkened. He noticed the poacher now looked afraid. "Do not worry. There will be money—lots of it—if we catch this man."

"I thought you were going to hit me."

Marais shook his head, his thoughts already elsewhere. He walked back to his Land Rover with a hurried gait. Looking at his phone, he cursed the lack of reception. He arranged the bundles of wire in the rear of the vehicle, representing three months of snare gathering.

* * *

Marais did not notice the message that appeared on his phone as he entered and exited a region with decent phone coverage: VENTER – URGENT.

* * *

As he drove to the ranger station, Marais noticed Sonja Venter running out to his Land Rover.

"Rebel activity?" Marais's hand drifted toward the rifle he kept behind his seat.

"Those wolves." She bent over after her run, putting her hands on her knees, puffing. "They are alive."

"Wait, which ones?" He forgot about the rifle, motioning to the younger ranger to get in the passenger side. The door closed with a bang and rattle, and Marais put the vehicle back into gear.

"The young ones. That Tick. Was going. The whole time." Her panting slowed.

"Are you serious? How did you find out?" Marais opened and closed his mangled hand which had begun to throb again.

"I expanded the search area, and there it was, two hundred kilometers to the south."

He cursed to himself, shaking his head. "I should have considered that possibility. So many of them had failed. I thought the signal disappeared same as the others. Instead, the signal just left Gorongosa." His jaw closed tightly, teeth grinding, as he swallowed a string of expletives.

She waited.

"So... where are they?"

"This will be hectic. You promise not to *strip jou moer?*"

Marais started to drum the steering wheel.

"When I found the signal, I was busy with elephant monitoring outside the park, and you could not be reached. This all happened very quickly."

The drumming continued.

"They were out of our operating region so I called someone who was available, and they found them. The pack was dying, probably distemper."

Marais stopped drumming. "And they were found in time?"

"Resuscitated with fluids, and transported away." She folded her arms. "There was no place that would help rehabilitate them. Game reserves did not want to be stuck with them, forced to provide a place for them to live." Remarkably, her blue eyes seemed to darken with anger. "Phone call after phone call went nowhere, and there was no time to find help."

"Around here?"

"No, nothing. Not in the South African parks either."

"So you found what you could." Marais was devoid of emotion.

"I was desperate."

"It was Dyk, wasn't it?"

She nodded. "He did not tell me where he took them. First thing he said was he will find another organization to take custody."

"You did the right thing." Marais sighed. "They would have died if somebody had not fetched them." He resumed drumming. "He is not going to give them up now, though."

"Dyk has been asking for wild dogs for some reason. He could not get them from the metapopulation of Kruger or the other game reserves. So he got these."

"He transported them across a border, and there is no way he got official permits that quickly. To give them back would be to admit to a crime."

He walked past Venter without another word.

She followed closely, matching his large strides with a faster pace. Her dark hair whipped about her head in the wind. At the ranger station, Marais retrieved the tablet used to track the Tick device.

She scanned the territory to the southwest, and stabbed the screen with her finger.

"There."

"North of Brits. Northwest province." He sighed, his large hands gripping the edge of the table. Under this, the wood cracked slightly. "He took them to his zoo."

"He denied keeping them." She stared at the floor.

"That is his place." Marais tightened his hold on the table. "I know it well."

After they watched for a while, the small blip reappeared. All too quickly, it faded.

* * *

"Did you notice?" Koorsboom blinked away the dust.

Olienhout lay by his side. As the sun descended in the late afternoon, it shone through the treetops. One tree glowed green amid the wild seringa.

"A fever tree." He managed to sound wistful. "Long have they been a good omen for me. A place of safety, perhaps."

Olienhout lapped his muzzle as they rested in the sun. The aching of her muscles was fading, the chronic headache was losing its sharp edges.

A loud, rapid drumming echoed through the wild pear and wattle as a Bearded woodpecker hammered its way into a dead tree. The beat continued, interrupted by a roar from a lion nearby, and then later a single rifle shot that reverberated off the hills around them.

Chapter 50

A cigarette hung from the mouth of the man behind the desk. It hung, ever threatening to drop, but it seemed pinned in place as he spoke.

"You have no legal claim to them."

"Legal claims are not relevant when dealing with endangered species." Marais sat with his heavy hands folded, working to hide his frustration. "You saved their lives, Dyk. This has not been forgotten."

Dyk gave a slight nod, his thin mouth curving into a slight smile.

"But their place is in the wild."

"They have a use when it comes to education and tourism." Dyk spoke in a flat voice, the cigarette still clinging on by unknown means.

"Sitting in a cage until tourists walk by?"

"Education. And do not take that tone with me. Tourism provides a lot of jobs here." A tendril of smoke worked its way past the man's utterly blank features toward the ceiling.

"Like the lions?"

"The kids love them. We get a school group in here each week." He picked up a pen to doodle as he spoke. "The cub encounters are hugely popular."

"And the volunteers love the cubs too, *né?*" Marais glared at him. "You still have tourists 'volunteer' here to pet cubs for ten thousand dollars per week?"

Dyk scowled. "Those volunteers value their time here. They learn a great deal working with the animals we rear." He grew more animated. "This is useful training for veterinary—"

"Useless." Marais raised his voice in kind. "No veterinary discipline trains people to cuddle with lion cubs. The cubs grow up fit for nothing more than canned hunting."

"We do no canned hunting here, eh?" The cigarette finally dropped to the ground as his voice raised by an octave. "Those lions are for tourism, eh?"

Marais nodded, sighing, knowing there was no point in arguing this. "The Painted wolves. They do not live well in captivity. And tourists are not going to make this worth your while."

Dyk did not respond, looking at the floor.

"You will try to make money with this new attraction, but it will not work."

"Well, the volunteer program has been great with taking care of the lions. They will be interested in the dogs as well."

Marais rubbed the old snakebite, as electric pains shot through the nerves buried in the scar tissue. "Wild dogs cannot be tamed. They will only bite the volunteers as they get bigger and lose their fear of people. No professional would ever recommend doing this."

Dyk kept doodling, no longer listening.

"And in the end they will not be able to return to the wild, once they get habituated to people."

The doodling continued.

"There are less than six thousand of these animals in the world. They can live only as packs. And there is only one alpha breeding pair for each pack of, on average, fifteen or so. Which means just over 400 breeding pairs for the entire species. Every one of them is crucial to the genetic bank of the wolf population." Marais sat on the edge of his seat, hoping this appeal would matter.

"Is there anything else?"

Marais stood to leave, adjusting the wide brimmed hat on his head.

"Those wolves have no permits to be here. And you took them across a border."

Dyk looked up, his eyes wide for a moment. Pointing a finger at Marais, he grinned. "Thank you most kindly for reminding me. I will have permits ready by the end of the week. In the meantime, do not bother to complain to Environmental Affairs, they have nothing to say unless you have cash in hand." Dyk's grin grew wider. "And I know how you feel about bribes."

Marais left the room, each step thundering on the stone floors. He passed one office after another, nearly knocking over a person carrying an armful of files. Outside the office building his boots struck the concrete walk, a steady knock. This progressed through an expansive warehouse, filled with antelope, wildebeest, and zebra behind thick iron bars. Dull eyes watched him stalk by. A white rhino paused to take a mouthful of grass from a pile on the grey floor.

The last pen contained a leopard, standing in the center of its tiny stall. Whiskers twitched as it examined Marais. The man stopped to regard the cat, who glared back with yellow eyes marked with a green tint. Small pupils were fixed upon him. It was alert, unlike the rest of the animals languishing here.

"You must be new." Marais's voice echoed throughout the warehouse. The scents of animal, hay, and waste were pungent in the air. His hands worked into fists the size of ham roasts. His path carried him from the holding facility and outside again. The path became loose rocks, crunching beneath his boots. This meandered past a distant outdoor pub overlooking a valley with a watering hole attended by several captive antelope. The polished wooden surface of the bar was festooned with abandoned glass bottles.

Before he reached the parking lot, he passed a pen containing two dozen lions, staring listlessly from inside a small enclosure. They lazed in the summer heat, fur matted with waste.

He walked past additional enclosures holding several cheetah, meerkat, two warthogs, a dozen eland, and handfuls of waterbuck and impala, ostrich, and various other game. Two transport trucks were fueling in the lot. Beyond this, he came to his lonely Land Rover.

Sonja Venter sat in the passenger seat, lost in thought. As Marais walked up to the vehicle, she spoke to him through the open window.

"He is not giving them up, is he?" She stared through the windshield, as though contemplating a crossword puzzle.

Marais merely frowned and considered putting dents into the door.

"Would it help if I had a chat with him?"

"No." Marais was curt as he climbed into the Land Rover and slammed the door. Somewhere within the frame a bolt banged loose. "Any discussion involving ecology and Dyk's eyes will glaze over while he stares into the middle distance."

"No use for science?"

"None." He scoffed. "I understand how he feels. Facts are disobedient."

"Whereas lies are malleable?" She furrowed her brow.

"Lies are fantastic. You can make the entire world whatever you want. And people will believe them. People love lies. They comfort and insulate us. Facts and the scientists who use them are obnoxious in comparison." Marais seethed.

"We can probably do better communicating with people. Bridging that gap." Venter sighed. "I made a mistake calling Dyk for help."

"Do not do that." Marais nodded to her. "You did what was necessary." He plugged the key into the ignition, the rest of the keys dangling below it. "Normally it can take several days to arrange a darting and extraction. They did not have days."

"Now they are stuck here."

Marais grunted.

"In captivity." Venter paused. "They may live a longer life here."

"They will live, until Dyk learns that tourists are not interested in dogs."

"*Wild* dogs." She lifted an eyebrow.

"Tourists may not know the difference, and I doubt Dyk will educate them. They do not have anyone here experienced with wild canids. Not a one." He issued a halting laugh, one that was unconvinced of the joke. "Not that they are experienced with cats. Or anything else other than foreign currency."

She stared at the parking lot, pondering this.

"It comes down to money." Marais drummed his fingers on the steering wheel.

"I remember my friend said he needed money, and fast."

"With all their lions?" Marais grumbled. "Between tourists going there to pet lion cubs and the canned hunting of lions, rhinos, and everything else, I thought he was doing well."

"My colleague tells me Dyk paid a price once canned lion hunting made international news. This brought on investigations and fines for animal neglect. Then, violations of endangered species laws took their toll. He sold most of his cheetahs to the Saudi royal family to pay the fines."

"The wolves will not change his fortunes." He turned the key. The engine rumbled with a wheeze, and the Land Rover was moving, back onto the dirt road, down to the blacktop highway.

"By the time we get to Musina, the border post will be closed." She checked her watch.

"We will stay on Du Plessis's farm tonight." Marais shifted into third gear as the road straightened out.

"Is that what the mountain is for?" Venter looked over her shoulder to the rear of the Land Rover, where there was a cardboard pallet with several cases of beer.

"Perhaps he can keep an eye on the wolves for us."

"Man, they are not our animals in any case." She planted a boot on the dashboard. "And the other packs are doing fine. We could concentrate on them."

"There is something special about that pair. No wolves that young ever led their own pack."

"The pack died, so maybe they are not so special."

"Distemper strikes down entire families, regardless of the experience level of the alpha." He shook his head. "And Venter?"

"What?"

"Every Painted wolf matters. Every last one of them."

Chapter 51

The Land Rover bounced over the rough dirt road as the sun was setting on the Lowveld. Somehow Johan Marais knew where to drive despite the dimming light, his steering anticipating the stones that could rupture a tire.

Mild rains had tailed off for the evening, and the rich scent of soil and leaf were in the air. Late summer left a lingering heat on the Lowveld even as nightfall approached.

"The *Kasteel* will need to rest before they are opened." She laughed, indicating the cargo area. The shrink-wrapped six packs emblazoned with CASTLE LAGER had shifted and rolled about. None had burst, a testament to South African engineering's ability to protect alcohol from the rough roads. The bottles appeared to strain at their captivity.

"Do not bet on Du Plessis having patience." Marais allowed a flicker of a smile to appear.

The winding dirt road was strewn with rocks and gravel, occasional washouts creating rough ground that tested the limits of the vehicle's suspension. It seemed to go on forever, past endless stands of flat-topped wild seringa, various acacias, and twisted wild olive trees heavy with fruit. Impala and wildebeest chewed on mouthfuls of the rich green grass, eyeing the Land Rover with suspicion.

The ruts wound carefully around a stand of several *Aloe candelabrum*, the hefty trunks skirted by brown dead leaf remains that hung down.

Thick green succulent leaves extended out from the top of the trunks. The crowns of golden florets stood two meters above the ground and resembled braziers, especially now as they caught the descending sun.

The path ended at a small red brick dwelling only slightly larger than a two-car garage. Corrugated steel roofing topped the dark red of the walls, glass windows encased with iron bars. The wooden door was open, and before it stood a man wearing dark green cargo shorts with a khaki shirt tucked in over a protuberant abdomen. The shirt was dark green in the upper half bib area, the rest the color of almond, with shirt and shorts covered with pockets. Dark brown boots and a faded brown cap completed his attire. His mustache and beard were greyed, and eyes stark blue, almost silver in appearance. As they coasted to a stop, the man raised his bottle in their direction.

Marais was calling through his open window before they were parked.

"Du Plessis! *Howzit!*"

The man in khakis tossed his bottle into a nearby empty metal drum as he walked out to them. His other hand already held a freshly opened bottle. "*Ag*, Johan. How long has it been, eh?"

"Too long, *vriend.*" Two hands clasped together in greeting. "Are you at work or play?"

"Mended the fences again today, but mostly tending to the impala. Work and play."

"When you live in the bush, those are one and the same."

Du Plessis laughed. "Well, it is like the difference between a ruck and a maul. Subtle but significant." He saw Venter hauling some of the cases out of the boot of the Land Rover. "*Dankie* for the beer, but what are you going to have, *meisie?*"

She managed to shake his hand while just keeping hold of the shrink-wrapped bottles. "Sonja Venter."

"So, you researching the ultimate underdog with this *oke?*"

"That's how we came to be here." Marais clapped him on the back as they walked around the back of the small house to make themselves at home.

Darkness took the bushveld, and the wide-open sky closed. The limitless space of the great savanna, seeming to hold the entire world, shrank at night. The far horizon drew close, to just beyond the wavering flames of a bonfire.

As they sat around a raised concrete surface where a small fire began to flicker, Marais told Du Plessis of the Painted wolves, the tracking device, distemper, and their cage at *Wildsplaas*. The kindling was aflame, the fire licking the more substantial hard firewood piled just above it. The four corners of the concrete platform had breezeblocks stacked, and these supported a large, wide grill grate. Off to one side was a heavy plastic cooler filled with ice. While Marais spoke, he removed several pounds of meat to a side table, and emptied the cases of beer bottles into the ice.

"So we left. There really was nothing more to do." Marais stared at the firewood, underside just beginning to glow.

Du Plessis nodded. He extended a hand into the fire, the tips of the flame dancing over his fingers leaving black marks. "Strange, isn't it?" He sat, bottle in hand. "The notion of owning animals. I own that *bliksem* just there." He pointed to an impala with long, curved horns standing on the edge of a line of acacia brush. Seeming to realize he was an object of attention, he withdrew behind the leafy border. "But he can leave whenever it suits him. He knows nothing of being bought at auction, only that he was captive, and now is back in the wild." Swig of the beer. "Sometimes I think aliens must come down and round us up. Explaining 'right, we own you, off to the farm'. A little reminder where we stand in this world."

"I doubt the farmers around here would agree with you." She spoke low, not sure what to make of this man.

"Yes and no." Du Plessis motioned to someone in the distance. "*Kom hier! Kasteel and vleis!*" From the night two other men emerged, both dressed in blue overalls. Their dark skin was covered with dust. Du Plessis motioned them toward the cooler, and they muttered to each other in Sotho. They each gave him a salute and kept walking into the night.

"Neighbors?"

"They live on my land." Du Plessis raised his brow, pointing his finger off into the distance. "Their families once lived here, hunting, raising cattle. Then along came farmers with guns. 'Right, we own this land, *voetsek* with you.' Before that, Nguni people kept their cattle, until Shaka swept through. 'Right, this is all mine, and take this *assegai* in your belly for your trouble.'" Tip of the bottle. "And before that, Bantu people in the Iron Age brought in their cattle to take the land, and slaughtered the *San* bushmen who were here for ten thousand years. The *San* had it right. They hunted with borrowed time, on borrowed land, killing meat that was borrowed as well. And they knew it was borrowed. That, my friends—" His finger pointing in accusatory fashion. "— is what we forgot." He adjusted the wood on the fire, his hands seemingly impervious to burning wood logs.

"So we return to the days of the *San* and our problems are over?" She stared at the flames licking over the wood.

"*Ag*, man, nothing is simple. Nothing ever can be. Voortrekkers came and took land from the Zulus, and the Zulus killed the white wizards whenever they could. Bad blood was the only kind on offer. And Chief Makapane, to the east of us, massacred Voortrekker families, and the Voortrekkers came back for revenge. And in the end, the British came roaring back to take it all, and invent the concentration camp just for us."

"More violent times." She murmured.

"*Ja*, well, at that time, ethnic cleansing was the way of the world. One people conquer another, the loser is wiped from the Earth." He took a drink. "The Carthaginians lost against the Romans. Gone. Any *oke* facing the Mongols lost for all time. Indians lost against the Americans, and the few left were moved to concentration camps by another name. Any tribe in the way of Shaka was exterminated. Sometimes down to the last child. Today, conquerors think genocide is bad PR, and so they only hope the conquered become docile customers."

Marais nodded. "The peace now is uneasy at best."

"Peaceful for who, eh? The whole world is either getting ready for the next war, or are waging an economic war on poorer countries. Nature is caught in between. Giraffe going extinct, your Painted wolves are going extinct. Elephants and rhinos are being hunted legally and poached illegally to extinction—what care do they have for whether the extinction is legal? In the end, nothing will be left but animals that make money. And a cage for all of them."

"Maybe a cage for us too." Venter muttered.

Du Plessis smiled at her. "And with so many cages in the world, and getting smaller and smaller, does it even matter if we are outside or inside those cages? When there is nothing but cages, there is no outside." He tossed the bottle behind him, and it went in the metal drum. After a few moments of quiet, She chanced to speak again.

"There is no going back to the way things were."

"Right you are." The finger pointed again. He adjusted his cap, and was pacing by the fire, which was now consuming the soft wood. "No going back. The wild is gone, except for the remote wastes of Antarctica or the Rwenzori Mountains where people cannot live anyway. We move ahead to the new wild." He uncapped another bottle and held it aloft. "To the New Wild." The other two returned his gesture, and he drained half of his at a gulp. Dragging a tarp laden with fuel closer to the platform, he hefted three heavier logs onto the burning softwood.

"Any chance you could watch those wild dogs for me?" Marais peeled the label from his Castle bottle.

"*Ja*, of course. Quiet." He had his hand up, and looked into the void beyond the fire.

Silence.

She mouthed 'what?' to Marais.

"Jackal. Nice." Du Plessis cracked an enormous grin. He was gazing into shadows beyond the fire. Only after a few minutes did they see some movement that betrayed the presence of the jackal. A branch cracked, and a creeping form disappeared into the darkness.

"I will expect a dead impala by morning." Du Plessis saluted the departing predator with his *Kasteel*.

Venter looked at Marais with some puzzlement. "Are you going to shoot it?"

"*Fokoff*, man. I don't shoot them." His grin was gone, swallowed up by his greyed beard. He shook his head. "Shoot them." He scoffed. "I was just starting to like you, *meisie*."

"You are farming impala, *né?*"

"I—" Another gulp emptied the bottle, which was placed more gently in the bottom of the drum. "— am a scientist."

Marais chuckled.

"I raise impala because I wanted to return this place to the wild. Used to be a farm for cattle and some crops. Soybeans, tobacco. The soil was ruined, and the farmer had had enough with Apartheid politics. So he left, and I bought it all cheap. Then I brought some impala, kudu, and duiker to the land. This is a desert country for the most part, and these animals have done well here for millions of years. Why farm anything else? They are doing *lekker*."

"My father would agree with you." Venter raised her bottle, a salute that Du Plessis answered.

"So I talked to the nearby farms, and they all have problems with carnivores. Mostly jackal, a few reports of leopard, cheetah. Some time ago there were reports of wild dog, even. If you kill a jackal, then another one will come along and take over the territory."

"A tradition since *boers* came to the Cape." Marais poked the fire with a stick.

"I am trying to convince them to get guard dogs for their cattle to repel any hunters. Then, I do what I do best—sit back and wait."

"You are inviting jackals to kill your livestock?" She took a drink.

"Livestock, shit." He waved a hand in her direction. "We will see if the farmers still report losing cattle to carnivores when there is wild game on offer. The New Wild." He raised his bottle again and drank without waiting for anyone to answer.

"Are going to publish your results?" Marais propped his boots on the concrete *braai* slab.

"*Ja.*" He slit open the butcher paper holding the meat, and threw each on the grill. Rump steak, tenderloin, and several coils of *boerewors.* "Right on the wall of the ladies room at the pub."

As the meat roasted on the coals, the cooler gradually emptied, and the fire burned down to glowing embers. They talked of rugby, friends, family, and of nothing as the fading sun revealed the star filled sky.

The Southern Cross twinkled in the endless black above, while higher rose the burning white of the star Canopus.

The grey bark of a tree overlooking the fire shifted. A scops owl, invisible during the day, opened its large yellow eyes to stare at its territory. Subtle *krrrup* calls were issued as the tiny hunter ruffled its feathers, preparing for the evening's hunt.

They drank into the night, eventually falling asleep where they sat, oblivious to the mosquitoes that could not interrupt their drunken stupor. A Fiery-necked nightjar whistled past, *whir-whrrr-whhhrrrr!*

As they slumbered, and Du Plessis snored, a leopard crept past the fire that was now cold out. It could scent the discarded charred bones, but a stronger smell wafted from not far away. It left behind the brick house through the acacia brush, finding an impala carcass. It was carefully laid out, stripped of hide and select cuts of muscle from the rump, the pelvic tenderloin, and ribs. Its viscera were in a pile next to the butchered remains. The leopard began the work of stripping it clean of meat before vultures found it in the morning.

* * *

Bright midnight, the moon above shining on a grass clearing devoid of tree or rock. In the distance indistinct sounds permeated the air, bird calls, grunt of herbivore. None could be identified and created an odd background noise like an audience in darkness.

A wolf and a hyena lay on the ground, nearly prone. Neither could gain their feet, neither could fight or flee. The wolf, old and mostly black in coloration that appeared grey under the moon, pulled himself toward the hyena and ripped away a chunk of hide and muscle. The flesh did not bleed.

The hyena raised his head on a long neck covered in sores. He blinked, gave a giggle, and took a heaping mouthful of the wolf's haunch. This did not bleed, either.

The wolf regarded his wound, then looked up, and his gravelly voice filled the clearing.

"Ponder this, Koorsboom. If we eat each other, will anything be left?"

***

The young wolf jerked his limbs in a spasm, and was awake, suddenly aware of the sun burning down upon him. He wavered, and with effort was on his feet. Fence, Giraffe-thorn acacia, dirt road. All seemed in order.

"The scents are growing stronger." Olienhout padded from her resting spot.

"Our sense of smell recovers." He stepped to the fence, sniffing the rusted iron. He touched it with his nose, feeling the hardened keratin surface that was present since his recovery. A portion of the fence was bent inwards. He took this in his mouth, and adjusted, until he could feel the link slip between his shearing teeth.

"That would be unwise—"

He bit down, harder and harder, the muscles of his skull locked upon the metal. A loud crack like a gunshot reverberated through his skull, and he let go as pain blossomed in his head. He sank to the ground and tasted blood in his mouth, already knowing that a tooth had broken.

Olienhout was by his side, lapping his muzzle. He let out a long, slow whine.

"My mother taught me of this affliction—for those who survive, they are weakened, including their teeth. Some are so badly affected, they never hunt again."

They lay without much activity for the rest of the morning.

A mechanical sound, and smell of burning gasoline and ash. The sound of the engine died, and then the stamp and shifting of gravel. Four feet on the ground. Two men, both in blue coveralls, approached the enclosure.

Koorsboom did not move, or pace, or attempt to flee. A hand went into the bucket, and a chicken soared over the fence and thumped to the ground beside the wolves. This was followed by another thump, another chicken.

Olienhout devoured hers quickly, holding the body down with a forepaw as she ripped it to pieces. Nothing remained but a carpet of white feathers on the ground.

Koorsboom gingerly took his bird apart, chewing with care to avoid the shattered tooth. "The scent of lion is more pungent now." Koorsboom sniffed the air.

"It troubles me." Olienhout sniffed as well.

"Lions often do."

"No, something more than just lions." She paced the enclosure. "It troubles me that I no longer mind the smell." She continued to pace, restless. "It is everywhere, and there is no escape. And so, one becomes accustomed."

Koorsboom saw a hole along the base of the fence. "Did you discover yet more fence as you dug?"

"Fence, and then rock. My claws could find no purchase." The padding of her feet faded as she circled around the acacia. "The fence is too high to clear."

He nodded. "*Ek verstaan, my bokkie.* This terrible feeling." He took another piece from the chicken and swallowed it whole. "Of not minding."

Koorsboom looked out of the enclosure toward the fever tree, standing away from the fence. It did not quite catch the sun at this angle, but he smiled, thinking of the way it would glow later in the afternoon. For reasons he could not explain, this reassured him.

* * *

Midafternoon, a pair of boots clomped toward their pen. Blue coveralls and blue jacket, bucket in hand. The wolves padded to the fence, saliva dripping with anticipation. A gloved hand went in, and out came a headless white-feathered carcass. A practiced fling, and Olienhout caught it in her mouth. The second corpse cartwheeled over the fence, and Koorsboom caught it neatly. He shook the kill violently in his jaws, and white feathers coated the ground with unnatural snow.

The wolves trotted to the far side of the tree and ate in the quiet. Their appetite had returned.

After the men had left, and the meals completed, they paced their enclosure yet again.

Corner, side, corner, side.

Walk, pace, back, forth.

Sniffing the air, same animals detected as last time.

Corner, side, corner, side.

Day, night, day, night.

Chapter 52

An engine stopped nearby, and the wolves stood at the fence awaiting their meal.

Something was different about this day, and the number of footfalls were much greater.

"On your guard—there is an entire herd of them approaching." Olienhout rasped.

A group of humans emerged from behind the brush, and walked closer. None of them held buckets, and there were no blue coveralls that they came to recognize as the uniform of the workers. They had seen none of these people before, and the air was alive with the smell of soap and perfume.

"What is that noxious scent?" Koorsboom's nose wrinkled. "A sweet version of decay?"

The people all held devices, none large enough to be a threat. They babbled amongst each other, pointing and talking.

"Sounds like wildebeest." Olienhout said with a chirp.

Koorsboom laughed with her, glad of the distraction.

The humans spoke, and the wolves listened without understanding.

"Are they dangerous?" A woman in an orange jumper and denim pants. One hand held a camera, the other held tightly to an obese child.

"Oh yes. Any wild animal is dangerous if you get too close." The person speaking looked familiar, clad all in khaki, a thin face marked with stubble. Though he lacked blue coveralls, he must live here as well.

"Do they kill people, Dyk?"

"Decades of observation have shown not a single attack on humans. Adventure writers from earlier in the twentieth century claimed they were capable of wanton slaughter, but this was based on wild imaginations. They view us with interest, but not as food. Watch."

Koorsboom did indeed watch as Dyk approached the fence and took hold of a metal box that hung on the fence. A click and a clack parted the box and magically the fence developed a vertical hole. He started for a moment, mind racing with excitement for the first time in weeks. "Olienhout—this may be our chance!"

"Do not be so sure."

The man did not open the fence very far, slipping just inside the enclosure and closing the fence once more. Koorsboom deflated visibly. They continued to watch this person with bemusement as he turned his back to the wild dogs, and then sat on the ground. The humans on the other side of the fence gasped audibly.

"As you can see, they are not interested in me as meat. A lion would have a hold of my windpipe by now."

"What if you run from them?"

Dyk laughed, and was back on his feet. "They would chase, just to keep me in sight, to see if I did anything strange. They like to know the goings-on of the bush. But they would never attack." He opened the gate again, keeping a wary eye on the wolves. Closing the gate behind him, he addressed the audience. "Would you like to see them eat?"

The group seemed too afraid to respond until one the children exclaimed "Yes!"

He snapped his fingers, and made a hand gesture. A man in blue coveralls emerged from behind a vehicle, and approached with a bucket.

Koorsboom and Olienhout fixated on the bucket. They began a loud twittering to each other, anticipating the hunt, such as it was.

"They sound like birds, or whiny dogs!" One of the children pointed, laughing.

Each wolf caught one chicken as they were tossed over the fence. The dinner exploded in clouds of white.

"A pillow fight!" The crowd laughed uproariously, and the wolves retired from sight to dine.

The humans ambled off, and the engine of the tourist vehicle rattled to life as the tour continued. Olienhout heard the engine stop and start again over the next two hours as it stopped at different enclosures.

Each day, tourists stopped, usually at feeding times.

Two meals per day.

The weeks ground onward.

Chapter 53

The white *bakkie* rolled up to a fence that enclosed a vast area, and a man in dark brown pants got out. He jogged to the fence, pulled it open, and the *bakkie* drove through, stopping on the other side as the fence was closed behind it.

"This is our private reserve. We are alone here." Dyk had one hand on the wheel as the vehicle coasted on the dirt track, now two ruts in the mud. He looked at his client in the passenger seat.

The man in dark brown pants got back into the rear seat of the *bakkie* after closing the gate, and remained silent.

"Very nice." The client was reclined back, relaxed. His pale complexion was already pink with exposure to the sun. Clad in cotton khakis, a khaki shirt, and tan safari vest, he was sweating heavily. He looked behind his seat.

"No need to worry. Your rifle is behind us. You will have it in hand when we have found the animal."

"Beautiful here." The man sat back again, drumming his fingers on the door, his arm hung out of the window.

"Yes, it is stunning. Most of the reserves here have the Big Five, you know."

"You sure I can keep my window down?"

"Yes, nothing will harm you here. We take good care of our people." Dyk laughed, adjusting his hat.

The engine roared as it wound down the dirt path, careening off rocks and grinding through mud. The land rolled gently down, thatch grasses dotted with stands of sickle bush, African olive, and various acacia trees. The *bakkie* passed near a medium sized monkey orange tree, pale grey trunk holding aloft a crown of leathery green leaves. The branches still held a few yellow bulbous fruits the size of cricket balls. Vervet monkeys were perched, wrenching loose what remained of the fruits, gnawing on the orange flesh and avoiding the poisonous seeds. No other animals were in sight.

The enclosure was gigantic, the size of a small town, with fences carefully placed to blend with the environment. It resembled open wild, and Dyk did not correct the assumption made by customers.

Dyk pulled around on the wheel and parked the vehicle behind a rock outcropping bordered by red seringa trees.

"You remember what we discussed?"

"Yes." The man's jaw was set, brow low, eyes hardened. "I am ready." His voice was unsteady, a waver in his flat midwestern American accent. His right hand drifted over his heart for a moment.

"Are you sure?"

He nodded with vigor. The two men exited.

The other ranger in dark brown khaki was already out, and he hefted a long case. In the open back cargo area, he opened the case, and removed a large hunting rifle. He handed it to the tourist with a nod of approval.

"You made sure to bring enough gun, yeah?" Dyk laughed.

"Ruger .375 caliber magnum." He grinned. He clacked the bolt and opened the chamber, sliding in the bullet. The bolt clicked home.

The three men continued on foot across the wet ground, heavy boots clomping on grass or squishing into the mud. Dyk was in the lead, and he held his hat tightly as the wind whipped around them. The other man in khaki carried a bolt action rifle of his own. After ten minutes of walking, Dyk held up his hand to stop their walk.

"We have stalked far enough, our quarry is just ahead. See through the brush, just there?"

He pointed, holding aside a thorn-covered branch of acacia, toward a white rhino.

The grey behemoth placed one heavy foot before the other along the uneven ground. Movement was made with care, arthritic joints causing pain with each step. His funnel-like ears swiveled this way and that, straining for sounds of a threat above the whistling wind. Brown eyes were flecked with white of cataract, rendering him entirely blind. Drugs still coursed through his system, rendering him unable to move quickly. In his drunken stupor, the rhino's head collided with a tree, and he backed up to change course. Wavering, he nearly stumbled, managing to stay on his feet, but only just.

An ear-shattering report cut through the air, and a hole appeared in the old rhino's side between two ribs. The bullet tore through the other side, and both lungs began to rapidly fill with blood. He sank to the ground, gasping for air.

Click clack

Another gunshot ripped the air, another hole punched into the rhino's side. Followed by a third.

The rhino's breathing was rapid and shallow. Minute after minute, its respirations slowed.

Dyk held back the tourist until the rhino finally suffocated.

Dyk took photos with the tourist's camera and his own camera as he posed with his rifle, arm draped over the rhino's head. The tourist still breathed heavily, sweat spreading across his shirt.

They drove back to the *Wildsplaas* reception area, and the men drank scotch on a veranda watching the sun go down. The orange of blooming lion's eye flowers blazed in the sunset.

"Ah, that was exciting." The tourist held up another glass with iced scotch. "No thrill like hunting one of the most dangerous animals alive."

Dyk clapped him on the back, and walked away as his phone rang. He answered with a terse "Dyk."

"The horn is off. Taxidermy will finish with the fake horn in the morning."

"Good. Call the exporter, and confirm the price—in dollars." He disconnected, and returned to his client, who was launching into a story about a lion hunt.

"After several hours of stalking that cat, we had it cornered, and it charged right at me. Bang!" He mimed the action of a rifle. "Right between the goddamned eyes." He laughed loud and long.

Dyk laughed in kind, accustomed to the exaggerated stories by his clients.

The tourist held up his glass, beaming. "To Wild Africa."

***

Koorsboom lay, snout on the ground next to the fence. He watched the dirt puff in front of his nostrils with each exhale. He stared blankly toward a seringa tree, surrounded by spear grass.

A Black-backed jackal padded out of the brush. It froze, and locked eyes with Koorsboom for a moment. The smaller predator regarded Koorsboom, its small, sharp snout held low toward the ground. The black and silver stripe along its back resembled a cape, and its bushy tail waved one way, then the next. It relaxed, and he stood at his normal height, head held up. Another branch snapped away as a female jackal walked through the foliage and joined her mate.

The jackals stepped closer to the enclosure, and their eyes played over the metal links that formed its surface. They sniffed one another and they resumed their gait, side by side, along the edge of the fence, and on down the path.

Koorsboom watched them intently, and the easy strides they took under the moonlight. He watched them for several minutes, until both left his sight beyond a stand of seringa trees. Even after they had vanished into the brush, he continued watching, waiting for another glimpse of the wild.

***

A rattling buzz jarred the wolves out of their sleep. The sun was just over the trees to the east. A man in blue coveralls carried a small machine that issued a harsh roar. They glanced at it, and him, and sat in fear and wonder.

A large rectangle was staked out on the ground within sight of their enclosure with stakes and cherry red rope.

Next to one of the ropes was the phosphorescent green trunk of the fever tree.

Koorsboom shifted his weight, whimpering where he stood.

The man rotated the chainsaw until its blade was parallel with the ground, and throttled up the engine as it bit into the soft wood. A spout of whitish green powder shot away from the trunk as the chainsaw ate its way through. Two more cuts and the man stood back as the crown of leaves shuddered. A crack, and the tree toppled over, thudding to the ground with a rattle of leaves and a crash.

Koorsboom trudged over to Olienhout and lay by her side.

He did not speak again that day.

* * *

A walk along the perimeter of the fence, one paw before the other. No defects in the fence.

A sniff. The scent was dominated by humans, other captive animals, a hint of gasoline and ash.

Walking. Looking. Searching. Needing.

A defect in the fence? None detected.

Ever searching.

A way back to the way things were. Beyond reach. Perhaps forever.

Pacing, searching.

And if nothing was found, then waiting.

Awake.

With time, sharpness of sense would ebb, decaying as all things decay with time.

Dulling, slowing, stopping. Hope becomes a scar, twisted, ever present.

Will an opportunity not come?

He paced, watched, and waited.

His fur became matted, dirty.

His world was reduced to the minutes of wakefulness, and the fifteen meters of fence at a time.

Yet nothing yielded. The voice of Blackthorn echoed in his head.

Ever taut.

So it would be, in this unnatural unlife.

Until there would be a defect in the fence.

One is all I require.

Chapter 54

The Land Rover struggled over the rocks poking through the dirt and mud road. Weaving their way around such obstructions over the remote hills, 10 kilometers per hour was all the speed they could muster.

"Wild dogs, or dogs gone wild?" Marais optimistically shifted into second gear.

"Wild dogs, verbatim." Venter looked through the sheets on her clipboard. "The translation from Portuguese is less confusing." She murmured to herself. "Definitely not feral."

"This is not the right area." He held up a folded map of Gorongosa Park. Two blobs outlined in pencil partially overlapped over the south edge of the park with another smaller red blob to the east of them. "These two packs tussled for space, the big pack the clear winner overall. Another group, independent of the two, inhabit land much further east. Here marked in red pen." He dropped the map as they hit a group of rocks, and the Land Rover rattled over them. "Right. So we are further east still from that territory. So either they are on the move, or this report is *kak*."

"It has been a few months since I came out here with the posters." She retrieved the map from the floor. She pointed toward the back seat, where a box rustled around with each bounce. The box contained rolled-up brilliantly colored diagrams of cheetah, Painted wolves, and hyena.

"That could all backfire, you know. Or already has."

She grimaced at another jolt. "How so?"

"We teach people what wolves look like, soon every cow killed by feral dogs will be claimed as a wolf kill. And word is spreading that the government is compensating farmers for livestock taken out by wild carnivores."

She gave him a look that acknowledged as much. "We still must try." After several minutes in silence she spoke as though there were no pause. "They depend on us to try." After several more minutes, she continued. "The packs elsewhere are getting along. The metapopulation is successful enough in South Africa that there are no reserves to take them all."

Marais sighed. "That is a sign of a lack of habitat. Not success." He massaged his mutilated hand for a moment as they eased off a tree root growing into the road. "Their genetic diversity has suffered over the years. Some dens have utterly failed from inbreeding. So much for living the dream."

"What was that?"

"Living the—never mind."

He drove in silence for nearly an hour before he continued his thought. "Was this your dream, Venter? To work with wild dogs?"

"Well, working with carnivores in general, yes."

Marais nodded. "Mine as well." He sighed. "Time and distraction eroded that dream. All of my work—I am not sure it made the slightest difference."

"You never really know until afterwards whether you or your work mattered."

"Dreams are useful only for the genius." Marais paused as he maneuvered over a collection of relatively flat boulders. "Visionaries can wield the impossible and bring about a new reality we didn't even know was there. For everyone else—" He avoided looking at himself in the rear-view mirror. "—dreams distort and poison you. They bring delusion, and they should, really."

"What does that even mean? Should we put you on suicide watch, man?"

She held tight as the Land Rover teetered over another boulder.

"Well, you know." He gestured with his four-fingered hand. "It is just as well the world changes little despite the best efforts of all involved. Bigots and fanatics want to change the world, too. So at least we all fail equally."

"I am happy with small changes. One moment, one person, one wolf at a time."

Marais sighed, as though giving up the discussion.

"I am enjoying this work, at least." She looked to Marais for some sign of contentment. "Glad to be a part of something important."

Marais did not respond.

"Or at least a job one would do for free."

"For free?" He glanced at her and shifted gears with a lurch. "You may end up having your wish."

"Works for me. I love nature."

"I do not."

"You do not love nature?" Venter could not help but sound incredulous.

"No." He paused, rubbing his hand. "I need it. As does anyone who wishes to remain alive."

"Well, I meant—"

"It is where our food and water comes from. Sadly, the world has forgotten this, food coming from the store, and water from the tap, and nature no longer needs to exist."

She was not sure what to say without provoking an argument. She folded up the map. "This is the road here."

They pulled off onto a smaller dirt road, and this carried them onto level ground. Small wood or mud dwellings began to appear. Before long, they approached a village. Before the Land Rover stopped, several men were striding out to meet them. Their faces were twisted with anger.

She greeted them with a firm handshake, and the village men began to speak while Marais stood by, leaning on the open driver door, watching from a distance. Each man joined in, more animated than the last, with wide arm gestures and finger pointing. This went on for nearly an hour,

Venter quietly listening for most of it. At several points she asked short questions, offering cigarettes to the men at each question. At the end, she spoke very briefly, and the men erupted at once with shouting and more finger pointing. She nodded, never breaking eye contact, nodding, nodding. Finally, she shook the hands of each man who had met with her, and walked back to the vehicle.

Marais got in, slamming the door shut with a bang and turned the key.

"Feral dogs." She shook her head.

"Was it their appearance or behavior?" He spun the wheel around and drove slowly back the way they came.

"Both. The dogs were of various colors, not painted coats, they fought one another over the kill, and then attacked one of the farmers."

"I hope you did not tell them what behavior is typical."

She could not help but laugh. "You cannot blame people for trying. If their own dogs kill livestock, that is like a life savings gone."

* * *

The Land Rover took a road south and west, trundling in dirt ruts. Eventually they reached a tar road, and the transition was almost shocking.

"Like a mattress." Johan Marais settled in.

"What is the farmer's name?" Sonja Venter put her boot on the dashboard.

"Luis Bonete."

They drove on in without a word for the next hour. She tapped her boot with a pencil.

"Johan—where do you go when you have time off?"

"Nowhere. Tent out on the Mountain with a bottle of Klipdrift."

"You have friends?"

"*Ag*, man. They are exhausting." Marais shifted his considerable weight in the seat and set his jaw.

"What, pick up the phone and you are exhausted?"

"No. What is tiring is trying to sound glad someone answered."

"You do not like people, do you?" She smiled at him.

"Some. Most disappoint. I suppose everyone does if you know them long enough." He gripped the wheel tightly. "My best mate lives in Pretoria."

"How long since you chatted?"

"Three years." Marais allowed a smile to briefly cross his face.

"Not much of a friend."

"He is. One of the best. A policeman. He was best man at my wedding. Gave me the best advice I ever had."

"What was it?"

"Don't."

She chuckled. "So why not call him?"

"After years? Nothing to say."

They drove on in silence on the way to Bonete's farm. Marais examined the map, a finger tracing the road they followed. It led into the red circle drawn in pen.

* * *

Three adult Painted wolves scampered about the den, sniffing at small, plump bodies obscured in the grass. Heads down in the green foliage, tails in the air. Tiny paws reached up to the muzzle probing them.

Even at a distance, they were unmistakable. Another pup bounded atop a rock and yapped to the adults that mobbed it.

Marais lowered his binoculars. He nodded toward Venter. They crept back to the Land Rover, and the engine rattled to life. They slowly made their way back to the farm house, where the owner waited for them, glowering.

"I need them off my land now." Luis Bonete was clad in dirty khakis, hands on his hips. "Not next week, I mean now."

"Have they killed any of your cattle?" Marais asked softly.

"You want me to wait until they start killing my herd?" Bonete leaned in, veins on his head bulging and nostrils flaring. "You want to come round a few weeks from now and collect the dead bodies?" His hand dove into a cavernous pocket, and fished out a white box. 'MAGNUM Packaged Explosives Type E' black text proclaimed boldly on the cardboard.

Venter and Marais shared a glance.

"Control these damn things, or I will control them for you." The farmer turned and lurched away, grumbling to himself.

"We shall work on a solution." She spoke to the man's back.

"Time is against us." Marais muttered.

"We do not have the staff to dart this entire group." Her hands were in her black hair, massaging her skull. "Do we have a place for them?"

Marais stared at the wolves in the distance. He raised the binoculars toward his face, but dropped them again, and stared at the ground, breathing heavily. His hand throbbed, and he cursed it as always.

Chapter 55

The slight cool of night touched lightly upon the sleeping wolves, neither stirring as the breeze rattled the fence on its brackets. Grass whispered, and the nearby boekenhout trees moaned.

They lay next to one another, sharing body heat. When the wind rose into a subdued roar, Olienhout shifted closer to him, and the wind retreated again. She ignored the internal urge to prepare a den, the beckoning force denied in this strange place. Koorsboom had tried to mount her, but the sustained stress of confinement deadened her interest.

She did not explain this to him, nor did she need to.

* * *

A fawn body tore through acacia brush, cracked branches ringing staccato through the veld. Hooves of the impala hammered the earth, chest heaving, ribbed horns curved back, whistling through the air.

Swiftly the shadow followed it, a flash of gold, black, and white, with glinting ivory of fang. Hazel eyes were locked on their target, ears folded back, lean and muscular body hewn for this moment by a million years of evolution. The work was taxing, but the joy in effort and pride in craft is what made Aalwyn a great hunter.

The chase went on for two kilometers, neither adversary willing to concede. The Painted wolf was in purposeful stride, the buck tilting into a burst of speed. In this brief moment the two were in a desperate race against hunger, time, and the season to breed. As they struck ground, so did their ancestors from hundreds of millions of years past, on this and other lands.

The predator chased the prey as long as there was prey to strike, a pursuit neither could afford to lose.

The ears of the wolf detected the increasingly heavy breathing of the impala buck before it, and she picked up speed.

Knowing the wolf was closing the distance, the impala increased its pace to break away. Marble eyes rolled wetly, looking for escape, thick brush or open water. Its flanks felt hot, then numb as it began to flag and stumble.

Aalwyn's pace was sure, and her strike was true.

A sharp cut was scarcely felt across the impala's haunch. The mind, dulled by oxygen deprivation, barely could tell it was upended. Final thoughts could only concede the chase as the world blackened.

Aalwyn's jaws slashed away hide, spraying blood over her head and ruff of fur about her neck. Kurkbos gurgled with a mouthful of heart muscle, filling his expanding stomach. The yearlings that gripped and ripped away muscle and tendon did so ravenously, knowing the pups at the den were waiting patiently for them. Only the lightest chirps were issued by the wolves, feasting in near silence.

The heat of the mid-April morning warmed the bushveld.

Aalwyn stopped, staring at the carcass. Kurkbos did the same, and they shared a glance while the rest fed.

"Aalwyn?"

She stared back at him, lost in thought.

Both returned to the feed.

* * *

The pups were already bounding from the aardvark hole, mewling and yipping as they scented blood in the air. The adults and yearlings met

331

them, and as the pups licked the muzzles of the hunters, the begging was answered with liter after liter of impala meat and organ. The pups greedily consumed every speck that touched the ground, and the larger pieces were tugged into manageable ones between them all.

Kurkbos lay next to Aalwyn, who after giving her share to the pups gazed into the distance.

"They may be ready to move soon with the hunting party, should we be compromised."

She acknowledged him after a moment with a distracted nod.

"Should we chance another foray across the river this evening?"

"No."

"Agreed. The risk is unnecessary." Kurkbos continued to study her face, a storm of emotions. "We have survived here, despite being on the edge of the wild."

She stared at the claw marks made in the dirt.

"And you have returned to form since rejoining the coursing." He grinned, a flash of canine. "I wonder how ever we made a kill without you."

Her torn ear fluttered, discouraging a biting fly.

"The pups will be fine, my love." Kurkbos regarded her, his face a blank.

She turned to look at him again, as though recognizing something long since forgotten. She could not explain what went through her mind, lost and at the same time utterly focused.

"And we shall endure." He stared in her hazel eyes.

"Yes." She answered absently as she stood and began to walk, her mind already elsewhere.

Kurkbos lapped her muzzle gently before she left the denning area. He returned to the pups who celebrated their meal by collapsing in a torpid heap.

In the rising sun, she felt the presence of wolves who were her forebears, dead for millennia. They padded with her, looking beyond her, through tree and rock, over mountain and stream. Brushing close with her fur, looking far ahead for danger, and clearing her path.

At once she felt a strange detachment, one that humans feel as though glimpsing part of a world larger than comprehension, before it fades without providing an answer. Every scent and sound became a language she could understand.

The sounds of the bushveld enveloped the rest of the *Dwalen* pack, although none reached Aalwyn, who listened only to a distant heartbeat.

Chapter 56

They lay prone in the mid-morning sun, slumbering far longer than they would in the wild. The weeks bled together into a collection of time that no longer held meaning.

The morning rally in preparation for a hunt had vanished, as there was no place to run, no land to navigate, and no prey to cut down.

Food was provided, twice daily in predictable fashion. This was eaten in seconds, and nothing more occupied the day. Tourists were brought round at odd intervals, but the wolves no longer took an interest.

This day was different.

Koorsboom was up, on his paws, ears swiveling about in search of clues. Was it a scent that set them on edge? An errant sound?

Olienhout was on her paws as well, and they shared a look of concern.

A low rumble to the east drew their attention. Standing on lean legs, now bulked up from the regular meals, they had recovered from the distemper. Each glanced about as the rumbling approached, a lower pitch than the usual truck that delivered the chickens. Pops were heard as gravel crunched under heavy tires. Looking, scampering back and forth, they anticipated a danger, seeking escape routes that did not exist.

A large truck rolled into view, engine straining. The cab contained two workers, while the sides covered with black tarps had more workers hanging off. The tires crunched down, biting the rocks as they made slow progress toward the enclosure.

"Something is afoot, Koorsboom." Olienhout uttered a low growl, descending into a light whine. "Prepare to run."

"Your instincts are not often wrong, my *bokkie*." He sniffed the ground. "That opening. That is the only way out. And we may just, this time."

The truck made a lazy circle next to the fence, pulling away, then stopped. It then reversed, backing up to the gate.

The wolves tensed. Paws were flexed, claws dug into ground.

Several men in blue coveralls dismounted, crunching more gravel under their black gumboots. From the rear they pulled a ramp, hooking it to the rear of the truck. Each man unfurled more tarps that sealed off the space between the gate and the rear of the truck, producing a tunnel.

"Even this." Olienhout muttered. "These humans leave us no flaws to exploit."

A man strode down the ramp and unlocked the gate, entering.

More workers then entered the enclosure with tarps, and they strung them together. A line of men, each holding tarps creating a wall along one side of the cage.

Koorsboom padded to the gate, seeing only the tunnel, and the dark interior of the truck. He whined.

The wall began to move, boots clomping, and the tarp barrier swung around the cage, herding them closer to the gate. As their space diminished, the wolves darted into the tunnel, and up the ramp. The cage closed with a bang, the ramp was secured, and the rear of the truck was closed with another bang.

"There will be nowhere to run when we leave this thing." Olienhout shifted her weight, the floor vibrating as the engine rattled.

"How do you know we will leave?"

"Scent of lion, zebra, antelope." She sniffed the floor of the vehicle in the dim light. "Many creatures trod this place, and none are here now."

"And where have they gone?"

A lurch, and the floor moved underneath them. Every bump and jolt were felt, and they struggled to stabilize their footing. The smell of exhaust burned their nostrils. They could scent fear from the men.

"There will be a time when their vigilance flags." Koorsboom tried to lap her muzzle, but the bouncing of the truck made this difficult. "There is always a time."

***

The humans gawped at them. They muttered to one another as Olienhout and Koorsboom whirled about their new enclosure, gigantic compared to the last. They padded about quickly, sniffing the ground with equal parts fascination and anxiety. Every centimeter of the fence line was explored, looking up and down, every link properly intertwined.

"This fence is buried as well." Olienhout intoned, her forepaws clawing away the dirt, releasing shovelfuls of dirt between her hind legs. "To stone." Her claws scrabbled against a concrete base. She continued her survey.

Soap and perfume wafted from the tourists, wearing mostly khaki or colorful dresses.

"Why are dogs here?" The man let his camera hang slack. "Did they run away from home?"

"These are African Wild Dogs, also called the Cape Hunting D—"

"Were they killing cattle?" A woman holding the hand of her two restless children.

The guide patiently listened to the question, and resumed his spiel. "Cape Hunting Dog. They do not normally hunt livestock, preferring—"

"You mean if they saw a cow, they would have no interest in it?" The tourist snorted.

"They prefer wild antelope, but if deprived of that, then they will take livestock."

"Well, why don't farmers just shoot them all, then?" The man with the camera let it hang, and started to wander off.

"Can we go see the lions?"

"Can we pet a lion cub?"

"Of course, sir." The guide led the tourists away. The customer is always right.

Koorsboom and Olienhout watched them leave, and continued their exploration. More trees were in this larger enclosure, some acacia and red seringa. A single weeping wattle stood in the center, now losing its luminous yellow flowers.

"The scent of lion is stronger here." Olienhout muttered.

"Are we closer to where they are imprisoned?"

"Perhaps, but they were also here once. Many animals once walked these grounds." She raised her head, breeze tousling the ruff around her neck. "But no more."

"The fences are far enough apart, it almost reminds one of home." Koorsboom managed to sound wistful.

"This time of year, there would be no cold biting in the night, and the pups would be growing older. Weaned from milk, and enjoying the savor of the meat." She lay on the ground under the wattle. "I sense home is very far away. And yet I can feel the grasses under my paws, at least in memory. On the run, never tiring."

Olienhout glared to the distance, where the fence stood an eternal vigil.

"There was a time when we commanded the land entire." Her hazel eyes flashed in anger.

"No longer." Koorsboom lay next to her. "The savanna is in thrall to those who control the gates."

Chapter 57

The familiar sound of the giant truck crunching its way across gravel to the enclosure inspired no further anxiety, after all these days in the new enclosure. It was the smell that agitated them.

It was all too familiar.

Olienhout and Koorsboom sprinted along the edge, back and forth, loudly twittering among themselves as it approached.

The truck performed the same lazy circle back to the gate, until it was very close. The ramps were attached, the tarps put into place, and the gate was unlocked by a man in blue coveralls.

The twittering between Koorsboom and Olienhout intensified. Sharp, short chortling with higher pitching whines filled the area with chaotic sound.

When the rear of the truck was opened, there was no movement. Only a growl emanated from the darkness within, soon joined by another. Then another. After several minutes in standoff, one of the workers climbed into the truck. He yammered in annoyed twitters of his own, before banging on the inside of the truck with a shovel. After several metallic clangs, three Painted wolves raced down the ramp and into the enclosure, promptly locked shut.

For one very long minute, the five wolves stared at one another. Heavy, rapid breathing, with an occasional snuff. Large dish-like ears swiveled about, detecting the slightest nuance in silent communication. The scent of wolf musk hung in the air. All protocol of nature was warped by this strange place, and its close confines.

Olienhout began a deep rumbling, almost ultrasonic, then rising to a grating call.

"What madness does this portend?" Her fur was on end, the air electric.

"It seems our food supply has dwindled with these *okes* in place." Koorsboom bared fangs, drool streaming from his open mouth. "Or perhaps they have come to claim what little we have."

The ground was littered with the feathers of the two chickens each that were portioned for the last several days for the two resident wolves. A gruff bark shattered the impasse.

Olienhout narrowed her eyes to slender triangles. *"What say you? Shall we have a blood river this day?"* She rushed the closest wolf, snapping her jaws shut just as her adversary withdrew with stunning speed.

And that wolf spun about, bearing fangs of her own. Both ears were in tatters from an old battle, and a deep slash along her jaw and throat revealed an old snare wound long since survived.

"Then we shall fight." Olienhout rumbled. "And it will be dark indeed when we have finished."

* * *

"Our admissions data indicates about fifty tourists daily on average, and we estimate about five to ten of those people at any time would be inclined to overnight if a bed and breakfast on the grounds were available." Dyk droned on to the two suits in attendance, already sensing they would not be inclined to invest.

"Do you have numbers on local accommodation capacity and whether the market can sustain another venture?" The tone of the dark grey suit was flat and disinterested.

"We are preparing a survey—"

"The information is available from the Tourism Business Council."

"We will be accessing that—"

"And it seems the area is already at capacity excluding holidays. So your facility would be unlikely to benefit from further expansion."

Dyk mused various expletives to hurl at the suits.

The door was wrenched open by a worker in blue. *"Baas!* The dogs are attacking each other!"

Dyk sprinted from the office, relieved to have the interruption. "What happened?"

"We loosed the three new dogs into the enclosure with the other two, and they went right at each other." In a jeep the drive took a few minutes, and they could hear the melee at a distance.

"Separate them!" He leapt from the jeep as the workers scurried to the gate. It was opened, and three more men attempted to create a wall with tarps. The wolves, however, were moving too quickly, and the area was too large to isolate the animals. As soon as the men sealed off a corner of the enclosure, the animals would dance around the edge and would resume snapping at one another. Each would lunge at their adversary, a bite would release a spatter of blood, then a dash back before a wound was returned in kind. "Fetch me the tranquilizer gun!"

"If we dart one of them, won't they be killed by the others?"

"Kak." Dyk was at a loss. He was new to dealing with Painted wolves, and did not consider this possibility. He clenched his fists, and cursed under his breath. "Let them kill each other, then."

The fight did not last long. Koorsboom was wounded on his shoulder, and Olienhout had an ear nicked, but the other three fared badly. One limped heavily on a foreleg, another sported a deep wound on his haunch. Koorsboom stood at his mate's side, and did not advance further. "Are they a danger, then?"

Olienhout continued her growling. "Only a shadow of danger. Perhaps we have impressed them after all."

The three new dogs retreated slowly, haltingly, one of them bearing weight with difficulty on a wounded paw. One began whining, no longer issuing threats of any kind. "We will not challenge you... we yield this ground."

The wolf with the ripped ears snarled. "I will not starve."

Olienhout ceased her growling. "There is no hunt in this place. The humans bring the food." She looked about to the men, just outside the fence. They no longer ran about like vervet monkeys. Not for the first time, she saw some similarities between a monkey and the pale man in khaki, arms folded with a sour look on his face.

Olienhout searched the faces of the men staring at them. Her nostrils flared, scenting the emotions pouring off them.

"Let us finish off these creatures." Koorsboom snarled.

"No." She ruff-barked. "I suspect they will bring more of those strange birds now that you have joined us."

The wolves shared their growls, but the tension seemed to deflate with the promise of meat.

They continued to pace, eyeing one another, and the fence all around them.

One of the new wolves slumped on the ground, easing off his injured foreleg and paw. It throbbed as the animal heaved. His coloration was lighter than theirs, a southern trait. He bore a white stripe longitudinally along each side, originating from the black and gold ruff that hung around his neck.

"Leadwort has been my name." He grimaced at ease with his wounds. "Though seasons have passed since I have had occasion to use it." He grunted to himself. "At times I have forgotten it. One tends to lose these things, in the world of fences."

Another still had teeth bared, and was slow to withdraw aggression. Hers were the ears shredded and throat scarred long ago. She did not offer words.

"Her name is Wildevlier, and you can expect to hear nothing further from her. Not today, perhaps not ever." Leadwort reclined on his side, as though with no care about what came next. "Since her pack died in an enclosure from the Sickness, she has had nothing to discuss."

Olienhout tilted her head toward the nearby fence. "Are you all from one of… those places?"

"As long as I can remember, I and my mother before me dwelt within an enclosure. Some vast, some diminutive." He thought for a moment. "Or perhaps they grew smaller as I grew older."

"And you?" Olienhout inclined her head towards the third.

"Hardekool." She concealed her canines behind lips, and bowed her head in deference. Her eyes, however, did not soften with the gesture.

Koorsboom and Olienhout shared a glance, not sure what to make of an existence in captivity.

"How do your hunting skills fare?" Koorsboom chirped.

Leadwort grinned in the way of wolves. "Whatever do you mean by hunting?"

Dyk watched this with some interest. "Well, it looks like they won't kill themselves just yet." He placed hands on hips with some satisfaction. "That purchase was a good one after all. Thembiso—fetch us some chicken carcasses."

White feathered bodies arced over the fence, landing on the earth with meaty thuds. Olienhout and Koorsboom seized theirs immediately, wrenching them back and forth creating an instant cloud of white that settled gradually to the dust. Growling began anew from the introduced wolves, until three more thuds quieted them. Leadwort took his quickly, Hardekool took another soon after it thumped in a cloud of dust.

Wildevlier left hers alone until an hour passed and it seemed to simply disappear along with her.

Holding the dead bird with his good paw, Leadwort ripped the meat and bone in two. Between gulps, he probed Olienhout.

"How did you know we would be provided with food as well?" A swallow, and a glance to the female.

"We have spent much time with these creatures. From the wild, far to the north. And now, as it seems, in our new home." She rested her bloodied head upon forepaws. "Such a price we paid for this understanding."

Chapter 58

Koorsboom paused before the sleeping bodies of the three new Painted wolves. Leadwort's chest heaved, the dust puffing before his nostrils. Hardekool's forepaws twitched, probably running in a dream. Wildevlier was motionless, barely moving to even breathe.

The sun was already over the horizon, the morning birds calling, and a hadeda ibis blasting a *HA! DA!* in the distance. He wanted to awaken them, but could not approach.

"You are feeling awkward." Olienhout had crept behind him.

"Though I am unsure why. They are... well, not part of a pack."

"It takes time for interlopers to become a part of a whole." Olienhout looked down upon them dispassionately.

"We are drifters as much as they." He glanced at the nearby fence. "Anyone would be in this place."

He looked down to see twin hazel eyes opened, rimmed in red. Wildevlier glared at him.

In an abrupt lurch, she was on her paws and loped off, disappearing behind a clump of feverberry trees.

"Not sure what to think of that one." Koorsboom mused.

"I suspect the decimation of a family weighs upon her." Olienhout paced away, toward the nearby fence.

Leadwort lifted his head, eyes blinking awake with effort. He placed weight on his injured foreleg with reluctance, and limped over to Koorsboom. He lapped the younger wolf's muzzle, and Koorsboom at first shrank from this, then accepted the gesture, returning it in kind.

"We are in this together." Leadwort grimaced. "Whatever this is."

"It is difficult to tell with these creatures." Koorsboom muttered. "What was your experience within the fences?"

"Elsewhere, not far away, we lived like this." He looked about, turned with difficulty on three legs. "Smaller cage. Regular feeding, daily. Humans were often walking by."

"Sounds as dull as it has been here." Koorsboom sighed.

"Dull, perhaps, other than the mating."

Koorsboom gave him a quizzical look.

"We were caged in pairs, and moved about, but always male and female." His brow fell, along with his tone.

"Does not sound all bad."

"I sired a few litters of pups." Leadwort's voice wavered.

Koorsboom thought once again of his litter, pups lost forever to the fog of the Sickness.

"Each litter, a mob of fat, whimpering pups." He smiled sadly. "They were nursed by my mates, each in kind. Growing, and becoming wolves. Ready for the hunt." His eyes met Koorsboom's. "As they grew bigger, and were weaned with meat, they left the den for the sun outside. Each pup walked... that eager stumble out into the stark light of day."

"I know that walk." Koorsboom whined gently.

"And then they were gone."

Koorsboom did not breathe, and his heart began pounding.

"There were no bodies. No fur or blood. No scent of enemy." Leadwort snuffed. "They simply disappeared. The next litter, the same thing happened. Gone just after they were weaned."

Koorsboom growled, and glared at the fence. "I can suspect what creature took them."

"Had you a litter, before coming here?" Leadwort's jaw hung open, panting.

"Yes."

Leadwort did not ask further, reading the answer in Koorsboom's eyes.

The young wolf padded over to Hardekool, who was beginning to rouse.

"Awaken, hunter." He lapped her muzzle, growing used to their presence.

She raised her head, jaws wide in a yawn, teeth glinting in the dawn.

"Shall we explore?" He gestured toward the interior of the large enclosure.

Olienhout trotted up to them, tongue lolled out in the rising heat.

"Everyone is roused, it seems." She lapped Koorsboom's muzzle. "It is so peculiar. No preparation for the hunt." She thought to herself of the twice-daily hunting rallies that their pack engaged in on the veld. "No hunt. Nothing." The breeze tousled the black ruff of fur around her neck. "Outside of the wild, there is nothing."

"Nonetheless, we shall patrol our territory." Koorsboom shook himself free of dust.

Hardekool shared a cold look with Olienhout.

"Yes, we shall patrol." She took a step toward Hardekool. "You and I." Her voice was hard, and the command was unmistakable. She began her lope, and Hardekool struggled to keep up. The two wolves faded into the distance along the fence line.

* * *

The two made their way along the rusted iron fence, slender forms bouncing along a dirt track worn bare by the animals that preceded them. Rounded ears listened to the savanna ahead. Wild seringa trees dotted the enclosure, their flattened and spreading crowns providing shade below. Olienhout searched them for signs of vervet monkeys, and saw none. She sniffed the ground briefly before returning to her tireless lope.

"Nothing else is living here." Olienhout examined the ground, finding no tracks. Their path took them further along the fence, twisted iron weaved together into an impassable wall, yet allowing one to view the world denied to them.

They wandered past more seringa trees, Giraffe-thorn acacia. They paused under a red leaved fig, a bushy tree that held a bulbous arbor into the sky. Green fig fruits were beginning to adorn the branches. Olienhout took note of this, wondering if monkeys or baboons would attempt to harvest them, even here.

She stopped briefly, finding a deep impression in the ground. A large central pad with four oblong toe blots above, lacking claw prints. Her nostrils flared. She placed her paw upon the print and found it hard as concrete.

"Lion print—but devoid of scent." Her voice did not waver. "There are none here now."

"There were once." Hardekool rasped.

"I wondered if you would speak."

She held her tongue, not meeting Olienhout's gaze.

"Living within these aberrant places, wolf behavior must become aberrant in kind." She stood tall, and stared at Hardekool. "And so I must be explicit."

Hardekool returned her stare, and stood almost as tall.

"A pack, if you wish to be of a pack, may only have one matriarch." Olienhout narrowed her eyes and stepped closer. "Dispute this at your peril." The wolf she faced looked to the ground. Olienhout nodded, taking no satisfaction in asserting dominance, though she was gratified at correctly guessing the reason for Hardekool's discontent.

"Were you the head of your pack before finding yourself here?"

Hardekool moved as though to go around her before pausing. Her paw in the air, she considered her next step. Rounded ears began to flatten, then relaxed again.

"I was." Her voice was barely a whisper.

Olienhout took a step back.

Hardekool's eyes bored into the ground between her forepaws.

"What has shaken you so?" Olienhout no longer saw her as a potential rival, and lapped her muzzle tenderly. "Tell me, my sister."

Hardekool hesitated for a moment, then lay on the ground.

"Far from here. Worlds away." She became still as a statue. "Cages. Many, and more." She spoke haltingly. "Wire. Bitten, broken."

"You escaped?"

Hardekool looked with annoyance.

"Go on."

"Out of the cages. Found a wolf." She exposed her fangs. "Of the wild."

"Other wolves as well?"

"Yes."

Olienhout nodded, sighing. "At least you reached the wild places."

"Farms." Hardekool glanced at her.

"Humans came for you." Olienhout stared at the ground.

"We scattered. I was taken."

"You came so close to being a matriarch." Olienhout lapped her muzzle.

Hardekool's features softened, her posture slumping.

"Take heart. Your time may come again, Hardekool."

Hardekool lay down, appearing deflated.

"Our time may come again." Olienhout rested by her side, snout next to hers. "For us all. The wolf. The wild."

* * *

"I was rather expecting more blood on those two." Koorsboom stated as he watched Olienhout and Hardekool approach. To his surprise, they paused to lock jaws, then stand on hind legs to box with their forelegs for a moment, before returning to all fours and padding closer.

"Hardekool is stalwart." Leadwort nodded. "A tough one, always. And uncanny at finding food in the cages."

"*My bokkie.*" Koorsboom met Olienhout, lapping her muzzle in greeting.

"Feeding time?" Leadwort inquired.

"The humans come at varied times." Olienhout shook her head. "Inexplicable, all of this. And the food arrives wrapped in a stench of loathing and contempt."

"Where has Wildevlier gone?" Koorsboom glanced about.

"It is best not to account for that one." Leadwort intoned. "The madness that destroyed her pack has taken her mind. Only the body still stalks the land."

* * *

The *bakkie* drove to the fence with the usual cracking of rocks and gravel on the road. If it were not for the food it promised, the wolves would scarcely notice its approach. Four lanky forms in black, white, and gold fur monitored the gate. Five beheaded chickens took flight over the fence, some thumping to the ground, the others caught in midair in eager jaws.

Olienhout gnawed the feathers off her catch, tearing open the flesh beneath. Her teeth pried apart the carcass, all the while watching the fifth chicken. After the wolves finished their meals, which took only a few minutes, they parted to lay in the grass, further from the gate.

Olienhout retreated slightly to sit under a seringa tree. Branches arose from low on the trunk, spreading widely, the ends holding broad clumps of compound leaves. The ends of each branch held drooping spikes sporting creamy white flowers.

Hours passed, and the last chicken remained untouched. Olienhout raised her head to the sun, now overhead, and closed her eyes to the burning heat. Eventually, the fatigue of midday brought her to slumber.

Upon awakening, she immediately looked for it.

The carcass was gone.

Chapter 59

The sun was beginning its descent before the *bakkie* rumbled into view. Olienhout rested under an acacia, her coloration blending with the shade. From her vantage, she watched as the men slung their meals over the fence, each bouncing once before coming to a rest. Leadwort, Koorsboom, and Hardekool grabbed their food.

Koorsboom tore into his, quickly devouring the meat. Feathers adorned him, gradually drifting away with the wind. He looked about, and saw no one else nearby. He took hold of one more chicken and padded off toward his mate.

Under an acacia she lay on the ground, and her tail waved one way, then the other, as Koorsboom approached.

"A fine hunt." Olienhout tore into the chicken as it thumped to the earth. A vicious shake loosed a cloud of feathers, and holding it down with one paw, she ripped the skin open. All the while, she watched the last carcass sitting by the fence.

"Perhaps this will one day seem normal to us." Koorsboom muttered.

"Many days will need to pass for that to occur." She made short work of her food. Shortly she sensed him creeping next to her, brushing close.

"It may pass that we could raise a litter here." He gripped her forepaw in his teeth. "They could slip through the fence and bring the hunt to us."

"Your attentions to me are on the rise." Olienhout purred to him. "Strange that we feel less inhibited in a larger enclosure."

"I remain ever hopeful, Olienhout." He lapped her muzzle tenderly.

She stood and presented herself to him, and they mated in the shade of the acacia.

"Take heart, my love. We shall find a way." Koorsboom lapped her muzzle and padded off to patrol the fence once more.

Olienhout remained in the shade, and continued to watch the gate.

Nearly an hour later, Wildevlier crept along the fence line, peering about for signs of movement. Her ears, or what remained of them, were folded flat against her skull, slender body crouched. Her tail was low, her movement almost cat-like in bearing. Pausing near the gate, she glanced around once more before snatching the carcass and sprinting off along the fence from where she came. After waiting a few minutes, Olienhout padded off to follow her.

She was expecting a longer search, but the trail of discarded feathers led her to a clumping of acacia.

Wildevlier was finishing off her meal when she saw Olienhout approach. Immediately, she was on her paws, and slinking away.

"How did you survive?" Olienhout ruff-barked, willing her to stay.

Wildevlier kept moving off.

"You are capable of speech." Olienhout stood firm, refusing to follow her. "Disregard us if you must, but I will know how you survived your snare wound."

Wildevlier looked back.

"Such knowledge can save an entire pack." Her hazel eyes were resolute, and did not waver.

After taking another step, Wildevlier appeared to reconsider. She turned back toward Olienhout. Her rasping voice rose above the surrounding winds.

"I did not."

"I have little patience for games." Olienhout intoned.

"The snare throttled me. Riven open, my throat was bare to the world." She exposed her teeth, releasing slaver onto the ground.

"And yet you stand here."

350

"My run had torn the snare from its mooring." Her rasping voice quickened. "When I regained my footing, it was loose. The wire travelled with me for days, before I could extricate myself. The wound festered long before healing." Her chest heaved.

Far above, a Jackal buzzard called to the veld: *weeaah-ka-kaka!*

"So I did not survive." Wildevlier hissed. "I am whatever is left."

"And your pack was lost to the Sickness." Olienhout's voice softened.

"Yes."

"As was mine."

Wildevlier chuckled.

Olienhout's heart raced. "I did not realize I had spoken of a tragedy in jest."

"There is nothing but tragedy for our kind." Wildevlier snuffed. "All notions of a Pack. Keep them. Keep them far from me." She turned and began to pad away.

"There is only the Pack for us." Olienhout did not sound convinced, but said it nonetheless.

"Keep your delusions. I shall die alone. There is less pain in doing so." Her tail vanished behind thornbrush.

Lost in thought, Olienhout stared at the ground. She nodded to herself.

"You may be right about that, Wildevlier."

Chapter 60

The yearling pattered through the *Combretum* shrub and twittered quietly.

"We have found the herd, Kurkbos."

He gave a nod, and the pack was off. They spread out through the thickets, winding their way toward a gathering of impala.

"What ever is that noise?" Kurkbos inclined his head, ears swiveling to find the source of a low-frequency buzz.

"That is a... bird?" Another yearling tilted his head to the side at the sight of it. "Or the largest insect I have ever seen."

The drone hovered above them, with adjustments to its independently functioning rotors to remain stationary in the wind. Eight arms extended from a central hub, vertical motors whirring. The octagonal center held an inferiorly mounted camera that captured the action. An optional mount adjacent to this was designed to hold a darting gun, but this was empty.

As the wolves bounded through the sedge, the drone kept them in view. The herd of impala bolted as the wolves made contact, and they leapt as one away from the threat. Powerful hind legs drove each antelope into a high pronk, with a rear kick declaring to all in view that the impala was robust, and may not be worth chasing. The antelope took towering leaps over the brush, while the wolves plowed through it or around it. Each individual prey strained to escape, while wolves pressed their attack to surround and isolate their targets.

At last one impala stumbled, and the twittering from the wolves erupted at once, calling all to take advantage. They surrounded and killed the antelope, and the drone slowed to hover overhead.

Marais sat back as he watched the monitor, clutching a pint glass in hand. He upended it, savoring the earthy flavor of the plum red pinotage.

"The Mozzy drone has made the chase easier, no mistake." He set the glass down on the dirt.

"I can almost hear the Land Rover voice its gratitude. Not to mention my spine." Venter held the remote in her hands, making small adjustments as the wind picked up. "Wonder if this puts us out of a job, though, in the long run."

"If anything, our positions will be busier than ever with all the data these things will create." He tallied information from the hunt, the kill, herbivore herd numbers and dynamics. Marais sighed. "I am glad you talked the administrators into getting this." He nodded toward the younger ranger.

"Good investment." She smiled. "*Dankie* for picking it up while you were in Joburg."

"I was glad to get away from that funeral."

Venter shifted awkwardly in her seat on the grass. She was unsure what to ask when it came to the death of someone she did not know, but like most people, had to ask something. "How, um. How was it?"

"Successful. The body ended up in the ground."

"Well, it must have been nice to see friends from home." She still did not know quite how to take these conversations.

"Not really. Nostalgia for those *okes* is a blood sport."

"I heard that your friend, um." Venter shifted her seat again. "Was it, um, he—"

"Was he a suicide?"

"Yes." She swallowed the word.

"Yes, as well as a regrettably excellent shot." Marais had not taken his eyes from the monitor.

"Still. It is sad. Sorry to hear about that."

"How is it sad? He found his way out, and on his own terms."

Venter watched Marais as he carefully refilled his pint glass, and set it down on the dirt again. Adjusting the control on the drone, she considered asking the older ranger many questions, each dying in her throat. The image broadened on the monitor as the drone was adjusted to hover higher overhead.

"What ever happened to the alpha female?" She asked aloud, eager to change the subject.

"*Ek weet nie*. Nobody has seen her for a few weeks. The male seems to be keeping them in order. And he seems to be in no hurry to choose another mate."

"I inquired amongst the rangers to look out for signs of Painted wolf kills elsewhere."

"I was not planning to ask around the local villages." Marais snorted. "They need no loose carnivores to be distressed about the park."

"Understandable. Each cow or goat is their insurance policy." Venter moved the stick on the remote, swinging the drone around for another view of the feast. "I heard that word is getting round about Dyk and his new carnivores. Like he is trying to promote something."

"What, come and see the doggies in their tiny cage?"

"See them hunt and kill, something to that effect."

"He has no idea what he is doing." Marais rubbed his temple. "I saw his enclosures. No double fencing, no fire breaks, no real care taken with anything other than the stalking enclosure and the pub."

"My colleague in Joburg mentioned that he seemed to have plans for captive wild dogs. Now I have to wonder."

"He thinks tourists will want to see them tear prey to pieces." Marais flexed his left hand.

"Speaking of, last weekend, while you were away, I saw to another complaint about wolves."

"Livestock kill?" Marais took another drink from his pint glass.

"Bloody *kak* in any case. A village reported two goats were killed. Sure enough the owner demanded compensation, and asserted it was Painted wolves. He had one of my posters open on the table, pointing at it." She laughed to herself. "I swear, when I drove up, his hand was already out as if I carried cash for such an occasion." She shook her head. "The funny part is, he had no body to show me. No, the goats were consumed whole, bones and all."

"I bet they were consumed."

"Oh yes. Asking around the village, there was a wedding feast a few days before. One guess what the main course was." On the monitor, the wolves finished and left behind the carcass. "I am sure these efforts will bring a dividend. Someday."

"Someday." Marais flexed his four-fingered hand.

Venter stared at the ground.

"Johan, would you recommend any other Painted wolf research projects?"

He shrugged.

"Should the grant expire, I want to keep an open mind, and look for opportunities to learn in different contexts."

"Maybe find another animal to study."

"Your pessimism approaches nihilism." Her barb was sharper than she intended, but Marais barely seemed to notice.

"*Ag.*" He shook his head. "You would do well to seek someone else's advice." He took another gulp from the pint glass, the dark red of the wine catching rays of the sun. "Of the big decisions I have made, I regret every last one of them." His deep voice resonated across the grasses, without inflection, as though he spoke to no one.

"I doubt the animals or the people who live here regret them." She smiled in his direction, but he was not looking.

"Even if all we do ends in failure, at least these wolf packs will die on their own terms. Instead of languishing in zoos."

A low distant rumble.

"Bring back the Mozzy, Venter. A storm is coming."

* * *

As the dirt road approached the ranger station, Marais took his boot from the gas pedal. The Land Rover coasted along the twin ruts toward a dirty white *bakkie*.

A ranger leaned against the door of the vehicle.

"One moment." He murmured, slowing to a stop.

The ranger lifted a cigarette to his mouth and took a long drag, the smoke wreathed about his dark face.

Marais got out and clasped hands with the man.

"Razak."

Razak did not speak, answering him with the slightest of nods.

"Have you heard any word of Augusto?"

Shake of the head.

"It may be soon."

Nod of the head.

"I hear any word of Buatoom, you will be the first one I call."

Razak gave a wide grin, revealing sparkling white teeth. A nod of the head.

They clasped hands again. The shake lasted longer than expected, and Marais's face grew red.

"Hey—trying to hurt me?" He extricated his hand from Razak's.

"First." His voice was low and booming despite the word being spoken nearly at a whisper.

The Land Rover shifted as Marais swung his considerable weight into the driver seat. The door banged shut.

"What was that about?" Venter waved to him with a smile.

Razak gave her a subtle salute.

"Poachers." Johan removed a black book from his jacket pocket and made a note.

"The ones working around the northern border of the park?"

"No—a big one. The guy who pays the guy who pays the guys." He wrote a date as a reminder, a phone number under that, and circled it twice. "Nattapong Buatoom."

"Is there something I can do to help?"

"You must let me know if someone calls looking for me." He wrote down a number and a name. "I am waiting for this man. A poacher."

"Informant?"

"*Ja.* He will call me. About Buatoom, or his middle man Augusto." He handed her the piece of paper and put away his black book.

Turning the key, the engine rattled and thrummed. Razak lit another cigarette.

"People are waiting for him."

Chapter 61

Feathers covered the ground, matted with mud and congealed blood in a patch near the gate. Four wolves waited expectantly as the truck approached. Each drooled in anticipation, shifting weight from one paw to another, tensed and loose as they wondered what to anticipate. Ears swiveled in a search for information, only able to verify that, indeed, a vehicle approached.

"Something is off, Koorsboom." Olienhout stood back from the others.

"I feel it as well."

"It has been two days since we were fed. The pattern is breaking."

Koorsboom padded one way, then the next.

Leadwort sidled up to her. "What do we do?"

"Stay alert." Olienhout took another step back.

Hardekool watched the fence closely. Wildevlier, as usual, was hiding.

The large vehicle appeared, making the usual lazy circle and backing up to the gate.

"They are bringing more of our kind?" Koorsboom whined.

"I do not scent that." Olienhout backed up further.

"Something other." Hardekool spoke for the first time that day, and her voice was tinged with anxiety. Her head was held close to the ground, paws splayed.

Another engine whine could be heard of a second vehicle, and it drove up more rapidly. Gravel crunched, and the sound of human voices rose above it. It parked near the larger truck that had backed up to the gate.

Men in blue coveralls set up the tarp tunnel and unlocked the gate. The rear of the truck was opened, and from inside came a low snort.

Tourists tumbled off the other vehicle, two dozen of them, and they nattered among themselves.

Dyk led them, leaving the driver seat.

"Normally wild dogs follow their prey for many kilometers before they kill them. They do so quickly, and eat more quickly, which gives the impression they are wanton killers." He spoke in a high, overloud voice, attempting to drown out the mumbling of the children present. "They must eat fast or a lion or hyena could ambush them."

He gave a nod to the men in blue, and the gate to the enclosure swung open. Banging noises inside the rear of the truck were answered with a metallic drumming of hooves on steel. Down the ramp and into the enclosure went a female impala.

Olienhout could not have been more surprised if she were presented with a humpback whale. It had been months since either saw an antelope, when the distemper had taken hold.

The impala stamped, snorting, and stared wide-eyed at the four wolves.

Each wolf gushed saliva, and took a step toward the impala.

The antelope bolted, and Koorsboom and Olienhout were fast behind it. The other two followed their lead, and gave chase.

The hunt ended within seconds as the impala sprinted headlong into the chain-link fence, breaking her neck instantly.

"Right. Well." Koorsboom ground to a halt beside it. The four tore into the antelope, ripping away the hide, removing the organs, spilling the intestines in a steaming pile. After Koorsboom and Olienhout demonstrated how to dismember it by seizing a limb each and pulling, Leadwort and Hardekool made quick work of the carcass. The hide was pulled away in sheets.

The tourists began to protest and stammer.

"Why... why are they doing this!"

"Ugh, this is disgusting!"

"Horrible."

"Is that all there is to a hunt?"

"Well, that was anticlimactic."

Dyk glared at the wolves, his arms folded. He put a hand on the shoulder of one of the workers. "There should have at least been a chase around the enclosure, don't you think?"

The man in blue shrugged, disinterested.

"No way am I finding a bigger pen for these miserable things." He shook his head as the tourists wandered back toward their transport. "Would you like to see the lions now?" He offered to one of the tourists, clad in oversized khakis.

"Yes, I think you owe us something interesting after *that*."

* * *

Dyk seethed as he walked down the hallway to his office, heavy boots clomping on the concrete floor. He pushed open the door to find Johan Marais seated in front of his desk.

"Johan." He closed the door behind him, depositing his hat on a shelf. He forced a smile onto his face. "How can I help you?"

Marais brought from his cavernous jacket pocket a fat yellow envelope.

"One hundred thousand rand." He set it down on the desk, but left his hand on top of it. "All five of them, plus transport."

Dyk stared at the envelope, avoiding Marais's stare. He shifted uncomfortably, and took a deep breath.

"They are worth more than double that." He met Marais's brown eyes with a withering glare.

"Nobody will pay that amount for them. You cannot find a game reserve that will take them even for free."

"Two hundred thousand is the price, if you want them so badly. You can fundraise."

Marais pulled the envelope off the desk and returned it to his pocket. He studied Dyk's face, but no emotion crossed it.

Resisting the urge to look at the ranger's bulging pocket, Dyk picked up a pencil and started doodling on a pad. "Tourists have been quite keen on them so far. The impala hunt just today made quite an impression."

"You put an impala in their enclosure?"

"Yes. They loved it."

Marais allowed a slight grin. "They ran it right into a fence, *né?*"

Dyk's face hung slack. "Who told you—"

"Nobody did. That is what wolves do with prey in fenced reserves." Marais resisted the impulse to discuss the unethical nature of captive feeding with live game. Surely, a seed upon barren ground. He withdrew the envelope again. "Last chance."

Dyk bit the inside of his mouth. "Look, my investors have expressed their interest in them, and they will not part with them for that little."

"I know you need the money, Dyk." Marais rubbed his temple, exhaling. "Canned lion hunting interest is waning. And you recently sold your last cheetah."

He opened a drawer with a metallic clang.

"I ate a lot of *kak* from you, Johan, over the years." Dyk sat back. "You talk a lot of shit about this place, with your self-righteous bunny-hugging. And now you ask me for a favor like this?"

Marais shut his eyes tightly.

"I think you lost your mind in the bush war. Instead of working in the real world, you hug your bunnies and sit in the bush like a loser. You hate everyone who works, who makes a profit. Well now you can take your wolves if you come up with *three* hundred thousand rand of profit for me." Dyk flashed a grin. "How does that suit you, my friend?"

"You are not my friend, you poaching shitgibbon." Marais growled, his hands locked on the desk before him. "I know plenty of farmers who do not need canned hunting, raising animals in filth, and doing business with poachers to make money."

"Prove a single word of that, bunny-hugger." Dyk dropped his pencil, a smirk curling his mouth.

Marais scoffed. "*Bliksems* like you." His face contorted with anger, he began to lift his side of the desk with a mind to put it and that smirk through the wall.

Dyk brought up his other hand from under the desk, now holding a pistol. He cocked the hammer.

"Back to your bunnies, prat."

Marais gently set down the desk back on its feet and stood up, scowling at Dyk with derision. He turned and stalked out of the office, slamming the door.

The front door of the building was kicked open, shattering the glass in the frame. Glass chips crackled under his boots. The long route through the offices, past the pub basking in the golden setting sun, and holding pen after holding pen of animals served only to intensify his rage.

He climbed into his Land Rover and turned the key, fuming. He pulled away, out of the parking lot and down a dirt path. Dull thudding stuttered underneath as he passed over a cattle grid at the guard shack. The man inside ignored him, staring with dead eyes out his window. Along the tall fence that bordered the property, a giraffe paced, its head bobbing back and forth. Between stands of trees, he glimpsed for a moment the enclosure that held the wild dogs, and it was gone. At the end of the long dirt road he pulled onto the tar surface of the highway. As more pressure was placed on the accelerator, he rubbed his deformed hand as it throbbed.

* * *

After a week, Dyk wished well the last group of tourists to comment on the wild dogs. None seemed enthused about their presence, and a second impala was sacrificed to the five predators before an incurious crowd. After their departure, he was on the phone.

"Van der Merwe? Dyk here. *Ja, nee,* well, fine. Look, I have five wild dogs, yeah, and I am not thinking they are working out." He nodded, listening. "Well, you warned me, *ja ja.* So do you think you can find some interested parties for what we discussed?" He nodded again. *"Goed.* I will move them to the stalking enclosure just now."

Chapter 62

The truck bounced along the road, metal shrieking with each jolt. The wolves inside balanced uneasily on the floor of the dark chamber, slivers of light piercing the edges of the tarp that covered the vehicle.

"We have been in here a longer duration than the last time we were moved." Koorsboom was rigid, steeled against the unpredictable lurches the transport took.

"Ours lasted days, it seemed." Leadwort groused. Nausea overtook him, and his vomit splashed on the floor of the vehicle.

"Day we entered. Night we emerged." Hardekool muttered.

"We shall find our fate soon." Olienhout was utterly calm.

The pitch of the engine rose as a gear shifted, and they seemed to slow down. Stopping with a whine from the brakes. A sudden reverse, causing the wolves to stumble a step. Stop again.

The engine rattled to a halt.

Talking. The odd wildebeest-like murmuring between several humans. The voices congregated near the rear of the truck where they were forced in.

Sure enough, the rear opened, revealing a tarp tunnel leading through a gate. Shovels banged against the walls.

"There is nothing for it." Olienhout padded down the ramp, and a quick look to the sides told her there would be no escape.

"Gigantic, this one is." Leadwort gasped in wonder as he padded after

363

her away from the vehicle. "Perhaps there are no fences this time!"

Wildevlier merely grunted in answer to that.

The smaller enclosure they were in was gone. There was no fencing here, or at least none they could see. Knob-thorn acacia, red seringa, and bushwillow trees dotted the veld. A bald *koppie* stood far away in the distance.

"There is blood on your shoulder." Olienhout sniffed Koorsboom, scenting the trickle of red high on his back. The dark grey Tick was gone.

"I feel nothing there." Koorsboom looked about. "Are we back in the wild, Olienhout?"

"I am not sure." She glanced all around her. "I suspect not." She sniffed the ground. "I can scent their vehicle, the noxious ash of their burning. Search for a barrier and listen for my call."

Leadwort smacked his muzzle. "Remarkably, I am famished after all that. When will we be fed, I wonder?"

"Perhaps we will not be." Olienhout trotted off.

"Whatever could she mean? There must always be food..." Leadwort looked about, worried.

"Desperate." Hardekool rasped.

Koorsboom was startled. Any time she spoke set him on edge.

"We are desperate. In this place." Hardekool glanced about, wary of every rock and tree.

* * *

Over an hour had passed. The wolves reconvened as the sun descended to brush the plateau to the north. Red light filtered through the atmosphere, the last before the following sunrise. The wolves hungered.

"There are indeed fences." Olienhout spoke first. "Our present cage is more expansive than the last. There is a gate that offers entry."

"No rivers or ponds." Leadwort scratched his side with a hind leg.

"Some trees, though not much cover on offer." Koorsboom lapped Olienhout's muzzle.

364

"No prey." Hardekool grumbled.

"We were brought to a place with no prey, and few places to hide." Olienhout paced, an edge of alarm in her voice. "There is something sinister at work here."

* * *

Dyk dialed the focus on his binoculars, and viewed the five wolves. Never were all in view at the same time. It annoyed him to no end that wolves defied even the slightest effort at surveillance.

In one hand he held the Tick. The disk still had a trace of blood and fur on it, from when it was wrenched from the filthy animal.

From a pocket he removed a pliers, closed the jaws upon the Tick, producing a satisfying crunch.

"Nobody is tracking you but me, *boykie*."

He held up his phone, noting the signal was nonexistent. Returning to his *bakkie*, he drove back to Wildsplaas. It was not until the nearby town he could make a phone call.

"*Howzit?* Do you have buyers yet?" He frowned. "Well, cast a wider net, then. See your people, put out the word. These things cost a lot of money to feed." He stuck a finger in one ear. "Of course it isn't legal, but nobody around here will give a toss. Just avoid being too explicit, just say 'A rare predator opportunity.'" He paused. "No wait—just this: 'Hunt the hunters.'"

Chapter 63

"Run, Olienhout!"

She dashed to her limit, but it was clear she was outmatched. Paw and claw struck the hardscrabble ground, and her deconditioning showed. The lingering after effects of distemper, poor nutrition, and the limited mobility of caged life had eaten away her stamina. She struggled to keep her footing as she weaved first one way, then the next, panting more heavily than a short sprint should require. Her heart fell as she realized time was up.

The scrub hare darted underneath the fence through a small flaw in the links, and into the veld beyond. Olienhout halted at the edge of the fence, looking wistfully at the departing meal.

"Bloody *kak.*" She and the others had not eaten for two days in their new enclosure. Olienhout showed no further interest in mating with Koorsboom during this lean time.

"Something will blunder in here again, and we will have another chance." Koorsboom lapped her muzzle with a dry tongue. "The others are in a bad state. Hardekool was taking a mouthful of dried grass when I saw her."

"It is my only consolation that with the time we have left—you are by my side." Olienhout returned his gesture.

"Lizards on the rocks just there." Leadwort trotted past them. "Not much else is on offer."

Hardekool joined them, face and paws obscured by dirt.

"Resumed digging at the fence?" Koorsboom inquired.

"The hole—deep as my chest." Hardekool was gradually speaking more around them.

"I can guess what you found."

She nodded, shaking her head, spraying dust and clods. "More fence."

Koorsboom looked up.

"Rather higher than the fences we last encountered." Olienhout looked up and across as well. "That would be up to the reach of a giraffe."

"Perhaps one was imprisoned here as well." Koorsboom remarked.

"They are not here now." Leadwort returned. "Faint scents of animals long past—have you noticed?"

Koorsboom shook his head. "Our sense of smell has suffered, I am afraid."

Leadwort held his nose close to the ground. "Everything is in the dust. Gazelle, impala, lion even." He continued to sniff, and his voice became more manic and bothered. "Some strange antelope I have never encountered. Giraffe, though faded. Some cats, perhaps a serval or caracal. And far on the other side there were the tracks from a medium sized elephant."

"Perhaps some of these creatures escaped." Leadwort managed to sound hopeful.

"Not a trace left." Hardekool was on her hind feet, looking at the horizon, then back on her paws.

* * *

The sound of a vehicle approached. All five wolves were at the gate, salivating and whining faintly. Even Wildevlier appeared, eyeing the other wolves with suspicion. Leadwort flicked his ear to dissuade the flies.

The truck slowed, but did not do a lazy circle, only stopping. The driver exited, leaving the door ajar and the engine idling. As the motor churned and the exhaust belched black smoke from the tailpipe, the man in blue coveralls retrieved a heavy bucket from the rear. He trudged to the fence, and set down the bucket. One at a time, he slung four decapitated chicken carcasses over the top of the fence. One at a time, they thudded to the dirt and each were seized by a wolf.

A fifth chicken banged ineffectually against the top of the fence, and thumped to the ground at the base. Koorsboom watched the others retreat with their meals while his rested on the wrong side of the barrier.

The man in blue coveralls did not notice, and returned the bucket to the rear of the truck. The door slammed shut, and the engine roared as the truck pulled away.

The white feathers fluttered in the breeze, one pulling free and floating away on the wind current. No blood seeped from the neck of the bird, now a part of the landscape.

"Olienhout." He did not tear his gaze from the carcass. "We haven't much time."

* * *

"Something is on your mind." Marais wrote his notes, tally marks in the appropriate column as the tablet display revealed an expansive herd of impala and wildebeest. The grasses of Gorongosa were productive beyond measure.

"What makes you say that?" Venter did not look up from the monitor for the Mozzy drone, making slight adjustments in guiding the device over a stand of acacia trees.

"You have said perhaps five words all morning." Marais mouthed the numbers as he counted the waterbuck present on the screen. Mark, mark, mark. "It leaves me to wonder."

She did not respond, other than a shrug. Her blue eyes met his, a crystal storm within.

"You need not weigh options for a plausible lie. Just tell me." Mark, mark, mark.

"Dyk is arranging a new hunt." The words left her mouth in an unprepared blurt. She regretted them immediately.

"I see." He paused in his marking, looking at the sky for a moment. "Lately he has been concentrating on rhino horn, I think. Commercial trophy hunters." More scratching on paper. "I take it this hunt is different."

"This one is not being advertised openly." She took a breath and decided there was no further reason to hold back.

Marais set down his pencil and began massaging his old snakebite wound.

"A veterinarian colleague of mine in Joburg found it online and recognized the contact number. A hunt, no details provided, to be held north of Brits." She was looking at the ground.

"Strange, most ads proclaim up front what animal, what odd mutant breed makes it interesting, to lure in customers."

"This one said almost nothing." Venter felt a burning in her chest. "She called the number, and the only information provided was that you get to 'Hunt the Hunters'. Her interest was really piqued, she paid the deposit, and found out what is on."

Marais folded his meaty hands together.

"Wild dogs."

Hands clenched. A joint popped.

"She called the provincial office, left messages, none answered. When she finally reached someone, they said there was nothing to prosecute." The ranger took a deep breath. "Not until afterwards."

Marais showed no reaction. He rubbed the scar over where the puff adder had injected venom that destroyed his middle finger.

"When is the hunt?" His affect was flat, voice devoid of emotion.

"Three days."

"I can make a few calls. No need to dwell on it." His voice had no tone.

Venter exhaled with a sigh of relief.

He only gestured with a head nod to continue their work.

Within the hour the survey of the herd was completed and the drone was returned to dock, and they packed up their equipment. The tally sheets indicated the date, time, sample count by species for the transect area, the temperature, weather, habitat type. The top of the sheet read "Road strip, south, 13km mark".

"Now you can tell me what is on *your* mind." She switched off the drone. "You are not upset?"

"Not in the least."

On the drive back to the field office the only sound was the thumping of rocks under tires, and the skitter of thornbrush against the doors.

Chapter 64

Leadwort and Olienhout lazed in the morning sun while Koorsboom paced the fence.

"As little food as we have had, it would be advisable to conserve energy. Do you not agree?" Leadwort flicked his ear against a biting fly.

"Against the diminishing resource of time, it may not be wise." Olienhout watched Koorsboom pace.

"When do you presume the humans will return to feed us again?"

"Their indifference suggests there will be no feeding. Who knows with these creatures?"

"Have you known a time outside of the fence?" Leadwort raised himself on a forepaw. "There seems to be so much more beyond these places. Though I have yet to venture."

"There is indeed a world beyond." Olienhout's voice was nearly a whisper. "It is vast, but barren of our kind. And vanishing, taken over by the humans. Theirs is a strange world, scented only by rubbish and ash."

"You have been in the wild?"

She raked the dirt with a claw.

"What of it?" Leadwort leaned towards her.

"It matters not. The wild is no more." She watched the trees of red seringa, crowns waving in the breeze. "Like you and your companions, I shall make my peace with it, as there is no escape. There are only the fences. If not this, then another."

* * *

The Land Rover sped along the tar road, careening hard to one side, then the next to avoid potholes deep enough to break an axle.

"Luis, we talked last week and you—" Marais held the phone, listening. "Yes, and you said you would leave them be." A bead of sweat ran down the side of his head.

"Did you tell him we would—" Sonja Venter gestured.

"We will compensate you for any cattle killed." Marais nodded to her, and gripped the wheel. The voice issued from the phone, metallic and distant. "We can move the wolves, but it is best if the pups are older. They only need a bit more time."

"We are maybe three kilometers away." She placed a finger on their map, held against the dashboard.

"We are coming just now, and we can dart a couple of the older dogs. Yes, we are on our way." Marais frowned. "What?" He held the phone away from his face. "He disconnected."

They drove on in silence, while Venter measured out a dose of sedative for the dart gun. Pulling off the main road onto a dirt path, they could hear the subdued rumble of rocks under their tires.

Whumpf!

The explosion sounded underwhelming, like a firecracker under a pillow, but enough to reverberate off the distant rock *koppies*. Marais and Venter shared a look, as though both were punched in the stomach. He cursed under his breath.

As they rolled up the dirt path beyond the gate, they could see Luis Bonete strolling leisurely towards them.

His dirty khakis were unchanged from their last visit, but his expression was brand new. His smile expressed triumph.

"All taken care of."

Marais rolled down his window. "We came to dart some of the adults."

"No need. I took care of them all." Giving a lighthearted wave, he grinned. "Never come back." He walked away, toward the great house in the distance. The engine continued to idle as they watched the man walk slowly down the path, following the gradual curve.

Step after step, they watched until he was out of sight beyond the tall grasses. Neither of them could speak.

Turning around the Land Rover on the narrow dirt road felt as though it took hours. It seemed even longer to reach the tar road.

The sun burned high in the sky, an accusing glare. Marais pulled off to a small *spaza* shop.

Marais waved to the owner, lounging on the *stoep* of the market. "Ten packs of Stuyvesant." His Afrikaans accent made his Portuguese passable at best.

"You started smoking, Johan?" Venter was confused.

"No." He muttered. "They are for a friend."

* * *

Dead, sightless eyes gazed on the two men who stood in the middle of the room. A sable antelope, its black shoulders and neck emerging from the wall on a wooden mount, held its head with twin curved horns high. The eyes were black glass marbles, staring through the wall ahead of it.

Joining the sable was a kudu with spiraled horns nearly scraping the wall behind, a cape buffalo with a head seeming to strain under the weight of its heavy horn, and the lighter head of a Thompson's gazelle. Lower on the wall was the protruding massive head of a white rhino, funnel ears extended forward as though listening carefully to the conversations of the room.

The head of an elephant took up a wall on its own, the great trunk hanging nearly to the floor from the wooden plaque that anchored the lifeless trophy. The real tusks had long since been replaced by plaster.

The men stood next to a table occupied by a half empty bottle of whiskey, standing next to three glasses. Next to this was a leopard, body frozen in a menacing pose with claws extended, jaws hung open in a mute snarl. The trophy was positioned on a stand with a tree branch, as though it was coiled in threat while high in a Giraffe-thorn acacia. The fur of the dead leopard was faded with age and dust, and smelled of must and mold.

"I hope their taxidermist got better with practice." One of the men poked the glass eye of the leopard, and the body shifted on its stand.

"Apparently we have a more expensive one retained for our catch. You get what you pay for, Don." The other man upended his glass, draining the rest of the whiskey within.

"The dollar goes a long way down here, Mike. One of the few good reasons to be in Africa." He spun the cap off the whiskey bottle, and it clattered to the floor below. "I like going to the exchange and getting a whole stack of blue and red *rand* with animals on it." His drawl drew out the 'rand'. "Damn good steak and lamb down here for cheap, too. Just make sure you tell them not to pour that syrupy shit on it. They put that stuff on everything."

"Wish I had that warning last night." Mike looked around him. "Sent that rump steak back to the damn kitchen." He looked about at the dead animal heads. "Hope this was worth the fifteen hour flight."

"You can't get this experience back home. Been comin' here for a few years now, and bagged an elephant or a rhino each time. Nothin' else like huntin' an animal that can kill you."

"Sounds like that lion hunt you went on last year was somethin'." Mike stared into the eyes of the sable. "You ever use this guy before?"

"Dyk?" The drawl slurred out the name. *Deeek.* "He's okay. Thought it would be good to try his place. Really seems to know how to navigate the regulations." Don slammed the whisky in one swallow.

"They have regulations here?"

"Better believe it." Don chuckled as he splashed more whiskey into his glass. "This third world country has a first-world bureaucracy. Every form requires another form, and whole ministries of government—" He pronounced this as 'guvr-munt'. "—are there with a hand out. The place I've used for years was shut down by some tree-huggers. You need someone who can get around rules written by people who hate hunters."

"I believe you." Mike poured into his glass while looking at the trophies on the walls. "Though, really, we coulda just stayed in North America and shot bears."

"This hunt's a good 'un to finish the trip." He paused to swallow. "I mean, so far, with bagging the kudu and a lion, we can't do that at home." Another pause. His face became redder with each drink. "And now, we hunt some real bastards."

"They really trying to get rid of wild dogs?"

"You bet. Just cruel things. They eat their prey alive." Don's brow was raised, given the gravity of this charge.

"They a challenge?" Mike swirled his drink.

"Too right, eh?" Dyk's high pitched voice echoed in the room.

"Dyk!" Don strode forward to clasp his hand with Dyk's, pumping it thoroughly.

"Been a year." Dyk's clipped accent caused the two men to lean in, concentrating. "Glad you decided to hunt on my land this time."

"Never forget that bull elephant from last year, on your friend's land." His drawl made Dyk lean in closer as well, straining to understand. He mimed a rifle in his hands, a buck, and a pump of the fist.

"Yes, yes." He turned to greet the other man. "Michael."

"Mike." He gripped Dyk's hand like a vise. "First time in Africa."

"Welcome to our country. Will you be taking in some birding, or sightseeing—"

"Just huntin'". Mike smirked.

"Very well. We have your payment in full, and we are a go at sunrise."

"Eight is fine with us." Don turned to look at the dead elephant.

"Yes. Eight." Dyk poured another glass for each of his guests. "You are familiar with the ground rules, Mike?"

"We're good." Don stepped closer to the elephant head, peering at the glass eyes.

"We will meet you in the morning and lead the tracking with a guide." Dyk put his hands on his hips as he spoke.

"And the trophies?"

"That will take time." Dyk feigned a look of concern. "The job is unusual as most taxidermy involves antelope, lion, and rhino. Not so many wild dogs, so it will take time to mount their heads and look right."

"About that." Don turned back and set down his glass, and pushed it closer to the bottle expectantly. "I want the whole body. Striking a hunting pose, looking real fierce."

"Very well." Dyk smiled widely. "I guarantee their delivery to the port."

"Good." Don lit a cigarette with a match, dropping this and his ash to the floor of the room.

"Very well, gentlemen. To the pub for the evening." Dyk clapped a hand on each back. They left the office, leaving behind a nearly empty bottle on the table next to the leopard, frozen in its eternal growl.

Chapter 65

That evening, the pub was filled with a raucous noise, with shouts, cheers, epithets, the blare of a rugby match in the background. The screen was not visible, but the action could be followed easily enough from the crowd's reaction.

Dyk held three fingers in the air, and the bartender gave a nod.

"We will begin the tracking at the gate." Dyk shouted above the din.

"Are we in an enclosure or something?" Don lit another cigarette.

"It is a huge piece of land, as big as a wild game park. This will require some stalking." Three pints were set down on the bar, and were quickly removed by eager hands.

"So you supply lions, leopards, all that?" Don gulped a third of the amber-tinted beer in his pint.

"Yes, you must come back again for another hunt." Dyk's grin widened further. "Whatever you are looking for, we will have it."

"Giraffe?"

"I did say anything."

Don laughed loudly, and drained another third of his pint. Mike smiled into his beer, sipping more slowly.

"We take good care of our clients, as we must. The animals of Africa are quite dangerous—and wild dogs are no exception."

"Are they really that scary?" Mike seemed skeptical.

"African wild dogs take down something every time they hunt." Dyk leveled his gaze at the two men, his smile gone. "Without fail. They kill their prey by eating it alive. Cruel and vicious. If they get behind you, we will be transporting your remains back home in coffee tins."

"And we are hunting these things *on foot?*" Mike was turning red, setting down his pint.

"That is the sport." Dyk gave a nod. "You are with hunters and trackers you can trust. And tomorrow, you will be glad you did." His smile reappeared, and the two men visibly relaxed.

"This will be good for a story." Don looked off toward nothing in particular. "You never know, you know."

"What?" Mike looked toward Don,

"When you get to be the last one to hunt an animal." He turned toward Dyk with a wide grin.

Dyk returned the grin, and raised his glass to Don's.

He laughed above the din. "To shoot the very last of them." He seemed far away as he weighed the gravity of this final kill, and his grin widened.

"That is why they are here." Mike gave a more reserved smile toward the floor, playing with his glass. "And why we are here."

Don nodded in agreement.

"Nature is here to serve mankind." Dyk held three fingers in the air again, waving them to be noticed by the bartender.

Don set his empty glass on the bar. The televised rugby match paused during an ad. *"Have dominion over every living thing."* His deep voice resounded across the bar during the lull, during which the bar was quiet.

"Spread the word, my friends." Dyk took the three pints that appeared as magic on the bar. The glasses were raised. "To *Hunting the hunters!*"

* * *

Disturbed sleep, plagued by shadowy creatures. The sounds of branches cracking, wind through leaves, all concealing the approach of a killer.

Koorsboom lay on his side, whining in his sleep. His paws twitched as he ran in his dream, ahead of his enemy.

It drew closer.

He jerked awake, and shook his head. Blinking away the sleep, he looked up to see the first rays of sunrise. The clearing where the other three wolves slept was bathed in a pale light. Wildevlier was missing as usual.

On his feet, he padded toward the fence, which rattled slightly in the wind. He placed a paw on it, and the iron gave slightly.

Clink-clink.

It sounded strange, loose somehow. He followed the barrier for a few meters and stared.

A vertical flaw in the fence. From just under the height of his head, down to the ground, the links were parted. A depression was dug a few centimeters deep in the other side, a failed attempt by some adversary to gain entry. An enemy powerful enough to bite through metal. Hyena? Honey badger?

He sensed the opportunity, and yet still was afraid. The danger that surrounded them in this place paralyzed him with fear.

The hunt is on, but I know not the prey.

He crouched, ears flattened, prepared for the attack. He sniffed the air, and the wind carried the scent of lion to his nostrils.

I failed my pack before. I cannot fail her now.

"I trouble the night with my sounding call." He raked the ground with a claw. "Against the bitter winds I howl. To my enemy I deliver fang and claw. And for my kind, the silence in passing." He crouched, every muscle strung tight. White knives unsheathed, a glint of teeth in the moonlight.

An echo reached his ears, as he strained to listen. He raised his voice, a howl to the wind.

"I sense someone out there in the darkness. Give your savage bellow." He bared his teeth, slaver released onto the ground. "You have heard my call."

The answer was resolute, as though carved in rock.

"Aalwyn answers..."

Chapter 66

The wolves bounded together, the six bouncing figures acquiring a golden glow with the rising sun. Olienhout spun about, scampering around Aalwyn in circles. Koorsboom was on his hind legs, boxing Hardekool, who managed a slight smile. Leadwort padded happily behind them, tongue lolling out, with the occasional glance back to the broken fence receding in the distance. Wildevlier managed to look somewhat less resentful with their freedom. She had been missing, but once the escape was underway, the wolf materialized from nowhere.

Again they stopped to greet one another, twittering madly, loudly, and heedless in their excitement.

"Back to the wild, Olienhout!" Koorsboom lapped her muzzle.

Aalwyn uttered a harsh growl and ruff-bark. "We are not in safety yet—keep your wits about you." She listened. "We have not much time." Her jaw ached from her work in the night. Each link of iron parted with extraordinary effort.

"We shall be quit of the fences, the humans, the dogs they keep..." He was too overjoyed to bring his voice under control.

"So as the father, the son." Aalwyn grinned in spite of her alarm. She batted her offspring aside. "You are still an impetuous pup in my sight."

Leadwort greeted the older female, dipping his head low in a subservient display. "It was an unexpected pleasure to meet you." He looked to

Hardekool and Wildevlier, who gave her the same gesture.

"Hardekool." She grinned, revealing serrated teeth. "To the far mountains?" She gestured to the distant *koppie*, her eyes filled with hope.

Wildevlier kept quiet, suspiciously eyeing the other wolves, and the grasses around them.

"So, on this fine morning," Leadwort shook his head free of flies. "Where could we be headed?"

Olienhout stopped her celebration, and padded to him. "What ever do you mean?"

"Will we find a place to be fed?"

Aalwyn looked at him, then the others. "Does this one have the Sickness?"

Koorsboom spoke with care. "There will be no feeding, my friend. I assure you, there is only death behind us."

"What shall we do? Humans are where we get food." Leadwort appeared crestfallen.

"Where does one even start with the answer?" Olienhout raised her brow.

A revving engine could be heard in the distance.

* * *

The *bakkie* stopped a dozen meters from the gate near a seringa tree, and the two hunters got out. Dyk and one of his workers picked up the elongated cases from the rear seats. The worker was clad in khakis in keeping with the appearance of a guide.

"Thando." Dyk motioned to him, without introducing him to the men. Thando handed him one of the cases.

Dyk carefully opened each case, inspecting the rifle, looking at the long axis, the trigger, the stock, and nodding with approval to the owner. This was for show, but an effective ritual to his customers. The rifles were returned to the men.

Dyk strode to the gate with his key, and unlocked it. The men made their way inside, and the gate closed with a clang. The lock was clicked shut.

Don and Mike hefted their rifles, eyes wide and surveying the distance for murderous animals. Each were dressed in the uniform of the tourist, with khaki pants and short sleeved shirts, each wearing a khaki safari hat.

Thando stood before them, holding a bucket. Dyk did not bother explaining to the tourists that the wolves had not been fed, and their approaching engine and the presence of a bucket was meant to attract the wolves.

None approached them.

Thando banged on the bucket with his hand, but nothing emerged from the brush.

"The hunt will soon be on." Dyk smirked.

Don and Mike began to slowly relax, their vigilance waning as they grew bored.

Thando set down the bucket and walked along the fence. He glanced back at Dyk with a frown, and Dyk sensed something had gone wrong.

Suddenly, Thando stopped, and ran back toward them.

"*Baas.*" He pointed down the fence line. "They are gone."

"What do you mean?" Dyk's clipped voice became more hushed as he rushed to Thando's side.

Following Thando's finger, he peered at the fence, and saw it.

He sprinted to the hole, gripped the links and pulled them wide. Plenty of room for a slender wild dog.

"*Shit.*"

"What's goin on, Dyk?" Don had strolled closer, and laid his rifle over his shoulder. Mike was close behind him.

"This is where they got out." Dyk ran a finger along one of the cut links while he knelt on the ground. The edges were jagged, bent. Drops of blood were on the ground along with bits of gold and black fur. Dyk, the tracker, and the two sport hunters were clustered around the opening in the fence.

"They bit the fence?" Don folded his arms. "Are you serious?"

"If they can shred an impala, they can bite metal." Dyk fumed. One hand was flat on the ground, and the other was a clenched fist on his thigh.

"The hell did you use this kind of fence for, if they could eat through it?" Don lit a cigarette with a match as he glared at Dyk. "Do you really know what you are doing?" He tossed the spent match, still smoldering, into the dried grass.

"Huh." Mike was bent over with him, empty hands playing with a brown stalk.

"They must bite like hyenas." Don had an odd grin on his face.

"So it would seem." Dyk's voice rose.

"You tellin' me you lost our damn trophies?" He took hold of his cigarette and exhaled, his wide face wreathed in smoke.

Dyk looked at the ground nervously, then forced a smile onto his face.

"This has turned into a *real* African hunt!"

"We paid for trophies, Dyk." His drawl was not as drawn out as it was earlier, and his face was set in a grim mask.

"You will get it. This man is the best guide in South Africa."

Thando looked at Dyk, eyes wide, mouthing 'What?'.

The four men returned along the fence to the gate. The lock was opened, and the gate was swung shut. The tourists wore looks of anger and disappointment, each carrying their rifles at ease. They began to walk back to the waiting vehicle.

"Back inside, then. We should have them in minutes—" Dyk closed his mouth with a click.

Don and Mike stopped short, the gravel kicked by their boots rumbling to a halt.

Leaning against the tourist *bakkie* was the stocky figure of Johan Marais.

"Friend of yours?" Don exhaled grey smoke.

His arms were folded, his jacket flapping in the moderate morning breeze. He was clothed in dark khakis encased in a layer of pale dust, heavy tan boots, and a brown strap over his shoulder. He looked up, his wide brimmed hat revealing brown eyes that verged on blackness.

"Gentlemen."

Dyk walked just ahead of his clients, an uneasy smile on his face. "What is the problem?"

"The hunt you had planned for today is off." His clipped Afrikaans accent lent a finality to his words.

"Like hell it is." Don coughed. "You a cop or something?"

Dyk held up a hand to calm him, looking back toward Mike, then again toward Marais. He took a step closer, eyeing the truck.

"That tracking device you removed from the wolf was the only invitation you needed to offer." Marais lowered his hands.

"Did you cut them free?" Dyk opened and closed his right hand. "That is illegal—"

"I did not need to." Marais, looking at Dyk's opening hand, dangled the ignition key of the truck from his own. "The wolves did that of their own accord." He shifted his weight.

"Look, you must—" Dyk froze as he noticed the barrel of a rifle swing just into view from behind Marais's back as he took a small step. His face grew pale as his heart slowed, and he came close to fainting. This passed quickly as he took a breath. "We can talk about this."

Marais nodded with a smile. "We have talked, and you refused my reasonable offer. Now the wolves are gone."

"Those are *my* dogs." Dyk hissed through clenched teeth.

Thando gradually backed away from them all, slinking along the fence. "*Jou dom stuk kak.*" He laughed. "There are only a few hundred of them in this whole country. When so few stands in the way of extinction, they *belong* to nobody."

Don's face grew redder still, and he dropped his burning cigarette on the ground. "You owe me a hell of a lotta money, you goddamned thief!" He hefted his rifle in both hands.

Dyk pointed a finger at the man and mouthed *shut up*.

In a singular motion, as quick as it was fluid, Marais shifted the strap off his shoulder and the rifle was in his hands. As he did this, the tourists gasped as one, and hesitantly began to raise their own guns.

Marais brought his rifle to bear, glaring down the sight at Don's throat. Don offered a wheeze in response, and lowered his firearm. Slightly.

Marais did not waver. The dark metal of the AK gleamed against the polished wooden stock, his hands tightening across the handle and barrel. Each of the men facing him took another step back.

"Hey now... hey..." Mike babbled, straining in vain for words that would change the situation.

"Drop them, or I drop you all." Marais's voice was crisp, quick, and uncompromising.

"Do it." Dyk gave this order as a rapid exhale.

Each hunting rifle thudded to the ground.

"Phones." He hefted the AK, angling the barrel ever slightly in their direction. *Plop. Plop.* Two phones laid at his feet. He lifted the rifle to his shoulder and took aim. *Plop* went a third phone bouncing to a rest. He nodded with satisfaction at the three phones, and crushed each under his boots.

"Johan, they are *animals.*" Dyk pleaded.

"So am I." Marais allowed himself a smile. "You wanted blood, gentlemen. You can still get your money's worth." He looked to Dyk, a mischievous grin crossing his face.

"My god. You are insane." Mike shook his head.

"Not at all. There are seven billion of us. The world will scarcely notice if we kill each other. I have no identification, no passport, and my death will not be investigated. The police in Limpopo drink too much to care about another *tsotsi* hit."

"The *polisie* will care about theft." Dyk clenched his hands, wishing for something to fill them.

"The wolves escaped your worthless cage. Insurance will not cover this."

Dyk was shaking his head. "You want to get killed, eh?"

"Your friend there was in the mood a minute ago. He will be again. And I am well aware this will ruin you."

"Load of *kak*, man." Dyk turned a bright red. "You have no idea about that."

"Nobody is going on a canned hunt with you after this. You took money and lost the prey. And you are running out of animals to sell to bored psychopaths."

"Let's do this. This lunatic is practically begging for it." Don attempted to whisper, but loud enough for all to hear.

"That's the spirit." Marais lifted the AK to his shoulder. He turned and fired two shots, one in each tire on the driver side. He swiftly moved to the opposite side and repeated the shots, followed by several into the engine block. Oil splatted on the ground beneath, mixed with other fluids. Dyk and the two hunters slowly picked themselves off the ground as Marais slipped another banana clip neatly home and chambered another round. "We have a lot of land to knock about in. This enclosure is several kilometers from your zoo. I have no intention of escaping." He climbed onto the vehicle and took a spare hunting rifle, emptying it of bullets. Tossing the handful of cartridges into the grass, Marais strode to where the men cringed on the ground, and did the same to their hunting rifles. Shells scattered amid the foliage.

Don was still trembling with rage. "We shoot rabid dogs like you where I'm from."

Marais continued to grin. "On the contrary—living out this day will be an uphill battle for you." His grin melted away. "Hunt the hunter." He sprinted toward the closest line of brush, disappearing rapidly into the hills.

Dyk bent over, dry heaving for a moment before standing up again. He took a deep breath.

"That sumbitch was right about you bein' ruined over this. I expect my money back." Don gritted his teeth. He lifted his rifle out of the grass, and pawed the ground for what bullets he could find.

"There is no... money." Dyk panted. "I have debts, that money—"

"Then we are going to get that man." Don chambered a round into his rifle. "I am either taking that money out of *your* ass, or his." He nodded to his friend. "Let's down this dog."

Mike shook his head. "Not for me."

"Are you shittin' me, Mike? He takes your money and you put up with that?"

"This ain't no drunk story you tell afterwards, where everything ends up okay. This is real. And I am really going." He gave a nod to Dyk. "I ain't shootin' at game that shoots back." He walked off down the long dirt road back to the tar, boots clomping in the dust. As he walked, he bent down to pluck a strand of grass to chew.

Dyk regarded his remaining client. "Are you ready for this?"

Don spat on the ground. "I have given this a great deal of thought." He set his jaw. "Let's kill this sumbitch."

The two men, each holding a hunting rifle, crouched and followed the path Marais took toward the high plateau.

Chapter 67

A slurred warble *trrr-chree-chrrrr* from a glossy starling punctured the dawn. The uniform blue-green plumage was brilliant in the light where it surveyed the dry savanna from a rock. The only other animal in sight was a man, concealed in the *Combretum* shrub. The starling took to wing to search for food amid the lush grasses.

Marais was crouched under dense brush, listening to the sounds of the meadow. The rolling hills made seeing any distance difficult. The roads were all dirt and gravel, washed out in some places from the rains. The tourist vehicle would be able to traverse even this if they were able to replace the tires. He suspected, however, that they would not risk losing him, and search on foot.

As he waited, he noticed a golden orb spider, suspended in midair between the branches. Vibrating as the breeze disturbed the web, the spider sat immobile, waiting for prey to blunder into its trap. The wind teased the vibrant green leaves of the seringa and wild pear trees, filling the air with the sound of rustling. Fighting against the force of wind, a butterfly fluttered through the sedge. Marais found himself hoping they decided to go home, and leave him to enjoy the peace of midday in the veld.

Crack

A rifle report echoed off the plateau behind him.

Marais lowered himself further, removing a pair of wire cutters from his pocket. This was cast to the ground. He was still amused by the notion of rescuing the wolves, only to find they facilitated their own escape. He could, at the very least, ensure they got away.

A rattle of gravel nearby, Marais could not tell where. He peered through the branches down a dried river gully. Checking again that his safety was off, his AK-47 rifle was pointed down the depression.

The wooden stock was worn, the steel oiled. His index finger brushed the trigger lightly.

Suddenly, the ranger heard a scratching beside him, and felt a pang in his chest as the unmistakable sound of a footfall reached his ears.

Turning his head slowly, Marais's brown eyes were met by the hazel of Aalwyn's.

He recognized her immediately.

The carnivore was less than a meter from him, yet he had no fear. Suddenly he felt far away, in another time, and another place, where humans and wild animals shared the land. The human regarded the wolf.

Aalwyn peered at him down a black muzzle, a vertical black stripe dividing the gold of her head. One ear was torn in a past battle. She stood at ease, scenting no panic, and detecting no malice. She sensed the presence of humans, long dead for millennia, hunting the veld under no threat from the Painted wolves that moved in packs fifty strong. In turn they were under no threat from these upright primates. The balance of an age long since departed passed between them.

"You are lovely, but for pity's sake, *voetsek.*"

Aalwyn, as though in understanding, vanished in the brush. She was followed closely by five other wolves, two of which he recognized from their coat patterns.

"You two." He smiled to himself. "I am glad you made it."

As the wolves passed, he became aware of the whine of an engine. His smile evaporated.

Marais was on his feet, shouldering the rifle, and ran along the riverbed. The wolves were ahead of him, moving in a line parallel to the riverbed.

Before him, he saw a line of dust rising along a dirt road, a small car racing at the head of the dust cloud. The wolves were headed right for it.

"Oh no." Marais was on his feet, in a dead run.

* * *

"There is no return, Leadwort. I will hear no more of it."

Leadwort sat on the ground in the middle of the dusty road. "Is there another cage where we are headed?"

The revving engine sounded closer and closer.

"This is folly." Aalwyn growled, refusing to speak loudly despite her anger. "Come with us, or return to your imprisonment. It matters not to us."

The engine stopped.

"We need not decide." Leadwort only grinned. "The humans have done so for us."

A shot split the air around them, echoing off the rocks. First close, then distant. Leadwort's eyes became glassy, then snapped back into focus. The promise of food forgotten, he darted into the brush next to Aalwyn, leaving the road.

Distantly, a whoop reached their ears.

"Hyena?" Hardekool rasped.

"Far worse." Aalwyn gave a ruff-bark. "Away with us, now!"

The sound of another shot reached them. Koorsboom heard a high whistle over his ear.

Two figures stood near a white car ahead of them.

"Got at least one of them." Don drawled, as he loaded more bullets into his rifle. He primed the bolt, sliding one into the chamber. "Hell, maybe that guy ran off."

"Do not be so sure." Dyk held a hand over his eyes, panting in the heat. One of his workers had been driving past, and he hastily took their car from them under threat of termination.

"Sure about what, the guy?"

"Yeah. Or that dog. I do not think you hit him."

"I never miss." Don chuckled. He put the rifle back to his shoulder.

"There—on the road." Dyk pointed.

"Got him." Don spotted the bounding rear of a wolf, rounded ears bouncing up and down over the grass tips. He lined up his shot.

A staccato crack from a rock by his feet left him reeling, and he dropped his rifle. He hit the ground, and looked over to see Dyk was crouched under a bush.

The white tail tip bounced out of sight as the wolves rounded a curve in the dirt road.

"Son of a bitch." Don seethed. "We can get back to the car and catch up to them."

"While we are being shot at?" Dyk looked at the man as though he proposed to sprout wings. He glanced back toward the squat white hatchback car.

"You owe me." His red face was twisted with rage.

"Worry about your trophy later." Dyk threw his hat to the ground. "The man shooting at us was in the Border War."

"So?"

"Those people brought back enemy soldiers as trophies." Dyk paused. "Are you clear about what you are in for?"

Don harrumphed, and hefted his rifle again. "Banana republic losers don't bother me." He poked Dyk in the chest with a finger. "And nobody robs me and lives out the day. Have some self-respect, boy."

"Those shots were only warnings, Don." Another whine split the sky as a bullet whizzed far above them.

"Warning understood." Don's grin grew larger.

Several ear-splitting cracks rang out across the plain.

"He ain't shooting at us!" Don got on one knee, shielding his eyes against the sun.

Metallic clangs reached their ears. Dyk looked back toward the car to see the windscreen shatter, a hole appear in the hood, and finally the two tires on one side hiss their air forth.

Dyk looked from the car, where the bullets had struck one side and the front of the car. He looked back over his shoulder, toward a steep rise up a high plateau, where green crowns of trees stabilized the crest, and smaller trees and shrubs anchored the slope. A flash of light, a reflection off metal.

Dyk crouched down, and looked back to see his client had noticed it as well.

The glaring sun baked the crimson rocks along the slope of the plateau. Further along, the rise was more gradual, with a tumble of rocks descending into a naked valley with few covering trees, and a dry riverbed at its base.

Dyk recoiled as a shot went over his head, and he looked back to see Don holding his rifle to his shoulder, smoke rising from the discharge.

"Careful, you idiot!"

"He is right, you know." He drawled. "This is your last hunt." He slid back the bolt, chambering another round. "He will make sure you lose everything." *Click.* "Or I will."

On one knee, he took aim, one eye closed, slowly moving the barrel along the slope. The shot split the air, and echoed off the rocky slope, followed by the higher pitch of a ricochet.

"There." Don was on his feet, and hustling as fast as his girth would allow, and Dyk was fast behind him. They neared the rise, and crouched under an acacia bush that provided some cover.

A cascade of small rocks came down the slope.

Further up the hill, a flutter of khaki moved between two thornbushes.

Dyk rolled onto his back and pointed up the slope that led to the higher plateau. "He is up on those rocks, eh?"

"Some scrub up there to hide behind." He scratched his chin. "Not so much on the way up."

They were on their feet and running toward the base of the plateau, ducking behind a leafy seringa tree. When they emerged from cover, more shots rang out. They returned to the shadows provided by a velvet bushwillow.

"We can try to climb using boulders as cover. Between us and—" He pointed carefully to a rocky outcropping where the last shots originated.

"No way out, though. Look." Don pointed beyond the outcropping, where the vertical rise appeared impossible to climb.

Dyk fished out binoculars and glassed the ridge. "Too right. We got him."

"Why is this guy so bound and determined to ruin you?" Don checked the breech of his rifle.

"Bunny hugger. Tried to get him to understand with these wolves, but *ag.*" He waved dismissively.

"Their time is up." Don scowled. "So is his."

"Well, I can make a go of this way up." Dyk looked up the slope.

"I will move further down and go behind that boulder just there." Their voices echoed across the plateau.

"I can take a few shots at him, and see if he gets flushed out."

"No—I can sit tight and wait for him—"

"What, so I can be the bait?"

"No, what—"

"*WILL YOU IDIOTS JUST GET ON WITH IT*" Marais's voice boomed across the rocks.

Don charged up the hill, rifle in both hands, stumbling on a loose rock with every other footfall.

Dyk loosed several shots, watching for a response from the ridge where Marais was hiding.

Don took position using a boulder as cover.

Observing the rock outcropping concealing their prey with binoculars, Dyk held his rifle close.

A shot rang out, and Dyk turned to see Don look toward the brush, ready to chamber another round. "I got him!"

Another shot answered, and Don's face vanished in a red cloud. His body collapsed, tumbling down the hillside bringing rocks with it. His body clambered to a rest close by. The twisted remains were thick with dust and blood, the deformed head marked by a shattered skull and large exit wound.

Dyk's heart raced with equal parts rage and fear, scrambling up the hillside on his stomach. Adrenaline allowed him to ignore the pain and bruises as rocks raked his underside, and he nearly broke a rib as he dragged himself behind a boulder.

Dyk glassed the ridge, across the rocky outcropping, and at this angle saw a small clump of vernonia, bristle-tipped purple flowers. Panning across this, a sharp white flash blinded him, and a rock next to his head exploded. Chips lacerated his cheek, and he could feel the wetness of blood dribbling down his face.

He brought the rifle butt to his shoulder, eyes straining to see down the sight and the outcropping from where the shot came. He could see nothing there but broken lines of shadow and rock.

Dyk pulled the trigger, and the shot rang with an echo across the ridge.

He heard it. Quiet, but distinct from the ambient noise of wind and bird calls.

An unmistakable *oof* sound.

Looking through the binoculars once again, he could see Marais trying to regain his feet. His right hand was on his AK rifle, his left was clapped over his right chest.

Dyk chambered another cartridge with the bolt action and raised the rifle again. Another shot, but it did not reach his target as Marais flopped behind another boulder.

Sprinting across the hillside, Dyk stumbled but covered the distance in a few minutes and rolled to the ground behind another medium sized rock. The sandstone was cream in color, layered with sediments from an ocean bottom.

Peering around the edge, he could see binoculars were no longer necessary. Blood spatters coated one of the nearby stones, and before him was a clump of Knob-thorn acacia that provided some cover. Another bullet found its way into the breech, and he took aim, eyes struggling to find some sign of his quarry among the bushes of acacia. The breeze tousled the branches, or perhaps they were moved by a man struggling to breathe. No sounds were betrayed. Suddenly, he saw it.

A subtle flash of light. The sun glinted off metal within the bush ahead of him. The Knob-thorn acacia shifted slightly in the wind, and there was another glint. He lifted the rifle, took aim, and fired, the kick powerful against his chest.

He stood to assess his prey, only to find his legs no longer supported him. He looked down to see he had dropped his gun without realizing it. A red circle rapidly widened across his chest and spread to his abdomen, his feeling of triumph seeping from him. He was lying on the ground, only vaguely aware of his fall.

He glanced up to see Marais emerging from behind another boulder, not from the acacia clump. He bent over to retrieve the signal mirror he had left wedged onto a branch of the acacia, now with a corner shot off.

"Why." Dyk mouthed, but no air gave it voice. The shell had ripped through the lining of his heart and lung, both filling with blood and collapsing promptly. His eyes were wide with disbelief as he took his last breath.

Marais stared at the man, taking all the while his own shallow breaths. Blood was leaking into his right lung cavity as well. Slinging the rifle over his shoulder, he danced down the hillside, desperation pushing him forward.

His breathing became more labored, his skin coated in a sheen of sweat. Bypassing the enclosure that once held the wolves, he took a route across the savanna to an accessory dirt road a kilometer distant. Every step was becoming agony as his chest tightened, his shoulder seared, and his breaths became shallow.

As he jogged with halting steps, hands fished in his pockets finding a pen and a pocket knife. Stopping his run, he wavered, dizzy, tearing open his shirt, buttons scattering.

He pulled each end off the pen, dumping the contents on the dirt. His right index finger probed for what he hoped was the second rib and plunged the blade of the pocket knife deep. A sputter greeted the steel as high-pressure air escaped around it with a bubbling of the blood welling on his chest. He worked the knife to widen the hole as his breaths became deeper and more substantial. For a moment he paused, struggling against losing consciousness.

He pushed the body of the pen into the wound, continued gasping for breath, and the pen spat droplets of blood and air.

He closed his eyes as he breathed, relishing the taste of air that was as sweet as marula fruit. The threat of the collapsed lung was staved off. Marais continued his march.

He still felt faint, and grew more so with time. Earlier in the day he had stashed a car a few hundred meters away in the bush. It contained hundreds of rand and the other half of the cigarettes he used to buy his way across the border.

Marais walked toward the car, each step a balancing act. He continued to replay the events of the day in his mind, wondering again how this came to pass, again coming up empty for an alternative. His left hand no longer throbbed, his head no longer creaked under the weight of a migraine. His thoughts turned instead to the wolves that followed his path in parallel, back to home. Or perhaps another home was in the making.

It is up to you now. Defy them all, queen of the veld.

He stumbled, regaining his feet quickly. His breaths became shallower despite the tube preventing further lung collapse. Close, the car was close. Then a short drive to the local hospital. He crossed a dirt road.

Marais stumbled again as he approached his goal, this time flat on his face. The blood seeped into his lung cavity, inexorably. Standing, with a deep breath, he approached a cluster of acacia shrubs and parted the branches.

No car.

He looked up and down the dirt road. Maybe it was in another direction. His mind spun, his breathing more shallow, quick panting breaths. North became South, all the same.

Johan Marais fell to the ground again, and was too weak to regain his feet.

Just need a little rest.

His thoughts drifted to Aalwyn. *How did you find them here? How will they get home?*

Paws upon earth, running, ever running, further and further away, returning to the wild.

To the wild.

Chapter 68

THE LOWVELD

Every hunt shall be the last.

Mist hung lightly over grasses veiled in fine silk, each thread sparkling with the dawn. Web remnants were strung loosely between the stalks, strands waving from shrub branches in the light breeze. A sea of blue green waves was topped in patches with pink-red tufts as the *rooigras* flowered through March. Each stem held dangling awns of furry seed, and these were caught by the wind to be blown far afield.

The expansive game farm appeared indistinguishable from any other wild place, apart from dirt tracks running through the land, allowing access to fences or shacks housing supplies. Throughout this and other farms, antelope could be found that were not seen in the wild of South Africa.

A narrow, black snout dipped toward the red tufted grass, mouth open and ripping free a knot from the ground. Black eyes rimmed in white took stock of the surrounding level savanna, and the six other tsessebe antelope that grazed nearby. Its single pair of horns, short but sharp, angled away from the top of its skull, then upwards in a wide 'V'. Chewing slowly, it surveyed for enemies knowing its dark reddish brown to black fur did not blend with the green of the grasses. The bull stood tall amidst his harem, and stood taller still as he spotted a possible threat.

Six wolves bounded across the grassy plain, ears back, tails down, heads held low. They seemed to spring along on legs so slight that they could scarcely bear a weight. The tsessebe bull was not fooled by their slender, wasted appearance. Though he had never seen a Painted wolf before, instinct commanded his heart to pound, adrenaline coursing in preparation for a fight. He snorted, hooves stamping to signal his herd to stay alert. They did not run, knowing such a small group was unlikely to be dangerous. Nonetheless, they were cautious until the killers left their sight.

"Ever taut, my dear wolves." Aalwyn twittered to the rest. "We shall happen on prey within a single beat of a vulture's wing."

"Perhaps this will be an unending wild in which we may linger." Koorsboom's tongue lolled out as they loped through the *rooigras*. "On our path thus far, every wild place began and ended within a single hunt."

"Expect nothing, my love." Olienhout lapped his muzzle as they made their way toward a stand of acacia. "That is all that we are due."

Koorsboom returned the gesture, stopping for a moment to rest his head alongside hers, eyes closed. "Do you think the hunt could carry on without us?" His hazel eyes gazed into hers.

"We must keep moving." Aalwyn ruff-barked, imploring them to keep up. "It has not escaped notice the roads that cross this place." She continued her lope. "And with roads come the danger of humans."

Koorsboom sprinted to his mother's side.

"The danger is ever with us, and so it is pointless to worry. After escaping that terrible place, the roar of a lion or the cackle of hyena fills me with elation."

"Your joy is apparent, my son. I understand your mind." Her voice lowered. "But you and Olienhout have been mating ceaselessly. You have been for some time in that place."

Koorsboom could only twitter happily, and ran a ring around her before racing forward into the thornbrush.

"Now we must search in a panic for a den." Aalwyn grumbled to herself.

She twittered to the wolves as they reached some bushwillow trees ahead of her. Koorsboom bounded back to her.

"Water hole ahead—a large one."

Leadwort and Hardekool gazed before them. Wildevlier still kept her distance.

"Wildevlier—what say you of the wild before us?" Olienhout resisted lapping her muzzle, given their last conversation.

"We shall see."

"You shall witness the power of the Pack." She indicated the water ahead with her snout. "There is more meat to be had when we act as one."

"And you draw the evil attentions of humans while you do so."

Olienhout did not speak further, watching Wildevlier closely.

The wolves peered through the edge of the acacia to see more *rooigras* descending to a broad but shallow waterhole. The stagnant water was as still as a mirror.

Soft mud ringed the verge, where a herd of impala drank their fill. Their heads were down, mouthfuls of water creating a ripple across their throat as they swallowed. Then all jerked up in alarm, and the herd remained still in watch. After a few moments, they would resume drinking, and would spring back up, heeding some unseen threat. Several waterbuck made their way to the water, creating a distraction for the impala herd as they watched the commotion.

Aalwyn stepped forward, and with the slightest of nods, crept from the shadows. Her legs were bent, her form hunched down as she moved through the tall grass. Each step brought them closer, and the grass stalks grew shorter. As the length of the foliage was reduced, she could no longer trust the grass to obscure them.

One impala turned its head toward the wolves, and spotted them approaching.

"*Strike.*" Aalwyn twittered, and the wolves threw themselves forward.

The impala wrenched its head up and neck forward with a startling alarm snort. The herd leapt into the pool, and toward escape. The one who called the alarm was last to move, the rest bolting the moment the call was issued. Hooves struck water, and the splashes spooked the rest of the animals in the vicinity. Each hoofbeat was into muck, and pulling free sapped each stamp of its power.

The waterhole was broad but shallow, and only the middle was deep enough for safety. Each impala struggled in the mud to reach salvation.

The straggler entered the pool, and gave a desperate pronk, kicking its hind legs high in the air. The show was meant to impress the predator, but served to bury its forehooves in the thick slime. Aalwyn's slight frame splashed in after the impala, and gripped the hindfoot. Koorsboom took hold of the other, while Olienhout held the haunch.

"Do not kill until we return to the bank." Aalwyn spoke through gritted teeth. The three pulled, resisting the bucking of the impala. With each yank backward they slid in the mud of the shallows.

Wildevlier finally joined them, bounding forth and locking her jaws on the impala's snout. Its struggles were weakened, its airway sealed by the wolf. She pulled sharply, and the antelope lost its footing with a *thwump*. On the shore, Koorsboom ripped open the belly as the impala spasmed, suffocated by Wildevlier.

A disturbance brought their feast to an abrupt halt.

"What is that?" Hardekool canted her head to the side, one paw in the air.

"It looks like a human only..." Koorsboom took a step back. "A giant?"

Standing tall on four hooves, the behemoth strode closer to the pool. An elongated head with a brown-haired mane looked toward the kill. A second head, covered with a broad brimmed hat, had a gaping mouth, and it nattered excitedly, extending a human hand toward the pack.

A second giant creature trotted out from the acacia sedge, also with two heads, one covered with a wide safari hat. A third, fourth, and more joined them at the side of the water hole. The entire group of humans were on horseback, which confused the wolves. They jabbered to one another, each pointing towards the kill. Several of them produced devices from pockets and held them up as they watched.

"Are we to run?" Hardekool backed away from the impala carcass.

"What say you, mother?"

Aalwyn hesitated. "I sense they intend no violence. Eat quickly—these will not be the only humans we encounter."

"Humans?" Wildevlier recoiled. The rest were startled by her voice.

"They are riding something. Another animal, much like the machines that spit ash and smoke." Olienhout spoke between gulping down chunks of meat.

"Hurry—there is no thunder from these *okes*. That may change if we linger." Aalwyn ruff-barked to the others, and with much trepidation, they resumed feasting.

Within minutes, the impala was skeletonized, only head, hooves, entrails and hide remaining. In that time a safari vehicle had found them and was approaching fast.

"Right. Away with us, before one of them decides to cut us down." Aalwyn led them around the pool to disappear into the bushwillow and acacia shrubs. A pair of scrub robins scattered at their approach with a flurry of *trrrrrr!* calls. The pack quickly found another road.

"There is time for another hunt later. The hunger is becoming constant for me now. Do you wish to rest?" Olienhout panted.

"With caution." Aalwyn looked around her. "A fine kill, all of you." She nodded her approval, greeting Wildevlier with a lapping of her muzzle. The wolf pulled back.

"You are unaccustomed to the company of the pack." Aalwyn regarded the female. "How long were you a captive?"

"For a turn of the seasons." She dipped her head in deference, though her eyes wandered the horizon. Her damaged ears flicked away the attentions of a biting fly.

"Formalities are unnecessary when you are with family." Aalwyn grimaced as she looked closely at her snare wound. Though long healed, the flesh still appeared twisted and angry.

"You are not family."

"When blood is shed together," Aalwyn dipped her head to meet her lowered gaze. "it is *always* with family." She took a step closer. "And I shall tear in two any who threaten you."

Wildevlier lowered her head further, but her face remained an impassive mask.

Aalwyn led them onward down the dirt road. Twin ruts were divided by a thin short grass stripe. A bleached antelope skull sat to one side of the path. As they padded along, the road grew wider and split into another roadway.

"This appears adequate for a place of rest." Aalwyn checked to ensure none were left behind or lost. "The sun is reaching its height." She exhaled as the wolves caught up to her. "Every belly present hangs low with the feast."

Olienhout padded by her, visibly winded.

"Though yours hangs lower than the rest." Aalwyn sniffed her as she lay down to rest in the heat.

Before the others were able to laze on the ground, the whine of an engine reached their sensitive ears.

"*Ag.*" Hardekool faced one of the roads. Dust rose in the distance. Shortly a safari vehicle was upon them, and slowed to a halt. Excited tourists prattled to one another as they made clicking sounds with unknown devices.

"They followed us all this way?" Leadwort twittered.

"No." Olienhout was on her feet with a sigh. "This one looks different somehow." Her ears perked up as another engine whine became apparent.

"Are they hunting us?" Leadwort sniffed the air.

Hardekool withdrew into the grass.

"No." Aalwyn hastened them with an agitated twitter. "Not yet."

They continued their lope throughout the day. Time and again they encountered people, some on horseback, some on vehicles. Somehow, they never seemed far away. The sun continued its slow meander across the sky, descending as the wolves wandered endlessly.

Koorsboom raced ahead, and quickly returned. "A tangle of thornbrush ahead, just by a rock slope."

"Let us see them ride one of those damned things down a rockfall." Olienhout snorted.

The air was close, the wind barely able to penetrate the thick foliage around the snarl of Knob-thorn acacia. They rested momentarily under the branches, the ground dry and mixed with large stones. Flies buzzed about them.

"The end of this place is close." Koorsboom ducked in amongst the wolves. "Just beyond is rocky hills, some human dwellings. It seems this wild place is as small as the others."

"If one could call it wild." Aalwyn tongued his muzzle as he settled, and did the same with Olienhout. She laid her head on the older female's shoulder, and heaved a deep breath.

"Olienhout, my dear, we face trouble ahead."

"Indeed we do." She sighed.

"You have fallen pregnant." Aalwyn looked deep into her eyes, allowing no chance for her to waver in her answer.

"Yes."

Koorsboom's ears were up. "Are you now?" He was at her side, and they lapped one another's palates with joy. "What *lekker* news!"

"You are very heavy indeed with pups." Aalwyn scratched a flea from her ear with a hind leg. "The timing could not be worse."

"*Ek verstaan*, Aalwyn." Olienhout rubbed her jaw on the older wolf's shoulder. "We face a difficult way ahead, in country we do not know. And into this cruel place we bring pups to face it with us." She sniffed. "So it must be. There may never, for any of us, be an ideal time or place for our young to join us."

A tambourine dove called just above them, toward the setting sun—*coo coo coo coo woo woohoo woo tutu tu-tu-tu-tu-tu*. Its muffled song seemed a cautious greeting to the end of the day.

"The time will be shorter than you know."

"How so?"

"We must find a den, and we must find it quickly." She rested her head on her forepaws. "And hope that we are far from humans when we do."

"This place will not do." Koorsboom studied the ground. "At any moment one of them could capture the lot of us." He eyed Olienhout. "We cannot allow them to find you."

"Then we must leave now." Olienhout paused, looking ahead to the areas of human habitation. Evening was upon them. "Farms are dangerous, but at the very least, there will be no lions at night."

The pack was on their paws, each with a newfound urgency. They threaded their way through the dense brush. As it parted, they could view the rolling hills to the east. They resumed their tireless lope through arboreal savanna. Scattered velvet bushwillow trees with broad green crowns had yet to turn reddish purple with the coming autumn.

Even as they crossed bushveld, there were roads, one after another. Signs of humans were everywhere.

Several informal huts were clustered nearby, shacks fashioned of aluminum and wood. Near one such dwelling a woman washed laundry, spreading cleaned garments to dry on the grass. The wolves crept past to ensure none were seen.

A broad stand of hornpod trees spread before them in a large horseshoe, the small drooping green leaves rustling gently in the evening breeze. The trunk of each split low to the ground, twisting and coiling to the sky as though a roaring fire had suddenly frozen in place and sprouted greenery. Thick grass and brush clumped about the bases of the trees, creating a dense curtain of foliage in every direction. The wolves probed their way at haste.

As they rushed through, an abrupt yelp pierced the quiet. Each wolf froze, listening. None breathed.

A plaintive whine reached their ears, and Koorsboom tore through the brush to the source. He soon found Olienhout sprawled on the ground. She was on her side, forepaws clawing the ground uselessly in front of her. A hind leg clawed as well, at nothing. The other hind leg was pointed behind her, suspended in midair. Dark wire encircled her leg just below the knee, knotted tightly.

Aalwyn and the others gathered by Koorsboom's side. None could speak.

Olienhout's jaw was agape, her chest heaving, eyes wide with quiet agony.

"What... has... taken me?"

The sun dipped behind the distant hills to the west, and the land was enshrouded in utter darkness.

Chapter 69

Blood trickled from the edge of the wire where it bit into the leg at the knee joint with a gradual patter of drips on the ground. Just above the wire knot, the leg was stripped free of fur, naked muscle and bone underneath. The trapped leg quivered.

"What is it?" Hardekool sniffed Olienhout's prone body.

"A snare." Aalwyn's voice was flat, devoid of emotion.

"Snare?" Hardekool still was reluctant to string more than a word or two together.

"A trap left by humans to kill animals and leave them. She tripped the wire as she ran."

"No escape?"

"No." Wildevlier's rasp brought a chill to their hearts. She twisted her neck, the scar of her own healed snare wound from long ago writhing like a snake on her skin.

Koorsboom seethed, and prepared to dart off into the dark.

"You will do nothing." Aalwyn spoke nearly in a whisper.

He tensed, claws dug into the dirt, but he was knocked down by her powerful forepaws. She held him down, surprising him with her strength.

"Where one snare is found, there shall be more." She hissed. "By morning we would all be hanging from the trees." Her breath was hot on his face. "Wound in the threads by a spider." Her forepaw left his neck.

Padding to Olienhout's side, she whispered to her, and the pregnant female's whining quieted, and ceased. Breathing became slow, calm, and steady. Each lay down around her, and rested for the night.

"What if a hyena scents her blood?" Leadwort wondered.

"Then we eat hyena." The bitter edge in Aalwyn's voice faded to a quiet rumble in the night.

* * *

"The pain is subsiding."

The voice, croaking in the dawn, startled the rest.

"Where are we?" Olienhout attempted to get on her feet, but quickly gave up as she remembered the snare.

"Leaving the wild, in a grove of trees." He sniffed her. "We were approaching farms. Do you recall?" Koorsboom was up, looking about, starting to run, stopping. He felt agitated, unable to act decisively. "The patrols must be underway."

"Walk." Aalwyn gave a ruff-bark which caused him to halt. "And move about slowly. The snares depend on speed to dispense their cruelty."

He gave a nod, and gestured to Hardekool. The two vanished into the brush.

"Has your throat been cut?" Aalwyn sniffed the younger wolf.

"The snare caught my leg." Her voice was hollow and resigned.

"Can you eat?"

Olienhout did not answer, only staring at a beetle that trundled its way to wherever past her snout.

"Then the hunt shall commence. You shall need the meat." Aalwyn nodded with authority.

"For what?"

Silence passed between Aalwyn and Olienhout. A series of warbling whistles trilled nearby, *thweeeloo thweeeloo* from a green pigeon hanging upside down from a fig tree. After taking its fill of the fruit, it was gone with a flap of its wings, free as the air around it.

Aalwyn grunted. "Leadwort?"

He looked up, hopeful for a distracting task.

"Come kill with me." She gave a nod to Olienhout. "We will return. And you shall dine heartily." She drew closer to the wounded wolf. "Your pups are depending on it."

Olienhout stared at the ground, eyes of glass.

The two padded off through the hornpod grove.

* * *

Koorsboom picked his way, one paw before the other, through the tangled branches and tall *rooigras* and under a lavender feverberry tree. He looked up through the sparse leafed crown of the tree, branches waving gently above him. Rounding the dark brown wood, he glanced back to see Hardekool following close behind.

He turned again to face a skull.

Stopping dead, he held his breath.

The creature before him was a wasted form, little flesh remaining on the exposed bone. Between skull, neck, and shoulder was connective tissue that seemed to hold together the skeleton of the animal by habit alone. Hanging suspended from a low branch, he could see the snare where it had strangled its victim. The jaw hung open in mute laughter.

"What was it?"

"Goat, perhaps. It does not appear to have had the robustness of an antelope." Koorsboom sniffed. The body scarcely had the scent of decay anymore.

"What killed it?"

He gestured to the wire around the neck.

They circled around, stepping carefully. After a few minutes, attached to another feverberry tree, Koorsboom found another large loop of wire hanging in midair. He turned to meet Hardekool's eyes, and they were swelled with horror. She stepped far from the wire, as though it would reach out to make contact.

Within the hour they finished their circuit, and returned to Olienhout.

"We found more snares. Soon we will patrol a passage. Find a way out with no further dangers." He lapped her muzzle. She did not seem to hear him. He stepped away and examined the wire. Gripping it in his jaws, he chewed. Each bite, the wire slipped between teeth, and out again. He gripped harder, and again it became stuck between his canines. It was thinner than a chain, yet was flexible, and would not give way. He followed the snare to the tree where the other end was secured, and further biting gave the same result. At the end he stared, the wire unaffected. He returned to her side.

"My mother will be back soon with a kill." A few more licks, and he was on his paws to continue the patrol. Hardekool followed him.

"Is there release?"

"Not with any means I possess."

"How long?" Hardekool gazed at him coldly. "Do we wait?"

Koorsboom stopped, and glared at the earth before him. "Until the bitter end."

Chapter 70

Suspended from the branches of an acacia tree were a handful of woven nests. The chatter from the resident sparrow weaver birds was incessant, emanating from the bundles of grass wedged between thorns along the branches.

The adults scattered from the nests at once as a large grey hawk descended on the acacia with a leisurely glide. Alighting on the canopy next to a nest, the harrier-hawk gripped the wood with sharp talons. Dark brown eyes set in a bright yellow face surveyed the area for threats. Examining the closest bundle of woven grass, it began to probe for nestlings.

Below the agitated chirping of the weavers, two Painted wolves padded by without concern for the drama above.

"While in captivity, have you learned to hunt?" Aalwyn shook her head to dislodge a biting fly.

"I have heard of this 'hunting', but the word means nothing to me." Leadwort spoke low, in flat tones, as they crossed the open field of red-topped grass.

"You know nothing?" Aalwyn shook her head with frustration.

"Teach me so I can be of use to you."

"Very well. The prey may be sparse here, along the fences. Stay close, and follow my commands." They had returned to the wild place, sensing the game was inside. Somehow, only livestock was to be found outside the fence. Between stands of acacia and Transvaal milkplum trees, the foliage was dense, and the sounds of the savanna did not travel far.

"Vision is of little use here." Aalwyn spoke in hushed tones. "Be wary of elephants, though I am not sure if they live in this region."

"Something so big could surely be seen coming?" Leadwort sniffed the air, wondering what the scent would be like.

"For a creature the size of a hillside, they move with stealth. Their footfall is as loud as a leaf settling on the ground."

Leadwort followed in silence.

As Aalwyn ducked under a low branch of Knob-thorn acacia, she raised her head to face a bushbuck, where they stood a meter apart. Her dark hazel eyes met an utterly black left eye in profile. Its charcoal nose led to a black stripe up the midline of its face, the rest of its body a brown-grey coat with white spots that rendered it nearly invisible against the shadows and leaves. Its diminutive face was topped with spiraling short horns that ended in needle sharp points. The jaw locked in mid-chew.

Each froze for a moment, but a moment only.

The bushbuck broke first, knowing it was too close to blend in with the plant cover. Aalwyn was upon it, and twittered to Leadwort that the hunt was unexpectedly on.

The bushbuck darted through the trees, charging through the brush rather than attempting to leap over it. The Painted wolves did the same, often receiving thorny branches in the face as the buck passed, bending each and releasing them as their body passed. The *whap whap whap* was repetitive, interspersed with the snapping of twig and branch that were too rigid to give way.

"Sweep alongside—there is no room to maneuver!"

Leadwort accelerated, and reached the bushbuck's flank.

"Drive it to the side!" Aalwyn spotted a thicket line of *Combretum* shrub, and Leadwort pressed his attack, driving the bushbuck toward it. As quickly as the hunt began, it ended as the buck reached the impenetrable *Combretum* barrier, and paused. Aalwyn tackled it, knocking the small antelope off its hooves, and tore the throat open. She took one of the limbs and gestured to Leadwort, who had paused to admire her kill, to do the same. He took a leg in his mouth.

She pulled, he resisted, and the corpse was torn to pieces. They packed away muscle and offal, leaving a skeleton and entrails after less than an hour.

"You were a help, Leadwort." Aalwyn panted, her fur coated with dark blood.

"Despite being frightened."

"Of a bushbuck?"

"Of having to make a kill. If it had been within my reach, I would not have known what to do."

"You will, Leadwort. With time."

"I do not understand your ways, but no mistake—I am grateful for the chance." Leadwort instinctively held his head at a lower level than hers.

"We are pleased to have you, though you have much to learn." Aalwyn wondered of his chances of survival, knowing so little of free living.

"I do not know the extent of my ignorance."

"You are at least aware of that." Aalwyn allowed herself a smile, tongue lolled out, and shearing teeth exposed. "You have not asked of Olienhout." She regarded him. "Our ensnared mother to be."

"I am not sure what to ask." Leadwort cast a grave eye on Aalwyn.

As they loped, the hornpod grove appeared in the distance. Within minutes, they were at Olienhout's side. The two wolves promptly discharged ropes of bloodied meat for the pregnant female, who required rousing to notice the food. She choked it down, though without much enthusiasm. Her trapped hind leg was strung tightly to the nearby tree, the wire glinting with menace.

"Your bleeding has stopped." Aalwyn examined the wound. Flies that were feasting on the exposed meat scattered. The flesh distal to the knotted wire was a dusky bluish-grey color.

"My leg feels strange, as though immersed in a cold pond." She laid her head down.

Aalwyn walked back and forth along the snare, despite knowing there was nothing further to learn. The wire was twisted in several places as the others had attempted to bite through it in vain. She longed for the brittle rusted iron of chain link.

Before long, Koorsboom and Hardekool returned.

"We have explored the path to the east. There are no further snares in that direction." He lay down next to his mate, and they rested in the quiet.

* * *

Morning found Olienhout shivering, and breathing heavily. Koorsboom remained with her, while the others hunted. By midday they returned with empty stomachs, and lay down dejected. Even if the hunt had gone well, Olienhout would have had little appetite as a fever wracked her body.

Koorsboom paced near her shivering form, unable to calm or settle. He looked up to see a Cape vulture watching them. Yellow eyes stared from a bluish face above a sharp beak. Cream colored feathered wings, edged with darker tail and flight feathers, were folded shut. It was perched high above them on the branch of a dead tree, the wood pale and resembling bone.

Koorsboom moved to threaten the bird, but quickly gave up, knowing he could never drive it away.

The Cape vulture continued to watch Olienhout with impassive regard.

Chapter 71

The following two days were without event. Koorsboom stayed by her side, absently nipping at the wire. Aalwyn left twice each day for the hunt, and returned with a small kill each time. Olienhout took in a few mouthfuls of each meal, but remained listless. The flies filled the air in a roiling black cloud. The leg was turning black, fur parting and falling off.

Wildevlier lay alone in the brush, apart from the rest. Each time Olienhout's body was wracked by chills, she glanced over, and after a time, laid her head down again. Since the night Olienhout had become caught, Wildevlier had scarcely spoken.

Aalwyn spoke to Hardekool and Leadwort at a distance from the snare.

"Another tactic that I employ is to surround the herd with a cordon of wolves." She glanced at them. "We do not create much of a cordon with our numbers. Nonetheless, one can drive the prey into a trap."

"What trap?" Hardekool wondered.

"The kill is easier to achieve if you know just where your prey will be. In formation, the Pack drives them to the wolf who shall make that kill."

"Does that work with other species?"

"Somewhat, Leadwort. Oribi are quick as falcons, and would evade a trap. Slower antelope can be corralled."

"And yet you did not let the swift bushbuck escape."

"We were near enough to close the chase. And even for the swift, we can outrun them over great distances, down to the horizon."

Hardekool was quiet after each answer, nodding to the ground.

"Tomorrow we may return to the wild place for another hunt, perhaps to probe for wildebeest calves." Aalwyn shook her head to deter a mosquito. "Though I fear Olienhout is growing weak."

"My world has become another." Leadwort mused.

Hardekool canted her head to the side. "What do you mean?"

"My world has grown, far beyond reckoning, in the short time we have known together." Leadwort lowered his head beneath Aalwyn, who accepted the gesture. "More than in every season I have experienced until now." His eyes met hers, but he was quick to avert his gaze.

"You are most welcome, Leadwort." She lapped his muzzle, for which he was grateful. "All are welcome who desire the wild."

Wildevlier moved further away, reluctant to watch Olienhout suffer.

"Will you be off soon?" Aalwyn stood over Wildevlier's resting form.

"Perhaps." Wildevlier muttered. She stared into the middle distance at nothing.

"There is nothing I could say that would convince you to join us." Aalwyn gazed at her wistfully. "To indeed be part of the Pack."

"I have no desire to see you or the others die." She grunted. "That seems to be all we do."

"The indifferent veld demands blood."

"Then it can have all it wishes." Wildevlier turned on her side, away from Aalwyn. "Leave me alone. Nothing shall convince me a Pack is worth the bitter tears."

Aalwyn glanced away to see Olienhout, sleeping, leg still angled toward the tree behind her. Her body shook with rigors, and her breathing was rapid, as though on a hunt of her own.

Chapter 72

"We met on the veld, a fence between us. And now we are parting, a wire to separate us."

He looked in her eyes, at this point closed more often than open. The lower leg was blackened and ulcerated. The dead limb had stopped bleeding long ago. Purulence oozed from where the snare bit into her leg. The smell was thick and inescapable.

"Our bond would be everlasting."

The flies were relentless, busily laying eggs in the decaying tissue. Koorsboom had long since stopped chasing them away. He did not comprehend what was happening to her as the infection progressed. Her panting was now slowing. Her abdomen, swollen with pups, no longer heaved with each breath.

"If I knew that bond would be so brief... I would change nothing, and remain by your side as now."

"My son."

Koorsboom laid his head on Olienhout's shoulder.

"The time to leave is coming soon." Aalwyn dreaded to utter these words, as she knew he would obey.

She turned to see Hardekool and Leadwort watching, keeping a respectful distance.

Wildevlier crept further away. She averted her gaze toward the distant bushveld.

Koorsboom studied the rotting leg. The wire had sunk into the twisted wound.

"Even now, it is eating." His voice was a tortured growl.

"Son?" Aalwyn prodded him with her snout.

"Devouring her... like a snake would."

"The snare knows nothing of—"

"The snare knows. And remembers." Wildevlier startled them with her abrading voice. She came from nowhere, creeping upon cat paws. Glancing at the wire, she began to wander off.

Koorsboom nodded gravely. "It took so many lives, as a snare nearly had mine, so long ago."

Aalwyn lapped his muzzle, but he did not respond.

"And now it must slake its cravings on my pups... even now who desire to run the wild."

"Do not torture yourself this way, Koorsboom. Madness will follow you." Her voice rose, the steel edge of alarm.

"The Sickness took my sons and daughters." He heaved a breath, slaver dripping on the ground. "And the wire shall take more." He glared at the snare, his mind hot and rolling with hatred.

"Koorsboom—"

"Grass may never touch their paws, nor the savor of the meat their tongues. All for the greed of the wire." His eyes narrowed to hateful slits, a growl burning in his throat. "And those who placed it here."

"Anger has its place, my son." She brushed against his side. "In a violent season, it may cause an enemy to flee. Now, however, anger will only corrupt reason. And your pack needs you."

Aalwyn left his side, knowing there was nothing further to say.

Koorsboom heeded the advice of his mother. His breathing slowed, and he calmed. Eyes closed, and his thoughts drifted far away. Laying down next to Olienhout, he felt her prone and unconscious body. The steel wire held fast her leg, and it extended up and away, suspended in midair. The thornbrush was gone, the pack was gone. The sounds of the day, gone.

The sun hung black in the sky, immobile.

"Helpless in a land that conceals our enemies." The voice of Olienhout returned to him. She had nearly been blinded by a spitting cobra, averting her glance at the last second as she recalled a lesson her mother provided.

"If not for a half-remembered remark."

"This wound would never heal." Koorsboom prodded the dead leg.

Then let it not fester. The voice of Blackthorn echoed through his mind. During their great *trek*, seemingly ages ago, he rested with the old wolf that took his father's place. Blackthorn was injured, and he lapped at a gouge in his hind leg that was rusty with blood. His rough tongue worked at that deep gash, even as his face contorted with pain. Finally, one last lick brought a thorn as long as his paw out of the wound and onto the ground.

The thorn is no longer my problem.

Once again, the bushveld surrounded them, the orange sun above, the rest of his pack waiting nearby. Koorsboom looked again at her leg, held fast by the snare. Suppuration oozed from cracks in the fur and skin.

His rough tongue over the decaying flesh scraped it, opened it, scattering the carrion flies. Amid the putrefying tissue, a grey-white length of bone terminated at the joint. It appeared as dead as the rest of her leg. Koorsboom thought on this.

The snare clings tightly to this dead flesh.

His eyes widened as he made a connection.

Then it is no longer her problem.

He closed his jaws gently upon her leg, where the knot of wire bound her knee, and bit down. His powerful canines locked upon the bone where it met the joint capsule. His head trembled with the effort. A dampened crack met his ears as the joint fractured and parted. He felt the wire shift against his lip. Tightening his jaw, the bite carried through fur and tissue with a click.

Olienhout's body lurched as the snare wire whipped free with a whistle, carrying the severed dead leg with it, thumping to the ground. The snare dangled loosely in the brush, as though awaiting its next victim.

Koorsboom blinked in stunned disbelief at the stump, gently oozing blood. He licked at the wound, and emitted a low whine.

"The pain..." Olienhout slurred, and gave a deep heave.

The young wolf jumped back as she spoke, then moved closer and sniffed her. Gnawing on the wound, the bleeding became fresher as the dead tissue was stripped away. He could taste the rust and cinnamon of her blood. The dusky color of the snare wound gradually disappeared.

Aalwyn stepped forward, watching Olienhout closely. Her breathing gradually steadied.

After several minutes passed, she whispered to her son. "You canny *bliksem.*"

"A half-remembered moment." He whispered.

Olienhout opened her hazel eyes.

"I thought of your cobra." Koorsboom nudged her resting body. "One never can tell what moment will be crucial, in a lifetime laden with such moments."

She blinked, not understanding.

"For me, recalling the way my father dealt with a wound, never leaving it to molder."

She laid her head down, and took a deep breath. And another.

"My *bokkie.* Your pups are eager for your return."

"She will live?" Wildevlier's voice startled the others. None noticed her approach.

"So it would seem." Olienhout murmured, eyes closed.

Without a word, Wildevlier lay close to her, watchful. Into the evening she studied Olienhout, a thing of wonder.

Chapter 73

"Koorsboom?"

He was already at her side, and had been for hours.

"Where are the rest of the Pack?"

"You do not remember. They left for the hunt this morning, and you watched them go."

"My mind is moving so slowly." Olienhout laid her head down again.

"I am heartened it is moving at all." He lay down with her, lapping her muzzle gently. "Does it still hurt?"

"A searing ache, but less as the day wears on."

"Your trapped limb somehow sickened you." His ear flicked as a biting fly settled on it.

"Then I am glad to be rid of it." Olienhout smiled weakly.

***

The hunters returned in triumph, galloping into the stand of hornpod trees. All four gathered around Olienhout, their bellies low with wildebeest meat.

"You are like me now." Olienhout's eyelids seemed heavy.

"How so?" Leadwort crouched down.

"Pregnant."

Hardekool and Leadwort shared a quizzical look. Wildevlier only gazed at her silently.

"The mind is addled from her ordeal." Aalwyn regurgitated the bulk of the kill, as did the other hunters.

Ravenous, Olienhout took up all she could bear.

Wildevlier added to the pile, and the rest of the wolves shared the balance.

"Those humans. Everywhere." Hardekool released her share of the meal. "Followed us in the hunt." She grunted. "Outran them. Only to find more."

"Go back the way we came, now that you have given Olienhout her measure of the kill." Aalwyn twittered to her. "If they follow us still, we need warning."

Hardekool bolted from the grove on patrol.

"There seem to be more of them in the wild than outside it. As though they gather there." Aalwyn padded to the young wolf.

Koorsboom sniffed her wound, now clear of the rich stench of gangrene.

Olienhout shifted her weight, and to the shock of all present, stood on her three remaining legs. Wavering, she shook her fur free of dirt.

"Are you... quite alright?" Aalwyn peered at her.

"It matters not." She composed herself, her features set as though hewn from leadwood. "The time grows short."

Koorsboom looked down, and noticed her belly hung lower still. He opened his mouth to speak, but Olienhout was already hobbling away. Pushing off with her good hind leg, and then both forelegs, she moved at a steady lope.

"Well, come along then." Aalwyn hoo-called for Hardekool to rejoin them, and they were soon on their way.

* * *

Hills to the east along the Lowveld rolled gradually, a rumpled blanket of green dotted with wild seringa and acacia trees. The itinerate wolves crossed the land with great care, encountering isolated houses and small villages. Rondavels of mud topped with straw thatch made up each house, with scattered people tending goats or patches of squash and beans. A dog barked in their direction, and they altered their course, adhering close to high vegetation and drainage gullies that concealed their progress. A tar road baked in the midday heat, and the wolves ambled across this uneasily. Their lope continued.

All the way, Olienhout was in the lead.

As time passed, she ran even faster.

As the sun declined behind them, Olienhout came to rest in a stand of olive trees. She angled her head up to gaze through the thick, dark green canopy.

"I was born under one of these trees. Far from here." She panted, utterly indifferent to exhaustion.

"Unless we find true wild, we are in dangerous territory." Aalwyn sniffed the air. "If humans find us, fortune may allow us to distract them for a while." She noticed Koorsboom inspecting the distant brush. "Over time, however... you will be compelled to abandon your litter." The older female paused, not knowing another way to express this. "Or you doom yourself alongside your pups."

"If that comes to pass, so be it." Olienhout's teeth were bared. "I have lost one litter to the Sickness. Every last helpless pup slain where it was born on the pitiless savanna." She took a deep breath. "As long as I carry the claw and fang, I will be their equally pitiless avenger." Every word was laced with venom. She shook her head, the ruff of her neck waving gently. Her eyes flashed with a dark passion. "The mountains shall be consumed before I surrender my young."

"You have the look of the last wolf on earth, Olienhout." Aalwyn stood in awe of her.

"Nothing shall stop me from leaving a mark upon this land." She bared her fangs. "Not these humans, their snares, their thunder."

Aalwyn set her jaw, and nodded in understanding.

"Whatever cruelties they hope to bring to me..." Olienhout wore a savage grin. "... they can *FOKOFF!*" Her ruff-bark reverberated across the veld, and the rest of the wolves turned to her. Each broke out in excited twittering, and they ran about her, up on hind legs boxing one another, exulting in the joy of the Pack.

"Very well." Aalwyn padded away, and Koorsboom joined her as they surveyed the area for a possible hunt.

"She is as resolute as the *koppies* that stand sentry over these lands." Aalwyn nudged her son as they hastened into a run.

"I admire her defiance. We shall need it."

"Quite." Aalwyn surveyed the valley before them in the dimming light. "Should Death come for her, it shall be left bloodied once she has finished with it."

Chapter 74

A lonely red seringa tree stood in the meadow, its flattened green top waving gently in the wind. The tall grey trunk was heavily scarred, bark worn through in places exposing the underlying reddish-brown wood. Punctures marked the trunk along its lower half, and the grass was worn through around the base of the tree with deep scuffs.

Around the gnarled roots of the tree sat a loop of solid iron chain link. This led away from the tree for several feet, and looped again around the neck of a white rhinoceros.

The rhino had poor vision even at the peak of his life, and was now almost completely blind. Skin nearly two inches thick provided a robust armor against animal attacks. Brute strength would have rendered the chain irrelevant, but the powerful sedatives coursing through his system made that chain a nearly intolerable weight.

Murmuring to one side alarmed the rhino, but he could only drunkenly wobble away from the sound. He bumped into the tree with his horn, gashing the bark. The murmuring rose into laughter. He tried again to wander the other way, until the clicking of the restraining chain held him back.

More babbling again, sounding like wildebeest, but somehow alien and noxious. Loud clicking, followed by a louder clack.

A deafening crack split the air around him, and he suddenly gasped for air. He tried to take a deep breath, but was stopped by a sensation like a binder around the rib cage that prevented taking air. His heartbeat quickened, and panic filled his dimming mind. He took a step to flee, but he sensed his head crashing into the ground. A raw terror seized him, and the rhino blacked out as his lungs filled with blood.

The rifle was stowed in its case, and the man that fired the shot gestured toward a Land Rover.

"Augusto!"

Leaning against the passenger door was Augusto, wearing fashionable dress pants and a shirt with a new gold chain. He nodded, and opened the door. After a moment, he reached in and pulled out a short, shy girl. He mumbled to her and she walked out. Dressed simply in a white T-shirt and jean shorts, she stared at the ground.

Augusto held her firmly by the wrist, leading her to the dead rhino.

Each step was taken hesitantly, as she looked at the animal in revulsion.

The other man handed her the rifle and motioned to her to stand next to the rhino. She did not move.

Augusto leaned close to her and whispered in her ear. His Vietnamese was choppy at best, but his master had taught him all that was necessary for these 'clients'. She went pale and stepped closer to the enormous grey carcass. He grabbed one of her hands and placed it on the head of the rhino between the funnel-like ears. In the other hand Augusto placed the rifle, nearly dropped on the ground from her reluctant grasp.

The shooter stepped back and took a few photos, and gave the girl a thumbs up.

Augusto whispered to her again, and she stepped gratefully away from the animal. She uttered an oath in Vietnamese and ran back to the Land Rover and slammed the passenger door shut.

"When is the next kill?" The shooter lit a cigarette as he picked up the rifle from the ground where she dropped it.

"Six days. I have four more girls coming from Bangkok." Augusto handed over a thick wad of *meticais*. "Four rhinos. Can you get them?"

"From Wildsplaas?"

"No, I have not heard from Dyk. Heard he was killed by some lunatic." Augusto shrugged. "Four rhinos, four hunters."

"That is still the limit? One horn per 'hunter'?"

"That is the law."

"You trust them to be quiet?" He pointed to the girl sitting in the vehicle, staring at the floor between her feet.

"I trust Buatoom to keep them quiet." Augusto answered.

He laughed, exhaling smoke.

"I will be staying in Maputo, then. Same number."

* * *

A well-worn trail wound its way through the brush, the dirt stamped flat from years of pressure by hoof and footpad. Close by, a dark grey box watched over this game path through its single black lensed eye. Attached to a short post, it held a black antenna in the air from one side like a hand raised to attention. Fresh batteries hummed within, the camera itself locked shut.

Sonja Venter picked up her machete and hacked at the grass and brush between the camera trap and the trail, cutting it short to allow an unfettered view of the path. She bent down to examine the camera's field of view, and slashed down several more stems of grass, then nodded her approval. Fishing in a pocket, she took out a compass for the third time. She knew the camera was pointed north already, but kept checking out of habit. The orientation meant the lens would never be pointed at the sunrise or sunset. Picking up several branches freshly cut down, she positioned this around the back and sides of the camera, rendering it less visible.

Boots crunched on the dirt and gravel as she walked away from the camera trap. After a short search, she found a large lump of grass-laden elephant dung. Sliding on a pair of gloves with a snap, she took handfuls of the dung and marched back to the camera. With great care, she smeared the dung in a thick layer on the post that secured the grey box, applying smaller amounts to the camera device itself.

After disposing of the gloves in a bag, and a quick wash of the hands, she packed away the machete, keys, spade, pickaxe, spare posts, drill, and a tackle box full of batteries and data cards.

The drive back to the ranger station felt longer than it really was.

At the station, she parked, and waved to one of the rangers with a smile. He returned the wave.

"How many more cameras to set up?" He placed a hand on his hat anchoring it against the wind.

"None—they are all set. All along game paths, all at angles to focus on rhino identification."

He nodded, glancing at the ground, then back at her. For a moment he stood there with an awkward pause before walking away to his car.

In the early afternoon, Venter drove the dirt road to the local village. As she did every day after knocking off, she walked to the pub. There was an overhang to the bar itself, leaving the rest of the tables under the open sky. As it was every day, the place was subdued. Music drifted from a radio lazily across a scattering of people. There was little conversation, but it hushed further once she walked among the tables. She smiled at the bartender who responded with a newly opened bottle of Castle lager, placed on the bar with a clunk.

"Anything planned for the weekend, Venter?"

"I may drive to Limpopo in the morning." She gave a nod. "Anything new today?" She laid her hat on the neighboring seat, fairly sure no one would join her.

"Only that the police are not looking for anyone else." His clipped Afrikaans accent reminded her of home, the rapid pace of his speech suggestive of Johannesburg origin. "Looks like Johan was alone."

She sighed. "So everyone knows it was a ranger."

"Ja. And they know it was over animals."

"Was the other man a farmer?"

"They were both farmers." His brows were raised, lending a damning edge to his comment.

"Dyk was not much of a farmer. Canned lion hunting and so forth." She did not speak with much conviction.

"No matter. A wildlife ranger killed two farmers. Over wild predators." He wiped the already gleaming polished wood bar with a white towel.

"It looks bad."

"It could not possibly look worse." He glanced over her shoulder.

Venter looked back in time to see two people averting their gaze.

"I do not suppose it matters that I knew nothing about it." She took a drink. The cold beer washed down, and she took a deep breath. "He gave no indication what he was planning to do."

"Well, I believe you, *meisie.*" He stopped wiping the bar. "Strange he told nobody, though."

"I suppose he wanted to keep the damage to himself." She sighed again. "Just before he left, a pack of Painted wolves was killed by a farmer. It did not occur to me at the time, but there was a hint of despair in his manner."

"The Border War left him the worse for wear."

"Is he still in the news?" Her dark hair was teased by the passing breeze.

"No, the *Star* and *Argus* have moved on to armored car robberies and the home invasions in Pretoria. The farm communities, though, have talked of nothing else." He took a drink from a water bottle he kept behind the bar.

"Do you think the talk will die down?"

"Even if it does, this bad blood will last years."

"Relations between farmers and landowners and conservation are so easily strained." She held her face in her hands. "Any attempt to calm a situation with a jackal or leopard on private land will lead to this refrain."

"'What about that bunny hugger', *ja, meisie?*"

She nodded with a halfhearted laugh. "*Ja.*" She checked her phone again. No messages. "He was a good man."

The bartender shook his head. "I liked Johan, but..." He shrugged. "What he did was evil. Killing two men in cold blood."

She gave a slight nod, measuring her words with care. "Sometimes I hear it in conversations, when people talk about trophy hunters. 'They must be shot. Hang their head next to their trophies.'" She shook her head. "This." She struck the wood with her finger. "This is why that notion is wrong-headed."

"Well, you saw how few people came to his funeral." The bartender moved off to clean the bar elsewhere. "Just you, a couple of rangers, and that guy who is as crazy as he was. Razak."

"Johan was just trying to help."

"You think it helped?" His voice acquired an edge.

Venter shook her head. "Desperation does that to people." She pushed away the bottle, losing all interest. Eventually the bartender wandered off. Drops of water formed on the surface of the beer bottle, eventually succumbing to gravity and sliding down the glass to the wood below. Her boots clomped in the dirt parking lot out to the Land Rover.

The streets were moving with more people now that the evening had come. Laughter erupted in one place, then another. A car passed, dance music thumping from the open window.

The ranger got into the driver seat and closed the door. She watched the street before her. Two children ran along a fence. One held a meter-long length of wire, driving a wire-frame car the size of a shoebox before him.

From her pocket Venter fished out a small black book. Among the very few personal effects of Johan Marais, it had not taken her long to find it.

She opened it to a bookmark. It had a name and phone number.

The poacher.

After some thought, she pulled out her phone and tapped in a number.

A voice spoke on the other end.

"Johan Marais was waiting for your call."

"I... have not heard anything yet." The voice on the other end was hesitant.

"When you do, this is the number you call." She listened to his tone.

"Where is he?"

She thought for a moment.

"I am the one with the money."

A pause.

"I will be in touch."

The line went dead, and she thumbed through the book for the hundredth time. Stopping again on the page with the circled number, she peered at the jagged handwriting. Below this was scrawled 'Orlando'.

She turned the key in the ignition.

***

At sunrise, Sonja Venter departed Gorongosa, taking the long, winding tar roads south and west. After a prolonged wait at the border post, and more roads laden with heavy trucks, she reached Limpopo province after nightfall, eventually turning off onto a dirt road.

The winding track was difficult to navigate in total blackness, though she did recognize the stands of *Aloe candelabrum*, the florets less brilliant in the headlights of the Land Rover. Eventually the small red brick house emerged into view beyond the wild seringa trees.

The door opened inward, and out strode the man, still wearing the same dark green cargo shorts, the same khaki shirt. Only the cap was missing, his greyed hair in disarray.

"*Welkom, meisie!*"

"Du Plessis." She extended a hand, which was ignored in favor of a binding hug. His hand clapped on her back, and he uttered his infectious laugh.

"The same. *Kasteel?*" He held up a bottle.

"After that drive? *Ja, meneer.*" She took it gladly.

Around the back of the house a fire was already going, the coals glowing red.

"Have you eaten?"

"*Dankie*, I am starving." Her hands were in her pockets, playing with the black book. "It is nighttime, and you still organized a *braai?*"

"An Afrikaner can hold a *braai* in ten seconds notice." Meat awaited his attention, impala steak and *boerewors*. One after another were slapped on the steel grid with a sizzle.

"For which I am forever grateful." She sat in the chair, the wood squeaking under the weight. She took a deep breath. "Thank you for having me here. I needed this."

"I know it." The smile disappeared into his salt and pepper beard. "I do." He sat down in his chair.

"Did he tell you?"

"Not a word." Du Plessis shook his head, grunting. *"Bliksem."*

The minutes passed, with the sounds of grilling impala meat, the calls of birds in the night, and katydid razzing. They stared at the glowing red coals. She would have happily continued staring for hours on end at the flickering red of the wood. The quiet got the better of her.

"How did you meet Johan?"

His smile returned immediately, requiring no time to think.

"Ovamboland." Du Plessis seemed sad and delighted at the same time. "Johan and I fought together in the Border War."

"You were there?" She was shocked, though she mused nothing should really surprise her about this odd man.

"Ja, though Johan is younger than me." He shook his head "He was an idealist then."

"About politics?"

"About everything." Du Plessis turned the meat on the grid. "He grew up fast. As did all the young men sent to war." He was quiet for a moment. "After he was thrown into the fighting, his ideals shifted to survival."

"Is that why he seemed so bitter?"

"Bitterness takes a lifetime to set in. Years of disappointment were to come, but back then, one lethal contact after another in that war took its toll." Du Plessis stared at the coals. "At least we found something else out there."

"What was that?"

"Black mambas." He smiled widely. "Lovely things. Four meters of grey beauty, whipping through the bush. Johan and I got to see, one evening after a contact, two snakes wrestling." He whirled together his forearms. "Two long mambas wrapped together like a single length of rope. One trying to push the other to the ground to tire the rival out, for rights to mate. The locals scattered when they saw the mambas, but we stayed to watch. Over half an hour." He laughed. "The insane things we saw in the war, and the snakes managed to impress us the most." Du Plessis nodded. "We wanted to work with nature after that. Nature made sense. Fighting a war... well, some people believed in it. We did not."

"He went into research, then?" Venter took a drink.

"After we finished our time, we read all we could on mambas, and tracking. And we tried to find ways to get involved in conservation ever since." He held a bottle of Castle aloft. "To being *bosbefok!*"

Both were quiet for some time, listening to the distant crackle of the flames.

"In the Lowveld. Johan felt it necessary to kill those men." She stared at the fire.

"He... took a narrow view. Johan saw to those Painted wolves. Their immediate survival. He missed the broader view. The survival of the wild itself."

"Did anything change?"

"Dyk's zoo is closing. Creditors are taking all the animals, everything to be auctioned off." Du Plessis smirked, then waved off the news. "Nothing changed. The system is the same. Someone else holds the canned hunts now."

"Who?"

"*Ag*, man, there are too many to count. They keep it quiet." He drained the rest of his beer and set it in a metal drum nearby. Taking hold of a pair of tongs, he turned the meat on the fire. "There will always be trophy hunters, and people to supply them with animals to shoot. You understand why Marais was so cynical about this work?"

"I think so." She took a drink, and seemed lost in thought.

"There is so much pressure, from every direction, on what is left of nature. Farming, urbanization, consumption of natural resources, the hunger for habitat. Hunters on top of it all, needing to kill rare beasts to show off to others. He thought disaster was inevitable."

"So he snapped." She sighed.

"Johan has left the whole community hostile to the wild." He glanced in her direction. "Be careful, *meisie.*"

"We will find a way. For the wild, and for us all." Venter seemed to be staring through the fire.

"Why are you so sure about that?" Du Plessis peered at her with grey eyes.

"Because the alternative is too dark to contemplate."

"Indeed." Du Plessis started to remove some of the meat from the fire. "There are people who understand. Some." He scratched his beard. "The talk from most people, however, is ugly. Very ugly."

She nodded. "So it was all for nothing."

"Well, there were no dead Painted wolves found near where they—" Du Plessis paused, and shrugged. "Perhaps he got what he wanted. Though I would not be too confident of their survival in all those farms."

Chapter 75

The fields once filled with maize were now cleared, providing no cover for the wolves. They raced across the open ground, rock and mud with dried stalks poking from the ground. A dog barked in the distance.

"I do wonder how long she can keep this pace." Aalwyn pushed herself to keep up with Olienhout.

"I worry about her, mother." Koorsboom panted.

"Worry for us all, son. These lands have no sanctuary."

On the far edge of the maize field stood a house, concrete exterior painted a pale orange and topped with a steeply sloping tile roof. A person stood on a platform outside of this, holding a hand saw. At the sight of the wolves, he dropped this and began shouting excitedly.

"We are in for it now." Aalwyn twittered to the rest.

"It was only a matter of time." Olienhout twittered back. Her three remaining legs were pistons upon the hard ground, a machine thrum that stopped for nothing. Her ears listened for threats, eyes locked upon the land before them, allowing no distractions.

Close behind her was Wildevlier, who had scarcely left her side, nor spoken a word in their flight. She struggled to keep the pace, but not once considered asking her to slow.

A tall barb wire fence lined a tar road, stretching off into the far distance. Wildevlier threw herself into an examination of the barrier, and quickly found a flaw in the wires that she could push her head through. She withdrew her head from the barbs, shaking it in a spray of fur and drops of blood. She twittered in triumph.

"Olienhout!" Wildevlier stood on hind legs for a moment to draw her attention. She thrust her head and shoulders into the opening, driving it wider, ignoring the furrows dug into her flesh by the rusty iron. Digging at the soil, clumps were thrown behind her, producing a larger hole. She squeezed through, shuffling her body side to side to widen the gap. Each wolf flew through the hole under the fence, and bounded across the road beyond. Leadwort was the last one across, and a car bore down upon him.

"Run, you fool!" Aalwyn ruff-barked to him.

As though a lion had been sighted, he sprinted across just as the car whizzed past with a blare of the horn.

"Were they trying to run me down?" He panted to Aalwyn.

"One can never know. Assume they mean you harm, and you will not go wrong."

Once off the tar road they penetrated another fence, and entered a green grass field. To one side stood evergreen trees, straight as soldiers. To the other stretched a vast green carpet into uneven rock and a hill.

"Quickly, now." Olienhout pressed forward, ears erect, eyes ever wary. The field unrolled before them, broken by seringa and Apple-leaf trees. Not a living thing was in sight.

"Strange place. The grass is clipped close." Koorsboom took a sniff of the ground. "Some animals should be found here, though none seem present."

"Not sure what it would be. Not antelope." Aalwyn paused to sniff the ground. "No lions, in any case."

Over the crest of the hill, they descended onto a vast lawn. Structures stood before them, canopy tents on poles, one after the next and number-ing a dozen at least. The canvas was blue and white striped, and the tents had no sides to them. The breeze pushed upon the canvas structures, and they yawned back and forth gently, the ropes creaking with the movement.

"What ever are these things?" Hardekool trotted closer to one of the tents. "A dwelling without walls?" She tripped over one of the ropes anchoring a pole and stumbled to the ground, freezing there.

"No need to worry, Hardekool." Aalwyn managed to laugh in spite of her worry. "There is no snare holding you."

"Yet." Wildevlier snarled, and even Aalwyn quieted at this. She sprinted forward to where Olienhout stood.

"Wildevlier seems a changed wolf." Koorsboom mused to Aalwyn.

"Indeed. Where once she saw us as a danger or liability, now she sees a Pack." Aalwyn looked after her, close to Olienhout's side. "Something changed when Olienhout stood tall."

"Wildevlier stood taller still." They shared a glance.

They loped further from the tents past a series of stacked plastic chairs and wooden picnic benches.

As they rounded this pile of equipment, they faced a human.

The human carried a heap of tablecloths, and these fell to the ground, as did the man's jaw. His eyes were wide, and he did not seem to breathe. One shaking hand dove into a pocket.

"*Run!*" Aalwyn was off, and the pack was close behind.

The man sputtered something into a phone, pointing toward the fleeing pack.

Within minutes they could hear an engine revving behind them. The open field before them was devoid of cover. A stream cut through the field and trickled down toward a grove of acacia, seringa, and palm trees.

"Follow me into those trees... and hope we vanish into them." Olienhout took the lead as a *bakkie* roared over the top of the hill. Its blue color was marred with rust, and one human bounced in back. The metal whinged with every jolt as it careened over the uneven ground.

A shot tore through the air, though the expected high-pitched whine was not heard. The human in the rear was firing wildly as the vehicle sped to close the distance. Another shot, this time closer, as a clump of sod leapt into the air beside Olienhout.

As they raced along the stream, they entered the shadows of the trees, but found it was no grove.

"This is their den." Olienhout twittered with alarm.

The stream was spanned with a wooden footbridge, on each side decorated with earthenware pots sprouting flowers. A second bridge of concrete was beyond this, covered with dirt tire tracks. Another canopy tent was pitched on their side of the stream, with more stacked white plastic chairs. The far side was filled with palm trees that cast shade over a grass lawn next to a large wooden deck. An expansive farm house of brick and corrugated steel roof was beyond this. A painted white wooden fence surrounded the house, up to a white wishing well with a sloped roof. Several people were busying about, carrying dishes and tablecloths. One held a crate filled with cut flowers, and the woman set this down next to a wooden gazebo that was already decorated with more flowers. The wolves could hear them chattering to each other, though this ended as the *bakkie* sped up toward the stream.

The people turned to see the vehicle approaching, and then noticed the wild dogs.

"Run—straight through them." Olienhout bolted across the footbridge.

"*Through* them?" Koorsboom was close behind.

"That thing will not chase us across. And the humans are too fearful to retaliate." She loped up the manicured lawn and onto the wooden deck. The humans there were setting up tables and laying out white tablecloths. As the six wolves raced across the deck, the humans parted, some leaping over the railing of the deck, crashing glassware as they upset tables.

Behind them, the engine of the *bakkie* rattled to a halt and doors slammed. They could hear the men hustling across the grass, shouting as they went. As the wolves reached the end, they vaulted over the railing, Olienhout barely clearing it with her distended abdomen.

A shot rang out, and she thudded to the ground.

Koorsboom was at her side.

She lifted herself up, shook her head, and bolted once more. The pack rounded the edge of the house, and across another vast green lawn. They could hear humans shouting behind them, but these voices grew more faint.

Over another hill was a field filled with sheep.

Baa.

Pausing only for a moment, the wolves streaked through the herd, the sheep jolting into zig zagging runs with fitful anxiety and perturbed *baa* calls.

"Time for a hunt?" Leadwort mused.

"Not even for the beat of a bird's wing." Olienhout's terse reply kept them focused. Through rough ground and more seringa trees, they reached a fence that they crossed without difficulty. Another tar road that carried cars belching ash and smoke stretched from horizon to horizon.

"Will there be no end to these things?"

"Stay alert for a den. Or a place where humans are absent." Olienhout panted, grunting with each step.

"Are you able to continue?" Koorsboom lapped her muzzle.

Olienhout answered him with a snarl.

"Do not ask me that again. Ever."

Koorsboom lowered his head.

She led them across, charging headlong without hesitation.

The fence on the other side of the tar road was much taller, and could not be jumped. As they approached, Aalwyn's hair stood on end.

"This one is poisoned."

"What ever does that mean? Do some animals eat fences?" Leadwort sniffed the fence, and could hear a low buzz.

"The wires kill you if you touch them."

He backed away in horror, his mouth agape as he stared at Aalwyn.

"The poison fence is protecting a bounty, I suspect." Olienhout panted as she sniffed the fence as well. The fine hint of ozone made her snout wrinkle in alarm.

"Right. Koorsboom, search along the fence in this direction. I will go in the other. The rest of you run towards whomever hoo-calls first." Aalwyn and Koorsboom sprinted along the barrier.

Wildevlier sat close to Olienhout, glaring in all directions, scanning the horizon for threats. Her bared fangs dared any to approach.

"How does she know these things?" Leadwort inquired, sitting down a good distance from the fence.

"A lifetime of learning." Olienhout lay down, wincing. "She killed a cape buffalo once with this."

Hardekool and Leadwort were stunned to silence.

"Through cunning she manipulated one of those behemoths into a fence such as this, and it died where it landed." She nodded. "You can learn much from her."

"*Bakgat...* a remarkable wolf. Dare I ask if she has a mate?" Leadwort wondered.

"Very much so." Olienhout laid her head on the ground, eyes shut tightly.

"Does your leg pain you?"

"Yes, though it has grown strange. I can feel the entire leg, down to the paw, ache with a constant shock." She moved her stump uselessly. "It returns again to sear me, as though beckoning to me from afar, inviting me to join it."

"We shall be resting soon." Hardekool nudged her with encouragement.

"There will be no choice." She breathed heavily. "They are coming soon."

A hoo-called startled them, and Olienhout was on her feet instantly. She began loping as fast as she could bear down the fence line toward Koorsboom. By the time they reached him, Aalwyn was at their side.

"A hole—it seems as though we are not the only ones to come this way."

Aalwyn sniffed the shallow depression dug under the fence. "Jackal. We need to dig this deeper to clear the fence." She began to work on the loose dirt, shoveling dust and gravel behind her. Ducking low, scooping the earth from below the fence, she took great care to avoid the buzzing wires. Hanging above them was a yellow plastic sign emblazoned with a silhouette hand with lightning bolts around the fingers. DANGER - GEVAAR - INGOZI.

"As low as a tortoise, all of you." She shimmied under the fence, dropping her tail down just under the low hanging electrified wire. Each of them did the same, Olienhout struggling to claw her way to the other side. Aalwyn gripped her by her shoulder and pulled her the rest of the way through.

On the opposite side, Olienhout was on her feet, and loping away across the grass field.

Here there were no signs of a farm. It was, by all appearances, savanna. As far as they could see, *rooigras* and russet grass stretched over rolling hills marked with Knob-thorn acacia, wild seringa, and milkplum trees. Rocky outcroppings jutted above the grass in places, and termite mounds dotted the landscape. Many of these were derelict, empty of life and reclaimed by trees that exploited the rich earth therein.

"Steady on—there is a smell of death ahead." Koorsboom gave an alarm growl. The rest of the pack slowed while he sprinted ahead. The rich scent of decay became apparent to them all.

Over the crest of a hill they found Koorsboom standing silently, the breeze tousling his fur. He looked down on the prone form of a Black-backed jackal. Silver ends of the fur stood still, speckling the long black stripe that ran from its head to its bushy tail. Four stiffening legs jutted into the air. The tongue hung out of the slack mouth, buzzing with flies. Its eyes were sightless, staring intently at nothing. A neat round hole was in its side behind the shoulder, dried blood running down to the belly.

The six wolves continued onward in silence.

After an hour of traversing this pocket of the wild, Olienhout twittered excitedly to the rest. She bounded forth to a distant stand of wild olive trees.

Light filtered through the leaves above on sparse grass and bare earth. Ground squirrels scattered to the trees as they approached. Koorsboom chirped excitedly to the rest.

"A denning hole!" A pause. "No death or disease within!" This sounded muffled as he spoke into the subterranean chamber.

"This is more shallow than the aardvark hollows we have used in the past." Aalwyn sniffed the edge. "I wonder what creature excavated this."

Olienhout hobbled to the mouth of the hole as Koorsboom poked his head out.

"What fortune is on our side!" He exited the den and stood aside as she eased her way down the hole. The bare earth sloped down for a meter, then widened slightly. It was cramped with a wolf inside, but the dirt within was dry, and absent of mold. She gave a nod over her shoulder.

"This shall be our home, our root and tree until the pups are ready to join us on our *trek*." Her swollen belly rested on the dry dirt.

"Indeed, Olienhout. At last, you are safe." They lapped one another's muzzles and held their heads together, with eyes closed for some time.

"This could not have turned out better."

A White-backed vulture took notice of the wolves as they entered the wild olive grove, filing this away for later use. Wild dogs meant wild kills, and that was always welcome for scavengers. Gliding over a squat granite *koppie*, the vulture caught the warm air rising from the bare rock. The thermal lifted the bird a kilometer into the air, and the raptor surveyed its territory.

Below, the wild olive trees sat near the edge of a gigantic game farm, where herds of impala, wildebeest, and blesbok grazed listlessly. The sprawling property bordered another game farm that was larger still, with a central pond from a natural spring. Various antelope species devoured the grass around the mud-banked pond with several white rhino grazing amidst the trees. To the west, the farm with fields now denuded of maize bordered both of these. To the south and east, the granite *koppie* sat, and beyond were still more farms boasting various game species and fields of hay.

The vulture glided lower to the ground, able to view all of these farms, their homesteads, and the tar roads between that provided kills from time to time. It did not for a moment forget about the presence of the pack.

* * *

"Yes, there is no doubt." The man barked at the phone. "They are wild dogs. I think they got through my fence somehow."

He looked out his window as though they would return to his farm despite having left an hour ago.

"You do not do removals? We can do this ourselves the old-fashioned way. Well who does?"

A pause.

"They do predator removal? *Goed*. When do they open?"

After taking some notes, he banged the phone back down, and picked it up again to call a neighbor. And another. And another.

Chapter 76

"What is this, then?" The man's voice echoed through the corridor of concrete, causing the people in the queue to look anxiously. "Is this your paracetamol?" He let the plastic bag filled with white tablets drop to the floor.

The man in the chair stared at the ground, a look of resignation on his face. His hands were folded on loose fitting dirty pants. Calloused feet were clad only in cheap plastic flip flops.

"This will be tested, friend. And if it is Mandrax, you will be going to prison for life." The border agent was bent over the man, shouting into the top of his head like a giant microphone. "And that SIM card you flushed down the loo was the last hope you had of seeing daylight."

He stormed away from him, leaving the man in the custody of local police.

"There is no point in being angry, Orlando. That man will be paid well to sit in jail." The other border officer leaned against the wall.

"I am sick of this border post being a place for drugs and horn to cross. The next man who gives me a stack of *meticais* to not search his bag is going in a ditch in the forest."

His colleague laughed as the man's phone rang.

"Orlando."

"*Hallo.*" A pause. "My name is Sonja Venter." Another pause. "I am a friend of Johan Marais."

"Then you are a friend to me." Orlando paused for a moment and bit his lip. "He was a good man. Did you know him well?"

"I think so." Her relief was easily heard through the phone. "I was told you were not a good friend to poachers."

"You did not hear that from a poacher." Orlando hissed. "When I catch one, they must learn to breathe dirt."

She laughed to herself. Everything Du Plessis told her about this man was true.

"Are you coming my way?"

"At some point, yes. I have been in contact with a poacher who may have information about your post being used to transit rhino horn to Maputo."

"Good." He chuckled. "There is so much cargo moving past it is impossible to check it all. I am glad to get warning that something shady is coming though."

"I will have dates and times soon, I hope."

"We should open a special queue for those bastards." Orlando shook his head. "Leads right through a door to a ditch."

"One poacher we are looking for is Augusto. He is a Mozambican national, and he may be traveling with horns."

"Smuggling?" Orlando sounded hungry.

"He may have legal permits for them."

"Damn." He grunted in disgust. "Still, these bastards are greedy, and they will always try to get more through illegally."

"And there is a Thai national named Buatoom who may be running it all."

"That name." Orlando inhaled. "I know him."

"You do?" Venter practically sang this.

"Yes I do. Rude piece of shit. Tried to walk right through once about a year ago, and just tossed money in our direction, as though all Africans are corrupt."

"We can intercept him if we have notice."

"No problem." He smiled widely. "I will be in touch."

* * *

The speaker sat on the rear of an open-back *bakkie*, the cargo area holding the rear leg of a recently killed impala. A wire led from the speaker into the cab of the vehicle. A button was pressed, and the speaker vibrated.

A loud roar shuddered across the grass plain, followed by silence. The distress call of an impala was repeated several times, with five minutes between each call.

Sonja Venter pushed the severed leg off the end of the *bakkie*. She closed the door and glanced about, pressing lightly on the gas pedal.

Before long, a swish of lion tail appeared about the grass tips nearby. Another joined it.

She stopped the repeated impala calls, and shifted into gear. As the lions approached, she slowly pulled away, watching the lions in the rear-view mirror. At a prudent distance, she stopped to watch. Two lionesses ripped into the impala limb, laying side by side.

She took a note, documenting the location.

CALLUP-0930

Lion - female x2

No darting, bait taken

As she idled the engine, she made sure the vehicle remained in sight, so the lions were habituated to its presence. Future callups like this would be used when darting was necessary.

Her phone ring was startling to her, unused to receiving a signal this far from any village.

"Du Plessis?"

"*Goiemore, meisie.*" His voice was taking its usual jovial tone. "Those Painted wolves are alive. And they are causing quite the stir in the Lowveld."

Chapter 77

The engine revved, and the complex of buildings receded into the background.

Sonja Venter eyed the border post in her rearview mirror, hoping she did not offend the agents there with her urgency. One never knows when memory of a good interaction would come in handy, or when a poor one would be cause for regret.

The nondescript veld passed by as she pushed the Land Rover to 150km per hour.

There was so much ground to cover.

* * *

Aalwyn awoke to the dawn, a slight chill to the air on an early autumn morning. The wild olive trees kept her in shade, wind hissing through the leaves. A lone vulture soared high above her, little more than a dot. Hazel eyes surveyed the area before the den.

Leadwort was standing out in the open.

"Get down, you fool." She growled, sprinting out to his side.

"Impala herd, not far away."

"Excellent. Now get low and be quiet." She crouched to the level of the wavering russet grass.

"Are we not in a wild place?"

"The treacherous fence that we crossed indicates otherwise. No matter how natural it seems, be on your guard." She crept back to the den and called the others.

"The hunt commences!" Koorsboom was on his hind legs, boxing his mother.

She knocked him back. "A hunt shall be undertaken, but with caution. Act as though we are on a farm."

"We may just be." Hardekool twittered, excited in spite of herself to learn more on the hunt.

Olienhout moaned in the den below.

"Off with us, then." Each wolf lapped one another's muzzle in greeting, and the rally was underway. With much scampering about and colliding of bodies, Koorsboom darted off, and the rest padded after him. The sun warmed the savanna, evaporating the dew clinging to grass stalks. A black sparrowhawk took flight, spreading wide wings black above and pale grey below. As it soared over the meadow, its sharp eyes searched for its prey, primarily smaller birds. The four wolves loped below towards the nearby impala herd.

There was no cover, and so there was no approach. Koorsboom accelerated to top speed, ears flat, head hung low, a streaking missile. Even at a distance the alarm was raised. The closest impala moved its head side to side to identify what approached, and rapidly gave a startling alarm snort. The herd bolted as one, and the pronking began.

"That male—he is not pronking with the rest." Hardekool twittered.

"Indeed—he is lame. His hind leg is in a limp." Aalwyn chirped to Wildevlier and Koorsboom. "Isolate that one—surround his flanks!"

Leadwort increased his speed to follow her order.

The rest of the herd split away, and as the chase left their area, they resumed grazing. The pursuing wolves boxed in the fleeing male, horns held aloft as it sprinted. One of its haunches bore a wound, bite marks from a survived attack from a jackal.

The hunt lasted for a kilometer. At the end Hardekool sprinted forth and dragged the antelope down.

"Well done, Hardekool." Aalwyn could not help but be impressed. "One would hardly have guessed you lived in cages most of your life."

"I am honored you would think so." She ripped open the abdomen and unrooted the heart. The kill was devoured by the pack.

The White-backed vulture that soared above spotted the carcass with no difficulty. Angling its wings, the scavenger lost altitude as it glided in a lazy circle. Soon it fluttered to the ground, taloned feet striking the dirt, and wide wings folded in. The wolves left with full stomachs, and the vulture hopped over. There was little food left over, but still made a banquet for scavengers with residual meat, liver, intestines, hide, and tendons. A spiraling funnel of vultures circled overhead.

* * *

A Jeep drove out to the carcass, easily found under the gliding vultures. The body was invisible beneath the writhing mass of dirty white feathers.

The driver stood by the idling vehicle and tapped on a phone.

"Get the men out to the fences. We have a carnivore on the grounds." He nodded. "*Ja, nee.* Make sure they have their rifles ready." Another nod. "*Nee,* not sure what it is this time. Not yet. Have we had any reports of carnivores from other farms?"

Chapter 78

Rapid breathing from the newborn pup made barely a sound in the den. She snuffled, the small pug snout still covered with secretions. Struggling onto its four tiny paws, she was shaking, hesitant, and thumped to the ground of the dry earthen chamber. Her small floppy ears were now covered in dust. She pulled herself back onto forepaws, dragging her hind legs and a stubby tail. Her coat was black and white, and would not acquire gold coloration for another month. Her eyes were still closed, blind to her dim world.

A tongue whipped over her face, clearing away the thick fluid that coated her head. Now free, she breathed more comfortably, and took in the rich, pungent musk scent. She knew nothing, but sensed who she was, and the beginning of a boundless love. The scent from her mother was the world, and the roughness of her tongue drew her close. She moved closer to Olienhout's fur and rested.

Another thing joined her. A small form, shaking, snuffling. She would come to know this new thing as her brother.

Another, then another. Olienhout's body was wracked with pain from the contractions, and she bore these in silence.

Olienhout pushed each small, helpless pup to the verge of her birth canal, and gently pulled them free using her teeth. Licking their pug faces, she ensured each had a clear airway before attending to the next pup that emerged.

Another, then another.

The den was filled with rapid, shallow breathing sounds, and sniffing from the already inquisitive young.

Finally, the last emerged, and was set carefully with the rest. She examined the pup, and was satisfied it was breathing, and surviving this first crucial test.

Olienhout knew the eleven pups, each by scent and distinctive coat coloration. Exhaling, she laid her head down to rest.

"Are you well?" Koorsboom poked his head into the chamber. His hazel eyes played over the new litter. Like all fathers, he was captivated utterly with a blooming love and aching fear. The memory of the litter that died under the Sickness faded, replaced by wonder and joy.

"It is finished." She took another deep breath and lifted her head again. She pulled one pup closer to her belly where it found a teat and began suckling.

The pup's throat filled with rich milk, and this overwhelming sensation taught her the existence of food. As she drank, she shook with excitement, only breathing with reluctance.

Olienhout pulled another pup closer, and it latched onto another available teat.

"Are you ready to eat?"

"Not just now." She pulled the rest over to her belly, and all took their fill. She gazed down at the suckling pups, content at last. She forgot her aching leg and her shoulder wound. Her entire world was within the den, lost in the savanna, hidden from the vagaries of the land beyond.

*****

"We need to extend the hunt to find that impala herd." Koorsboom rested under the olive tree, one forepaw folded over the other.

"A risk, my son." Aalwyn was on her back, working herself back and forth to scratch her shoulders on the rocks beneath her. She rolled onto her belly. "The more we chase one impala herd, the further they may move away from us. Excessive attacks may scatter them, and our work is greater."

"I found some tracks that were not impala during our last hunt." Hardekool shook her head, the ruff beneath her chin rustling. "Larger ones."

"Likely wildebeest. I do not venture our numbers could bring an adult down. And there may not be calves in their herd." Aalwyn mused, almost to herself. "That impala herd has been wandering south, so we move in the other direction to see how the land favors us."

Within minutes, the rally was underway, and the pack struck out to the north.

***

The *bakkie* idled on the ridge, surrounded by grasses waving in the wind. The stalks had begun to slowly dry as the winter approached. A man stood in the rear, holding binoculars in one hand. He glassed the field below him, and saw only the herd of impala. He wore a green fabric shirt and khaki shorts. Though he was towering in size with a bulging gut, he moved as quickly as a rugby forward. He sighed.

"Did your father have similar problems with carnivores, mister Grootes?" Another man in a bicolored green and blue denim shirt and khaki shorts paced on the ground by the *bakkie*. He held a hunting rifle with a scope.

"*Ja*, he and his father before him. There were always predators." He took the binoculars away from his eyes and rubbed them.

"Predator mitigation has really changed with technology, eh?"

"Not really. A few new tools, some chemicals, electric fencing. But it all comes down to the same method." He resumed viewing the herd. "This farm has been in my family for decades. And we had to fight for every single one of them."

"Should we continue waiting?"

"*Ja*, for now. If we find another carcass in the morning, then we are dealing with a nocturnal hunter. Lion, jackal. Maybe hyena." He fished a packet out of the large pockets of his shorts and pulled out a stick of *droëwors*. Biting off the end, he chewed fitfully. "Apparently a farm nearby thought they spotted a wild dog, but I doubt they did." Another bite. "We will find what has invaded our *plaas*. Only a matter of time."

* * *

The five wolves sprinted to their very limit.

"Forward, my wolves!" Koorsboom attempted to take the lead, but faltered.

The impala had long since stopped pronking, all of its effort spent in pounding the earth with hooves to escape the hunters. It was strong, but that strength was beginning to flag.

Unlike most of the impala of its herd, this one had a coat of ghostly white.

"It is trying to reach that acacia thicket!" Aalwyn barked to the rest. "We may lose it in there!"

Wildevlier clawed forward, snorting with the effort. The sedge barrier drew close. She gave a wild snarl, and threw herself at the impala, catching a glancing blow of a hoof to her head.

Instead of stumbling, Wildevlier scrabbled forth, frothing at the mouth, and clamped her fangs on the lower part of a hind leg. The impala flailed its forehooves against the thornbrush that was to be its salvation.

The wolf dug in her paws, halting the impala, dragging it down. Reddened eyes wide with rage, she released her grip to close her jaws on the abdomen, and tore an enormous gash that flooded the ground with crimson.

The pale impala died with a fading moan as the wolves mobbed the corpse, each taking hold of a limb and pulling, until each joint popped and the body was dismembered.

"Well done, Wildevlier." Koorsboom lapped her muzzle.

"She shall never hunger." Wildevlier's face was locked in a rictus of

453

rage.

Koorsboom took a step back, for a moment thinking her anger would be directed at him.

Her eyes lost none of their ferocity as they ripped into the impala's side, tearing loose muscle in flaps to swallow.

The rest of the wolves packed away the precious meat with all haste, each glancing about for hyena or lion, any approaching enemy.

When the hunters finished, they left behind a discarded fold of hide, the skeleton in several large sections, and the untouched head. There was the faintest hint of golden coloration on its cheekbones, and black tips on its ears. These were the last vestiges of its natural color, the work of careful breeding yielding the unusual coloration.

The sightless eyes like black marbles gaped at nothing, its jaw parted in a frozen wail.

* * *

The *bakkie* sat on the ridge, its engine now stilled. The driver surveyed the horizon for carnivores for a moment, and continued thumbing through a magazine.

Grootes was not distracted by anything, and continued searching the horizon.

There was a ringing from the pocket of the driver, and he answered.

"What? Bloody hell." He tossed the magazine into the rear of the cab and jumped into the driver seat.

"What is it?" Grootes jumped in the passenger seat and slammed his door shut.

"Another impala killed, on the other end of the ranch." He looked to his employer. "The white one."

"Shit." Grootes spoke this as a long exhale. "That was set to auction next week. Nearly a million rand's worth up in smoke."

* * *

As the sun was setting behind the distant mountains to the west, Grootes examined what remained of the white impala.

"How long did it take to breed this one?" The farm hand was almost afraid to ask.

"A long time. This color is quite rare." He stood up and kicked a stone. "Insurance may cover a little of its value. Nothing like what we could have gotten at the auction." He paced around the body. "These kills were far apart." He placed his hands on his hips while walking about. "Six kilometers at least. Whatever we are dealing with, it is moving fast."

"No tracks, not in this grass. And no scat." The farm hand pawed through the grass, slick in places with blood.

Grootes answered another call, walking away.

Flies buzzed around the decapitated impala head, alighting on the protruding tongue.

"*Ja, nee.* Nothing here. Thanks for the call." He pocketed the phone and walked back to the *bakkie*. "That was a ranger from Mozambique, name is Sonja Venter. You ever hear of her?"

"*Nee.*"

"Make some calls when we get back. She wanted to come here, look around. Apparently there is a pack of wild dogs about."

Chapter 79

A week had passed, and the pack had managed at least one kill every day. Aalwyn kept their movements varied, hunting on all the surrounding properties, probing the land at random. Fences were crossed quickly when necessary, and they learned where these flaws were located.

The pack moved its hunt to the east, finding a herd of two dozen wildebeest. They milled about, uttering the odd *gnu*.

"There will be little yield from this herd." Aalwyn padded toward the gathering, followed closely by the other wolves.

"How are you so certain?" Hardekool shadowed her, ever curious.

"Their numbers. They are well aware we are a threat only if we force them to run. And they will not flee when they have a thicket of horns against so few of us."

As the wolves moved closer, the males stopped grazing and stood in a line. Drawing this together tightly, each adult bent down slightly, their horns angled toward the predators.

Aalwyn feinted to one side, and the wall of wildebeest shifted like a shield, and grew longer still as other males joined the barrier. She padded quickly back, and rushed the edge of the wall. It stood strong, and the male wildebeest did not back down.

Hardekool bolted forward, giving off alarm barks. A few of the wildebeest were momentarily startled, but with snorts and *gnu* calls, they quickly rejoined the line.

Aalwyn shook her head.

"Enough of this. Come, before we waste any more time."

* * *

The fence was as high as the last one the pack encountered, and at the base there was an almost inaudible buzzing.

"The day is fading." Aalwyn turned about and twittered to the rest to return to the den.

She froze, breath caught in her throat.

On the crest of the hill facing them, a dirty white vehicle trundled along.

"Nobody move."

The *bakkie* moved along the hill, bumping about as the tires encountered depressions and holes in the rough ground. It resembled a tortoise to the hunters in its awkward gait. Interminably, the vehicle worked its way along the ridge. The wolves crouched lower in the wavering grass.

"Is there a danger?" Hardekool spoke in a whisper.

The vehicle passed out of sight.

"We must make haste. We are not the only hunters out here."

As the wolves loped along the fence opposite the direction of the *bakkie*, they noticed a roll of wire fencing. A pair of pliers lay on the ground.

An engine revved in the distance.

Aalwyn turned to look, and saw the *bakkie* moving quickly along the fence line towards them.

"Run!"

They tore along the fence, onto a dirt path. Their speed increased without the need to clear the long grass.

The engine throttled up, and closed the distance.

"Off this path—they can outrun us here." Aalwyn bolted at a right angle to the fence, and the wolves followed. Behind them, they could hear the engine change pitch, and steel banged as it bounced over the grassy hill. Sprinting at top speed, they left the vehicle behind.

The engine stopped behind them, and a human voice shouting reached them. A single shot echoed over the field, but it went high over their heads.

* * *

The wolves rested outside of the den, and none spoke. Aalwyn stared at a knot in the bark of the olive tree, tracing the concentric circles within. A beetle scuttled over the bark, oblivious to the consternation of the wolves.

Her mind was in turmoil. She considered the options, and none being palatable, she kept to herself. At last, she stood and padded to the den hole. Dipping her head and folding back her ears, she crawled down the tunnel into the larger chamber.

Olienhout lay on her side, and the pups suckled greedily.

"The hunt was aborted." She took a deep breath. "We are on a farm. A large one, but nonetheless a farm. Humans chased us today in one of their things."

"They have chased us in the past, the great wild hunting lands." They had no words for Gorongosa, other than 'the wild'. "And there was no threat."

"The threat here is all too real. They were not trying to watch—it was a hostile pursuit."

Olienhout sighed. She paused to scratch herself, forgetting that hind leg was lost, her shortened limb flailing for a moment.

"Every hunt we take is a risk. And I fear for you if they find you." Aalwyn's voice was edged with anxiety. "Lions will seek our den and destroy it. Down to the last pup. I suspect humans will do the same—for the same reasons." She ran a claw along the earthen base of the chamber. "They want no other predators here."

"There must be a successful hunt soon. I will need it to maintain the milk." Olienhout nosed one of her pups back onto its feet.

"You must abandon this litter."

Olienhout breathed quietly, the only sound that of sucking and shuffling of pup bodies.

"Else they will find us, and slaughter us. It is only a matter of time before they track us here." Aalwyn panted.

One of the pups left her teat, and stood on all four tiny paws. She no longer trembled with weak newborn muscles. She placed a paw on her mother's shoulder. Olienhout looked down to her.

The pup opened her eyes, gazing upon her mother for the first time. Olienhout ran her tongue gently across the pup's snout, and the little one moaned with pleasure.

"Whether we are run down on the open savanna, or struck down here in this den, it matters not. There is nowhere to run, and so I may dispel your worry."

Aalwyn sighed.

"I abandon nothing." Olienhout raised her head, jaw set. "This stand shall be my legacy." She touched noses with the older female. "Your family awaits you in the great wild lands, far from here. I am grateful to you for freeing us from that terrible cage. Even if we die in this place, the time we have gained was precious. In the midst of our *trek*, we knew happiness."

Aalwyn took a breath. She knew what Olienhout was suggesting. "I am honored to have been your alpha."

"We never had a choice, here in this part of the world. Stay or run, it is the same. And that is a comfort in a way."

Aalwyn gave a long exhale, her eyes on the earthen floor, but her mind far away. Her jaw clicked as her teeth came together, muscles locked in grim determination. She looked up toward Olienhout, and gave a nod.

"Then I am with you to the end."

Olienhout allowed herself a smile in the dim chamber. "To the living edge—always."

Chapter 80

The farm house was a flurry of activity. Men rushed about, carrying tools and implements. A woman in faded grey coveralls dried her hands while ushering the children out of the way. One man in blue overalls hustled outside into a chaos of barking dogs.

Two men in bicolored green and blue cotton shirts and khaki pants stood in the great room chatting. One held a photograph.

"Insurance is reimbursing me less than a thousand rand." Dawie Grootes tossed the photo on the table. It was of the decapitated head of the ghostly white impala. "Not even the cost of a normal one. Backing out of the auction cost me as well."

"*Ag*, man, these things happen. Part of the risks of farming, *né?*" Marthinus Louw was from a neighboring farm where he raised wild game.

"It has been two weeks now since the first impala kill. I have not had losses like this outside of severe drought." He tapped his fingers on a table. "If this was just a jackal, it would not be such a big deal. Shoot it, and the problem is done."

"Well, shoot it, and then their mate." Louw swirled a rocks glass containing brandy and soda.

One of the farm hands bounded into the house and panted to Grootes. "Sir. We saw them. Wild dogs, five of them."

"*Nee*, man. They have not been around here since... well, ever."

"We saw them close enough, there is no doubt."

Louw poured more brandy out of a bottle marked 'Klipdrift' onto the melting ice in his glass. "Wild dogs can be tough to get rid of."

"They do have a nasty habit of surviving." Grootes drummed his fingers on a table.

"At least if we shoot these, there will not be any others to take their place. Before long, they will all be extinct."

"That was bound to happen eventually." Grootes' ample gut seemed to strain at the buttons on his shirt.

"How is the rest of your stock?" Louw swirled his glass.

"*Lekker,* dropped calves all spring. Should see a profit this year. Are you still farming rhino?"

"*Ja,* and I cannot turn down the offers I am getting. Millions for each one." He snorted. "I had one tourist ask for a baby rhino for their kid to shoot."

"I hope you said no."

"I did. They are worth so much more as adults."

A third farmer joined them, holding a bag. She wore a dark cotton shirt, open at the throat, with denim pants and heavy boots streaked with mud. Every move she made was with haste, as though loathe to waste time. She reached into her bag and showed the men the contents. Several white boxes with red symbols on them were marked with 'Magnum', and in smaller lettering 'Packaged Explosives'.

"*Dankie.* I am not sure if we will need them, but it is good to have them on hand."

"I thought you could use them." Riana Myburgh closed the bag and set it on the ground with care. She patted her pockets for cigarettes absently. "I have been blasting tree stumps on my farm."

"Are you still on about 'invasive plants'?" Louw laughed.

"Those black wattle trees do not belong here." She found a loose cigarette in her pocket. "If I wanted Australian trees, I would live in Australia."

"Do your antelope care?"

"I care." She stuck the filter end in her mouth.

"Did you hear about that Marais *oke?*" Louw's face darkened.

"He killed Dyk. And a tourist." Myburgh rolled up her sleeves.

"Both farmers." Louw corrected her. "Over some wild dogs he had." Grootes shook his head. "I heard he was *bosbefok* since the Border War."

She shrugged.

"Still." Louw continued to swirl his glass, the ice clinking. "If they think they can just shoot farmers and expect us to give a toss about wild animals, they have lost their minds."

"Have you identified what is killing your herds?" She found a lighter in her other pocket and raised it toward her face.

"African wild dogs." Grootes raised his brow as he spoke the words. Myburgh struck the wheel of the lighter, but paused, the flame dancing a distance from the cigarette before it whiffed out.

"I thought they were wiped out around here." Grootes muttered.

She stared at the floor for a moment. "Dyk's wild dogs escaped from his zoo. When he was killed." She chewed on the filter, nodding.

"Are you sure?" Louw swirled his brandy.

"That is what I heard. Marais freed them. Or helped them get away."

"You think these are the same wild dogs?"

"Probably." She eyed the explosives in the sack. "That *oke* never knew how to take care of animals. *Domkop.*"

"Well, they will soon be wiped out of the Lowveld once again." Louw smiled.

Myburgh glared at him.

"Are you okay?" Grootes caught her look. "You are still helping us?"

"I said I would." She stalked away, slinging her unlit cigarette into a nearby rubbish bin.

"These wild dogs may be denning." Grootes stared grimly out the window. "If that is the case, they will stay until they have killed my entire stock." A pause, and he picked up a set of keys. "We will need to work quickly on this."

"Before the wild dogs decimate the farm?" Louw appeared somewhat nervous.

"That, and the inevitable arrival of conservationists." Grootes rolled his eyes. "Always ready to stick in their nose. Where are they when we have real work to do?"

"Making a fuss in the press."

Grootes nodded. "Quickly, then."

* * *

The White-backed vulture landed softly, curving its wings forward in a scoop that brought its speed to zero as it touched down. Walking gingerly over to the carcass of the young wildebeest, it looked about for only a moment before tucking into the entrails. For whatever reason, there were no hyenas or other threatening scavengers here.

More vultures were in a circular mass overhead, and they glided down to join the feast.

Five Painted wolves trotted away from the kill, bellies hanging low.

"I sense danger in the air... make haste." Aalwyn began to run, and the others followed in kind. Over the rolling hills of open grass, the sky loomed over them, as vast as an ocean. Yet this felt claustrophobic, pressing down upon them, the open spaces a narrowing trap.

A scent of ash and gasoline became apparent. Within minutes, a hum of engine reached their ears.

"To the tree."

They raced towards an Apple-leaf tree, standing tall with a green crown. The pack rounded its base and kept on, hoping it would obscure the sight of them.

The engine grew closer.

"Faster, you lazy *bliksem!*" Aalwyn ruff-barked to them, and they ran flat out across the savanna.

"Shall we divide?" Hardekool twittered to the rest.

"No—we shall outrace them." Aalwyn spoke with confidence, and hoped it would be so.

The banging of metal behind them began to subside, and the engine cut off altogether.

"The thunder is coming—be quick!" Her head lowered further still, and her pace was stretched to the limit.

No sound of a shot reached them, however. The pack crested another hill, and she commanded them to slow.

"We may have outlasted them again." She panted to herself. "This is what survival must be here. Each day is a fight to the death. And once the season passes, you fight for the next."

A rumble caught their ears. Sprinting over the top of the hill the pack just descended was a domesticated dog. Pale brown, almost fawn in color, it was a thick and powerful beast, with floppy ears and a black snout. Built like a lion, with a nub of a tail, the *boerboel* was all rage. Its hide rippled with muscle as it bounded toward them. Never having encountered wild dogs, it feared nothing.

They had never seen a dog like this.

"Make haste again—they are upon us!" The five wolves darted away, and rapidly accelerated. Though Painted wolves have far greater endurance than any dog, they were not able to reach escape speed before the boerboel pounced.

Hardekool rolled as it collided with her. Powerful jaws were bared, and sank down for the kill.

Before the teeth found their mark, Aalwyn and Koorsboom had latched onto the dog's haunch. Koorsboom pulled the dog away from Hardekool, and Aalwyn ripped away, leaving the hide hanging in a flap. Blood cascaded down its hip.

The injured boerboel snarled, apoplectic at these invaders. It did not speak in words, knowing only guttural noises. Instinct guided the dog, as it faced a pack of killers, and realized what was about to happen.

The Painted wolves reformed their line, and gave no chance for it to respond.

Koorsboom charged, drawing the jaws of the guard dog. He withdrew at the last second, as Aalwyn darted around to grip the haunch. Wildevlier flung herself at the dog, and her jaws locked upon the powerful neck.

"Take him!" Aalwyn pealed.

Hardekool and Leadwort took hold of a hind leg and the nub of a tail, and Koorsboom tore it open.

"Let it go."

The wolves parted, and the boerboel lifted itself off the ground. Its eyes were a fog of confusion. It emitted a low growl, then a whine. Another growl as it stepped closer, and a lower sustained whine as it slowed to a stop. Another step and a stop. Behind the dog dragged nearly two meters of intestine. Each additional step was an agony, and despite this, the dog pressed its gradual attack. After a few more steps toward its enemy, it simply stood, heaving deep breaths. Laying down, it panted, paralyzed between anguish and duty.

"Back to the den." Aalwyn turned to leave.

"Should we finish it off?" Wildevlier looked at the hulking black form.

"We should. But there is little reason to risk a fatal bite." She looked the dog up and down. "The mother is waiting for us."

The wolves bounded off, and the pale dog watched, panting. It stood, and lay down again with a whine.

* * *

Koorsboom regurgitated his measure of the meat, and Olienhout bolted it down as each chunk hit the dirt. There was no chewing, only swallowing. He cleared out of the den, and Hardekool yielded her share as well. The remaining wolves shared the rest amongst the hunters.

"We need another kill tomorrow, no mistake." Koorsboom lay down next to his mother. "She will need to leave to get water as well."

"There is a pool close by, so that at least is reassuring."

"To the south?" Hardekool paced the ground under the olive tree.

"Yes, that should do. Best to spread out our hunting as much as possible." Aalwyn muttered. "Every day is under threat."

Aalwyn looked to the looming sky above. Clouds swirled, obscuring the sun.

"And every hunt may be the last."

* * *

The two men stood with hands on hips. Between them lay the prone body of the eviscerated mastiff dog. Its tongue hung out, mouth hanging open. Rigor mortis had not set in.

"Bloody vermin." Grootes kicked a rock and gritted his teeth. "Each of these kills are spaced across the whole farm. And other farms as well. There is no bloody pattern, and I do not have enough men to patrol the whole damned place!"

The farm hand stared at the dog. He cradled his chin in one hand, tapping one finger on his cheekbone. The dog's guts trailed behind it like the tail of an arrow. He pointed in the direction the dog had dragged itself.

Far distant across the farmland savanna were low rising hills, a few rocky outcroppings, and a grove of olive trees.

Chapter 81

"Shouldn't we drive around, Mr. Louw?" The younger man held his rifle in both hands at the ready, and paced incessantly.

"*Nee*, the engine spooks the wolves." The older farmer watched a group of impala grazing. Some were heads down, clipping the grass. Most were glancing about, heads high, on the alert for an attack. His binoculars were laying on the bonnet of the vehicle. "Just keep watching." His face was weathered, covered in part by a shaggy mustache. His dark brown eyes never seemed to blink, ever trained out toward the horizon.

"For wild dogs?"

"For anything." Louw peered out toward a hill. "Birds taking flight, antelope on the run. How long have you worked the Grootes *plaas?*"

"Seven years." He checked the breech to ensure a bullet was chambered. Brown hair in an unruly clump on his head was rustled by the wind.

"Never seen wild dogs, have you?" Louw never took his eyes off the hill.

"Not outside a book." His finger brushed the trigger before returning to the guard.

"Well, you can rest assured they will not eat you alive." Louw nodded at the younger man. "African wild dogs do not attack people." He looked at the rifle, which was still held stock to shoulder. "No need to be nervous. And no need to shoot me by mistake."

The younger man blushed before lowering his weapon, and attempted to relax. "Mister Grootes appreciates you taking time from your farm to help out."

"*Geen probleem.*" He looked back to the younger farmhand and clapped his heavy hand on the boy's back. "Us farmers must look out for each other." His gaze returned to the hill. "Nobody else will."

As the hours ticked by, the herd milled about, grazing. They were clustered around a large waterhole that stayed full in all but the driest of seasons.

"The grass around that pond looks diseased." He rested the stock of his rifle on the ground.

"Just overgrazed. They like to be near water, so they just hoover up the grass by the water's edge and work their way outwards. Most every pond looks like this unless they are chased off."

The younger man continued pacing.

The sun slowly crawled across the sky as the hours passed, and began its inexorable dip to the horizon.

"Look alive." Louw's voice rasped.

He stopped pacing and looked up. The entire herd was headed their way. The thunder of the hoof beats was muted, but growing louder as they approached. Behind the herd were pairs of large rounded ears, bouncing above the grass tops.

"Give me the rifle." Louw motioned with his hand. He ratcheted the bolt of the rifle open, and seeing the bullet in place, closed the breech. He took a deep breath and exhaled slowly as he looked down the sight at the approaching herd.

The crack of the gun made the herd slow, but only for a moment as they again pressed on with their run.

"Got it."

The younger farmhand held up the binoculars and saw four wolves standing around the prone figure of a fifth. "The stupid things are waiting for you to shoot again."

"I know." He opened the breech and chambered another bullet. Taking aim, he saw the wolves running off in the opposite direction.

Crack!

The rest of the Painted wolves continued their run, disappearing over the hill.

"Let's see where they retreat." The men got in the *bakkie* and followed the racing wolf hunters. Their pace was glacial compared to the predators, but the open savanna of the farm gave them no place to hide. The vehicle threw dust onto the dead wolf as it drove past. The chest did not heave another breath.

"They are heading toward that group of trees just there, I think."

"Should we kill the rest off?"

"*Ja*, but call the house. Night is coming and we will need help."

* * *

The wolves panted as they entered the grove. They found Olienhout above ground at the mouth of the hole. She stood silently and watched them approach.

Koorsboom lapped her muzzle, but his eyes were filled with sadness.

"What happened?"

Aalwyn shook her head. "Hardekool was killed."

Olienhout nodded. She turned to reenter the den. The rest of the pack clustered around the hole, listening to the subtle whimpers of the pups within. Wildevlier took position next to the den entrance, fangs bared slightly. Her glare penetrated hill and thicket, daring any to attack her alpha.

Leadwort lay down, closed his eyes, and emitted a low, plaintive whine. As the sun set, the calls of nightjars and katydids began to rise. Beneath it all, the low whine continued into the dark.

* * *

The vehicle coasted to a halt not far from the wild olive grove. Grootes wound down his window a small amount.

"We stay the night." He peered at the fading sunlight on the western horizon. "We cannot track them in the darkness."

"What if those wolves attack us?" The farm hand was anxious, and was not expecting to sleep in a truck.

"Then piss your pants if you must. Just don't wake me." He shifted his ample weight in the seat and folded his hands over his belly. "Let me know if they move."

"I am supposed to stay up?"

"If you want to get paid, yes."

"What if the wild dogs leave in a different direction?"

"Another *bakkie* is coming just now."

The creaking of metal became apparent as another vehicle crested the ridge behind them. It rolled alongside Grootes and the window came down.

"How many others are coming?" Grootes muttered, keeping his voice low.

"Three others—your neighbor volunteered as well. A fourth *bakkie* is waiting at the house with the dogs." Louw scratched his mustache.

"*Goed.* We leave the dogs at the house for the night, and have your men bring them in the morning."

"We will be on the other side of the olive trees just now." He saluted and his *bakkie* rolled off.

The farm hand dug into a pocket and removed several foil-wrapped bars, each bearing the image of a tiger with the word 'Jungle Oats'. He handed some to Grootes, who wolfed one down, possibly with the wrapper still on.

"Wild dogs are not usually nocturnal, but you never know." Grootes waved to another *bakkie* that trundled up toward them in the twilight.

The dust covered window came down to reveal Myburgh. "*Howzit,* Dawie." She spoke around the cigarette dangling from her mouth. "Where will the others be?" Her black hair was pulled tight into a short ponytail.

"In a ring around those olive trees just there. Space of a hundred meters between each *bakkie*." He paused to look at his watch. "Come morning, Louw's dogs will flush them out of the woods and drive them towards us."

She gave a nod after hesitating. "I will be at the far side of the grove just there." She paused to blow smoke, wreathing her head in a blue-grey cloud. "Do you have the explosive?"

Grootes nodded, patting a bag at his side.

Her mouth turned down as she thought for a moment. "Did you know Dyk?"

"Not well." Grootes scarfed down another snack bar.

She sucked on the cigarette, and the tip glowed a blinding orange in the dark. "I knew him for years." Her face melted into the shadows as the burning tip of the cigarette faded.

"While he ran *Wildsplaas?*"

"*Plaas?*" She grunted as her fingers drummed on the door of the vehicle. "That was no farm." She fumed quietly. "He had animals, but that was no farm. He gave that up over a decade ago. Working the land was too much work for that lazy *oke.*"

Grootes eyed her uneasily.

"He took pleasure in calling himself a farmer." Her eyes were a translucent grey, shining with what remained of the fading sunlight. "He bought and sold stock, ran some hunts. Some were even legal." She stared toward the olive trees. "That jackal praised his own tail, but he was barely a step above a bloody poacher."

"Myburgh—"

"That step is a charity from me."

"You think Marais did the right thing, killing the man?"

Her stare was ice. She chewed the filter as she drummed the steering wheel with her fingertips.

Grootes stared through his windshield and sighed. "I appreciate your help with what we must do come the morning."

"Unless there is another way."

"We *will* be killing the lot of them, Myburgh." He eyed her, wondering for a moment whether he made a mistake calling her. "They will cut down my entire herd."

"We will see." She shrugged, indifferent. "They are a part of Africa too—"

Grootes clucked, but was unable to respond before she finished her thought.

"—as are we." Her grey eyes softened as she shifted into gear, and her *bakkie* rolled away. He watched the red beacons of her brake lights bounce as she made a large circle around the olive trees and parked.

"There will be others to give us a hand come morning." Grootes dipped a hand into a rucksack on the seat between him and the farmhand. He removed one of the boxes marked 'Magnum'. He opened one end and removed a tube still wrapped in white plastic. "If there is a den, we will need a few of these."

* * *

As dusk set, the men muttered to themselves outside of the vehicles. Clinking and clacking was heard as rifles were loaded and set. Doors opened and slammed as the men paced about, bored and excited in equal measure as they anticipated the hunt.

None noticed the Painted wolf creeping past them, a wraith in the wind.

Wildevlier trotted back into the shadows under the trees, returning to the den.

"We are surrounded." She rasped to the others, gathered around the denning hole.

They were quiet, hardly able to breathe.

"What shall we do?" Leadwort asked.

"Are you afraid?" Aalwyn's tone was flat.

"I am beyond fear." He smiled, jaws open and sharp teeth gleaming. "After a life behind wire, even starvation and death in the wild thrills me. Come what may, I am filled with pride to die under your command."

Koorsboom was on hind legs and boxed him. The two wolves grappled in friendly play before they slumped to the ground again to rest with the evening.

Aalwyn could not help but smile weakly at them.

"I remember, before you were born, Koorsboom, the great river to the west." Her mind filled with images from Botswana, from years past. "So many seasons ago, my sister Essenhout and I taunted the elephant herds that ambled through the thick forest. Those were good times for hunting, so long ago.”

“Was he born under a fever tree?” Leadwort wondered.

“In a way.” She turned her head toward Koorsboom. “You received your name after we fled our den in the night when hyenas set upon us. You attacked one of the hyenas that stalked you. A tiny pup with equally tiny teeth, and you made your enemy scream.” She chuckled to herself. “And after you saw off your enemy, we found safety under a fever tree as our great *trek* began.” Her smile faded. “Your father and the siblings of your litter were killed by lions not long after. We found another life on a path bearing east.”

“Always on the move.” Koorsboom spoke, almost to himself.

“So it must be. Ever on the move in the face of threats. Until the time comes to den, and hope that time affords us one more generation to raise.” She looked above as the stars began to appear in the sky. “We *trek* forth, and the land shall be redeemed, as ever, with sacrifice.” Her voice was nearly at a whisper. “Once more against the void.”

“We shall know when the sun rises.” Koorsboom scuttled into the den and touched noses with Olienhout before backing out.

“We know already what we face. Against the forces arrayed against us, there can be no victor.”

“You have beaten your foes before, mother.” He lapped her muzzle. “Wherever we have been, you found a way. Even in this place, the savanna both strange and familiar. You are cleverer than they, and to that I hold.”

She was quiet for a time, and in the dimming light, the rest thought she had fallen asleep. Aalwyn startled them when she spoke.

“My son, we have one last gambit to take.” Her ears swiveled, listening. She could hear the sound of an engine, and that of a door slamming more distant. Her heart fell with each human sound. “Even if it works, it could mean the doom of the pups.” She could hear boots on the ground, but they did not come closer.

“No challenge shall be unmet.” Koorsboom parted his lips in the dimming light under the leaves of the olive trees, and his serrated teeth twinkled.

"The humans do not hunt in the darkness. With first light, however, we will make our final run from this place."

"And leave Olienhout and the pups behind?" He canted his head to the side, bewildered.

"We shall run, and the humans will follow us."

"If we return to the den, they will only come back." Koorsboom lowered his brow. "They know we are here."

"They have a thirst for blood, these humans. Perhaps if sated, they will never discover the litter." Aalwyn smiled. "We shall run, and we shall die."

Once again, the young wolf smiled in kind, revealing his fangs.

"And so we have crafted our elegy, at the bitter end." Aalwyn sighed. "Blackthorn would have agreed."

"Blackthorn." Wildevlier rumbled. "You spoke of that name before. When was his end?" Her eyes glittered darkly.

"Every moment of his life." Aalwyn whispered. "Death knew his name."

Chapter 82

Dawn.

Three wolves stood toward the edge of the olive trees, still in deep shadow, facing away from the den. They did not make a sound. Somewhere beyond the edge of the wood they had heard humans gather, making some sinister preparations. Engines revved, tires crunched upon rocks, and the gibberish of humankind reached their ears.

Wildevlier gave Koorsboom a nod and began to pad back toward the den.

"Give her my regards." He managed a slight grin.

"Any who approach her shall bleed." She did not share his smile.

Koorsboom looked over his shoulder and saw Olienhout standing at the mouth of the hole. He gave a nod, jaws parted in a smile. She could only look down at the bare earth.

Aalwyn, Koorsboom, and Leadwort padded forward, through the shadows under the olive trees.

The light grew brighter, reaching the edge of the grove.

Picking up speed, they raced forward, into the light.

The three hunters worked their muscles to the very limit, and left the grove as though shot from cannons. Heads low, ears flat, tails down, their legs pounded and claws gripped the earth in a fight for every meter of ground.

"Hold!"

Aalwyn stopped. Leadwort and Koorsboom did the same on her command. Leadwort bumbled into a heap, such was his shock. They looked about with bewilderment.

The *bakkies* were gone. The humans were gone.

Chapter 83

"Well who the bloody hell is it, and why did I need to meet them this early?" Grootes held the wheel of the *bakkie*, gripping it as through strangling the life from it.

"She offered her help, I did not catch the name." The voice at the other end crackled.

"*Ag.*" He tossed the phone into the passenger seat

"How did the wildlife authority find out about this so quickly?" He fumed as the vehicle bounced over the rough terrain. As the tires slipped onto a dirt path, they bit into the ground, pulling them quickly forward. More *bakkies* followed close behind them, raising a dust cloud into the air.

Within the hour they were back at the farm house, boots stamping on stone floors, doors slamming shut.

A farm hand sprinted out the front door and met Grootes on the *stoep*.

"She is inside."

"I wonder who called her." Grootes brushed dust from his khaki pants.

"I did." Myburgh paused her stride to light another cigarette. She looked none the worse for being up all night, her black hair still pulled tight into a ponytail.

"You? Why?"

She met his withering glare. "Let us hear what she has to say." The cigarette took its position at the corner of her mouth.

He bit down on the words threatening to spill forth and opened the door.

He stalked through the house, boots clomping on the ceramic tile floor. He crossed the great room in a few strides, and found a young, slender woman dressed in faded brown khakis, turning to greet him.

"Yes, we are quite busy just now. *Wat is jou naam?*"

"Sonja Venter, *meneer*. I am here to help with your wild dog problem."

* * *

The table took up much of the expansive dining room. The top of solid acacia wood was devoid of splinters and worn smooth over decades of use. Occupied mostly by farmers from this and neighboring lands, the dozen chairs were filled by Grootes, Louw, Myburgh, and several more. Venter faced them all alone.

Staring down upon her from the walls were photographs of family members. A man, broad face, hair brushed to the side, with a neatly trimmed beard, and dressed in a dark suit. Another man, narrower face, clean shaven save a mustache, eyes frozen in a terse gaze. A photo of a family, over a dozen people together in a hall. Some of the people in the photographs were long since deceased. A few of their descendants stood in this room.

"I have recalled my men as you asked, but you must be quick. We have tracked them, and do not wish to lose them." Grootes seemed to be standing despite being seated at the table. His girth was enormous, arms the size of beef roasts, and a head that appeared to be made of granite. His mustache was trimmed like a privet hedge. "I have lost a great deal of money already."

"First, we can guarantee reimbursement for stock lost." Venter placed a hand flat on the table.

Some of the farmers relaxed visibly. Louw raised a finger. "Who is paying?"

"A combination of the Wildlife Trust, the provincial government, and supporters of Gorongosa."

"Gorongosa?" Grootes sat forward in his chair, the wood groaning as he shifted his weight. "You worked with Johan Marais."

She took a deep breath. "I did."

"Killed enough farmers, has he?"

Venter flushed a light pink. "Nobody knew what he was planning to do."

"You did not know." His thick fingers drummed the hard wood of the table. "You worked together, and had no idea that he was preparing to, say, shoot dead two farmers."

The ranger stayed silent.

"Over a wild dog."

"I think they had a falling out. Between he and Dyk."

"Did they?" Grootes' sarcasm was met with some snickering around the table. "I would hope a murderer would be on bad terms with his victim." Tittering among the farmers.

"You do not know it was murder." Myburgh's voice ceased the grumbling of the men. "None of you."

"You do not know it was not." Louw shot back.

"How does this relate to the wild dogs out there?" Myburgh pointed toward the door.

"Farmers have a dangerous enough life in this country." Grootes intoned. "Without dealing with lunatics like that."

"Agreed." Venter gave a slight nod.

"Then why are we entertaining this nonsense?" Louw raised his voice. "That *oke* kills two farmers and we still listen to this *kak?*"

"Marais is dead." Myburgh snarled. "How dead do you need him to be before you let it go?"

The room erupted in argument, with calls for blood, men shouting across the table toward the ranger. Myburgh sat with her arms folded, staring at the floor.

Grootes spoke with another farmer, each gesticulating, words lost in the noise other than a booming "PEOPLE LIKE THEM" from Grootes, as he pointed in Venter's direction.

Louw and another man stalked toward the ranger, still seated.

"It is time you left, *meisie.*" Louw shouted, to be heard above the din.

She looked up at Louw, then the other farmer, her face betraying no emotion, and her body giving no ground.

The other farmer thrust hands into his pockets. "Your kind can piss off. You think you can kill our people and show your face?"

"He was never one of us." Myburgh's voice, reedy but low, resonated through the room and brought the conversation to a halt.

"How is that?" The farmer next to Louw sounded incredulous.

All eyes in the room were on her, but the tone of her voice never changed. "Farmers worked the land in this country for hundreds of years." She stabbed the table top with her index finger, sounding like a hammer strike. "Work the land. Build the country." She looked up, grey eyes staring back with resolve. "Dyk never built a thing with his zoo. He inherited it from his family, and sold it off, piece by bloody piece." Her finger continued to stab the table with each word. "People like him will sell off all of South Africa for so very little."

"His land. That is his right." Louw furrowed his brow, not expecting the discussion to make this turn.

"It is his right." Myburgh stood, her chair pushed back along the tile floor. "He did whatever he wanted, including courting dangerous *okes* with deep pockets. Poachers, smugglers. Who saw our country as a cheap shopping trolley." She knocked on the table with her knuckles. "It was only a matter of time before something put him in the ground."

"Are you saying he deserved it?" Grootes asked.

"I am saying I am not surprised." She popped another cigarette in her mouth, but did not move to light it. "He can sell all the rhino horn he wants to poachers. Just don't call him a bloody farmer." She pointed at the men around the table. "It dishonors everyone here. Dyk gave hunters a bad name with the *kak* he did. It is time someone rejected his kind." She stalked out, boots clomping in the now silent room.

Just before she left, she stopped and turned.

"I will have those explosives back."

Grootes frowned and gestured to one of the farmhands slouched against a wall. Running off, he returned quickly with the sack. She left without another word, and the door banged shut in the distance.

"Rubbish." Louw scoffed. "She chose the wrong side."

"You do not know what you are talking about." Grootes muttered. "The Myburgh family has been here for longer than mine. Her roots trace back to the burghers of the Cape." He folded his hands before him. He cast a withering glance at Louw.

Venter cleared her throat. "We can dart the lot of them." She glanced about to ensure all were listening. "We can remove them from your lands, but we do need time."

Grootes did not answer her, waving her off as he strode about the room. The morning sun blazed through the open windows, though the room was already quite hot.

"Where were they seen last?" Venter asked the rest of the men at the table.

None answered her until she stood to leave. Louw coughed. "Several kilometers from here." He thrust his hands into his pockets, looking at the table before him, in search of something that was not there.

"Will one of your people show me?"

* * *

Venter drove the Land Rover over the rough earth, shifting up a gear whenever she found level ground.

"Just there, the olive trees." The young man in the passenger seat was the son of Dawie Grootes, and was keen to see how this problem would be handled. Louw was seated in back, watching them quietly.

"Right. I am going to just creep a little closer. Keep an eye open if they flee the woods."

She slowed the vehicle to a crawl as they approached the grove, and then edged forward with care.

"Anything?"

"No movement over here." The young man peered into the brush.

The engine rattled as the Land Rover edged between scattered saplings.

She revved it once to get over a knot of roots, and the springs bounced as the front tire rolled forward.

"There!" Louw shouted.

Venter whipped around to see the white tip of tail disappearing behind a tree. She brought the wheel round, and through the windscreen she saw another head poke out from behind brush and watch the movement of the vehicle.

"There is another one!" Grootes' son pointed to a wolf loping past.

"Same one. They are running a circle around us." As the Land Rover eased forth, she thumbed through a stack of photos of the wild dogs, all taken at Gorongosa.

"Why?"

"I think I can guess." One photograph was set aside, matching Koorsboom. She dwelled on a second photo, of Aalwyn. She looked up in surprise. "How on earth did you get here?"

The older female looked back at her, seeming to examine the vehicle.

"I must push into the olive trees, just there."

She edged the vehicle forward, and the brush parted slightly. She peered all around, searching for more as the Land Rover eased to a halt.

"Why are the bloody things here, of all places?" Louw grumbled as the pack made another circle around them, twittering with high pitched chirps to one another.

"Dyk transported two of them to this area from Mozambique." She said carefully. "Though the antelope are the prey wild dogs have hunted for the past million years, they would rather not be anywhere near farms." Venter shrugged, not sure what to say without making them even more defensive.

From a distance, a wild dog watched them from underneath an olive tree. It was a female, and stood on three legs, one shortened hind leg held in the air. She found a third photo, and the coat coloration was a match.

Hanging from her belly were distended teats.

"They are denning." She scratched her chin for a moment. "How long has this been going on?"

"Stock has been found killed over the past two weeks."

"Then we will need to wait." Venter rubbed her temple, sensing another headache would soon explode behind her eyes. "And that word 'wait' will not go over at all well." She pressed numbers on her phone and lifted it to her ear. Listening to the interminable *bong bong* as it rang, she pleaded silently that a voice would emerge from the other end.

* * *

"*Denning?*" Grootes began to turn red. "Shit, man, they will not stop until there is not an animal left on my farm!" He began to shake his massive head.

"*Meneer—*" Venter spoke low.

"No, we must take care of this now." He gestured to his son to join them, and the young man jogged to his father's side.

"I will take care of them." She raised her voice, but only slightly. "I need until tomorrow morning." Jaw set, heart pounded within. "And nothing more."

The afternoon sun dipped toward the distant hill and *koppie*, glowing in the warm light. The farmer folded his massive arms, scarred by numerous encounters with barbed wire and farm equipment.

"Very well, we will wait the day." Grootes glowered.

"*Baie dankie, meneer.*" She resisted the urge to shake his hand. "I will fetch the sedative just now." She ran off, jumped into the Land Rover and tore down the road with all speed.

"Where is she going?" Louw was at his side.

Grootes held a hand up to shade his eyes, watching as the Land Rover drove off down the gravel driveway to the main tar road, leaving a cloud of dust in its wake.

"She said she must fetch the tranquilizer, and will be back by evening." The young man brushed some of the dust off his jacket. "Though it is strange, *Pa.*"

"*Ja, seun?*"

"I saw her kit in the rear of the *bakkie*. A rifle and some vials. Would a vet carry any drugs other than tranquilizers?"

Grootes glared at the receding vehicle, now a dot on the grass horizon. The men walked back into the farm house.

"Tell the workers to get those *bakkies* ready to leave at first light." As they ascended the steps to the house, he struck the wood railing with a fist, the dull reverberation ringing across the yard.

"You promised her we would not harm the dogs today."

"I know." Grootes stared at the wood slats that made up the *stoep* of the main house, wood taken from a tree felled more than a hundred years before. "A *boer* must keep his word. This *juffie* is only stalling for time. We will hit them at dawn."

* * *

It was not until evening that the Land Rover crept back along the gravel road. The sun was sinking slowly toward the hills to the west. Rocks popped underneath the heavy tires as it gradually made its way next to the house and parked. A groan of metal was heard as the doors opened.

"Thank you for coming, Du Plessis." Venter spoke quietly. "I hope you can turn the tide."

"Do not worry, *meisie*. Grootes is a good man, and more important, a practical one." He grabbed a bag from the passenger seat and closed the door to the Land Rover with a bang. "Why did you drive out to meet me? I know how to get here."

"It was to avoid questions for which I had no answer. Then."

Their boots clattered on the *stoep*, and Du Plessis doffed his cap before he knocked on the door. Loud conversation spilled onto the yard as it opened. She muttered her greetings to the young man who answered, and with handshakes, they went inside. Du Plessis put his cap back on as the door closed again, leaving the yard to the sawing of crickets and the purring *kuk-KOORR-ru* of a cape turtle dove.

Chapter 84

"This is ridiculous." Grootes was seated, arms folded, stern mouth hidden by the mustache. They were back in the great room, frowned upon by the ancient portraits on the walls. The windows, framed in faded curtains, looked out onto the evening light of the grass plain outside. The farmers had gathered again, milling on the edges of the conversation at the table.

"Another week or two is all we ask." Sonja Venter sat on the edge of her seat, and a bead of sweat ran from her temple.

"The time you ask for keeps growing like a cancer." Louw uttered with a chuckle.

"Reimbursement or not, I am not waiting for them to kill two or three antelope a day while you enjoy the show." Grootes fumed.

The crowd of farmers muttered amongst themselves, casting angry glances toward the polished acacia wood table.

"This is the best way—"

"Look." Grootes closed his eyes, gripping his nose bridge between thick fingers. "I understand where you are coming from. You care about the wild dogs. There are few of them, and you want to protect them." One hand was on the table, palm up. "But I have a business to run. I sympathize, but if they are killing off my stock, what am I to do? Carnivores cannot get along with game farmers."

"A little time. And we move them away." Venter's voice was low and even.

"And then they will come back." His eyes opened again. "They return where the killing has been good. Whether a day or a month from when they leave. I have read about these things—their home ranges are greater than most game reserves." He folded his broad hands together. "You are fighting a losing battle here. Some animals can adapt to changes like the ones the human race have created. Some cannot. Wild dogs no longer belong here." His eyes softened, devoid of hostility.

Venter nodded, her eyes drifting once again across the photographs of the *boere* staring down upon them all.

"There is another way through." Her voice echoed in the room. "The new wild."

"What does that mean?" Grootes shrugged.

"There was a time when these conflicts did not matter so much." She stepped forward, her blue eyes flashed. "Farms were few, and there was the rest of the wild to escape to, for a predator." She gestured toward the great table. "Then farms spread across the entire land." Her hands indicated the coverage of the table. "The wild places shrank. No more places to escape to. What is a wild animal to do?"

"Farms are not going anywhere." Grootes lifted his brow, as though to head off this suggestion.

"Of course. We all need to eat." Venter smiled. "There is a way to get along with the wild, and we all can eat." She placed both hands on the table. "We all belong here."

"Wishful thinking—" Grootes interjected, as muttering rose around the room.

"What you need is your stock left alone." She raised her voice, and the voices died down. "And the wild needs a place to hunt. A way to hunt. That is fair." She pointed out Louw, who was leaning against a wall. "Do you hunt on Grootes's land?"

Louw glanced around, as though this were an accusation. "N—no."

"Of course not. You know what will happen. You read the signs." The ranger extended her hand towards Grootes.

"And are you going to teach carnivores to read?" Grootes leaned back in his chair, which creaked in protest. "I can always make signs for them."

Venter beamed. "I am glad we are in agreement, then."

The farmers all frowned, Grootes most of all.

"We teach the animals to read." She pointed across the table, her grin widening. "Your signs. Your land."

"You must start making sense." Grootes was not smiling. Voices rose again.

"We shall make signs for the carnivores to read." Venter met his stare. "And the wild can run free."

At this the voices of the farmers began to turn more hostile.

"*Meisie*, the world is changing." Grootes looked almost sad as he spoke. "There was a time when wild animals ran across this country. That time is over." He stood, and the room quieted, as though the air fell to the ground.

"Some things never change. Unless hunting has gone extinct." Her smile did not waver. "Will you all stop hunting since the *slaghuis* has all the meat you need?"

"A *boer* will always want to hunt." Louw scoffed.

"So will the wolves." Venter extended a hand to the far side of the room, before any further argument could ensue. "Du Plessis? What do you think—will the predators have a place to hunt?"

He was leaning against the far wall, in an alcove near the front door, until now silent and in shadow. Now he rocked forward on his boots at the sound of his name. He stepped toward the table. Clad in the same bicolored cotton shirt and khaki shorts he wore when Marais visited his home, he seemed to have no other outfit in his closet. His salt and pepper beard was as scraggly as before, and pale blue eyes danced. His hair was greyed and unkempt, wild as the thornbrush that covered his property.

"Gentlemen."

"Been a long time, Dup." Grootes shook hands with him.

"Likewise. Your family well?"

"Very well. Daughter just got into University. Stellenbosch."

"*Lekker, man.*" He smiled widely. "I remember when she was shorter than my knee. You raised a winner. Your family always has." He gave an exaggerated nod. "I have a solution for you. Not just for this wild dog pack, but for every carnivore you will ever meet."

Grootes looked at him quizzically.

"I can see you are skeptical." He pulled a paper bag from his pocket and upended it on a plate at the table. A kilogram of biltong plopped onto the plate, the savory scent of dried beef, coriander and pepper filling the air. He dished half of the pile onto another plate, setting one close to the owner.

Grootes reached for the biltong, almost as a reflex.

A whistle broke the quiet as a black shape whickered through the air and struck the table with a hollow *whap* that echoed through the great room. The crowd of farmers took a step back in unison. In Du Plessis's hand was the black leather *sjambok* that made the sharp noise. Until now, no one had noticed it.

"Go ahead, have some." Du Plessis had not changed his expression.

"What is your problem, man?" Grootes had furrowed his brow. He did not seem disturbed, though the *sjambok* was more than capable of laying his arm open to the bone.

"Have some biltong. You remember how good I make it."

He reached again, and Du Plessis brought down the black leather weapon again, with another *whap* upon the thick wooden table.

"This plate is not for you." He pulled back one of the white dishes, and pushed the other one closer to Grootes. "And you will learn to stop reaching for it."

"Under guard against the predator." Venter interjected.

He reached over and took a handful from the other plate. "I see what you are getting at, but it will be too expensive. We looked into this before."

"What will be?" Louw spoke, his arms folded.

"Miss Venter is suggesting we protect the game ranches with guard dogs, and the predators will leave them alone." He took another handful from the undefended plate, managing to talk around the mouthful of beef. "Farmers tried that in the past, but it was not practical as a deterrent. This property is nearly forty square kilometers. We cannot fill that with enough dogs to keep watch."

"You will not have to, man." He took a mouthful as well from his own plate. "This biltong isn't spread over the entire house. I am keeping this plate right here next to me, and you are not getting any of it. You are going to the other plate."

"The antelope stock needs to be herded." She watched Grootes closely.

"Exactly. Herded around with guard dogs protecting them." Du Plessis was animated, waving his hands about. "Right now we rely on fences." He took away the plate before Grootes, to his disappointment, and shoveled smaller amounts onto several other plates that were scattered on the table. "We need to cut them down." These plates he pushed toward the other men around the table, and returned the first plate to Grootes. "Train the dogs to watch over the herds, and if a predator comes, they chase it off."

"Dogs have been used to guard goats and cattle. Not wild game like antelope." Louw noted.

"Then we work to find a way." Venter answered. "And the dogs will still protect the livestock herds in the area."

"And who is going to pay for that?" Grootes folded his arms.

"Can it work? That is the question that matters." She leaned in. "If so, the number of animals killed plummets by *ninety-five percent* in studies done in this region. Between you, NGOs, and the insurance companies looking for any way to reduce losses, the dogs pay for themselves."

"We just need to all do it as one." Du Plessis took another mouthful of beef. "Otherwise the wild dogs and other predators will cause losses at any farms that do not cooperate."

"And what will the predators eat, then?" Grootes was unconvinced. "Eventually they will find a way to kill. And we are right back to where we started—shoot the predator."

"Ah." Du Plessis smiled widely. "That is where I come in."

"Are they going to eat you, then?"

"A little stringy, but a good thought. *Nee*, I am raising impala of my own. Not killing them, just raising them. My property is filled with the bloody things."

"I was meaning to say, Du Plessis." Louw sat straight at the table. "You are herding way too many animals on your land. They will overgraze and then starve to death in the dry season."

"Not on your life. The soil is better, the grass is richer with all that manure. In fact, I need even more of them. And I need carnivores on my land so the antelope herd properly and keep moving about. Once the dry season is here, my land will retain more water than yours." He grinned widely somewhere under the beard. "When the wild dogs see my place without guard dogs, they will kill. And we shall see if the problems on the neighboring farms are solved."

"Is this a research project?"

"Quite. And it is well underway. You need only transport the wild dogs to my land, and I get to enjoy the view." He put his hands in his pockets, reveling in having an audience. "Apart from my property, there are antelope wandering about between farms, and other animals from scrub hares to lions that escape our notice. One can still farm in the wild without being at war with it."

"If your experiment goes badly, then? I lose out, Dup."

"*Ag.* So do I. But there is nothing for it. Without carnivores, the land will go to shit." He swept the air with the *sjambok,* and the leather produced a *whoosh.* "The land goes to shit, the livestock will suffer. We need to find out if this will work. And if it does, not only will I still have impala—I will have even *more* impala because of the carnivores."

"We will be a part of this plan to protect the land. The farms. The people." Venter projected her voice across the room. "And we always will be."

She looked from one man to the other, straining to read their minds. There was still muttering amongst the farmers who clustered around the table, but there was no more anger.

The sun cast a golden glow across the veld outside, and reached in through the window. The room eventually grew silent while the farmers looked at one another, then at Grootes.

She resisted the urge to say more, merely meeting his gaze.

He scratched his mustache and sighed.

"*Reg so*, we give it a go." Grootes stood, seeming to fill the room with his girth. He clasped hands with Du Plessis. "You had better be right about this. *Kom*, I need to show you my brand new baby. Barrett REC7 - you could take out a vulture a mile in the air."

"Let me fetch my AK. That rifle is fifty years old and would still outclass whatever new toy you have." He grabbed a glass of brandy that was sitting on the table and downed it. "First, let us go see this wolf pack." Du Plessis and Grootes strode from the room. "Oh, and whoever's brandy that was, *dankie* and I am sorry."

Venter followed them out the door.

* * *

"Here they come again. If they approach, the plan is the same." Aalwyn tensed.

The *bakkie* trundled its way close to the olive trees, and three humans exited the vehicle. One pointed in her direction. She crouched, unsure if she was seen.

"Something is different." Koorsboom stepped forward. "They carry nothing."

The two men walked toward them, relaxed, with an easy gait. They sounded like wildebeest to the wolves, with a droning *gnu gnu gnu* sound between them.

The big one and the slender one laughed, and loudly at that. The woman stood away from them, and watched the wolves, doing something with an implement in her hands.

Koorsboom walked out from under the shade of the trees. The setting sun fell on him, a burning warmth.

The three humans turned and looked at him.

Koorsboom looked back.

The slender man, older than the other two with a grey, wild beard, pointed to him and gave another laugh. He clapped his hands and gave a hoot. The woman just stared at Koorsboom, writing furiously in her notes.

491

One man then shook hands with the other, and they walked back to the *bakkie*. She followed them, reluctant to leave. Getting in, they drove away.

A snap behind the young wolf made him turn. Aalwyn was standing at the edge of the grove, watching.

"Forgive me, mother, for taking that risk. I needed to know whether they were hostile."

Aalwyn padded to his side, and did not speak.

"So is that it?" Leadwort ran a circle around them, stood for a moment on hind legs, looking toward where the vehicle drove off, and was back down on all fours. "That was the great battle?" He trotted up to Aalwyn, who did not move.

Even after Koorsboom and Leadwort returned to the den, she continued to stare at where the humans had stood outside the olive tree grove.

The image of the men shaking hands haunted her, and she could not put this gesture out of her mind. It stayed with her, into and through the night.

In her dreams, one paw clasped another. And somehow the world changed.

Chapter 85

The wildebeest took halting steps, casting its head side to side, looking for an escape that was not there. Its mind swam as the drug flooded its bloodstream and the dart dangling from its side fell to the ground. The beast soon did the same, and the men prepared to haul it onto the bed of the *bakkie.*

"Is that the last one?" Grootes watched with satisfaction.

"*Ja, meneer.* The rest are in the enclosures."

The wildebeest breathed heavily under the sedation. Its coat, unlike that of its brethren, was a glowing golden hue. The mutant coloration would have doomed it in the wild. Utterly unable to blend with the foliage, it would be a target for carnivores. To a tourist with a rifle, however, it was literal gold.

"Right. The wild dogs now have nothing to hunt but the cheap prey." Grootes scratched his mustache.

"Strange, not simply shooting them."

"I know. Tradition is hard to break, but we should ignore tradition when there is a better option."

"And if the pack comes back here?"

Grootes did not answer. He was not accustomed to taking questions when his mind was made up.

* * *

Sonja Venter studied her map, a copy made from a central filing obtained from Pretoria. Kill sites were marked with Xs, and the olive grove was a lonely circle on the southern end of the property. The wind tousled the edges of the map, where she sat on the *stoep* of the great house.

"Will you dart them soon?" Louw watched her work.

"Yes, any day now." She made additional marks near the olive tree grove.

A *bakkie* made its way up the gravel drive, spewing pale dust into the air. The squeaking suspension grew louder as it approached. Slowing to a halt, the door banged shut, and out walked a woman in khaki pants and shirt, hair black as nightfall trailing in the breeze.

"*Howzit*, Myburgh." Louw raised a hand in greeting.

"*Howzit*, Louw."

At the sound of her voice, the ranger looked up. "It was you who called me, *né?*" She stood. "Sonja Venter."

Myburgh shook her hand with unexpected force, nearly pulling her arm from its socket.

"I heard that the wolf kill was off." She spoke softly, hesitating. "Glad that something worked out." She patted her pockets absently.

"It will be some time before this works out." Venter took a stone from her pocket to weigh down the map as its edge lifted with the wind, threatening to join the currents.

"Let me know if I can help." Myburgh gave a half smile.

"I will, *dankie.*" Venter smiled back.

"Is Grootes through here?" She pointed into the house. "I was hoping to chat."

Louw nodded, and Myburgh hastened her way into the farm house.

He went back to peering at the ranger, who sat back down on the *stoep*.

"Why wait for the darting?" The farmer from the neighboring property watched the ranger with interest.

"Weaning. If we accidentally kill the mother before they can eat meat, then the pups die. Though without the alpha female, the pack will not survive in any case."

"They split up?"

"In the wild, often they will. We would place them in the South African metapopulation, maybe at Hluhluwe or Madikwe." She made a quick note in a book on her lap.

"Would another female become alpha, then?"

"Well, the other female is from elsewhere. Somehow, this one." Venter fished out the photo of Aalwyn. "This one found her way here." She shook her head with disbelief. "All the way from Gorongosa. No idea how she found it. But she is the mother of this one." He pointed to Koorsboom's image. "So she may go back to her pack. If there are no other females available, they disperse."

"I shot one of the other females." Louw was quiet. "I thought that..." He sighed. There was no thought to finish.

She turned to meet his gaze.

"We are on uncharted ground." Venter smiled. "Imagine being able to live side by side." She glanced out at the bushveld beyond the *stoep*. "With the Africa our ancestors knew."

"That was no peaceful time." Louw took a stalk of grass and chewed on it. "Between people."

"There will always be some fighting." Her smile widened. "Bad blood can be left in the past. Between people. Between us and the wild." She took a deep breath and exhaled with an elated 'hah'. She watched the sun rising into the late morning sky before her. "This is an exciting time."

"*Ag, meisie.*" Louw chewed the grass. "This may not work."

"*Ja,* it may work, or not, to be fair." Her smile did not fade. "Months of preparation, millions of rand, and a lot of guard dogs and the training that goes with them. Maybe we will figure out how dogs get along with and herd wild game. Maybe not." She returned to taking notes on the map. "When has 'maybe' ever stopped us?"

"Have you always been this optimistic?"

"All South Africans are optimists at heart. Why else would every farmstead or town in an arid country have *'fontein'* in their name?"

The farmer remained quiet. He did not say anything, nor did he motion to leave.

Her pencil continued its scratching. From the Apple-leaf tree nearby a hadeda ibis gave its *HA - DA!* greeting to the day.

Louw dug into his pocket and removed his address book. He removed a card from it.

"Here is my phone number." Louw gestured, unsure what to say.

"You want to help?" Venter beamed.

He gave a curt nod, and began to stalk away.

"I will be in touch, *meneer*." She was on her feet, and walking toward him with a hand extended.

Louw shook it, and smiled in spite of himself.

"We will do very well together." Her smile grew wider. "Farmers and rangers. The way it should be."

***

Over the next week, Venter continued her watch on the den. All the while, she worked on writing grant applications for what would become a grand project in the region: predator surveillance and mitigation with guard dogs.

The pack killed an impala each day, still varying their hunting pattern so no one herd was harassed with regularity. Even as she watched them from the edge of the trees, they seemed at leisure.

As the four wolves returned from the hunt, the mother joined them above ground. The greetings proceeded as usual with licking of muzzles prompting regurgitation of food.

This time, the mother did not eat. Venter could barely make out a subtle growling noise.

A small head poked up from the hole. Another one. Then several diminutive bodies bounded out of the den.

"Eight, nine, ten." She counted them several times, as it was difficult to keep track of the constantly wriggling and running forms. "Eleven."

The rest of the hunters gave up their portion of the kill, and the pups pounced on it. In less than a minute, there was nothing on the ground but dirt.

After watching them over the next hour, She eased away from the edge of the wood and back to her Land Rover. Retrieving a phone, a wide grin crossed her face.

"*Goeie dag.* Venter speaking. I would like to get the veterinary sedative I put on hold. When will it be ready?"

* * *

As the pack rested, Olienhout could not resist nudging each of the pups in turn. They lay paralyzed by the meal, bellies protruding so far they would brush the ground if they walked. She nosed each one lightly.

"I do not understand this turn of events." Koorsboom craned his head to look for the human who had just left. "I fear that they are only waiting for an opportunity to kill us all."

"The river that sweeps us along will not alter its course." Olienhout mused while licking the belly of the pup closest to her. "In fighting it, we will still end where it will end."

"We fight nonetheless, however we are able." Wildevlier rasped.

Olienhout nodded, and lapped the muzzle of her stalwart guardian. Wildevlier accepted the compliment, then resumed glaring at the world outside the den.

"Hardekool would have liked to have been a part of their lives." Leadwort released a plaintive whine to the veld before him.

The day passed slowly, broken only by the loud buzzing of a beetle. Alighting on what remained of discarded impala hide, it folded fragile wings back under its hard wing covers. Scissoring into the hide, it fed along with the carrion flies.

"The time has come for me." Aalwyn spoke, abruptly on her paws. "I must return to my home in the wild."

Koorsboom was by her side instantly. "What troubles you, mother?"

"Nothing worries me here. That is why I must leave." She regarded the rest of this new pack. "If those humans wished to kill us, they would have no reason to delay. However this ends for you, your impulse to live amongst these strange creatures may have been the correct one." She turned out to face the veld outside the grove. "Somehow." She shook her head. "Somehow you both found a way."

The young wolf embraced his mother, holding his head alongside hers, and lapping her muzzle tenderly.

"Much I have learned from this." Her voice trailed off, her mind fixed upon the gesture between the men, the shaking of hands. "They left us in peace where bitter violence was anticipated."

"I do not understand, mother."

"I am not sure I understand myself." She looked to Olienhout, where a pup crawled under her head, small open jaws seeking something to nip. "Under the watch of your alpha, your pack is safe." Aalwyn strode towards the mother and, after a moment, dipped her head toward Olienhout.

Olienhout's jaw dropped in shock to the subservient gesture, and hobbled closer on her three good legs. The pup behind her tumbled in the dirt, shaking its head free of dust. Olienhout lapped her muzzle.

"You have my gratitude, Aalwyn. Without you, we died in a cage. A prison of numb apathy, fear, and disease." She dipped her head further still than the older female.

"Aalwyn, you are the Alpha. Of the wild entire."

The rest of the *Gambiet* pack bowed their heads to her.

"I will guard all you have taught me." Leadwort lapped her muzzle also.

Wildevlier approached her to lap her muzzle once, an effusive display of emotion given her taciturn nature. "The veld will run with rivers of blood before Koorsboom or Olienhout shed so much as a drop."

"Return well, mother." Koorsboom twittered happily. "May the wild favor you, resplendent with herds of prey."

Aalwyn padded away as the sun burned down on the savanna below. Within the hour she reached an electrified fence and dug a channel underneath it. After traversing this barrier, she looked back.

She sensed this was the last time she would see her son. Turning her head to the sun above, she closed her eyes and felt the burning heat upon her face. Smiling to herself, she sensed as well that he would never need her help again.

Chapter 86

"Yes, all of them." Du Plessis was in a fever, on the phone all morning. "I told you I would pay, there is no downside for you." He paced in front of his small brick house past the metal barrel still brimming with discarded bottles.

A farm hand from the Grootes property shook his head as he watched the older man rant.

"If you shoot a wild dog because you refused a gift like this, I will not help you again through a drought." He was nodding his head furiously. "Right. Right, you think on it. And remember what you owe me."

"You had to know there would be resistance." The farmhand checked the batteries on the camera. The waterproof cover was snapped into place. A long fiber optic cable streamed from the device and terminated in a small lens.

"There will always be some push back. Still, you would think people would want free things." Du Plessis shrugged.

"Nothing is free. They can tell strings are attached." The farmhand hefted a power drill, with a meter-long custom-made drill bit in place, as thick as the cable.

"Just that they must tolerate predators."

"A big string for a farmer." The bit was tightened in place.

"In any case, every time the rains fail, their wild game is allowed to graze on my property. And still they do not trust my methods." He motioned to the farm hand. "The den is marked, you cannot miss it. Drill through the top into the aardvark hole, link it up, and trail the cable toward the hide."

The farmhand drove off on a motorcycle, one hand holding the loop of cable and the camera in a clump of wires.

An engine growled in the distance.

"Ah, here they come. My *wildehonde.*" Du Plessis beamed.

The large truck crunched up the gravel path, dust stirred by the heavy tires. The trailer in the rear was utterly dark, concealed by tarps. Du Plessis waved them on, and jumped into his *bakkie.* Tires sprayed gravel on his house as he sped in front of the truck, leading them into the savanna beyond.

An hour of agonizing slow driving over the rough ground brought them past a stand of wild seringa trees. The broad flat crowns cast their shadows on the truck as it passed. On the edge of this stand stood a solitary fever tree. The yellow bark gleamed in the sun, up to the similarly colored branches and the scant shade from the leafy arbor. At the base of the tree was an aardvark hole, abandoned some time ago. Close to the hole leading to the den below a cable emerged from the ground, where it was stapled in place to the tree trunk. This waterproof cable trailed away along the ground. The farmhand who installed the cable gave Du Plessis a salute and got back onto his motorcycle and puttered away with the drill.

The truck labored up to the verge of the den.

The rear burst open and Venter heaved.

"Gah!" She gasped. "There is no bloody air in here!" Breathing deeply, as the dense fumes of musk, urine and stool cleared away, she tasted the clear air that was as sweet to her as honey.

"Hurry! They could wake any minute!" Du Plessis waved frantically to her. The ramp was set in place, and Du Plessis and Venter each worked to carry out the prone bodies of each Painted wolf. They were eased down carefully next to the den hole, and a towel was removed from each head.

"The pups." She strode into the truck and dragged a large wooden crate to the ramp. They carried this down and set it next to the aardvark hole. "One more." The other crate was set next to the first one.

The ranger thought for a moment and nodded. She brought several tarps from the rear of the truck and unfolded them. Positioning each of the crates on opposing sides of the hole, she wrapped the tarps around both crates with the den opening between them, giving the pups no place to go but the comfortable darkness below.

Undoing the latch on each crate, she swung them open over the denning hole.

At first, nothing. Then one pup poked a head out of its crate, then another head poked out. Seeing the den hole, they sniffed carefully. The pups looked at one another, then looked around wildly for their mother.

She grinned, glancing at Du Plessis. "Watch this." She brought out a recording device and pressed a button. It emitted a barely discernible hiss for a moment, then a sharp, low growl.

The effect was electric, the pups scurrying down the den hole as though poured from a jug. Light thumping was heard below.

The rest of the cable was then connected to a longer length of cable that had been threaded into a long pipe that laid in a shallow trench, now covered with dirt. The end of the pipe was sealed with caulk and duct tape. This trailed off into the bush. The crates and tarps were removed and packed into the rear of the truck.

"That one is stirring."

Olienhout raised her head, and laid it down again.

Du Plessis put away the ramp, and the driver moved the truck away from the den. Du Plessis hurriedly got into his *bakkie* with Venter and drove a short distance away, to avoid spooking the wolf pack.

Koorsboom kicked his hind leg out.

The engine of the *bakkie* rattled to a halt. They entered a thatch-roofed wooden shed, rough but sturdy in appearance. Du Plessis carried a monitor, which he set down on a wooden bench. Venter retrieved the end of the fiber optic cable and plugged it into the monitor. After a moment, the image cleared and they could see the black and white shapes of the pups in the den below.

"Rustic." She patted the wooden walls.

"Best I could arrange in the past week." Du Plessis hefted the monitor onto a table next to a battery pack, just below a viewing hole. From where they sat, the fever tree was just visible.

Olienhout raised her head again, and was on her paws. Around her neck was a leather tracking collar, snug and securely fastened. Drunkenly weaving from one side to the other, she shook her head and began sniffing the ground. She stuck her head into the den hole, and even from where they were, Du Plessis and Venter could hear twittering and yipping as the mother discovered her pups.

Koorsboom was on his paws now, along with Wildevlier and Leadwort. They greeted one another, and Olienhout. Sniffing about, they investigated their new home.

"Well. One step done." The ranger nodded happily while she looked through the binoculars.

"Another hundred to go." Du Plessis clapped her on the back. "You smell like wild dog, *meisie*."

"You know, Dup." She scratched her head. "I sat in that truck for two hours with those wild dogs. What is your excuse?"

"*Voetsek*, woman. I am not here to impress you." He grunted. "We watch them for a while. Then, time for some *Kasteel*."

***

"The earth and trees have moved around us." Koorsboom lay down, his head still swimming from the sedative.

"I feel like I did when we found ourselves in that terrible cage." Olienhout licked the face of one of the pups.

"Are we in one of those places now?" He looked around, bewildered.

Olienhout thought for a moment. "No. Somehow, this place feels different. I sense no malice from the people watching us from afar. And they will continue watching."

Wildevlier padded past them. "I see no enemies. Yet." She trotted off, in search of those enemies.

Leadwort stretched on the ground. "What ever are we doing here?"

"Living." Olienhout nodded. "Just living. And we will explore our world, finding its limits, and its dangers. One day, one hunt, one kill at a time."

"Every moment a negotiation." Koorsboom lapped her muzzle. "Every day of survival a victory on the way to defeat."

"We have a place in this world." She nudged the pup between her paws, and he looked back at her. The pug face was shaped in a frown, but there was no mistaking the happiness he knew in his mother's embrace.

* * *

Du Plessis raised his bottle and clinked it against Venter's. "To the ocean of indifference."

"A dubious toast." She upended her bottle, looking about the clearing before Du Plessis's small house. The sandy soil was crossed with innumerable animal tracks.

"We ride the swells toward storm or shore." He took a long drink and pointed out toward the savanna before him. "Except here. The ocean parts, and emergent is the new wild." He drained the rest of the bottle and tossed it onto the ground next to the full steel drum.

"You are a strange man, Du Plessis." She laughed. "Shame there is not more of you."

"Look alive!" He pointed over her shoulder.

Staring at them was a wild dog.

"Well, that is fascinating, eh?" He adjusted his cap, hands on his hips.

Koorsboom watched them, taking in the sights and sounds of the house, the humans, the ashes of the previous night's campfire. His hazel eyes looked into the pale blue of the man's.

Du Plessis looked back, into eyes from an ancient world. They sensed the generations past, when humans first came to the veld, hunting with spears and arrows alongside the predators. Their gaze crossed millennia, when the land was owned by none, and survival was for all.

Koorsboom turned to leave, the white of his tail in the air, padding away with a relaxed gait. He took in every detail, every rock and tree, the slope of the land. He filed this away in a mental map as he returned to the den.

Koorsboom's eyes adjusted to the dim light within the former aardvark hole, and he could make out Olienhout. The pups crawled over her and over each other. He lapped her muzzle gently.

"You are my world, Olienhout."

"And you shall know no other."

Chapter 87

Stalks resembling bone jutted from otherwise bare ground that had cracked and fissured in the dry season. The maize crop had failed again after onslaughts of heavy rains were followed by searing drought. In central Mozambique, the farmers sifted through cassava fields, pulling up spindly root vegetables that had drowned in the wet season and now yielded only their desiccated remains. Vast areas cleared of trees for farming were now blasted by the sun, and the erratic weather wreaked its havoc.

The wolf padded through this field, unconcerned about whether people would discover her presence. She had crossed fields like this, running into humans too fatigued with fieldwork to bother with her. As June wore into July, even the patches of wild between farms took on a golden hue in the deep of the dry season.

Aalwyn gave a halfhearted look for prey in the ruined maize field, knowing from experience these places were sterile of life. On the edge of the field, within an arid drainage ditch, a scrub hare fell to her attack. The blood would sustain her, and she knew another day would be survived.

As she slowly worked her way north, she began to scent the faint signposts. Covering up to fifty kilometers per day, she found tracks of her kind. The musk of Painted wolf, faded over time, had been left to linger on the bushveld. Urination and defecation left chemical markers that could only have come from her mate.

Following these, the markings became fresher.

In a damp riverbed, she found her quarry.

"Kurkbos." She loped to the sleeping form, the head jerking up in response to her twittering call.

They met each other in a sprint, leaving deep paw prints on the sandy bed. Galloping past, each turned and the two wolves spun around one another, up on hind legs to happily box before lapping muzzles in greeting.

"Aalwyn." He spoke the name as though savoring fresh impala. "You have consumed my dreams."

She did not speak, only relishing the touch of her mate.

After this embrace they rejoined the rest of the pack. Effusive greetings went around, and each wolf shared this gentle touch.

"What news of the veld?" Aalwyn rested in the shade of a Giraffe-thorn acacia.

"The hunting is poor on this side of the great river." Kurkbos inclined his head in the direction of the Pungwe River that ran along the southern edge of Gorongosa National Park on its way to Beira and the Indian Ocean. "North of it, the herds still run. To the south there is little to pursue."

"Even the cattle and goats the humans keep have been few and far between." Blackthorn grumbled. The yearling appeared ill-fed.

"Perhaps they are killing their own animals." Rukato rasped. "Between our numbers, and the litter you left behind, these are lean times indeed." He rested his head on forepaws. "Since the death of Essenhout, matters are worse."

Aalwyn looked at the ground. "My dear sister." She sighed. "She called her pack the *Droom*, as though life here were an unending dream."

"If this were a dream, I would prefer never to sleep." Rukato was on his paws and padded off.

They watched him go, across the river bed and into the brush beyond.

"He has been wandering off between our hunts." Kurkbos spoke quietly, almost at a whisper. "And when our hunts have failed, he disappears for most of the day. I fear he is preparing to wander again."

"That is how he came to Essenhout's pack. Perhaps it would be best for us all to disperse." Blackthorn ran a claw along the soil.

"Take heart, young one." Kurkbos probed the yearling with his snout. "The dry season can be good hunting." He gave a slight smile. "If only we could return to the north."

"And have you ventured past the great river?" Aalwyn sat up.

"Only once. The hunt was prosperous, but it was not long before we sensed pursuit."

"Did you encounter the *Selous* pack?"

"Only their tracks. Once we made the kill and started back, we crossed them several times." He shook his head, and a streamer of drool fell from his open jaw. "They were all over our trail, and did not seem inclined to suffer our presence for long."

She rested her head.

"What ails you, Aalwyn?" Kurkbos lay by her side, nudging her with his snout. "It has been so long, and we wish to hear of all your adventures."

She did not speak, and closed her eyes. There, in the dark of her mind, she saw the men from the south, where she left Koorsboom and Olienhout. The shaking of hands, and the following peace.

Chapter 88

Sonja Venter pulled a key from her utility box, unlocking the housing on the camera trap. Quickly changing the battery with a fresh one, and replacing the data card, she then locked it shut. Using a wooden tongue depressor, she spooned a sample of elephant dung from a bucket in the rear of her Land Rover to smear on the camera housing and post. Refreshing the pungent scent would often protect it from destruction.

The ring from her phone startled her, and the wooden stick flipped in the air, landing in her breast pocket.

"*Ag*, perfect." Grumbling, she answered her phone. *"Hallo?"*

"Venter?"

"This is she." She recognized the voice on the other end.

"I have something." He sounded muted, as though trying to avoid drawing attention.

"Go ahead." She took out her notes and a pencil, the dung-laden tongue depressor still jutting from her pocket.

"You will pay me?"

"Give me your bank details." She jotted down the account number as he continued to mutter in a monotone.

"Augusto is running a poacher gang in a reserve not far from Gorongosa this week." A rustling sound came through the speaker of the phone shifting in his grasp. "They left just now."

"Gate details?" She quickly wrote down the name of the reserve and the entry gate they would use. More precise directions would not be possible.

"I will send you a third now. The rest when we get them."

"Half now."

"Very well."

The call disconnected. She quickly arranged the bank transfer. She blushed as the transaction was finalized, wondering if she were the fool parted from her money. This was her first informer. Shrugging this off, she made another call immediately.

"Razak?"

A grunt on the other end was the only recognition.

"We may have a lead to catch them."

* * *

There seemed to be no shadows upon the ground as the sun glowered overhead. The savanna was still, every herbivore sheltering under a tree, somewhat reassured that predators would be doing the same. A solitary man was the only thing moving on the veld, creeping forward one step at a time in the quiet.

A black boot took a step, and dark eyes would peer at the ground. Another step, every blade of grass examined. Step. Pause. Examine.

The dry ground was cracked in the heat, and one such crack had collapsed. Pressed into this was a round shape. The hoof of a zebra had made this impact. Another hoof print was ahead and diagonal to this, but Razak ignored these. They were spaced as expected, a normal gait for a zebra that was uninjured.

A sleeve wiped his forehead free of beads of sweat. Scarred hands straightened the beret atop his head, then held aside faded tall grasses as he stepped forward. Ever scanning the ground, he showed no signs of tiring. Padding his shirt absently, he plunged a hand into a pocket. Only crumpled, empty cigarette packets. From the other deep pocket he pulled out the last foil-wrapped nutrition bar, the label proudly announcing 'Jungle Oats'. Wolfing this down, he took a bulging handful of foil wrappers and stuffed these along with the empty cigarette packets into his small rucksack, which only contained a water filter and a jacket.

This supply had sustained him for the two days he pursued his quarry. He did not need much when tracking.

No tracks were visible on this barren patch of earth. Onward.

Walking faster over ground bare of animal or human signs, he slowed again as the brush became thicker.

Step. Pause. Examine.

Holding aside grass, he glanced about for disturbed branches. Nothing. Onward.

He made his way toward thornbrush not far from a watercourse. And there he saw it.

A boot print in the soil. Relatively fresh, devoid of weathering or debris.

He retraced a few steps and saw a shallower imprint due to harder ground. The soft, more moist dirt held the shape. Now that he recognized the print, he could spot them more quickly.

Following these into the brush, he needed only glance about to see the pace of the walker, and picked up one more set of boot tracks.

The prints were similar in size and make. The boots lacked tread, unlike store-bought boots, indicating they were custom made.

Money was backing these individuals.

These led further into an acacia thicket, and he followed them past broken branches, with fresh leaves scattered on the ground. A fast walk, then slowing for a moment as the grass grew thicker. Dark hands swept aside the blades to clearly see the imprints. Then faster, following the tracks where they were deeply pressed into wet soil.

The tracks each had widely-spaced prints, toes pointed outwards.

Men, both of them.

Toes pointed outward more than one would expect, with a wide straddle.

The men were carrying loads. Or a single load between them.

No other tracks were present. Razak weaved through the brush, eyes ever on the ground, then scanning the horizon for moving figures. He walked quickly past a feverberry tree, pausing momentarily when a yellow-billed hornbill took flight at his approach.

Kok kok kok kok korkorkorkorkor!

He watched carefully in all directions, and saw no movement in response to the noise. Still he waited, cautious not to warn his prey that he was coming.

Here the bootprints were closer together. Then together. Standing still. A bum print, next to disturbed dirt. Razak dug into this with a knife, yielding a handful of spent cigarette filters.

Walking in a circle around where the poachers had rested, he made out a rectangular imprint on grass.

A crate. Heavy, by the way the foliage was crushed.

The tracks led away from here into grass, and the boots had left less of an impression. Nothing escaped Razak's eyes as he peered under and between the grass stems. He found a snapped branch of acacia brush, the core still wet and fresh.

He peered across the horizon. Normally a tracker had at least one armed escort. Paying attention to tracks meant potentially neglecting the threat that made them. Razak reflexively felt for the AK-47 slung over his back on a strap. He brought it around, reassured by its weight. Glancing again around him, he saw no people in the area. He tightened his grip on the handle of his rifle.

The tracks of the poachers then disappeared into heavier grass. His pace slowed as he struggled to pick them up again. Making wide circles, he saw nothing. Listening for any noise or movement. None. Only the sound of his breathing.

He moved away from the dense scrub towards more barren ground. Making large circles further from where he lost the tracks of the poachers yielded nothing. Two hours passed this way, his heart pounding all the while.

His frustration was relieved by the sight of a dry riverbed ahead. Razak smiled, hastening to the edge, and was rewarded by the reappearance of the boot prints, pressed into the soft sand. Wide straddle between right and left prints.

And the distance between prints was decreasing.

They were tiring.

A finger slipped inside the trigger guard.

His pace grew faster, his muscular form crouching as he advanced. If he had the ears of a predator, they would be folded back, nostrils would flare, scenting for his prey. He walked upon bare ground where possible, his footfalls silenced by the dust.

The tracks continued to indicate a slower walk—closer together, wider straddle than before, toe points outward. A rectangular shape was pressed into the ground. More tracks, close together.

A third set of tracks became apparent. He slowed, now using both hands to steady the aim of his rifle. This set had a normal pace, normal straddle, evidently not carrying anything heavy. The boots lacked tread, like the others. The footprints stopped, side by side. An oval shape in the dirt.

A rifle stock imprint.

The tracks continued, off in a different direction from the other two. They were not walking together.

Razak glanced around, more wary with the notion that the poachers were not necessarily moving in a group. He stayed with the pair carrying the load, and the boot prints continued to appear, close together and clumsy.

Weaving through a thornbrush thicket, he abruptly came upon a dead rhino carcass. It was still as rock, and was partly under the shade of an acacia tree. This may delay its discovery by vultures, but only for a short period of time.

Blood had seeped from the large open wound where the horn was hacked away. This pooled beneath the ponderous head, eyes devoid of life. Multiple holes punctured the side of the mighty beast, each with trickles of red leading down from the bullet entry wounds.

Razak placed a hand on the side of the rhino, feeling the thick hide of the giant. He gave a brief sigh, and pushed on.

The third set of tracks made another appearance, with another oval shape indicating the armament of the poacher. All three sets remained together now, as they led into the veld. Earlier, care was taken to avoid leaving too many tracks, but no longer. They were easily followed for over a kilometer.

Suddenly a scent reached Razak, and he could not help but grin at the unmistakable sharp tang of smoke. Not of a campfire, but of cigarettes. Being a smoker, and having run out the day before, he was particularly attuned to the odor.

He threaded with care into a stand of feverberry trees, contiguous with a thicket. The boot prints continued, widely spaced and occasionally stumbling. In multiple places, he noted a corner of the crate had punched into the ground. They were truly fatigued, but also in a hurry. Razak suspected they were hiking toward a vehicle that was not able to cross the rough ground.

Easing through the branches that reached out to brush his khaki uniform, he entered a clearing that held three men, lying in the shade of the tree.

The men were dozing in the heat of the early afternoon, one snoring gently. He held a still-smoldering cigarette in one hand. His other held a hunting rifle by the wooden stock. The other two were seated against the trunk of the feverberry, faces nearly invisible in the dappled shade and light from the leaves rustling overhead.

An axe, coated with rust and crimson, was propped against the feverberry tree.

A fresh horn sat atop seven other horns in a large wooden crate nearby.

The stock of the rifle was placed against his shoulder, finger resting on the curved steel of the trigger.

With the tip of his boot, Razak kicked a stone across the clearing and against the crate with a hollow knock.

The three men were jarred awake, eyes wide. The two against the tree sputtered, hands reaching for things that were not there. The man with the rifle sat forward and coughed, lifting the remains of the cigarette to his mouth. The filter had reached his lips when he turned to see Razak.

The ranger was a hole cut into the daylight, eyes warped by a scowl and partly obscured by the steel sight of his rifle.

In one swift move, the poacher gripped the handle of his rifle and brought it around toward the ranger.

Three sharp pulls, and three ear–splitting cracks filled the air.

The poacher collapsed at once, dropping his rifle, three holes in his chest oozing blood, mouth wide in a gasp of air that never reached his lungs.

Razak pivoted to the other two men. One had unsheathed a knife and was halfway to the ranger. The stark white of his eyes was visible all the way around, his jaw hanging open with the beginnings of a shout bursting from a throat unready for words.

Four cracks in quick succession, and the lanky body of the poacher jerked and spun as the bullets caught him in the chest, torso, and throat. The words never came as his mouth filled with a wet, pink froth.

The third man never moved. His hands were up, palms toward the ranger. He wore a strange smile, an alien gesture striving for something relatable and friendly, despite neither making sense in this situation.

Razak stepped closer to him, finger never leaving the trigger.

He did not speak. He never spoke. He almost never needed to. His left hand extended toward the poacher, palm up, fingers curled.

Hand it over.

The poacher, taking the greatest care, felt for a pocket, and withdrew a phone. A piece of paper also fell to the ground as the phone left his pocket.

He attempted to crawl toward Razak to hand over the phone, attempting to retrieve the paper with some degree of subtlety. Razak motioned for him to stop. Hand lowered toward the ground, palm down.

Drop it now.

A dismissive gesture with the fingers.

Back away.

The poacher scuttled backwards, crouched.

Razak retrieved the phone and the piece of paper.

Dark eyes regarded his prey. The AK remained trained on the poacher, unwavering. His lips parted, and his deep voice filled the clearing.

"*Augusto.*"

The poacher began to shake his head, mouth opening to issue a flimsy lie.

Razak in two strides closed the distance and pressed the barrel against the man's knee.

"Hyena." His voice was a resonant thrum. *"They smell your blood."* His face contorted in anger, irate from having to waste words on a fool. *"They kill their prey. By eating it."* He motioned as though to squeeze the trigger.

The poacher uttered a slight whine, and tears began to fall. His head, with great reluctance, began to nod.

* * *

The black smoke billowed into the dry evening sky, the pillar rising high into an accusatory finger. Three rangers cleared a wide space around the burning rhino corpse, ensuring this did not spread into an uncontrolled veld blaze.

Razak's eyes were trained on the base, where wood was heaped against the dead animal. Though it would have made as much sense to let scavengers reap their harvest, he had found a container of cyanide poison in one of the poacher's sacks. He could not be sure whether they had laced the kill with it, to cover their tracks by killing vultures that would announce the location of a poached carcass. This measure was safer. Some poacher kills like this could be found surrounded by dozens of vultures, marabou storks, hyenas, jackals, and even a few lions. The men who left the poisoned carcasses did so without a second thought.

Retrieving his phone, he dialed a number. With his other hand, he continued to play with the poacher's cell phone. Cycling through the contacts, which were few, it took very little time to reach the name 'Augusto'.

"Hallo?" Venter's reedy voice reached through the speaker.

"Razak."

"Razak! Howzit?"

"Augusto." He read off the number for her.

"That is the poacher Johan was hunting." She sighed, which came through as a hiss. "He mentioned that Augusto works with the receiver who exports horn to Thailand."

"Buatoom." His voice was tinged with malice.

"Now we need Augusto."

"I captured one." He paused. "I do not trust him. I need a seller."

"If you took down one of his gangs, he will need time to recruit and set up another."

"Weeks." The ranger continued to study the phone.

"So he will need to buy horn from whatever source is available." She hummed to herself for a moment. "I met someone who could help draw him out." He could hear her smile through the phone. "A legitimate game farmer. He can pose as a seller."

"Chips." Razak rumbled.

"For the horn? Yes, we will have time to install tracking devices in the horn before the sale." She spoke quickly when excited, and sounded to him like a vervet monkey.

"Razak—are you smiling?"

He grunted. "Not yet."

Chapter 89

"Are you comfortable with this plan, Louw?" Venter's dark hair whipped in the wind about her. The phone signal was weak, but the voice on the other end came through crisply.

"I am. This will be coordinated with the local police?"

"Yes. I have contacted the department and made all the arrangements. Razak will link with them."

"Remarkable you convinced the police to work at all." Louw scoffed. "They barely show up to murders around here."

"Razak helped with connections. He has a way with people."

"He is either charming or frightening, then." Louw used his free hand to shield his face from the afternoon sun.

"You will see." She smiled. "Here are the contacts for the rangers involved, and who to call for help."

She read off several numbers. "Be sure to make the sale price reasonable."

"Big pleasure."

She turned to watch a dozen wildebeest saunter past. Pausing to watch for a moment, the ranger relished the silence broken only by the buffeting winds and the grunting calls of *gnu gnu gnu* uttered between mouthfuls of foliage.

"How is the predator management project going?" Louw asked.

"Quite well. The Wildlife Trust is taking the lead on it now, though I have been giving a hand with some parts of the project. Du Plessis has been instrumental in obtaining buy-in from local farmers."

"I have put in a word with the community about you."

"Thank you for your help with taking Augusto." Venter smiled.

The reticent farmer could not help but smile back. "*Ag, meisie*, happy to help." He paced away for a moment, a hand on his hip. "I felt bad about shooting the wolf." He shook his head. "Which makes no sense, since we have been shooting predators since we have had farms. From the Cape to the Transvaal. This time, though." He stared at the ground. "This time it just felt wrong. And after this all worked out." He waved off his thought, staring at impala in the distance as they fed on the hay.

"I hope we can work together in the future."

"Any time, *meisie*. I would like to find a way."

* * *

"Razak?"

"*Ja.*"

"We are set in South Africa." Venter was unnerved by the silence on the other end.

Static.

"Your policeman friend in the community will endorse the arrest and allow transport across the border." Silence. "Since the crimes occurred in Mozambique."

Faint sounds of wind.

"There is a farmer in the Lowveld named Louw who will be our contact. He will call our target about the horns for sale."

After a moment: "Good."

"I worry about Gorongosa."

"Why." This was phrased as a statement rather than a question.

"The rebel army covering them. They may retaliate against the park and the rangers."

There was a subtle rumbling noise on the other end of the call.

"We need to grab both Augusto and Buatoom before the soldiers know what we are doing. They have protection."

It took her a moment to realize the rumbling was a laugh.

"Had."

She had heard stories circulating in the village, but was not sure what to believe until now.

"Take care, Razak."

The call disconnected.

Chapter 90

The crate was surveyed with a scowl. Razak watched flies crawl over the rhino horn within, alighting for a moment on residual tissue and dried blood before flying off for another place to gather its food.

His face was normally carved from stone, but now appeared to crack. A fingertip traced a darkened line down the rhino horn to its base, and to a piece of dried hide at the edge. Here it lingered, feeling the texture of the skin. Withdrawing from the horn, the fingers curled into a fist. Knuckles popped under the pressure.

He dropped the tarp back into place and turned to face the farmer.

He was dressed in what seemed the uniform of a farmer, with khaki shorts and a bicolored cotton shirt, green higher on the shoulders and tan below the breast pockets. The bushy mustache completed the look.

"Louw?" Razak's voice was devoid of inflection.

"*Ja.*" He stepped forward to shake Razak's hand, though with some trepidation. "Sonja Venter sent word that you would meet me with some horn."

His nod was nearly imperceptible.

Louw walked toward the rear of the *bakkie* and lifted the tarp.

"This man is going to buy from me?" Louw's crisp speech sounded like a small yipping dog compared to the ranger's baritone.

"Augusto." Razak handed him a scrap of paper.

"Chuffed to help." He peered at the number written down. "Why would he buy from me?" Louw scratched absently at his mustache. "He has gangs that hunt rhino for him, *né?*"

Razak shrugged.

"Unless something happened to his gangs."

Razak gave the slightest nod.

"Right." Louw felt palpitations in his chest. "What... uh. What price?" He had never dealt with illegal horn before.

"I do not care." Razak's face remained cryptically blank.

"Hmm." Louw scratched his mustache again. "Well, whatever I get, it will go to your rangers in Gorongosa."

Razak gave a subtle grunt.

"These guys...." Louw felt very uncomfortable. "I was told they had killed some of your men."

Razak's face darkened, and one hand instinctively felt for his rifle. It was in his car.

"I will do my best."

The ranger did not respond.

"Right." Louw nodded with conviction. "Which horns have GPS trackers?"

"All of them."

* * *

Twisted acacia, tree and shrub, formed a barrier that obscured the barn from the main house of the farm. The barn was a newer structure on the land, having been built fifty years ago. The red brick walls were topped by a green corrugated steel roof. Windows for the structure were covered with wooden shutters, secured in place over steel bars to deter theft. Behind the sliding doors stood vehicles used to gather grass for the wild game that populated the land, reserves of seed, spare parts for the *bakkies*, and a single crate.

Louw eyed the crate while he scraped out his pipe with a metal implement. The residue of tobacco was already gone, but he continued working on the bowl of the wooden pipe, staring at the crate.

Skrip skrip skrip

He paced in and out of the shade of a marula tree that stood away from the barn. From a central trunk the branches spread far and wide, seeming to eclipse the sky. No fruit was scattered underneath the broad arbor, the bare ground crisscrossed by hoof prints.

The rise of the whine of an engine reached his ears, and he put away his pipe.

Down the long straight road that led across his property he could see a distant puff of dust. The vehicle approaching passed a dilapidated cattle feedlot which stood unused for over a decade, and beyond a circular dam that held a modest amount of water. A windpump spun gradually in the breeze, emitting a periodic knock of metal.

As the vehicle grew closer, Louw lifted the phone to his ear and dialed. There was a click on the other end, but no greeting.

"Stand by. He is here."

Another click as the line went dead.

Louw smiled to himself. He rather liked the ranger, taciturn though he was. The Mozambican had a way with silence he found agreeable.

The white *bakkie* slowed, and pulled off the dirt and gravel road, bumping over the grass. It was muddy up to the windows, and the glass was coated with dust so it was nearly opaque. Coasting to a stop, the engine died and a man got out of the passenger side.

"Are you Louw?"

"Howzit." He waved.

"You have something to sell?"

"*Ja.*" He gestured toward the barn, the crate visible in the opening where the door had been pushed aside.

"Do you sell such things often?" Augusto made no move in that direction, seeming content to do nothing.

"When I can." Louw folded his arms, in no apparent hurry.

Augusto glanced around, eyes on the horizon, past the building, past the trees.

"This farm looks deserted. Anyone working today?"

"It is a big farm." Louw retrieved his pipe and resumed scraping the bowl. "A lot of space to carry out work without prying eyes." *Skrip skrip skrip.*

Augusto chuckled. "Since when do you sell horn?"

"Oh, I have always sold horn whenever I get hold of a rhino. Auctions. Some farmers in this area sell off their stock to me as they go out of business." He concentrated on the pipe. "So, I have rhino hunts for tourists, and they take home a trophy with real-looking horns."

"A lot of farmers in the area doing this?" Augusto asked eagerly.

"Very few. Most prefer working through regulators. Lots of oversight." Louw looked up from his pipe. "I like to deal direct."

Augusto nodded. "You are not working with police, then?" He stared at the farmer.

Louw was not perturbed. "The only people around here who work with police are the bottle stores. The lazy drunks even forget to demand bribes sometimes."

"How did you get my number?" Augusto peered at him.

"A friend who works in Mozambique. In shipping." Louw stared back. "Someone who knows how to be discreet. Shall I ask him for another contact?"

Augusto gestured toward the *bakkie.* The engine gunned to life once again, and the unseen driver edged forward toward the barn. Augusto walked into the entryway and lifted the tarp on the crate. He dropped it again and clapped his hands together, rubbing them greedily.

The poacher returned to the rear of the vehicle after it stopped and removed a scale. Augusto carefully placed each horn on the scale, verifying the weight that Louw provided in their initial contact. Returning them all to the crate, Augusto gave Louw a thumbs up.

"Sharp, sharp." He handed over a brown paper bag. Inside were several bricks of rand, bound by rubber bands. "Will you have more?" Augusto was still rubbing his hands together.

"There will be plenty more." Louw wondered for a moment whether

Augusto was the one who killed the rangers.

"Then I will call."

The driver still remained out of sight, though as he shifted in the seat, the man seemed to cut an enormous figure. Louw guessed he carried a gun so Augusto did not need one.

Augusto heaved the crate into the rear of the white *bakkie*, and slammed the door shut.

"Let me know your needs going forward." Louw returned the pipe to his pocket.

Augusto grinned. He waved, and the engine roared as they made a circle to return to the dirt road. Dust rose in a cloud that followed the vehicle until it left his sight.

"Razak?" Louw spoke into his phone.

A barely audible grunt on the other end.

"He has it. One other man with him. Probably armed."

"Good." The line went dead.

Louw hefted the bag, and began counting. Two-hundred-rand notes, some with Mandela's smiling face, others with the blank stare of a leopard. Stacks of them, each bound with rubber bands. He shook his head and dropped the brick into the bag.

* * *

The dirty, weathered Toyota followed the *bakkie* at a distance, beyond the next rolling hill. The reassuring *beep* on the locator kept Razak informed. His dark eyes flitted from the GPS screen to the road ahead, immune to the numbing monotony of the highway.

WHOOM

A long haul truck flew past on the right, with two trailers carrying lumber.

Each time he encountered a slow-moving car, he passed quickly on the right with little regard for the oncoming traffic. For some, he returned to the left lane with seconds to spare.

The blip remained where it was, just beyond his sight.

Suddenly the blip grew closer to him. He was nearly upon it as he slowed. Over the next rise a petrol station loomed into view. The green SASOL sign advertised the current price of a liter of fuel.

The white *bakkie* with the poacher was rolling to a stop at one of the pumps. A worker in a green SASOL uniform jogged out and leaned into the driver side window. He gave a salute and flipped a switch at the pump, plugging the nozzle into the tank opening.

Razak drifted to a stop at the periphery of the petrol station and watched.

The worker moved to wash the windows, but the driver got out and waved him off. His bulk suggested a lumbering oaf, but he moved as quickly as a rugby flanker. Adjusting his belt, a hand went to the small of his back, feeling for an object just under his shirt. He spoke to Augusto, and gestured toward the station. He strode toward the entryway, where dozens of people were walking in or out after buying snacks or drinks for the road.

The ranger slid out of his Toyota and followed him inside.

Several minutes later, Augusto peered at the station, looking for his driver. Fishing in his pocket, he paid the worker for the petrol, tipping him with a small coin.

The driver side door opened and abruptly banged shut. Augusto turned to see a ranger seated behind the wheel. First, he noticed the uniform of khaki, topped with a beret. Second, he recognized the pistol in his hand, held with a firm grip. Third, the knuckles of the hand that were perched upon the steering wheel were covered with blood. Last, he looked into a pair of coal-black eyes that burned with a fierce intensity, and Augusto knew he had minutes to live.

His jaw opened, but could utter no words that had meaning.

Razak gave the slightest shake of his head, silencing the poacher. While his right hand held the pistol, his left turned the key and took the wheel.

The trip down the highway was brief, and the *bakkie* turned down a side road.

Augusto's head bobbed slightly from his bounding pulse, each beat filling his skull with blind sound.

When they stopped, Augusto moved to open his door, and saw stars. Dully aware of his face smashing into the dashboard, he regained consciousness seated on the ground. He was not sure how he got there.

His vision swimming, it focused on the ranger staring down at him.

"Are you going to kill me?"

Razak shrugged. He handed Augusto a phone. His phone. The ranger had taken it while he was unconscious. Augusto took the phone in hand, his eyes filled with questions.

"Boss."

Augusto merely panted, his mouth hanging open.

"In Maputo?"

Augusto slowly began to shake his head. "He... he will kill me... My family..."

"Chimoio." Razak's expression was of stone.

"How do you know where my family lives?" Augusto was breathing rapidly.

"Everyone knows the poachers." The ranger's voice boomed in the quiet, far from the highway. "We all know you. The money you throw about." Razak's features began to twist in anger. "The people you kill."

"That... that was not me..."

Razak glared.

Augusto gulped air in deep breaths.

"Boss." He spoke this as a hiss, eyes rimmed with red. "In Maputo?" His scowl deepened, growing increasingly angry at having to speak when it should not be necessary.

Augusto nodded slowly.

He handed the poacher a sheet of paper to read.

Augusto dialed.

"Mister Buatoom." He breathed rapidly.

"Yes." The voice on the other end was annoyed.

"I cannot deliver the horn to Maputo. I..." He glanced up to Razak, whose hand tightened on the pistol. "I was detained by police, but managed to hide the vehicle before they stopped me. The horn is in a white truck in Komatipoort. Keys are under a rear tire." He read the directions to Nattapong Buatoom.

On the other end, there was a muttering grumble, and the line went dead.

Stars again. A ringing through his head that faded as his vision went red, to a pale rose, then cleared. He had no idea how much time had passed while he was out, but the sun seemed to have moved across the sky.

From the ground, he looked up to see police officers speaking to the ranger. The ranger said very little back to them, but they seemed satisfied. One hand was offered to the ranger, and he took it, prompting the policeman to wince in pain.

Beyond them, he could see a *bakkie*, all white with a stripe of blue bordered in yellow running along a side, with the word POLICE marking the lower part of the passenger door. Leaning against the vehicle was Augusto's driver. His hands were zip tied behind him. Both eyes were swollen shut, covered in bruises. The shirt he wore was a curtain of blood and clots.

One of the policemen leaned down toward Augusto, and laughed as he said something in Tswana. It was one language Augusto was unfamiliar with.

Razak did not look down to the poacher before he left, getting into the white *bakkie* and driving back down the dirt road to the highway.

Chapter 91

Dust hung in the air, ever stirred by passing cars as they flew down the black ribbon. Some were larger vehicles carrying tourists toward the Crocodile Bridge gate of Kruger National Park. Others were cars overstuffed with luggage for families heading to local vacation homes. Most were people bound elsewhere, to the west and the industry of Joburg, or to the east and the business they had beyond the border. A great deal of money was in the area, foreign currency feeding the innumerable shops and shopping of Nelspruit. Services ranged from local guides, auto shops and panelbeaters for the many car collisions that occurred, groceries, medical for tourists who perhaps should not have traveled, and drugs and alcohol for the long, dark nights of the winter season.

Razak had little need for any of these things, though he appreciated the local petrol station for replenishing his stocks of cigarettes, and the *slaghuis* for providing him with two pounds of biltong. In one hand he held the lit cigarette that sustained him. In the other he hefted binoculars, usually trained on the *bakkie* that sat in the shade at the roadside.

The land here was abandoned, the derelict remains of a petrol station rusting in the distance. The pumps were overgrown with vines, and the concrete platform of the station was riddled with cracks from which weeds sprouted reaching for the sun. A tangle of brush obscured the white *bakkie* from the highway to avoid prying eyes that would make quick work of a vehicle left alone for more than a few hours.

Razak continued watching. Clad in shadow, he allowed no possibility for light glinting off his equipment. He had not moved for the last eight hours, unsure of how quickly his target would come for the horn. Neither day nor night was reason enough to leave.

A car stopped for a moment at the roadside. Out came a man dressed in khakis. He ambled over to a bush that had grown over a steel cage that once secured natural gas canisters. After a moment, he urinated, whistling tunelessly. Returning to the car, he got in and the car moved off.

Hours passed. And hours more.

A coffee tin held a pile of cigarette butts. Razak dropped in one more, still smoldering. Night passed without any visitors.

The sun was rising, lighting the veld with its auburn glow. Razak remained where he was, watching the *bakkie*. He raised and lowered the binoculars, keeping the vehicle in view.

Three crushed paper cartons had joined the pile of cigarette ends.

A royal blue BMW coasted to a stop at the roadside. It sat for a minute, motionless except for the subtle vibration of the exhaust pipe, releasing invisible smoke.

The door opened, and a man exited. He wore white silk, shirt and pants, shimmering even at this distance. Walking over to the *bakkie*, the man kicked at the rear tires, eventually picking something up from the ground. He opened the driver side door, then the rear of the vehicle. The tarp was lifted, the crate underneath examined. A minute passed, and the tarp was released.

He walked back to the BMW and the engine started. Edging forward, the weeds skittered across the underside of the car as it passed. Stopping again, the man opened the boot. He lifted the crate for a moment, then set it down. Retrieving one horn at a time, he delivered each into the boot of the BMW, setting them down with care. The crate was left behind, and the keys were tossed indifferently into the rear of the *bakkie* with a jingle of metal.

The driver door was closed with a bang, and the BMW pulled away, tires spinning gravel across the concrete.

The car pulled away. Joining the black ribbon of tar, it roared down the road past a sign that indicated KOMATIPOORT 20km.

Razak retrieved his phone.

"Orlando. Blue BMW. Ten minutes."

* * *

The cars were lined up along the road, the sun baking the black tar and filling the air with the reek of petroleum and asphalt. Each car idled, adding to the stench. Hour by hour, one car after the next stopped at a small temporary lot, and the people inside trudged into the concrete building holding their passports and cash. After more than an hour, the drivers left the building, returning to their cars, and drove on to the gate to pay the vehicle tax. Border agents examined very few of the cars, looking underneath, in the seats, and in the boot before waving the drivers by. Palm trees on the edge of the lot waved in the wind. The forest edged up to the grey bricks that made up the car park, stopping abruptly at the chain link fence topped with loops of razor wire. Men in dark uniforms and fluorescent yellow vests peered at the cars, selecting some for more intensive investigation.

Orlando was not wearing a yellow vest. Smartly dressed in a shirt and tie, he stood away from the line of vehicles on the South African side of the border. Ignoring the cars waved through the post, he paced back and forth. He had stayed outside nearly the entire day, glancing at the cars moving through, handling pressing matters inside the post with great speed before invariably returning to the car park to watch the traffic.

For the last several minutes however, he stood next to the border post, a statue staring down the approaching road, appearing to see nothing, disregarding even the words of his colleagues.

When he finally walked out onto the lot, the other men took a step back, eyeing one another anxiously. Two of the security guards nodded to one another, and picked up their rifles.

"What is he doing?" The guard ratcheted the bolt back on his AK-47.

"He would not tell me. He does not stare down that road unless he knows something big is coming. Just be ready." His finger was not on the trigger, but resting on the guard.

Orlando strode out into the lot, toward a vehicle edging off the road leading to the post. The BMW was royal blue, glistening chrome standing out from the other cars. The glass was tinted darkly, an impenetrable shield. Edging forward, the car rolled not toward the designated parking spots for passport clearance, but directly to the gates.

Orlando stepped in front of the BMW, which screeched to a halt. The window was lowered, but he did not move.

A head poked out of the window. "Get out of my way!"

The border agent pointed toward the parking spaces where the rest of the people crossing the border parked. He did not say a word.

A hand extended from within the car. Held in its grip was a thick wad of *meticais*.

Orlando's only response was to again gesture toward the parking spaces, face empty of expression.

"Do you know who I am?" The voice barked from within the car.

Orlando looked over his shoulder to see the two guards jogging over. Their fingers were on the triggers now. He returned his glare to the BMW windshield.

Abruptly, the BMW bucked, then reversed, and quickly moved over to the parking lot, sliding across two of the parking spaces and screeching to another halt. Melted rubber joined the smells of the lot.

The door slammed. The driver, dressed in pristine white silk, stalked out toward the border agent, his voice high and insolent.

"Do you know. *Who. I. Am!*"

Orlando's face was a stone edifice. His voice was calm and even. "Step inside, sir."

The driver fumed, seeming overheated despite the flowing white garments, but bit down hard on the words in his mind. As the men with the rifles approached, he took a long, anxious look at the boot of his car. Nattapong Buatoom walked to the building, his feet making scarcely a sound. The boots clomped close behind him as he passed through the door to the concrete building. As his eyes adjusted to the dim light within from flickering fluorescents, he found himself lifted into the air.

The men rushed behind him, carrying their rifles with one hand, and the other wrapped around each arm, and carried him with feet off the ground down a hallway. He had time for exactly three obscenities before the door at the end of the hall was opened with his head.

Tossed onto the concrete floor, he struggled to right himself, dabbing the blood from the corner of his mouth where he struck the hard surface.

The guards took up station at the door, each still holding their rifles at the ready. They said nothing to the man.

"*WHY?*" His voice echoed endlessly.

No response. The room was bare of furniture, no chairs, desk, or even a phone. The single window was barred. The shadows cast by the bars crawled lazily across the floor as hours passed.

As those shadows melted into the dim of the evening, the knob on the door rattled.

Orlando walked through, as calm as the dawn.

"Sir, I will need the keys to search your car."

"No!" He seethed, spitting on the floor.

"Very well." He depressed a button on his radio. "The blue BMW in the lot. Open the boot with the drill."

"Wait!" He fished his keys out in a hurry. "I have the—"

"You had your chance to leave with your car intact. Now you get it in pieces. By the time we are done, you will be able to put it in a sack. *Buatoom.*" He glared at the man, finally betraying a sign of emotion.

Buatoom furrowed his brow. "You are making the wrong enemy today."

"Ah, you will be very glad to know I need neither friends nor enemies." Orlando laughed, his dark face broken by the appearance of perfect white teeth. "I think you meant the magistrate in Maputo? Will he help you this time?"

"You will be out of a job, and I will be free." Buatoom gave a thin smile that resembled a twisted scar. "With the stroke of a pen."

"If you want to be freed, your friends will be needing a shovel." Orlando smiled big again.

The guards strode forward, and took hold of Buatoom. He protested once, and was silenced with the butt of a rifle.

* * *

When he awoke, he tasted dirt. Raising his head, he noticed the smell of damp earth filling his nostrils. Rolling to one side, he found resistance, as though against a wall. Rolling in the other direction found the same. As his vision cleared, he took hold of one of the walls, and got only a handful of clay.

A smattering of voices. The ringing in his ears began to abate.

"Yes, Venter. Thank you for helping arrange this." A phone beeped. Orlando was beaming. "She will be waiting to hear how it went."

Buatoom suddenly remembered the word 'shovel'. He was very much awake now.

Sitting up, a wail began in his throat, silenced with a boot to his chest. The white of his silk was now heavily soiled, stained brown in many places. Thumping back to the dirt, he realized he was looking up at three people standing at the edge of a shallow grave.

"I—I—I have—I have—"

"I have something for you." Orlando grinned. Fishing in the breast pocket of his shirt, he pulled out a green bill emblazoned with a picture of a man, 'REPUBLICA POPULAR DE MOCAMBIQUE' and '1000'. He crumpled this in his hand.

"You gave this to one of my men on the way in. You think all Africans can be bought?" He revealed gleaming white teeth. He tossed the one thousand *meticais* note in Buatoom's face.

"And this, of course." Orlando held up a plastic bag.

"He actually posed for pictures with that ridiculous thing?" One of the border guards asked incredulously.

The bag contained a chrome plated pistol.

"After he murdered my men with it." A voice boomed.

A fourth man, who Buatoom had never seen before, stepped into view and looked down at him. He wore nondescript khakis with the long sleeves rolled up past the elbows. His head was capped with a beret. He wore no insignia, but had a rifle slung over his shoulder.

With the quickness of a cobra, Razak bent down, and gripped the man's soft silk shirt and the throat underneath. Before Buatoom realized what was happening, he was held in the air by two arms, black as ebony up to the sleeves. His face was pulled close to the man wearing the beret.

"Careful, Razak. This one cries easily." Orlando chortled.

The man usually did not speak. He never spoke. Today, however, he felt the need to utter one more word.

"Boss."

***

Awake.

He had been awake for several minutes, having no idea of the time of day in the darkness. He first recognized the gnawing ache in his temple where he was struck with the rifle. He also felt his wrists were bound with zip-ties. And his legs. He scissored his legs back and forth, unable to move much as he bounced in this tiny container.

It was the boot of a car. There was a sliver of light entering through a crack opened by rust. His head had struck an object, and by the smell he could tell it was a spare tire. He hammered on the inside of the car, striking the quarter panel.

The car abruptly slowed and stopped. Stomping of boots. The jingle of keys and his world was suddenly flooded with light.

Rope was wound around him, rendering him completely immobile, and duct tape sealed his mouth. The lid of the boot slammed shut.

The car drove on for hours.

* * *

"Your friends." Razak moved a sheet of paper in front of the man, and laid a pen before him.

Buatoom glared at his tormentor.

"Vietnam. Thailand. Importers." The ranger held his phone. "All of them."

"When do I see the magistrate?"

"When you fill that paper."

"I will be free by morning."

The ranger nodded. A shrug of his broad shoulders, and he continued to stare.

He shook his head, chuckling to himself. "You people never learn. You go through all this trouble." The pen scratched on the paper. Names and numbers took shape. "Instead of taking the money like sensible people, you beat up businessmen like me." Scratch, scratch, scratch.

Razak said nothing.

"You were hoping for more money?"

No response.

"All you will get is a call from the magistrate. A poaching charge is a small fee for someone like me." Buatoom glared at him. "You do not speak much. Probably do not think much, either." His Portuguese was broken but easy to understand. "A nation of idiots." He continued writing in the quiet, until the paper had a small collection of names and numbers.

He sat back, and flipped the pen onto the table.

The ranger walked around, and glanced at the paper. Picking up the pen, he crossed several numbers out.

"These are not real."

The paper was crumpled into a ball and left on the table. Razak left the room, locking the door.

When he returned the next day, he opened the door to the cell of concrete, and found Buatoom getting to his feet. He squinted at the light, and rushed toward Razak, hands outstretched, mouth open emitting the beginnings of a shout.

The shout abruptly cut off as Razak struck him in the abdomen with a fist, gripped him by the throat, and threw him to the stone floor.

As the prisoner retched, Razak left again, locking the door.

The following day, the cell was unlocked, and Buatoom picked himself off the floor and sat at the table. Razak placed a clean sheet of paper before him with a pen.

The poacher began writing, the ink forming a phone number.

"More." Razak's voice was devoid of inflection or emotion.

Buatoom glared at him as though the ranger were an object.

"A week, then." Razak met his glare, and motioned to get up to leave.

Buatoom resumed writing, and did not stop until the paper was filled.

The ranger nodded to another person. Buatoom had thought they were alone. The other man was clad in khakis and a beret, same as the silent ranger. He took the paper and walked away, typing numbers into his phone.

The other ranger listened to the ringing, and when a voice picked up on the other end and spoke in Vietnamese, he hung up quickly.

"Now give me a phone." Buatoom slurred.

The silent man ignored him, while the other ranger tried more of the phone numbers. Each time, a voice answered, each with a different language. Chinese, Japanese, Thai, French. The last was English. Each time he hung up quickly.

He gave a nod.

Two men emerged from the shadows and held Buatoom's head down on the table. His wrists and ankles were expertly bound with zip ties again. A gag was bound around his head.

Footsteps, hard soles of dress shoes echoing off the concrete walls. A figure stopped before the bound man. He was wearing a suit, pressed and tailored with an immaculate fit. Despite the dark, he wore wraparound sunglasses. He removed this, revealing eyes that seemed to be dancing.

"Hello, Buatoom." His grin pulled wide. "You remember me."

Buatoom mouthed something into his gag, his eyes widening.

"Yes, I thought so." He extended a hand. "Zhou Yu."

Buatoom raged into the cloth that filled his mouth.

"Your manners have not changed." Yu's hand returned to his side. "Not to worry, I will not move to extradite you to China. You will be comfortable here."

The prisoner's glare burned holes in his captors.

"And I thank you for giving me your connections." Yu's smile grew bigger. "And the connections they will lead me to."

Yu chuckled to himself and walked off, the click of his dress shoes reverberating off the walls.

A ranger stepped in front of the poacher, arms folded together.

"And now you go to your cell, Mister Buatoom."

He screamed against the gag, a nonsensical rant into nothing.

"Your trial will be in a few months. Maybe six. And your usual magistrate will not help you. This is not a matter of poaching, though the horns you bought illegally facilitated your arrest."

Buatoom had a red eye, a vessel burst from the screaming.

"You see, this is a murder charge you face. Two of them. My friends, working in Gorongosa last year." He lifted the plastic bag containing the chrome pistol. "I thank you most humbly for your cooperation."

Buatoom was dragged from the room, and every moment was spent shouting into the cloth gag. The metal door slammed shut behind him.

Razak did not speak, enjoying the silence for a moment. He pulled out his own phone and dialed. A clipped voice picked up the other end.

"Sonja Venter."

"We have him."

"The families of those men will be pleased." She sounded relieved.

Razak grunted his agreement.

"I wish Marais were around to have heard the news."

Razak thought for a moment. "He made his choice."

"I doubt he would have made a different one, even if he knew what would happen. He did not think things could change."

"Or that people change."

"*Ja.*" She sighed into the phone. "I am glad to be working with you, Razak."

He hung up, and walked from the concrete cell, down the spartan hallway. Opening the door at the end of the hall, he flooded it with light, as the golden dawn greeted him. Taking a deep breath, he washed away the scent of prison grime, concrete dust, and poacher from his nostrils, and enjoyed the waft of nearby fruit trees grown near the border post. Winds stirred the broad leaves of palm trees that grew in a stripe further from the highway.

He straightened his beret again before making his way to the battered Toyota. Pulling away from the parking area of the post, he returned to the highway, settling in for the long road to Gorongosa.

Back to work.

Chapter 92

As the winter season wore into September, the drought had continued. In the rest of the Lowveld, rivers were reduced to trickles, and the reservoirs of the great city of Johannesburg to the south were reduced to mud. Grass fields were brown, the foliage of poor quality. A secretary bird stepped through the dried grasses with a long striding gait. The grey plumage of its breast and neck transitioned to grey and black of wings, now folded up as it peered into the grass. Stopping for a moment, its head lowered slightly. A clawed foot stomped the ground, and stomped again. A brown house snake, disturbed by the secretary bird, twitched and began to slither away from the threat. Another stomp crushed the snake, and the still-writhing prey was retrieved with a sharp beak. There was no shortage of food for the meter and a half tall bird, as the fields were still full of rodents and snakes.

The larger animals such as antelope were having a terrible time of it. A single klipspringer lay by the side of the road, tongue protruding, and ribs standing out. There were no wounds from bullet, tooth, or fang on the animal, only the lingering signs of starvation. Flies buzzed over its eyes and mouth. Flies were doing very well.

Giraffe-thorn acacia trees shaded the dead body, the branches swaying lightly with the breeze. The white thorns rattled as they scraped over one another with the movement. The stalwart trees were hundreds of years old, and had seen arid seasons many times, weathering this and other insults.

Along dirt roads leading away from the tar highways that linked the farms, a group of wild dogs trotted. Each side of the road was lined with fences, barbed wire, razor wire, with some sections of electrified barriers.

"The pups have taken well to the hunt." Koorsboom lapped the muzzle of his mate as they padded along a track.

"If only the hunts were not so hostile." Olienhout shook her head. "The change of the season since we found ourselves in this land has been harsh." She slowed. "Steady on, Koorsboom." She rasped.

"I smell it as well." His snout wrinkled. "Death on a great scale lies ahead."

The small hunting party detoured through a flaw in the fence. The wires were wrenched aside, with tufts of fur snagged on some of the bare ends. A buttonquail hopped away and took flight at their approach. A brown feather seesawed through the air to the ground.

"Growing stronger." Koorsboom muttered. "Be on your guard, Wilde-vlier, Leadwort."

Each wolf gave a nod.

Pushing their way through a stand of seringa trees, they encountered a wall of carrion flies. The buzzing was incessant and disorienting. Koorsboom shut his eyes and backed under the trees, and the rest of the pack did the same.

The flies were thick as smoke from a tire fire. Through this they could make out two hyenas gnawing on the remains of an impala before a giant mound of rocks. Remarkably, there was no fight amongst the hyena, each working to open their own carcasses. A slight breeze disturbed the insects, and they roiled along the air currents.

"Impossible." Koorsboom gasped.

As the cloud of flies shifted and their sight adjusted, they realized the massive mound was not rock. Bodies of antelope were piled high, in an advanced state of decomposition. Some were unrecognizable, while others appeared fresher. The newer corpses appeared wasted, little more than bones held in by hide.

"This was the work of humans." Olienhout whispered, careful to avoid startling the spotted hyenas working before them. "Although I suspect these animals were dying already."

Koorsboom took more steps back. "The Sickness?"

"Or starvation. The drought has been taking its toll on the antelope we have seen on these farms. The dead have been everywhere." Olienhout thought to herself for a moment. "With the exception of lands with waterholes."

"Let us be away from this place." The wolves withdrew, glad to leave behind the oppressive flies.

Down the road they went, scenting on the wind the promise of prey. Another flaw in a fence allowed them to slip through with ease.

Koorsboom took the lead, with one of their pups watching over his shoulder. Loping over the vast expanse of savanna, they weaved between acacia trees and wild seringa.

"There, my son. You see the herd?" They stood at the crest of a hill. This was overlooking a great pond, somehow retaining water in this awful drought.

"Yes, father."

"And what do you discern?"

"Impala." The young wolf scanned the field below them.

"There is more." Koorsboom took a step back.

"A smaller antelope." He cocked his head to the side. "More stocky and muscular than the lithe form one would expect."

"That is a dog."

"Do we hunt it?"

"We avoid it." He turned back and rejoined the rest of the hunting party, his son close behind. "More of those rather large dogs are on this farm."

"Are they fawn in color as well?" Olienhout wondered.

"Yes. Same as the others."

"Every farm we have probed has had them in force. They have all been fair in coloration. Perhaps this is a trait of their species."

"In any case, there will be no hunting here. They will come straight after us. They have done so every time we have approached them this season."

"Back to one of the tangled wild places, then."

The wolves slipped back through the fence and sprinted down the dirt road. After a few kilometers, the thrum of an engine reached their ears.

"Take cover, all of you." Olienhout ruff-barked her alarm.

The pack crouched as best they could beside the nearest fence, but this would not obscure them. As the *bakkie* rumbled toward them, it slowed, and stopped.

"Prepare to bolt on my mark." Her ears folded back, head down.

The thunder did not come, and there was no shouting from the people on the vehicle. They pointed devices in their direction, and after some clicking sounds, they restarted the engine and continued on their way.

"We were fortunate." Koorsboom mused, as they resumed their pace along the dirt road.

"I wonder about that." Olienhout lapped his muzzle as they walked. "There was no scent of anger from them. Apart from those dogs all the farms seem to have, we have seen none of the enmity to which we have become accustomed."

"Indeed. I am not quick to trust these creatures, but we have not detected a scent of hostility from humans since we awakened at that den." Koorsboom sniffed his mate, and the light but durable tracking collar she now wore. The tough leather was studded with steel bolts, designed to catch and cut snare wire should the bearer be caught in such a trap.

"We are back to hunting one of those small wild-like territories." Olienhout had found multiple small properties, all heavily fenced and filled with antelope.

"Strange, is it not?"

"What is strange?"

"When we hunted in the past, we lived in terror of the human thunder." Koorsboom mused. "Now, when we kill, the humans surround us and seem at leisure." He laughed. "What a bizarre turn for our world." The small private game parks of the region became a regular part of their patrols, and the humans inexplicably followed them whenever they visited.

Down another dirt road the pack loped, eventually moving away from the traffic and into green savanna. No fences were present here, the impala wandering freely, but reluctant to stray from the vibrant bushveld.

The wolves ambled past a twisted column of wood, resembling a titanic knotted rope standing on end. The gnarled pale tree appeared to have dozens of small trunks rather than a single large one, and all were wrapped over a Knob-thorn acacia tree. The Strangler fig had put down a multitude of roots into the soil, and spreading broad green leaves along its trunk and branches. The crown had already overtaken the acacia tree, which had only managed a few small leaves of its own. Within a few years, the acacia would die, and the strangler fig would consume the rotting wood until after a few centuries only a hollow center would remain. Koorsboom sniffed the roots, and studied where the trunk of the dying tree was subsumed under the fig.

"I worry that one day the dogs will appear here."

"We endure the trials as they come, Koorsboom." Olienhout took the lead, and they tore through the thick savanna. Wild seringa and acacia trees blended with wild pear and olive, opening to vast carpets of grass. Here the fields were still green, the trees blocking desiccating winds and retaining the rains of the previous summer.

The hunters joined with the rest of the pups where they were hidden, and together raced away to the open veld.

On their way to the nearest impala herd, they passed an area that was drier than the rest of the property. There they found the strange human who seemed to live here, wearing dirt-stained khaki shorts and cotton shirt, scraggly salt and pepper beard, and dirt-streaked cap. This time he was with another man, with dark skin and khaki pants. They were both armed with pickaxes, and they sank the tools into the rock-hard ground. As the wolves passed, the light-skinned man raised his cap in greeting and watched them. The dark-skinned man pointed and laughed, hefting the axe on his shoulder.

Holes half a meter deep trailed behind them, hundreds of them close together in an area the size of a rugby pitch. Each of these contained a ball of manure. Many of the holes had dirt scooped over the top of the manure, sealing in the moisture.

Over the last three months since Koorsboom and Olienhout found themselves in this place, they had seen these being dug seemingly everywhere. One week a dense pattern of these holes appeared, and the next they were all filled in. Du Plessis had excavated these holes throughout his property over the years. Termites were drawn to the manure, and proceeded to dig a deep network of tunnels around and beneath them. The deluge of rains would sink into the spongy soil rather than run off into flooded rivers. As a result, his land was thick with brush and tree, and the grass green and rich.

"I can scent the impala ahead—they are close!" Leadwort sprinted forth, and the rest of the pack were on his tail.

Du Plessis watched until they were out of sight, laughing to himself.

"You keep on those impala, you *bliksems.*" He raised the pickaxe and hacked again at the dirt. "Keep them moving about. There is work to do."

"You are the first farmer I have known who did not shoot them on sight." The other man attacked the ground with his pickaxe. "Now there are several. Some farmers, though, still think you are a lunatic."

"A lunatic with a beautiful property. I am telling you, Zai farming is ingenious. This is being used to fight the Sahara Desert, you know." He hacked another hunk of concrete-like earth free from the hole beneath him. "They do this in Burkina Faso. Want to learn how to fix Africa? Ask an African."

"Now you only need time."

"And some elephants." He removed his cap and wiped his brow. "I need some *ellies* to knock down some of these trees. Over time, the trees will overtake the grasses, and then where will my antelope be?"

"They would wreck a lot of your acacia trees."

"*Ag* man, they do land management better than we do. They like grass, so they prune the trees. *Ellies* farm grass, you know."

"Or the grasses farm the *ellies.*" The other man dislodged a rock in his hole.

"A philosopher, eh?" He laughed and continued hacking away.

The impala herd just beyond the men milled with wildebeest and cape buffalo, munching on the grass. When the Painted wolf pack appeared, they bolted. Sledgehammer hooves upon hard earth broke up the ground, leaving behind loose dirt. As the antelope departed, their droppings decomposed on the soil and seeped into the ground carrying seed and nutrient.

The savanna flourished, and the new wild continued the slow process of healing.

Chapter 93

MOZAMBIQUE

Ours is the veld.

Under the acacia tree there was a flurry of activity with the dawn. Seven pups bounded about with the adults, golden coloration flushing into the black and white coat of their birth. Aalwyn watched them with fascination.

"It is a wonder how much they have grown in my absence." Aalwyn mused.

"Bold and mischievous, the lot of them." Kurkbos lapped her muzzle. "But no use for hunting. That much is certain."

"It is early for them to have acquired those skills, let alone the stamina required of a hunt." She watched them scurry around and box on hind legs with the yearlings from Essenhout's pack. One gathered up a leftover impala hoof from a previous hunt. Small hazel eyes flitted in the pup's direction as he paraded it before the others. Suddenly he was mobbed by several squeaking forms, a tumble of black and white fur, and a victor emerged with the hoof.

"They have been surprising, I must say." Kurkbos admired them. "Not the vanguard of the attack, but quite keen." He nudged her. "They need you to teach them."

Rukato loped on the periphery of this rally, not quite taking part.

547

Blackthorn harried him, drawing the older wolf back into the fray.

"I am glad to see you with us, Rukato." Aalwyn loped beside him.

He parted his jaws, panting with the activity. His smile extended up the side of his head, the grisly bullet graze never having healed properly. He turned his head to peer into the distance.

"So many appetites." She mused quietly.

"Indeed." Kurkbos studied her expression.

"And no real fighters."

"You are casting your gaze to the north." He watched Rukato wander off. "And I am not sure that one will stand and fight if the need is dire. Challenge the *Selous* and we will be facing a massacre."

"First comes the hunt." She shook herself free of the night's chill. "One challenge at a time."

* * *

Lappet-faced vultures were first to descend on the waterbuck kill. Their broad wings swept them high over the bushveld, their piercing vision spanning many kilometers. The first landed with a thump on the moist soil next to the river.

"Time is running short." Kurkbos looked up to see more circling.

"Pull it apart—make haste." Aalwyn seized one of the limbs, Blackthorn another, and the yearlings moved in to dismember the carcass. The pups dove into the abdominal cavity and ripped away at the pelvic muscles and deep organs. Aalwyn bolted down all she could carry until something else caught her eye.

Standing apart from the waterbuck, she peered across the open veld to the palm trees that lined the river further away.

A figure was watching them. The black, white, and gold coloration, bullet snout and dish-like ears left no doubt.

"We run."

"There is so much more meat to take—" Blackthorn whined.

"We *RUN!*"

The pack distanced itself from the corpse, now in pieces. Lappet-faced vultures were joined by White-backed vultures, and they swarmed over the remains.

Aalwyn beckoned to the pack. She looked again to the palm trees.

The wolf was gone.

"We must create distance between us and the kill." Her eyes were fixed on the line of trees. "And the pups are slow indeed."

Returning to the shallow place in the river where they crossed, the *Dwalen* made their way back to the other side of the Pungwe river.

"The *Selous* are wise to these forays, it would seem." Aalwyn muttered, casting one more glance to the lush savanna across the waterway.

** * **

The pack rested on the verge of a small village as dusk took the savanna. There was little activity from the humans who seemed at a loss for what to do after a failed harvest. Even their domesticated dogs were silent.

"This cannot go on." Kurkbos spoke to no one in particular. "We will stray into *Selous* territory once too often."

Aalwyn lay in the shade of a feverberry tree, fuming as she stared northward. She had spoken little since they crossed the river.

"When is the patrol to return?" One of the yearlings twittered.

"Blackthorn is coming just now." Kurkbos answered.

Blackthorn padded toward the rest of the *Dwalen*, resting under a collection of palm and fig trees.

"We have not seen any movement from the *Selous* wolves." The young wild dog was alone.

"Blackthorn." Aalwyn ruff-barked, setting the rest of the pack on edge. "Where is Rukato? Did you not leave here together?"

The yearling sat and panted. "He wanted to continue the patrol." Scratching behind an ear, he dislodged a tick. "He assured me there was no need to wait for him."

They were quiet for some time as the wolves thought upon this loss.

"And so we recede." Aalwyn slumped to the ground, laying her head on her forepaws.

Kurkbos raised his head. "What do you mean, love?"

"Recede into the brush, fading one wolf at a time." Her eyes seemed to blacken in the approaching twilight, as the sun descended behind the mountains of the west. "A muddy bank, so slippery. Eroding with time into the rushing waters."

"Are we the mud in this story?" Blackthorn asked.

Aalwyn lapped the yearling's muzzle, but quickly returned to glowering at the veld before her.

"There is nothing for it." Kurkbos rested his head again. "Wolf packs under pressure fall apart over time. They come." He exhaled, blowing a puff of dust from the ground under his snout. "They go."

"*Gatvol.*" Aalwyn rumbled as a lip curled upward, revealing a glint of fang.

Kurkbos became aware of a rising growl from her, subtle at first.

"The vultures are at work on us."

Kurkbos looked to the dark blue sky, seeing nothing more than a wisp of cloud.

"Steadily. Working. Waiting." She harrumphed, a strange sound for a wolf to make. "Ever watchful. And so we wait in kind." Aalwyn raised her head, and looked Kurkbos in the eye.

He recoiled slightly. Her eyes had gone entirely black. Canting his head to the side, he thought perhaps it was an illusion of the approaching night.

"And for what?" Her voice rumbled. "For what. While we rest, our decay grows stronger." The growl continued rising. "And that corruption is coming for them as well, they will not be saved." Aalwyn looked to the north, in the direction of the river and the wild beyond. "Not be saved."

"What are you on about?" Kurkbos stared at her.

"We are in the teeth now." She bared her fangs for a moment, and breathed heavily.

"Aalwyn?"

She did not answer him, staring at nothing. Her voice dropped into half-murmured growls and threats, words, thoughts.

We are in the teeth.

These sounds melted into the coming noise of darkness.

Chapter 94

The morning rally was subdued, with a few of the yearlings inquiring after the disappearance of Rukato.

"He is no longer with us." Aalwyn informed them coldly. "We move up the river, and strike across later this day."

The column of Painted wolves bounded in the rich green grass bordering the river, moving further away as they traversed another small village of subsistence farms, mud and thatch huts, cattle and maize fields. Once they had left the dwellings behind, they crossed the great river where it slowed, silted, and developed sand banks that could be crossed in safety. The cool waters burbled as they left their clawed prints in the sand and reached the opposite grassy embankment.

On they loped, moving in haste, threading through the thornbrush that grew sparser as they left the river behind. Wending their way through a tangle of acacia trees, they rushed past an elephant herd. The matriarch barely took notice as she laid her trunk vertically along the tree, and rested her head against the hard wood that was between the mighty tusks. With a sudden heave, the towering acacia tree toppled, ripping up a cloud of dust as the root system saw the light. She backed away from the tree before feeding on the rich leaves now brought within reach, trumpeting at the pack that coursed past her. Deeming them no threat, the matriarch coaxed her son to take his share of the greenery.

The alpha wolf kept to herself, padding steadily, hazel eyes upon the distant trees and on the ground before her, allowing no details to escape her notice. All the while, she muttered to herself.

Gatvol.

Hyenas, all of us.

In the teeth.

Kurkbos sidled closer, unsure what to make of her subdued ranting.

"We are heading further north, I see." He watched his mate closely. Her murmuring paused for her answer.

"Yes."

"You are quite sure of this, Aalwyn?" Kurkbos attempted to lap her muzzle, but she did not seem to notice. "This territory where we are headed has been held by lions, no mistake."

"Trust in me." Aalwyn gave him an icy glare, and without thought he dipped his head lower in deference.

"You have it always." His breathing was rapid, and his hazel eyes darted about. He looked behind him toward the distant Pungwe river, which they had crossed this morning. The golden sun was still rising, the rays alighting on silvery webs still coated with dew, wavering from grass stalks across the field.

They raced into the veld, followed closely by Blackthorn and two other yearlings. Their lithe forms bounded through the tall grass, tireless and graceful. Before them, a herd of impala grazed upon the nile grass.

She twittered orders for one of the yearlings to mind the pups.

As the wolves closed in, Blackthorn noted a line of lion prints in the soil. They were everywhere.

Aalwyn caught his alarmed glance.

"Were you hoping to live long as the acacia?" She took the lead, and drove straight into the grazing impala.

A cough, followed by another, and the impala herd bolted when they sighted the assault.

"Follow me!" She twittered her command, and the Painted wolves of the *Dwalen* stayed close. "Kurkbos—take the point!" She ruff-barked, and her mate raced closer to the clump of impala.

She fell back, and took up station next to Blackthorn.

"Mother—I have seen only their prints." He panted lightly, growing more accustomed to the pace of the hunt.

"They shall find us before long with this commotion." Aalwyn kept her eyes on the periphery, in the tall grass, the edge of brush.

After a kilometer of the coursing, all but one of the impala had escaped to the sides, and Kurkbos concentrated on an old impala male. He and another yearling traded places to wear it down.

"Mark!" Blackthorn ruff-barked to his mother.

"I see her." Aalwyn twittered, as she spotted a lioness duck down into the grass, the swishing tail making an appearance once, then twice as the powerful cat followed their hunt.

"Come forth with me, hunter." Aalwyn raced to the front of the column, twittering warnings to the others.

"Lions approach—do not fall behind!"

One of the yearlings kept the pups together, and away from the danger of the hunt.

Kurkbos leapt nimbly over a squat Knob-thorn shrub, and lightly upon the ground he landed. His lean frame closed in on the impala, now beginning to stumble.

"Allow it to run a while more." Aalwyn was at his side. "We cannot kill it too soon."

He nodded. The wolves closed around the impala like a horseshoe, and after another kilometer finally brought it down.

Hoofed legs kicked as the heavy body was pulled to the ground, kicked once more, and stopped as a gush of blood spread beneath the body.

"Feast quickly." Aalwyn ripped away muscle from the hip, and the others gorged themselves on the blood and exposed muscle. She watched the veld from where they came.

"Nothing." Kurkbos looked over her shoulder.

"The lions shall be here. Listen for my signal." She bounded off, and began to retrace their path, back the way they had come.

Soon she stopped in the midst of a large grass field. She could smell the wolf scent their paws had left as they chased their prey. A breeze picked up, blowing in her face.

There it is.

The waft of lion reached her sensitive nose, and again with another light gust. Distantly, a swish of tail. She padded closer, and could see another lioness moving towards her. Powerful shoulders worked above the grass, her pace steady as a machine. The yellowed eyes of the lioness were upon her. Lips pulled back, muzzle wrinkled, their conical fangs were flashed.

Aalwyn glanced to her sides, and spotted a second lion closing in.

"You are not so cunning, lion."

Aalwyn bolted back toward the kill. Leaving the grass field, she crossed a barrier of Knob-thorn and sweet thorn acacia, and waited.

Several minutes passed.

A heavy head edged out of the brush, glancing about. Fore shoulders bulging with muscle emerged, sensitive nose raised to sniff the air. Another lioness followed close behind. And a third. They continued sniffing the air, looking toward the horizon. They could not find her where she watched downwind.

Tails twitched, the black tuft at the ends making wide arcs. The three lionesses began to spread out to search for her.

Aalwyn trotted from cover, and twittered in their direction.

Yellow eyes locked onto her. And the powerful bodies lunged toward her.

Aalwyn ran off, but took them away from the kill, leading the lionesses into another dense thicket of sour grass. Again, they looked for her, unable to see far in the dense sedge.

She called out, and continued calling until they zeroed in on her position. This time, their approach was less hurried, and seemed less aggressive.

Aalwyn bounded off, more than once turning to twitter in their direction. She made no further effort to hide. One of the lionesses appeared to lose interest, looking elsewhere. Tails no longer flicked rapidly from side to side. Their pace was not as quick, their fangs no longer on display.

Aalwyn padded closer, provoking one, then another lioness. She led them on with care, returning to the kill.

She padded into the field where the carcass was located, and found Kurkbos and Blackthorn standing well away from the impala. Though the pack was well able to strip it entirely down to bone, half the meat still remained.

Aalwyn looked back once more, and twittered again to the lionesses. They no longer focused on her, instead drawn to the meat before them.

As the lioness closed in, she snarled at a vulture that stood close to the kill, and it took flight with broad wings to escape. The other two lionesses dashed to the dead antelope. Once there, they milled about next to it, seeming to be at leisure. They looked about, shook their fur free of burrs and thorns acquired in the chase, and eventually settled down next to the carcass. They did not move to eat.

Aalwyn loped to where Kurkbos watched, further from the kill.

"Are the pups away?"

"Far away." He never took his eyes from the lionesses, his heavy breathing not the result of fatigue.

"Come closer with me."

He looked at her as if she suggested mating with them, but thought better of questioning her motives.

The two wolves bounded toward the carcass, and she twittered again in the lions' direction. One stood, seeming to hesitate. Aalwyn did not flee, instead turning to box Kurkbos. Her forepaws batted his head, and he looked from her, to the lionesses, and back.

"What are you doing?"

"Whatever I choose." Aalwyn smiled, revealing her fangs. She glanced at the lionesses, noticing the one that had stood and considered chasing her had laid back down. She turned to ignore them.

The lions began to gnaw on the exposed rib cage, tearing away succulent meat.

"Why are they not chasing us?"

"My guess was correct." She loped away, with no haste whatsoever. "It was important that they did not chase us off. We left of our own volition."

"And what was your theory?" Kurkbos lapped her muzzle as she smiled to herself.

"They would focus on feeding." She twittered happily. "And know that I led them to it."

* * *

Dark eyes pierced the savanna, in search of beetles or grasshoppers on which to feed. Perched on a thorned branch, the Lilac-breasted roller gripped the wood with taloned feet. The rich lilac color of its breast, underparts of greenish blue, with rump and outer flight feathers of violet was a striking sight.

Underneath the roller rested the *Dwalen* pack, with several snoring noises from the pups. Aalwyn rested in the early evening light. She continued muttering to herself, the occasional growl rising from within her. Kurkbos joined her side, and she stopped her quiet raving.

"I do wonder what that lion hunt was meant to prove." Kurkbos settled down on his belly.

"That is what I intend to explore." She said cryptically. "What I know for certain is there is no future without adaptation."

"We may be able to gather food from villages. The people may not always venture out." Kurkbos peered at grasses beyond their clearing.

"When they venture, they do so with thunder in their hands." Aalwyn sounded far away.

"See what the day shall bring." Kurkbos gave a smile. "There are other waterholes south of the river. Usually the animals kept by the humans frequent them, but perhaps..." He sighed.

"Your optimism is not shared by me."

"There are times when that is all a pack survives upon."

She watched the others, asleep on open ground. The pups, the yearlings, all huddled together in a few separate heaps.

"How ever did you bring them this far, Kurkbos?" She resisted the urge to wake one of the pups. "The hunting has been poor."

"Indeed it has. When desperate, we have hunted across that river, where all of our substantial kills have occurred. On this side?" He shook his head. "There have been nights where the young ones feasted only on their dreams. Otherwise, we have survived on scrub hares, the odd duiker or impala, and the dead."

She glanced at him.

He nodded. "Hyenas do as they must. As have we." Raking the dirt with a claw, he grunted. "The humans throw out meat that is more than serviceable. The villages around us have kept us alive. As have the corrupted remains of the southernmost *Selous* hunts."

Aalwyn thought about that.

"Perhaps with the passing of the seasons, our pups will survive long enough to be able to fight for territory. Then we can strike inward across the great river." Kurkbos nudged her.

"Time is against us. The humans could destroy us all with little warning. Their thunder, diseases of their animals, starvation. And the *Selous* will only grow stronger." She sighed. "We are in the teeth."

Kurkbos did not speak for a while, nor did Aalwyn. They watched as the Lilac-breasted roller took flight.

"You are leaving again." Kurkbos spoke in a flat tone.

"Yes." She did not take her gaze from the distant savanna to the north.

"Will I see you again?"

"Fangs sharper than mine shall answer that."

He moved closer to her, brushing against her fur, the sensation electric to him.

"I shall listen for your whispers with the waving of grass." He ran his muzzle along her head. "And wait for your return, even until the rivers flow back to the mountain."

"I will not return here." Aalwyn turned to look at him, and he saw the black glare had returned to her eyes. Her jaws parted, a streamer of drool pattering to the ground. Her teeth were unsheathed knives at the ready.

Kurkbos wondered for a moment if he would be attacked.

"Make your way north. I shall rejoin you." Her voice hissed. "I am *gatvol* of this slow death." She stood abruptly.

Kurkbos folded back his ears. "We fear to tread their ground."

Aalwyn looked over his shoulder. The rest of the *Dwalen* had aroused, and all the yearlings and pups had gathered to listen.

"Very well. Fear, if it grants you strength. Anger, if it drives you. For we cross that river, never to return, and take command of our hunting grounds."

One of the younger pups whined, and was silenced by Blackthorn, and he gnawed playfully on their snouts. Every wolf gave her their attention.

"By my side are wolves long dead. My mother and father, and theirs before them. A mighty army we shall be. Those who will not cross the river are not wolves, but their prey." Aalwyn returned their gaze, and as she watched, young and old alike seemed to grow taller, heads held higher.

"Should my negotiation with the void go well, my tracks shall lead to the north."

"We shall be there." Kurkbos growled.

Aalwyn gave a smile, the warmth returning to her eyes for a moment before turning black again.

"If the veld demands blood, then I shall drown it."

Chapter 95

Traces of animals, some long since passed, lingered upon the ground. As night approached, the sensitive nose sniffed the grass tussock. Chemical spoor was intentionally placed, such as the two markers of dark, then white paste left by brown hyena several weeks ago on high stalks of grass. This had faded, almost beyond recognition. Fecal matter left behind by jackals had decomposed, but left a lingering hint on the topsoil. Tracks of eland were pounded into the dirt. The slender snout breathed deeply, knowing the heavy antelope was far beyond the elderly wolf's abilities.

"I could not hope to fell this one." Laeveldvy wondered whether any of his kind had taken an eland. His mother had uttered stories of great packs of wolves, dozens strong, dragging down prey of virtually any size.

"Perhaps you lack ambition, old one."

The voice caused him to jump, spin about, and face his adversary. The enemy he faced was familiar.

"I know you. From not long hence." He folded his ears back, his jaws parted.

"You need not worry. I am not here to kill you." Aalwyn purred, her twitter slow and calming. "I am on the hunt for a greater prize." She loped off into the brush.

Laeveldvy realized with horror that she was on his own trail, leading back to where the *Selous* was resting for the night.

He tore after her through the brush, loping as fast as his aged legs could carry him. Throbbing joints crackled and strained. Even so, he could only just equal her strides, and then only on open ground. Aalwyn leapt over thornbrush in a tall arc, picking up the trail on the other side with ease and leaving him behind.

His aching legs cursed him for every kilometer of the return. Weaver birds scattered as he clawed his way through a sickle bush to gain ground, and impala bolted at his sight as he sprinted past.

When he loped into a clearing, he faced a hulking wolf that snarled at his approach.

"How kind of you, Laeveldvy." Ratel ruff-barked, a heart-stopping sound. "You have invited an enemy to us." His fangs sparkled in the twilight.

"I did not—"

A swift bite silenced the wolf, and sent him running with blood trickling down his haunch.

"Precisely." Ratel growled. "You simply did... not." He turned to face Aalwyn. A single hazel eye regarded her balefully. The other, blinded and milky white, stared through her.

She stood in an open area of grass, surrounded by acacia and the small canopies of wild custard apple trees. Her face was upturned to the moon, black of nose and muzzle to the eyes, yielding to gold up to the base of her rounded ears. One of her ears was partially torn and healed from her last encounter with the *Selous*. A gash on her shoulder had long since scarred over, as had several bites to her sides. The ruff of her neck fluttered in the breeze. She seemed at ease, even as the rest of the *Selous* pack closed around her. The ring shrank in size as more than a dozen adult wolves stepped slowly inward, the ring gradually working into a dot.

"And so you return." The rattling growl startled the rest of the pack, as Varkoor emerged from the sedge. "Your failure on the river has become your legacy." She walked slowly around Aalwyn. Her hazel eyes were tinged with red. "Why have you brought the song of your dying breaths to my young?"

Aalwyn seemed to ignore her, only making eye contact furtively. Her hazel eyes danced, alighting on one wolf, then another, and on the varied acacia trees around them.

"How fare the hyenas in your vantage?" Aalwyn chirped.

"I keep them destitute, through meat denied." Varkoor continued circling her. "An absurd inquiry from a—"

"They are greater than our kind, Varkoor." Aalwyn locked eyes with her. "You know hyenas are our betters."

"That filth knows wolf-kind is far greater." Varkoor snarled, her muscles roiling beneath her gold, black, and white coat. "We range across the veld, from mountain to valley. The land is under our claw. We kill as we wish, in ways no other killer could equal." The *Selous* matriarch chuckled with a twitter. "The hyena are welcome only to what we reject." She snorted her contempt. "If that is what you regard as greatness, then I truly understand why your pack is forsaken."

"Hyena eat the dead, and plague the living." Aalwyn spoke as though she had not heard a word. Her eyes met each of the wolves of the *Selous*. "They challenge your kills, and take when they will. I know it is not only lions that have driven you south. The hyenas have driven you as much, if not more. And they fight amongst themselves like rats over the leavings of better hunters." She looked into the trees again, following the path of a kestrel. "Nonetheless, they thrive. They adapt, and so they thrive, whilst our numbers dwindle in the wild." She stepped toward Varkoor.

The ring of wolves closed within striking distance.

"These humans." Aalwyn continued, as though unaware of the others, ignoring the hot breath on her fur. "I have learned much of their kind, so very much." She stepped slowly forward, starting to make a circle slowly around Varkoor. "Strange and wondrous, beyond what I thought were random and petty cruelties. They destroy, they kill, they raze to the ground what was beautiful. And they control the land entire."

"What does it matter—"

"Fences. Walls." Aalwyn interrupted, ignoring the larger alpha female. "The strange beasts they ride. And when they feed, their teeth are nowhere near the throat of another human."

"Have you the Sickness?" As Varkoor uttered this, the rest of the pack took a few steps back. "If so, disperse with—"

"And do they feed." Aalwyn mused. "Hunting is no concern. The thunder strikes down from afar, and the humans take what they please."

"You neither stumble nor salivate. Yet you show every sign of madness, confronting us here." The alpha growled.

"They have neither fang nor claw, and run with the grace of a boulder. Yet they command the world, from mountain high to the endless waters. *They adapt, and so they thrive.*" Aalwyn's eyes were wide, wild seemingly with delirium. "With a clasp of their paws, an accord is struck, and thus fences erupt from the earth and cover the horizon." Aalwyn stared ahead, at nothing, stalking in a circle around Varkoor. "That accord... is their claw and fang."

"You weary me with your diseased ramblings." Varkoor shook her head.

A subordinate female bolted in and nipped at Aalwyn's hip. She drew blood and retreated.

Aalwyn disregarded the wolf and the wound completely. "They may yet decimate our kind, and will do so should the desire occur to them."

"None can run as fast as we." Varkoor snarled.

"Swiftness matters not when the fences are everywhere." Aalwyn twittered, unshaken by her wound. "As our paws strike ground, that very ground recedes. All the lands are behind the fences." Her voice was agitated, a rising growl. "Our packs in union would hunt without equal, and thrive in what is left of the wild. Our enemies would tremble. And yet we snarl at one another, *bickering like rats!*"

"The wolf whose life I ended on the riverbank. That was your sister, was it not?" Her sneering growl taunted Aalwyn.

"Spoken as a true hyena."

Varkoor withdrew a step, and gestured to another wolf.

The other subordinate female rushed Aalwyn and ripped her shoulder. The fur hung off in a flap, exposing a bloody wound.

"Trapped in this world, without device to escape our fate." Aalwyn did not seem to realize she had been attacked, her gait unaltered. She curled her lip, exposing fangs of her own. Her hazel eyes darted again toward Varkoor. "I am *gatvol* of this pitiful fate that you seem to have accepted." She snarled, and the ring of wolves about her paced. "I shall adapt. *And I shall hold sway.*"

Another female darted forward and flashed her teeth. Aalwyn ignored her utterly.

"*Ours is the veld.*" At Aalwyn's unnatural growl, the *Selous* took a step back. "*Should we have a pact.*"

Varkoor charged and fastened her jaws upon Aalwyn, finding her injured ear. This she ripped beyond recognition, and red dripped down the side of her head.

Aalwyn cackled, the rising growl in her throat resembling a hyena.

The *Selous* pack took several steps back from Aalwyn, glancing at one another, not knowing what to do.

"An accord is lost, and your greatest ambition remains a tattered remnant. Your lack of vision will leave your family weak, doomed against the might of lion prides and hyena clans." She lunged toward Varkoor, who recoiled in fright. "*None of you shall matter!*"

The *Selous* pack closed in, then backed away. None knew what to make of the mad wolf in their midst.

"The Pack—and nothing beside—shall survive." Aalwyn crouched, at the ready to attack. "That clasp of forepaws—that greatest of creations—shall somehow be my device." Her eyes were wild, fangs glittering, chest heaving.

Varkoor backed away from Aalwyn, and the rest of the pack looked to her.

"Let her go. This *thing* has brought the Sickness to my den."

"Shall I kill her?" Ratel growled.

"Keep your distance. We shall find her body in the days to come." Varkoor retreated to her den.

"She is not mad, Varkoor." Ratel cast an eye toward this strange female, bold and without fear. Blood trickled from the gashes in her head, shoulder and flank, and she did not appear to care. "There is no Sickness, nor the

Rage. Only a resolute darkness. Whatever did she mean with her ranting?"

Aalwyn merely stood her ground, glaring at Varkoor.

Varkoor moved under the shade of a custard apple tree, peering over her mate's shoulder into the brush. "Unthinkable." Her voice was a muted growl.

"What is?"

She did not respond, withdrawing further underneath the tree.

The rest of the *Selous* wolves milled about the strange interloper, but none were bold enough to approach her.

Aalwyn stepped away from the gathering, and the rest of the wild dogs parted to make way for her. Walking, then loping through the bushveld, she left the *Selous* pack far behind.

Northward.

Chapter 96

The following morning, Aalwyn sat listening to the relative quiet of the dawn. The calls of katydids had faded, as had the calls of Fiery-necked nightjars. Her wounds had already stopped bleeding, though her ear still seared after nearly being torn off by Varkoor.

Stepping forward, she sniffed the ground, the grass, and took in the news of the bushveld. Her pace was gradual, taking care that none of the *Selous* followed her.

Within the day, she had found her beloved *Dwalen*, and the entire pack was well underway.

Aalwyn saw a pair of rounded ears bouncing just above the grass tips. Kurkbos broke into an open run upon sighting her, spun in the air and lapped her muzzle enthusiastically.

"You are injured." His face was creased with worry, and he stared into her rich hazel eyes.

"I scarcely noticed."

"My heart was consumed with fear that..." Kurkbos glanced at the grass between her feet, unable to complete his thought.

"You need fear nothing, Kurk." Aalwyn prodded him with her snout. "Fear shall be *their* problem." She parted her lips, fangs revealed in a knowing smile.

Days passed as the *Dwalen* moved with haste through the brush. Even the pups were moving with discipline, kept in line by the yearlings, with Blackthorn taking the lead.

Pausing only to kill an impala, the pack worked they way to the northwest of Gorongosa Park. The sentinel mountain towered in the distance. Aalwyn had never seen it so close. The rivers here were swift moving, the land inclined downward toward the distant floodplain of Urema.

Eventually, their pace slowed, and Aalwyn began to mark with feces and urine her territory, clawing the ground with each signal left in the grass. She lapped Blackthorn's muzzle.

"Well done." She tongued his palate, and the young wolf returned the gesture. "Your father would have been proud that you have borne his name, Blackthorn." Aalwyn touched noses with the yearling."

Aalwyn twittered to the rest of the pack. *"My beloved Dwalen!"* The pack, pups and yearlings, turned to her. *"Welkom* to the wild of the north."

Chapter 97

A soft patter of rain tapped on the moist ground. A scent of rich soil filled the air.

Aalwyn cast her eye toward the great mountain of Gorongosa, shrouded in mist. Several weeks had passed into memory, and their labors would not be forgotten.

The rains of October had come.

"It is time for the hunt, my love." Kurkbos admired the view.

"Time indeed."

The harrumph of lions gave their territorial call. Kurkbos eyed her with anxiety.

Aalwyn gave a nod. "Death comes to us all."

* * *

Laeveldvy glared at the female spotted hyena.

Her powerful fore shoulders pulsed, long neck dipping toward the dead remains of the impala, her heavy head already coated with blood. Lethal jaws yawned wide to take another mouthful of flesh.

Laeveldvy rushed forward to nip the scavenger's flank. The hyena brought her head up to meet the threat, and bared her teeth with a cackling giggle.

The wolf backed away, knowing he would make no headway with a dominant female. He loped away to fetch others of his pack to see her off.

The fields were still somewhat green on the northern aspect of the *Selous* territory, fed by the trickling rivers from the mountain. Along one of these rivulets he found others of his pack. Black, white, and gold bodies moved forth with a searching gait.

"There is a hyena just over the river."

"They must always press inward." One the wolves responded, batting at his muzzle with a forepaw.

In the past year, the *Selous* had settled into their vast hunting grounds, ever on the move on the southern half of Gorongosa. The lion prides had continued their pressure upon their pack, pushing them around the map. At this time, their hunts had shifted somewhat north to evade them.

"Shall we deal with it, then?" The others trotted over to him.

"Varkoor would be very disappointed indeed should a hyena clan gain ground against us."

The patrol quickly covered the ground, over the drying river, past the termite mounds and sweet thorn acacia, to find the hyena speeding away from them. Varkoor watched her enemy leave, before turning to glare at the approaching patrol.

"Laeveldvy." She spoke in a rumbling growl, her ears ever folded back on her bullet shaped head.

"Forgive me. I was just summoning—"

"If you cannot compel a hyena on your land to *voetsek* with all speed, then I have little use for you." She peered at the kill. "And she had been at work on this kill for some time." The corpse was eviscerated, most of its deep muscles eaten and limbs pulled off. "Your prints are everywhere. How long did you agonize over whether to intervene?" She turned her back on him and trotted away.

"My prints?" Laeveldvy examined the ground. There were paw imprints all around the kill. Some appeared to be underneath it. The hyena tracks were easy to differentiate, with broader marks than those of the wolf.

After a moment, he realized the wolf prints were of varying size.

"Varkoor!"

She sprinted over, her fangs bared.

"Have you discovered a new way to waste my time?" She boxed him with a swipe of her forepaw, and not in a playful manner.

"Aalwyn has returned."

* * *

Bodies bounced as their loping gait accelerated across the grassland. Each with a pair of dish-like ears, coat of black, gold, and white, flashing of teeth. The *Selous* were on the move, and their pack was nearly two dozen strong.

Varkoor called to the others.

"Search the veld—and no paw prints shall escape your notice." She seethed. "This wolf thought to defy us—and take our hunting lands from under our claws."

"There will be nothing of her but those prints when we are finished!" Ratel uttered his tortured growl. "Vultures and hyenas will consume her pups."

"No hyenas." Varkoor's abrading voice reached her pack. "Slow decay for the sport of the flies."

Ratel gave a wide grin, canines on display. He charged the other wolves, one after the next, lashing them into a frenzy for the hunt ahead.

"We make our kills as we search." Varkoor rasped. "And we sleep only in the deep of night."

"How did we not detect her through this past winter season?" Ratel shook his head. "Each time they have violated our territory, it has been within dashing distance of the great river that is the southern edge of the wild."

"They walked around us, my love." Varkoor nipped his ear. "They skirted the hunting lands, and went north." She glared at the veld ahead of her. "I only hope the lions have not finished her off. I can taste the blood with my every breath."

Chapter 98

The house snake weaved its way through the grass. In the broken light, the olive coloration rendered it indistinct, the thin yellow stripe running along its body further breaking up its appearance as it slithered in shadow. A tongue tasted the air, straining for signs of insects or rodents that would fall victim to the hunter. Creeping along, it sensed food was ahead. Its eyes were of little use, especially in the shade of foliage. The ability to scent and taste was a formidable weapon, though sight would have alerted it to the predator armored in orange and black.

Before the house snake could react, the enormous centipede pounced, and powerful mandibles cut the snake cleanly in two.

Each half squirmed in shock, but further struggle was futile. The centipede set to devouring the snake piece by piece. It paused as a large paw struck the ground close to its head, but resumed as the threat passed. Just as well, as any curious paw would find itself filled with venom.

"Take notice of every sign on the veld. Leave nothing to chance." Laeveldvy called to the yearlings under his charge.

"We have seen nothing." A female yearling protested, sniffing the ground.

"Then the search continues." He loped off.

"What say you of this?" The other yearling cocked his head to the side.

A brown bird glided to the ground not far from where they stood. Its broad wingspan could only have been a vulture. They trotted closer, and found the bird stepping carefully toward an impala kill. The drably colored body was topped by a head with brilliant pink skin and a light blue and orange beak. It began the work of ripping away exposed muscle.

Wolf prints surrounded the kill.

"The alpha will want to know."

* * *

Varkoor glared at the pack, each member with heads down, snouts in the grass sniffing about and searching for tracks. She surveyed the horizon, seeing no threats within sight.

"The wolf trail stops here. We may pick it up if we keep moving." Laeveldvy twittered.

"Keep looking."

He departed without argument.

"Their markings are few and far between. We have yet to reach what we assume will be her territory." Ratel was at her side with rumbling growl. "Lion prints, however, are not difficult to find." He scratched his ear with a hind leg. "We must be on our guard for their patrols, and we will be exposed at night on the open bushveld."

"My one burning concern is the usurper." She breathed heavily, voice nearly shaking with rage. "I allowed her to escape, Ratel." A streamer of drool dropped from her mouth to the ground. "The Sickness. Heh. I mistook stupidity for illness."

"It shall be remedied, my love." He lapped her muzzle, but she chased him away with a ruff-bark. The other wolves looked in her direction at the sound, but quickly resumed their search.

* * *

Rich green grass, thick enough to make walking through it a trial, covered the plain. The flat area was just beginning the slow rise toward the foothills of the great Mountain to the northwest. The vast lawn was interrupted by a rock outcropping adjacent to a longer ridge that rose toward the sky, with a tumble of boulders next to it. The green wavered in the breeze, creating a barely audible hiss. Grazers were absent, despite the wealth on offer. A single vulture stood upon the reason.

"She is becoming rather easy to track." Laeveldvy muttered.

Varkoor stared at the dead wildebeest carcass, reduced to bare bone and in two pieces. There was no meat remaining, most of the hide gone. Padding closer to the dead, and sending the vulture on its way, she sniffed around the edges of the kill. There were the narrow prints of wolf, pads and claw marks, all around the kill in various directions. Larger prints were made atop these.

"Lion." Ratel sniffed these depressions, broad based without claw marks. The scent of urine was dense and lingering, resistant to dispersal by the wind. "They took what Aalwyn left behind." Sniff. "The lions took a great deal. Perhaps they ran them off?"

"It does not seem that way." Laeveldvy twittered from the distance. "Their tracks are close together over here, where they departed." He shook his fur free of moisture. "And not at haste."

"What shall it be, Aalwyn?" Varkoor rumbled. "A fight? Or an ignominious retreat for you?"

"Neither."

The scattered wolves of the *Selous* looked about before they realized the voice came from above, an ethereal echo from the rock outcropping.

A single Painted wolf stood at the crest. Black, gold and white, a hole cut into the sky. A rounded ear was trained on those below, and her muzzle parted in address.

"We adapt, and so we thrive." Aalwyn's voice drifted to the pack below, each looking up toward her. *"Trapped in this world. I have found a device."*

"Ever seeking your death, interloper?" Varkoor ruff-barked toward her adversary. She motioned to Ratel, who nodded.

"Death has come for me every day of my life, and here I stand." Her voice was stark and penetrating. *"And Death's every failure has become my weapon against you."*

"Your painful end will come before this day is done." Varkoor snuffed. *"You will soon discover the hollowness of your threats."*

Above, a ringing *kewee-kewee* call from a crowned eagle drew the attention of the wolf pack. Aalwyn did not waver.

"Lions abound in this land of plenty. And they are a danger. To all but the Dwalen."

The other wolves of the *Selous* glanced at one another, not knowing what to make of this. Varkoor noticed their hesitation.

"The formidable packs of ages past numbered as great as the herds we now hunt." Aalwyn paused, her jaw hung wide, releasing a streamer of drool onto the rocks below. *"Greatness shall once again be ours."* She paused again, before emitting a shriek that caused all below her to recoil. *"OURS!"*

Ratel bounded onto the rocks, followed closely by several other wolves. Their claws clicked on the stones as they ascended.

"For there is only the Pack. And the Wolf Pack shall be one."

Clicking, scrabbling on rocks, as powerful hunters lunged forth along the ridge.

"You hunger for my hunting grounds, Aalwyn. You shall have them." Varkoor parted her black lips in a grin as her vanguard raced to the top. "When you are underneath them."

Back and forth from one ledge to the next, they climbed up the outcropping, and topped the crest.

The silhouette was gone, the space once again filled with sky.

"What of Aalwyn?" Varkoor ruff-barked again, unaccustomed to waiting for news.

"She is gone." Ratel's growl made its way down to his mate. A flurry of twitters came from above. Some muttering, followed by a loud growl from Ratel before he answered her. "There are no prints to follow."

Varkoor twittered to the rest of the *Selous*, and they scrambled up the plateau.

"I shall find you. As I will find an end to whatever plot you are crafting."

Chapter 99

Pattering of rain on the waterhole made the surface dance with every drop. There were no animals in sight, the rain chasing every antelope underneath the cover of trees. Birds did not attempt to fly in the deluge, as their feathers would become drenched. They stood amid the grass tussocks or underbrush to wait out the storm. The only things moving in view were the Painted wolves. Their fur was matted with moisture, ears down, eyes blinking with each impact of raindrops.

"We could seek shelter until this passes. I cannot see very far." The male wolf was young and inexperienced, and was prone to giving voice to his whims. Shortly, he could detect hot breath on his flank.

"Did you have a suggestion for the alpha?" Varkoor stared at the recoiling wolf.

"I would not dare."

"The wisest thing you are ever likely to say." She padded ahead.

The wolves endured the downpour that quickly soaked the ground, leaving a sloshing layer of water.

A snort to one side of the wolf column caught their attention. Next to a rock, two warthogs crouched in a dug-out depression that was now a muddy slurry. It was deep enough to hide their hindquarters. The two mates backed up further into their hole. Any approach would be met with tusks more than capable of impaling an enemy.

"They seem quite prepared to fight—they did not even need to run to their burrow." Laeveldvy inclined his head toward the warthogs. "Our approach was seen. How they managed to tell we were coming in this mess is unfathomable."

"Perhaps it is not us that alarmed the warthogs." A yearling offered.

The wolves pressed on, leaving the warthogs behind their flank.

The rain intensified. The sound of the water on leaves and grass was all they could hear.

Larger paws upon wet soil made no sound they could notice.

A guttural grunt was heard first. The wolves looked about, seeing nothing. Then a splash as a body hit the ground.

Varkoor bayed the *Selous* to her. The wolves quickly surrounded her position and their fur stood on end, ears folded back.

Facing them was a lion, ears folded back and large conical fangs exposed. The female grimaced in the rain at the pack. One broad paw rested on the neck of a *Selous* wolf, its spine broken. A rivulet of blood ran from the gaping jaws of the lion. The chest of the wolf heaved once, and ceased.

Against the might of the pack, the lion would normally back off. Instead, she stood her ground, a rising growl in her gaping mouth.

A rumble to the rear could be heard just above an echo of thunder.

Another lioness emerged from the gloom behind them, muzzle wrinkled with fangs bared.

"We are ambushed—we take to the plateau!" Varkoor gave her twitter-ing call to the others, and they were galvanized out of their frozen caution. The wolves fled as one, loping up a slope they could barely see. Scrabbling against the rocks with claws, they could hear the roar of lions just behind them.

Another yelp penetrated the rain. One of the wolves was struck across the body, falling to its death down the rocky slope.

Varkoor and Ratel made the crest of a flat rise of rock, one that was clearly visible to them before the rains had started in earnest. They continued their ruff-barks toward the pack, encouraging them to make the ascent.

Quickly the survivors assembled, and as the last wolf scrambled up the rocks, a male lion was fast behind it.

Ratel lunged, and his teeth clicked shut just shy of the muzzle of the male lion.

The lion drew back, jaws bared. The raindrops ran down his matted dark mane, collecting around his broad paws. His face was contorted in anger, fangs at the ready. He was isolated on the rocks just below the wolf pack, and he faced a barking horde. Another snarl and the lion backed down the rocks.

The rain began to dwindle, revealing the greater plain beneath them. Six other lions were gathered at the foot of the plateau.

The bodies of the two wolves were visible from where they stood, one on the drowned plain, the other lying motionless at the feet of the rocks. A lioness gripped the dead at her feet, shaking the limp form until satisfied that no life remained.

"This night, we shall not sleep." Varkoor glared down the incline as the rain pattered steadily on the stones.

* * *

Hraaaah!

The peal of the jackal resounded across the veld, and the wolves were startled. Each looked about, and finding no threat upon them, settled to rest. The sun was peeking above the horizon to the east, the red hue resembling a forest fire.

Varkoor and Ratel shared a glance, and examined the field below them. The lions had departed in the night.

"We press on." Varkoor spoke this with a grunt.

Ratel ruff-barked to the rest of the pack to get them moving.

"My exhaustion from a night of terror is bone deep." Laeveldvy moaned. He realized he uttered this too loudly when Ratel sent him reeling from a batting forepaw.

"Unless you wish to join the wolves below."

Laeveldvy glanced down at the two dead bodies. He kept quiet.

Each wolf picked their way down the rocks and resumed their canter across the grassy plain. Loping slowly with fatigue, their pace quickened as Varkoor made her way up the column to take the lead. Ratel moved to her side, glancing over with his good remaining eye.

"I would not question your judgment, my love." He murmured. "I must not."

"The wisdom of this foray is in doubt." Varkoor chirped, her voice flat.

He sighed, with a nod.

"Any time we cross the territory of a lion pride, it may end in tears. So it must be. If we allow Aalwyn to gather her strength, her territory could eclipse ours, one season into the next." She growled. "That cannot be left unchallenged."

She stopped short, her ears erect, a paw in the air.

Wolf tracks, relatively fresh, were on the ground. Four toes over a central lobe, each toe tipped with a claw mark.

Lion tracks were also present, wider central blots with four toes, claws absent.

Varkoor sniffed the ground, and recoiled in surprise.

"The scent of the wolf persists here." She padded forward and continued to sniff. "Everywhere."

"Strange that the markings of lions have not erased them." Laeveldvy sniffed as well, following the tracks. "Considering the density of the lion tracks, we are clearly within that pride's home range."

"Something strange is at work here." Ratel peered at the horizon. "The hunt for Aalwyn shall resume. I keenly anticipate its end."

Varkoor continued her lope, following the tracks of Aalwyn, each marked by her pungent musk.

Looking back, she could see Ratel following. The others, with reluctance, fell in behind him. Each wolf padded forward, but looked about constantly, rounded ears searching fearfully for signs of the next attack. Muted whines whispered in the grasses.

The *Selous* wolves were driven forward throughout the day, and collapsed in exhaustion in the night.

Chapter 100

"The *Selous* is closing in." Blackthorn panted as he bounded up to Aalwyn. The sun rose to the east, illuminating the thick brush with rose colored tones.

"So it begins." Aalwyn's fangs shone in the morning light. "Take the pups to safety and conceal yourself, until we have made the second kill."

"I will keep them in the aardvark den until your hoo-call." Blackthorn rounded up the young pups, and with a few twitters and a growl, they were off across the grasses and disappeared in a thornbrush thicket.

Kurkbos sniffed the wind. "How did you know she would chase you this far?"

"Varkoor is persistent." Aalwyn padded away. "A great alpha requires little more." Aalwyn twittered to the rest of her pack. Yearlings lined up before her. "If one is persistent, the qualities of greatness emerge. Hunting. Tracking enemies. Rearing young." She touched noses with each of them. "And now Varkoor will find the outcome of challenging the *Dwalen*. All of us must be prepared for a fight to the death."

One yearling growled.

"You are malice, cloaked in fur." Aalwyn twittered. She glared at another yearling, standing tall. "Enmity, given flesh."

A third yipped to her, tail waving back and forth.

"Malignant savage, fanged." She trotted before them. "They know not what we have become."

With her nod, Kurkbos bolted across the plains, followed closely by the yearlings.

* * *

"The tracks are all over—I am not sure what to follow." Laeveldvy cast his eye over the grounds as the pack milled about.

"I suggest you go in the direction of the claws." Varkoor snarled. "Spread out in search. Give a hoo—call if you find them."

The deep, sonorous warble of a hoo-call reached their ears.

"Who was that?" Varkoor canted her head to the side, listening.

The call repeated, reverberating through the ground.

"That is not from our pack." Ratel rumbled.

"Aalwyn's rats have hunted." Varkoor's growl reached the rest of the *Selous*. "Converge upon that call!"

* * *

Eyes wildly searched the brush, ears strained for another sign of their quarry. Varkoor went from a sprint to a stop, peering for tracks on the ground, a sniff, followed by another sprint for the next sign. Between her searches, she bayed the pack to vigilance.

Ratel ruff-barked, calling the throng to a halt.

"There is our prey." His single hazel eye locked onto Aalwyn at a distance, standing atop a rise of fawn colored rocks. His lips drew back, revealing jagged teeth.

The rest of the *Selous* pursued, scrabbling up the rock outcropping, bundling past the alphas.

"She was expecting us." Ratel bounded up along a path up the spine of sandstone after the others. "That was *her* call."

Once they ascended the height, they found Aalwyn dashing away, threading into a thicket.

The entire *Selous* pack bounded close after her, rounding through a stand of feverberry as a flock of wattled starlings rose into the sky with wheezy cackling.

They burst through tall grasses into a clearing as Aalwyn turned to face them all.

Varkoor opened her jaws to issue a final threat, but the words froze in her throat.

Aalwyn stood next to Kurkbos and their yearlings.

Just across the clearing was a pride of several lions, tearing into a freshly killed impala. The antelope's throat was crushed, tongue hanging out. The abdomen was ripped open, contents pulled away. The lionesses were tucking in. Rough tongues licked the hide to remove the fur before tearing the skin open, feasting on the meat within.

They were not perturbed by the presence of Aalwyn or Kurkbos, or even the yearlings that helped corral the impala.

When the rest of the *Selous* arrived, however, the lions abruptly ceased eating and took to their paws. Walking from the kill, each lion and lioness bared their fangs, a low rumble reaching the *Selous* wolves.

"I would advise you to turn your tail." Aalwyn hissed to them.

Varkoor sneered. "We shall not run."

"Your pack already has."

Varkoor turned to see the rest of the *Selous* distancing themselves from the lion pride. Turning back, she faced the approach of a lioness.

The whiskers of the lioness danced as fangs were unsheathed, musculature rippling underneath her tawny hide.

When Varkoor bolted, the lions returned to the impala.

The *Selous* pack scattered, hiding in the feverberry brush. Varkoor stood on the periphery of the clearing, staring at the lions as they resumed eating, relaxed despite Kurkbos milling nearby. Each wolf uttered their dismay at the sight.

Kurkbos twittered to the yearlings of the *Dwalen*, and they gradually left the clearing, melting into the brush.

Aalwyn padded closer to the *Selous* alpha, her face impassive.

"At the end of the hunt, we are not at odds." She sidled up to Varkoor where she seethed in the bush. Her head was held high, torn ear wavering.

The *Selous* alpha snarled, and turned to give chase. Aalwyn raced away from her, leaving behind the clearing with the lions and entering thick thornbrush. Varkoor pursued her, enraged. Ratel was close behind, and called the rest of the *Selous* to join them. Excited twittering reached the ears of the racing wolves. The chase did not last long.

Entering another clearing, Varkoor found Aalwyn rejoined with her pack. Kurkbos and Blackthorn were there with the rest of the yearlings and pups, tearing into a second impala kill, with no lions in sight.

Ratel caught up to them, along with the rest of the *Selous*.

"Steady on, my young wolves." Kurkbos ushered the rest of his pack away from the dead impala, and the approaching host of the *Selous*. "There are words to be had."

The pups withdrew from the rich meat with great reluctance, mewling. The yearlings crouched, prepared for an attack.

Aalwyn stood her ground.

The alphas glared at one another across the dead impala.

"Lions aside." Varkoor rasped. "I will not suffer your presence."

"We have been watching them, and so closely since we made our way to the north." Aalwyn paced behind the impala carcass. "We have been here an entire season." She nodded to Blackthorn, who crept closer and lapped her muzzle. "Watching the behavior of others, one can learn all one needs. Including where their territories are, and the herds they hunt."

Kurkbos touched noses with one of his pups. "These lions struggle to make the kills they need."

"While we kill all we wish, one day after the next." Aalwyn chortled to herself.

A resounding roar reached them from the nearby clearing where the lions devoured their meal. The *Selous* pack glanced anxiously in that direction.

"And so our hunts coincide." Aalwyn grinned, flashing white knives toward Varkoor. "Lions are not so very vicious when their stomachs are full."

"You fools are *baiting* these things? I wonder if the Sickness has not taken you after all." The alpha of the *Selous* pack grunted. Ratel nodded his agreement.

"Baiting has given way to dependence." Aalwyn angled her face toward the sun, the golden ruff of her neck tousled by the breeze. "They are ours now."

"We shall, then, take what you have." Ratel rasped.

"Then try." Aalwyn met his stare, her jaws parted.

"The lions will close in upon you before you realize your blunder." Kurkbos grinned.

Ratel looked from Aalwyn to Varkoor, and had no answer. He could not be sure of the truth.

The alphas continued to scowl at one another, neither willing to yield. Only the buzzing of a fly broke the silence between them.

"Too much blood has spilled for this to pass." Varkoor rumbled. "I have lost two of my hunters chasing the rats of your pack."

"You killed my sister." Aalwyn's voice was entirely void of emotion. "A transgression I shall forget in the name of survival."

"You speak as though allowing *us* to stay."

"We may all hunt these lands."

"This is so desperately what we need, more competition for land, and for the hunt." Varkoor leveled her sinister glare at Aalwyn. "How *ever* can we help?" A growl rumbled within her.

"What precisely do you want, other than having your throat ripped open?" Ratel grumbled.

"We are in the talons of an eagle." Aalwyn stepped closer to Varkoor and Ratel. "Here to pick over our remains. The lions, hyenas, scavengers, diseased dogs from the villages." She stopped before them, feeling the heat of their breath on her fur. "And the hind talon of humans to sink in to the full."

Ratel glanced at his mate, unsure of what to do.

"If you must have conflict, Varkoor, then we shall have it. I shall exact blood you cannot spare. Your best hunters, beloved yearlings shall fall before it is finished." She lifted her lips to expose ready fangs. "Starting with you." Her ears folded back.

Varkoor took a step back.

Kurkbos, Blackthorn, and the rest of the *Dwalen* tensed, awaiting the order from their matriarch.

"Step forth and join the wind." Aalwyn stood, poised, and stared at her adversary. The *Dwalen* alpha was as resolute as the great mountain in the distance.

For a while, none moved, none spoke. The breeze coursed through the trees, rustling the grass and rattling the leaves. A yellow-billed hornbill took to wing with a piercing cry.

Aalwyn remained rooted to her spot, content to stare.

"There is only so much prey." Ratel grumbled. "And we are in competition with lions and hyenas. There will be too many wolves to get by here."

"On the contrary. Our mounting numbers may be all that would save us." Aalwyn rasped.

Varkoor thought upon this.

"Consider our true enemy." Aalwyn inclined her head toward Varkoor. "Not lions, hyena, or even those strange humans with their strange ways." She lowered her gaze slightly, baring her fangs. "Our true enemy is time. And if we fight one another, it shall bring us all to ruin."

Varkoor quietly watched Aalwyn, a tempest of emotions behind her eyes. At long last, she relaxed, and twittered to her pack.

"We shall see about this."

Varkoor gestured to Ratel, and they padded away from the clearing. Beyond, the rest of the *Selous* horde waited for them, each glancing around fitfully for another lion ambush.

The clearing returned to an uneasy quiet.

KooRookuku, Kooku, called a red-eyed dove from an overhanging Giraffe-thorn acacia.

"What is to come?" Blackthorn asked to no one in particular. "Will there be a fight?"

"This is the great battle." Aalwyn closed her eyes, raising her head to bask in the glow of the morning sun. "Conflict, to end our conflict." Amber eyes opened again to regard her yearling. "That is the challenge of our age. Indeed, of all ages." She nodded, almost to herself. "To set aside distrust and acrimony. And build our future." She paused to gnaw on the exposed rib cage of the impala.

"Should we ready for an attack?" Kurkbos whispered to his mate.

"No." She swallowed as three Painted wolves emerged from the sedge and walked toward them. Aalwyn sniffed the air and scented neither fear nor animosity.

"Varkoor has bid us to join your pack." The female dipped her head below the level of Aalwyn's, as did the other two female wolves in deference.

Aalwyn acknowledged the gesture. "*Welkom* to the *Dwalen*."

"She would enjoin you to send two yearlings to her." She allowed a smile. "They will teach them the meaning of savage."

"Quite." Aalwyn gave a warm smile. "Then we yield this kill to Varkoor." She gestured to the impala with her snout. "For their return journey. Please inform her."

Two of her yearlings crossed the clearing to join the *Selous*.

"It is time to leave." She gave her nod to Kurkbos and Blackthorn, and they mobilized the rest of her pack.

Aalwyn led the *Dwalen* away, with their three new recruits in tow, until they reached a bramble thicket in which to rest for the night. She lay down in the tall grass, biting at ticks as Kurkbos joined her side.

"You never cease to amaze me." Kurkbos twittered to her. "Your gambit was a fruitful one."

"So it would seem." She lapped his muzzle.

"How did you know this would work?"

"I did not." Aalwyn shook her head, warding off biting flies. "When without hope, one has the freedom to be daring."

As they rested, a large wolf bounded in from the tall grass to greet them. Ratel twittered to the *Dwalen* as he approached.

"The *Selous* shall depart to the south, and hold that territory, as you hold yours. We shall be watching for your markings. News of the veld."

He regarded them with one good hazel eye, and a clouded white one. His jaws parted, tongue out, panting in the heat.

"Our hunts shall unify as we need, holding the lions in check." Aalwyn stood tall, and regarded the wolf before her.

Ratel cackled to himself, sounding like a hyena as he turned to leave. "You are a mercurial *bliksem*, Aalwyn. Perhaps you are of use to us alive."

EPILOGUE

The wolves were on their paws, anticipating the violence to come. Aalwyn could taste it, and it aroused her. She nudged Kurkbos, and the pack was running circles around their camp and one another. Black, gold, and white flashed in a flurry of excitement. Wild dogs held muzzles together, tongues eagerly lapping teeth and palates, on hind legs batting one another with forepaws. The twittering grew more agitated, and the pack tore away across the veld. The hunt was on.

Aalwyn loped alongside Blackthorn.

"Every day upon the savanna is the first of our lives." She nudged Blackthorn, and he pushed back against her.

"For either hunter or prey." Blackthorn peered ahead. "Every hunt shall be the last."

The throng crossed the plain, still covered with dew of the night. Splashing through a shallow pond, the wolves tussled in the water, soon covered in mud. Kurkbos bayed to them to press forth, and soon they encountered an impala herd.

Another Painted wolf pack converged upon them, and joined the mighty hunt.

Coursers from the *Selous* and *Dwalen* probed the herd and it took flight across the plains. Dozens of antelope streaked before the hunters as sleek fawn bodies pronked with hind legs high in the air. Twitters erupted from Aalwyn and Kurkbos as they guided the impala towards a patch of tall grass. On this signal, the wolves divided the herd, encircling one of the halves.

Lions burst from their cover in the tall grass and tackled one of the impala driven their way.

The rest of the antelope were pressed away from the lions. Aalwyn and Kurkbos separated one impala from their herd, while Ratel and the *Selous* hunters isolated another. Each wolf pack killed their quarry.

The lion and the wolf eyed one another across the veld. Cats pulled flesh from their impala, while the wolves devoured the remains of theirs.

One lion was on her paws, preparing to close the distance and take the impala kill from the *Dwalen*. On the instant, the pack formed a wall of claw and fang. Aalwyn stood strong, glaring at the lioness. Varkoor was by her side, unsheathing white knives. The lion quickly lost interest.

The killers resumed their feed, and none were left hungry.

When the impala was reduced to hide and bone, the wolves departed, and the lions watched them go.

Aalwyn rested with the pack in the scant shade of a fever tree, lazing in the noon sun. She placed a paw on the phosphorescent bark of the tree. Nearby, the river ran strong with fresh, sweet water from the mountain of Gorongosa, on its long journey to the Indian Ocean on the coast.

Blackthorn harried his mother, running off to play with the others of the great pack. Aalwyn watched them bound off together, and rested her jaw on a tangled root of the tree. Her mind turned toward her son, far away in the South African Lowveld.

Koorsboom rested as well, full from the morning hunt that had felled a duiker in the acacia forest on Du Plessis's property. He rolled over in the burning sun, and looked to the aardvark hole where Olienhout had established their new den. She emerged from the hole, moving more quickly on her three remaining legs than other wolves did on four. She gave him a nod, laying on her side in the shade. Harboring the denning hole was the golden crown of their fever tree, a familiar sight in their changing world.

Aalwyn watched the combined forces of the *Selous* and *Dwalen* packs, running in circles, boxing one another, splashing through puddles left by the rains. The lions kept their watch, and the wolves kept theirs, respectful of the distance.

"Ours is the veld, Koorsboom." Aalwyn whispered. "Our story, and we shall be the ones to tell it."

THE END

Author's Note

As in the first two books of the series, *Wait a Season For Their Names* and *Death Will Know My Name*, this novel was written to reflect natural behaviors of the African Wild Dog and Painted Wolf, with some dramatic license. The species name has been in motion for decades now: African Wild Dog, Cape Hunting Dog, African Painted Wolf, Painted Dog. Every textbook varies, but I stayed with 'Painted Wolf'. Names matter, and 'wolf' reflects its wild nature, though I use other terms as well within the book for the sake of variety.

The interactions between the people are an attempt to reflect the complicated economic realities faced in southern Africa, where the people struggle for survival, same as the wild. Without considering the needs of local people, no wildlife area will survive. Gorongosa is a model for this new way of integrating the needs of the wild ecosystem and that of the people.

The poachers depicted are based on advice of professional rangers, and in particular a notorious poacher best portrayed in *Killing For Profit* by Julian Rademeyer.

The 'Tick' described in the text does not as yet exist, but is a concept that would allow tracking of carnivores without the need for sedation and collaring, as dart sedation carries some risk.

In addition to my experiences with these complicated and elusive hunters, the following sources have been essential to understanding more about their tactics, movements, and family structure. Other sources have been useful for correct details on plant life, herbivores, and all the moving parts of an ecosystem.

The African Wild Dog – Behavior, Ecology, and Conservation by Scott and Nancy Creel c2002

Running Wild – Dispelling the Myths of the African Wild Dog by John McNutt and Lesley Boggs c1996

Painted Wolves – Wild Dogs of the Serengeti–Mara by Jonathon Scott c1991

A Window on Eternity by E.O. Wilson c2014

The Behavior Guide to African Mammals by Richard Estes c2012

The Safari Companion by Richard Estes c1999

African Wild Dogs on the Front Line by Brendan Whittington–Jones c2015

The Antelope of Africa by Willem Frost c2014

The Field Guide to Insects of South Africa by Mike Picker c 2004

Sasol Birds of Southern Africa by Ian Sinclair, et al c2014

Snakes of Southern Africa by Johan Marais c2004

Field Guide to Trees of Southern Africa by Braam van Wyk c2013

Organizations protecting and researching the African Painted Wolf:

Painted Dog Conservation

Peter Blinston, managing director

Endangered Wildlife Trust

Dr. Harriet Davies–Mostert, head of conservation

Wildlife ACT

African Wild Dog monitoring and research

African Wild Dog Conservancy

Dr. Bob Robbins, director

African Wildlife Foundation

African Wild Dog Conservation Malawi

African Wildlife Conservation Fund

Dr. Peter Lindsey, Africa director

If you have enjoyed reading this novel, I would be immensely grateful if you were to post a review on Amazon. They do help, and spread the word about the books, therefore improving sales and thus the contributions I make to the organizations protecting this endangered species.

All proceeds from the sale of this book will go to organizations serving the African Painted Wolf.

About the Author

Alex is a practicing physician in the United States with interests in carnivore conservation, community health, and South African history and politics. He is transitioning to living and working in South Africa to be a part of the changes taking place, and to continue working with wildlife conservation and community health education.

All proceeds of this novel will go to wildlife groups working to protect the African Wild Dog/Painted Wolf.

You can connect with me on:
- http://alexkendziorski.com
- https://amzn.to/2UhHjL9

Also by Alexander Kendziorski

Death Will Know My Name

Book Two in the series.

"Death comes for us all. When it comes for Blackthorn... it shall know my name."

From the author of *Wait a Season for Their Names*, comes another engaging, thoroughly researched, wildlife story in the series of African Painted Wolf Novels, told through animal eyes.

Blackthorn, a lonely old African Painted Wolf, wanders through the African savanna searching for other wild dogs of his kind. His longing and instincts for the pack initially lead to him hunting with a hyena.

Eventually finding a group of captive wild dogs to hunt with, the old and wily Blackthorn struggles to teach this pack to survive in the wild. Survival is the key theme in their world full of dangers. This primal drive to survive is richly woven into a tapestry revealing an occasional sense of hopelessness, and an existential dread of a dying, disappearing wild.

Take the journey through animal eyes, and discover Blackthorn's fate in a well-written, gripping wildlife epic for fans of *Watership Down* and *White Fang*.